Waiting for an Echo

Words in the Darkness

by

Jann Rowland & Lelia Eye

One Good Sonnet Publishing

This is a work of fiction based on the works of Jane Austen. All of the characters and events portrayed in this novel are products of Jane Austen's original novel or the authors' imaginations.

WAITING FOR AN ECHO: WORDS IN THE DARKNESS

Cover art by Dana Rowland

Published by One Good Sonnet Publishing

ISBN: 0992000017
ISBN-13: 978-0-9920000-1-1

Dedicated to our spouses and children,
the inspiration for our perspiration.

ACKNOWLEDGEMENTS

We would like to give thanks and recognition to everyone who has helped bring us to this point:

Our families, for their love and support and for allowing us the precious time we needed to write.

Jann's sister Dana, for creating the cover art and assisting with proofreading.

Lelia's brother Pete, for providing general commentary.

And finally, we would like to thank everyone who has provided encouragement along the way.

We really appreciate your support.

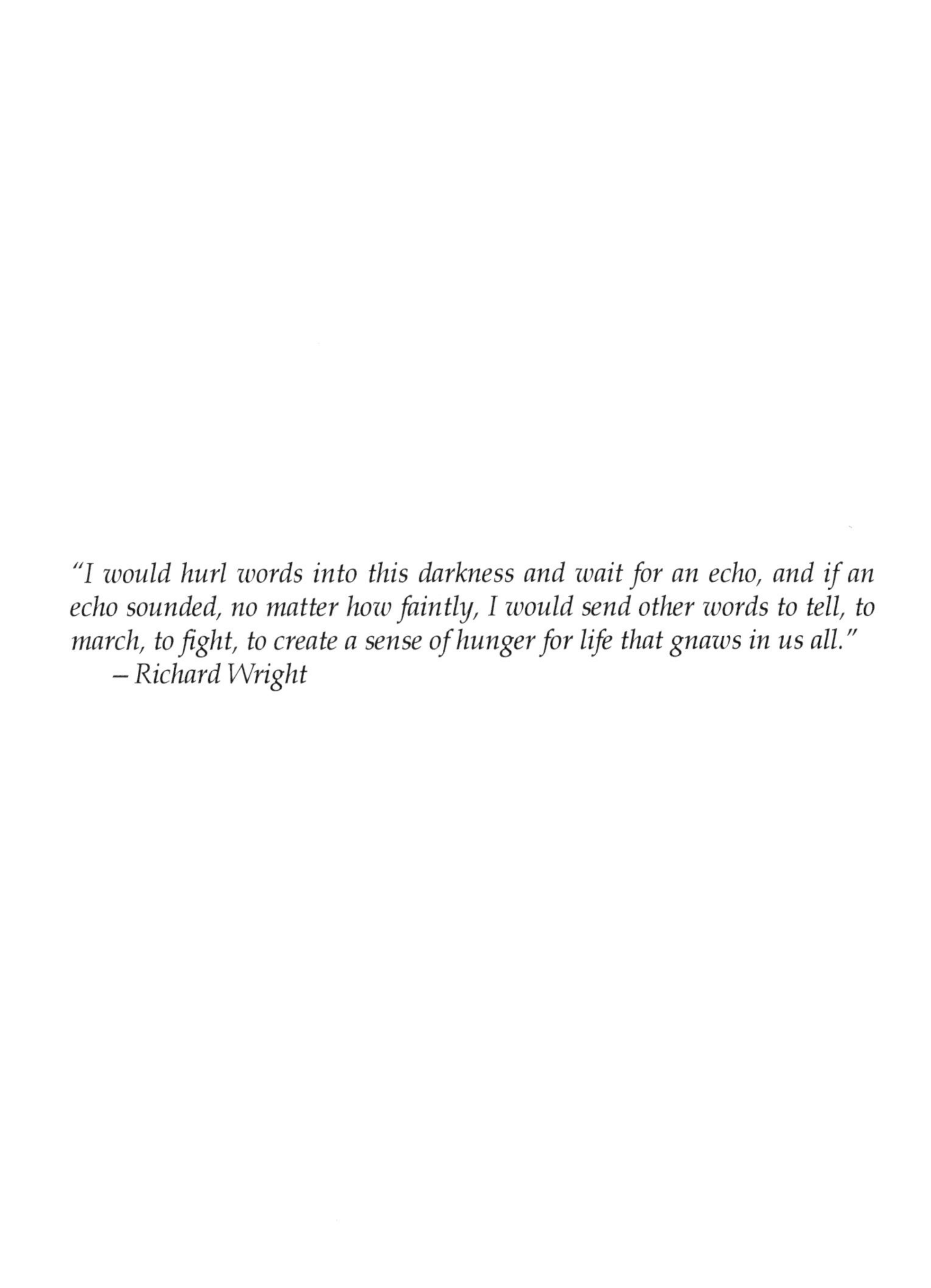

"I would hurl words into this darkness and wait for an echo, and if an echo sounded, no matter how faintly, I would send other words to tell, to march, to fight, to create a sense of hunger for life that gnaws in us all."

– Richard Wright

Chapter I

It is a truth universally acknowledged that when a single man in possession of a large fortune attends a public assembly, he is desirous of finding the companion of his future life.

On one particular night, the inhabitants of the area surrounding the little town of Meryton were quite enjoying the unseasonably fine weather, which had remained moderate and warm despite the fact that the calendar showed it to be the fifteenth of October. The upcoming assembly was of special significance to the locals, as the estate of Netherfield, which had remained vacant for many months, was now let at last to a young man of some means who happened to be accompanied in his residence by his closest—and more importantly, single *and* wealthy—friend. The above maxim was thus put to the test.

Of course, the mothers of the area—at least, those with unattached daughters—were assured of the universal nature of the aforementioned truth. Indeed, the relative sizes of the newcomers' fortunes were already being canvassed throughout the area within two days of their arrival at Netherfield. Ever since the estate had been occupied, these mothers had been whispering fervently about the situations of the young men, and many maternal imaginations were awash with manic dreams of daughters marrying into such wealthy situations. Rarely was so fine a catch to be found in the area; for there to be *two* such available and wealthy men was a matter of some astonishment! It went without question that the mothers of the area would gladly assist them by putting their daughters forth as suitable companions. Such an arrangement would be mutually beneficial, of course, as the men would find their quest shortened and the mothers would no longer need to fret over their daughters' futures.

Unfortunately, one of those men—a Mr. Fitzwilliam Darcy, who was said to have at least ten thousand pounds a year—defied any efforts these mothers made to ensure their daughters' situations. At first, Mr. Darcy was proclaimed to be the handsomer of the two men, and from a merely physical standpoint, that much appeared to be true. But though many could be heard to say that the existence of a fine fortune was a balm to cover up personal defects such as a severe countenance and incorrigible pride, the more astute among them noted that a marriage with such a disagreeable man would be most unpleasant, regardless of the grandiosity of his house or the extent of his holdings. Thus, it was soon proclaimed that Mr. Charles Bingley—with his four or five thousand a year—was infinitely more agreeable. He, at least, would dance with the young ladies of Meryton. Mr. Darcy, on the other hand, refused to do anything but converse with his sister Georgiana, though he did admittedly make occasional tight-lipped exchanges with others as necessary.

The seventeen-year-old Georgiana, it was soon decided, was a delightful young girl; it was quite unfortunate that she should have such a terribly proud and unapproachable man as a brother. That Mr. Darcy danced with Miss Darcy did not assuage the feelings of those assembled in the slightest—he would be *expected* to dance with her, after all, as she only had her brother and Mr. Bingley for dance partners due to the strictures placed on her for not yet being out. The fact that Mr. Darcy initially refused to dance with anyone else in attendance quite overshadowed any other consideration.

But perhaps before discussing the assembly any further, an event which occurred before it should be examined, so that the subsequent happenings of the evening may be more fully understood.

Elizabeth Bennet, being a single woman who was by no means desirous of finding her future companion at this juncture in her life, chose not to go to the assembly. Her decision was railed against by her youngest sister, Lydia, and even her dear twin Jane expressed some distress at her decision to forego such an entertainment. Elizabeth's mother was the most vocal of them all.

"Not attending the assembly? Good heavens, Lizzy! Next you shall be telling me you never intend to catch a husband! Whatever shall I do with you?"

"Do not worry, Mama," said Kitty. "I am certain Lizzy would never impart such dreadful news to *you*. She has much more sense than that."

"I should hope so!" proclaimed the Bennet matron, completely missing the slightly sarcastic note in Kitty's voice. "I dare say that my girls are some of the loveliest in the neighborhood. Certainly much lovelier than the Lucas daughters—"

"Mama!" cut in Elizabeth, flushing. "Charlotte is a handsome woman in her own right—and very intelligent and agreeable."

"Yes, yes, I suppose you might call her somewhat pretty. But of course, she was not able to marry, the poor dear. I will not have my daughters forced into such a wretched fate as she was if I have anything to do with it!"

"I think Charlotte is quite a beautiful girl," said Jane, "and I also believe she is very happy acting as a governess. I always thought she got on very well with children. Her younger sister is also very lovely."

Elizabeth smiled at her in gratitude. "Thank you, Jane."

"I should think that becoming a governess would be one of the most boring things in the world!" proclaimed Lydia. "I can think of a thousand things I should much rather do!"

"Well," said Jane, carefully guiding the subject back to the upcoming event, "I do believe Mama has a point, Lizzy—are you certain you do not wish to attend the assembly? I do wish you would come. We used to have such a merry time at assemblies together."

"I am quite certain," said Elizabeth firmly. She knew her sister only wished for her to be happy, but attending an assembly was not likely to produce such an emotion in Elizabeth Bennet. "I am afraid I have a bit of a headache, and I would derive no pleasure from dancing."

Mrs. Bennet shook her head, mystified. "I dare say I shall never understand your aversion to dancing! Such a thing is unnatural for a girl your age! After all, not very long ago, you were just as eager to dance as the next. Though, of course, that was when a certain young man had struck your fancy—"

"Mama!" said Elizabeth sternly, her cheeks coloring.

Kitty came to Elizabeth's rescue, calling out in a voice fraught with feigned uncertainty: "Do you really believe my dress is fine enough for the assembly, Mama?"

Mrs. Bennet, who could not help being tempted by a chance to bring her maternal knowledge to bear, turned away to inspect the item of clothing, thereby inadvertently allowing Elizabeth, her eldest daughter, to escape further notice.

"Our Kitty times her love of fashions well, I see," said Mr. Bennet from where he had been watching the flurry of female preparations.

Mrs. Bennet, of course, missed her husband's slightly sardonic quip, but Elizabeth, being of an uncommon intelligence, was attuned to every nuance in her father's voice, and she told him in a low tone, "And for that, I am grateful, I assure you."

"I am sure I cannot imagine why," returned Mr. Bennet with a laugh.

Stepping forward, he bade farewell to each of his departing daughters with a smile or a kiss on the cheek before ending with his wife, who had finally ceased fussing over Kitty's dress. Elizabeth looked at her second-youngest sister fondly—Kitty was well aware of Elizabeth's character, and she seemed to have an uncanny knack of knowing when Mrs. Bennet's effusions were starting to wear on Elizabeth. She also knew how to deflect their mother, a talent for which Elizabeth had often been grateful.

"Now, Mrs. Bennet," said Mr. Bennet to his wife, "if you should have the good fortune to induce some young man—or even, I dare say, the new master of Netherfield—to offer for one of our daughters this night, please send him on to my bookroom directly."

Mrs. Bennet gazed back at him with no small measure of horror. "Of what are you speaking, Mr. Bennet? I do *not* intend for one of them to be compromised this evening—or any other evening, for that matter!"

"In that case, I am glad to hear it. Though they are in essence silly young women, a few of them share a rational thought on occasion, and I find myself loath to part with any of them just yet."

With that, Elizabeth's father quit the room to return to his study and his beloved books, leaving his wife to stare after him, no doubt wondering at the meaning behind his statement. It was a scene which was played out all too often in the Bennet home.

But greater things were afoot, and the time had come to depart the house. Elizabeth watched her sisters go, glad she had been able to escape yet another assembly. She was certain she would enjoy being with her father, her solitude, and her books much more than she ever would enjoy being led around a dance floor.

Chapter II

Assemblies could be fickle occasions. Sometimes, they could be light and jovial affairs; other times, there was an indefinable tension in the air. Fortunately, Charles Bingley's first assembly in Hertfordshire was more of the former type. Though disappointed that his friend Darcy was not inclined to enjoy himself, Bingley found the night to be quite a success for his own part. After all, he was able to stand up twice with Miss Jane Bennet, who was widely considered to be the local beauty. Though he did attempt to dance with other young ladies, he could scarcely take his eyes off Miss Bennet.

In addition to being introduced to Miss Bennet, Bingley also met her sister Mary, who was mentioned as being very accomplished at the pianoforte and did not seem interested in dancing; her sister Lydia, who was perhaps more exuberant than was wise; and her sister Catherine, who had been afflicted at the age of ten with an illness that robbed her of her sight. One might have expected this last sister to have been withdrawn from the world as a result of her situation, but apparently Miss Catherine Bennet was made of sterner stuff. Bingley could soon discern that she was a pleasant girl who refused to let her blindness turn her heart to bitterness. He was even surprised to learn that Miss Catherine had memorized the steps of various dances with the aid of her sisters and was thus able to dance a few times that night with close family friends. It was a strong testament to how much her siblings cared for her.

Watching how Miss Bennet kindly tended to her sister's needs warmed Bingley's heart, and so near the end of the evening, he asked Miss Catherine if she would dance with him. On seeing the kindly expression on Miss Bennet's face quickly change to one of concern, he was certain to hurriedly add: "I assure you I will be most careful and attentive. Miss Catherine will come to no harm in my care."

Miss Bennet—who was obviously protective of her sister—reluctantly assented, but Bingley did not miss the fact that her eyes did not stray once from them as they danced. Realizing her concern, he brought the young woman back to stand by her older sister after only a fourth of a set.

With Miss Catherine safe, Miss Bennet was able to relax, and she gave Bingley a grateful smile that made his heart soar. "Thank you for taking such tender care of my sister."

"It was my pleasure," replied Bingley, beaming. "She is a fine dancer."

"I thank you, Mr. Bingley," said Miss Catherine, "but I assure you, all the grace was in the leading. I found it quite pleasant to dance with a new partner. I dare say this assembly is—without a doubt—one of the best I have attended!"

Though the look given to him by Miss Bennet made him happy indeed, Bingley soon became displeased as he realized that his close friend was still doing his best *not* to enjoy the assembly. Determined to rectify the situation, Bingley stepped over to talk to Darcy. Miss Darcy, seeing him approach, gave him a slight smile, her cheeks turning pink. Bingley graced her with a smile of his own before turning his full attention on his dour friend.

"Darcy!" cried Bingley. "Why *are* you standing about in this stupid manner? You must really find a partner and dance—I do not believe I have seen you go out on the floor *once,* other than with Miss Darcy, of course."

"You know I detest dances, Bingley, unless I am especially acquainted with my partner."

Bingley refused to have his efforts countered so easily. "But I simply must have you dance, Darcy! Why, there are many pretty girls who I am sure would not turn you down should you choose to ask them."

"The young lady with whom you have become enamored is the only handsome woman in the room, apart from my sister."

Miss Darcy, whose face was bright red by now, muttered something unintelligible.

"Now, now, Darcy," scolded Bingley. "I believe that your vaunted fastidiousness has once again made its appearance. Miss Bennet's sisters are certainly handsome."

"They are tolerable for a country dance, perhaps, but they are certainly nothing compared to ladies in town. They are not enough to turn my head, Bingley."

Bingley was mortified to realize that Miss Catherine and Miss Mary were sitting close enough to have heard their conversation. It soon became evident that they *had* heard when Miss Catherine stood and Miss Mary guided her over to stand in front of Darcy.

"I dare say, Mr. Darcy," began Miss Catherine, "that I had not taken you to be a man to judge another solely by appearance. I should have thought that someone of your stature would know that looks are a poor way to measure a woman."

And with that, Miss Catherine, a mischievous smile tugging at the corners of her mouth, requested that her sister take her to their mother. They were gone before either man could form a reply.

Bingley shifted his feet awkwardly, exchanging a grimace with his friend's sister. Trying to deflect attention from what had just happened, he suggested: "Ah, Darcy, if there are no young women who particularly catch your eye, perhaps you should stand up with Miss Bennet."

The expression on Darcy's face was very dour indeed. "Perhaps you forget that I am having difficulty determining how I should act with two women of my acquaintance in Kent. I would much rather not add one in Hertfordshire to the list."

"Darcy, one dance is hardly tantamount to a declaration," replied Bingley with some exasperation. His friend truly did take his unsociable disposition to the extreme at times. "All I suggested was that you attempt to make a good impression upon *my neighbors* by deigning to ask a truly handsome young woman—as you owned yourself—to dance. You need not include Miss Bennet any further in your troubles, unless you should suddenly become enamored of her, which, at this point, hardly seems likely given your performance this evening."

The full force of Darcy's gaze swung to Bingley's face, conveying the strength of his displeasure. Truly, Darcy could be intimidating at times, even though Bingley was aware the man was not as forbidding as he sometimes seemed.

"Be that as it may, I am in no mood for dancing this evening, and I would ask you to cease your attempts to induce me to do so!"

Sensing Darcy's hostility, Bingley shook his head and turned to Miss Darcy in hopes of more pleasant conversation. "So, Miss Darcy, how are you enjoying your evening? Unless I am mistaken, I believe this is one of only a handful of such experiences. You must be truly anticipating your coming out."

Georgiana smiled shyly at him. "Indeed, I am, Mr. Bingley. I do so wish to be able to dance more, though."

"Georgiana," admonished Darcy, "you are well aware the only reason you were allowed to attend was due to Bingley's rather persuasive arguments in your favor."

"Now, Darcy—" began Bingley before being cut off by a slight wave of Darcy's hand.

"No, Bingley, you were correct. A small country assembly in Hertfordshire is an ideal place for Georgiana to become accustomed to attending a ball. I thank you for the suggestion. However, I must own that I shall be more comfortable with the idea once your aunt arrives to assist my sister with her social education. But regardless of whether your aunt is here or not, the fact remains that Georgiana has *not* yet been introduced to society and, as such, is only allowed to dance with family or close friends. And since we have not been in Hertfordshire long enough to have made any close acquaintances, that leaves you and me. I am sorry, Georgiana, but for now you must consign yourself to dancing with your ancient elder brother and his silly friend."

This last was said with affection and energy and made Bingley smile. The Darcy siblings truly were close, and sometimes Bingley almost envied them. His relationship with his two sisters was in no way similar.

"Speak for yourself, old man," retorted Bingley good-naturedly, "I am not the one who has categorically refused to dance with *any* of the pretty young ladies in attendance tonight. By my calculation, that makes *you* both ancient *and* silly!"

Darcy waved him back to the dance floor. "I will state once again, Bingley, you are wasting your time with me. Return to your dancing and your parading before your new neighbors, and leave me to my brooding."

Darcy's eyes turned from his friend, and he seemed to be contemplating something on the other side of the room. Bingley, seeing Darcy's attention was engaged elsewhere, took his advice and turned to the young lady by his side.

"I seem to have been neglecting you, Miss Darcy! I may be poor compensation for the wonders of London society, but perhaps you would favor me with the next dance?"

Georgiana shyly let it be known that she would indeed enjoy a dance with him, and he stepped away from Darcy with her, that they might have some pleasant conversation before the next set. Bingley intended to enjoy the evening, even if Darcy was determined to do otherwise!

Chapter III

Darcy watched his sister and his friend step away to converse—his foul mood threatened to ruin their good ones, so he could hardly blame them. Perhaps he should feel guilty, but attending assemblies had never yet brought him any semblance of pleasure, and he regretted their necessity—they seemed like nothing more than a flimsy excuse for those who considered themselves to be paragons of fashion to parade in front of others. And that did not even take into account the matrimonial games that most attendees indulged in. Still, there was something more important to think about than the current emotional state of his friend and sister and his own hatred of assemblies. Taking a deep breath, he forced his feet forward and went in pursuit of the two young ladies who had been victims of his ill temper. They certainly had done nothing to induce him to speak so unkindly. Still, despite knowing he had made a cruel blunder, he could not help but frown and reconsider whether to approach them when he found them standing with their mother.

Mrs. Bennet was shaking her head and speaking about how unpleasant-looking he was in a remarkably low tone; once she noticed his approach, however, she was quick to raise the volume of her voice. "My daughters have informed me of what just occurred, Mr. Darcy, and were it not for my utmost confidence in them as honest girls, I might find myself unable to believe the horrors of which they have accused you! But knowing now as I do of what your opinions truly consist, I fear I must command that you cease all contact with my daughters. Of course, if you so detest our country society, I should wonder that you deigned to attend our assembly at all."

Darcy spoke stiffly. "I am aware that I have wronged your daughters, Mrs. Bennet, and I have come to offer my apology to them. My mood of late has not been a pleasant one, and my ill-spoken comment was not meant as an attack on their persons, but as a means of convincing my friend to cease his persistent appeals for me to dance. Regardless of that fact, I am aware that it is no excuse for my ill-temper, and I apologize for my words."

Mrs. Bennet appeared to realize she could now afford to be a little gracious, and she backed away from her righteous anger. "Did you indeed come to us with such intentions, Mr. Darcy? Well, I suppose my daughters might deign to accept your apology since you have been so gracious as to acknowledge that you were in the wrong."

Both young women muttered something about agreeing with their mother, though Darcy could tell that their acceptance was offered unenthusiastically.

A gleam came into Mrs. Bennet's eyes, and Darcy suspected that she realized she was now in a position of some power—and that she planned to use it to her advantage. It was nothing more than he had seen any number of times in London, but it was still difficult for him to suppress a shudder.

"There, Mr. Darcy!" said Mrs. Bennet, almost before the girls had finished their mumbled acquiescence. "You see how amiable my girls are. They would be quite a catch for any man—"

"Mama," interjected Miss Catherine, who appeared more than aware of the turn of her mother's thoughts.

But though Mrs. Bennet backed off her initial comments, still she ignored her daughter. "You know, Mr. Darcy, my dear Kitty has hardly been able to dance tonight, and she does love the activity so. Why, I believe that if you were to take her out onto the floor, she would be much obliged, and your previous comment would be quite forgotten. We do not trust her to just anyone's hands, you know, but I dare say you are capable of aiding her!"

Mr. Darcy was well aware that he bore the expression of someone who had just swallowed something sour, and when he replied, he did so in a tightly controlled voice. "I did not come to this assembly with the intention of dancing, Mrs. Bennet."

"Nonsense, Mr. Darcy!" cried Mrs. Bennet. "One cannot come to an assembly such as this without intending to dance. I simply must insist that you take Kitty through at least half a set."

"Mama," pleaded Miss Catherine once more.

But Mrs. Bennet kept her attention on the man before her. "I do not see you standing up with any other partners, Mr. Darcy. So, you are quite out of excuses!"

Mr. Darcy looked between the young woman and her mother, trying to judge whether it would be more unpleasant to argue with the woman whose daughters he had insulted or oblige her by taking one of those daughters to the dance floor. It was the woman's next loud exclamation—"Do not be so hesitant, Mr. Darcy!"—that decided him. He would much rather go through a quarter of an hour of dancing than continue to speak with such a woman for even a few more minutes. And so, he agreed to dance with Miss Catherine.

His thoughts upon going out to the dance floor were initially black indeed, but Miss Catherine, it seemed, had agreed to the dance to placate Mrs. Bennet just as he had. She did not appear interested in finding a husband at this assembly, and his realization of that helped ease his misgivings.

He felt awkward initially while leading her to the floor. He had never danced with a blind girl and had never aspired to do so. Yet despite her handicap, she was a pleasant enough partner. She seemed shy—at least in comparison with Mrs. Bennet—and she was, most fortunately, not in possession of the garrulity which plagued her mother. Despite her quiet nature and her condition, however, she possessed a strong confidence which led her to hold her head high. Though he was a stranger to whom she had trusted herself, she appeared undaunted by her situation. For that, he could only commend her.

The only thing that cast a shadow on the dance was the conversation taking place between Mrs. Bennet and Lady Lucas. The latter was a much calmer woman than the former, so he was unable to hear her words, but he could certainly make out Mrs. Bennet's. Indeed, he wondered that the woman could not be heard in London!

"Oh, look at them dance!" he heard the Bennet matron exclaim. "I dare say I can practically hear wedding bells ringing already! That Mr. Darcy is not so unpleasant a man once you get to know him, it seems. And his friend, Mr. Bingley—why, he is absolutely taken with Jane! Perhaps my girls will do very well for themselves after all. If only

Elizabeth had seen fit to come! I do not know if she will ever catch a good husband with the way she avoids these assemblies. We had hope once, of course, but it all came to naught."

There was a pause in which Lady Lucas presumably replied, and then Mrs. Bennet continued: "They are indeed lovely girls, are they not? Well, perhaps Mary is a little plain, but Jane is especially handsome!" And then Mrs. Bennet began to extol all the virtues of this "especially handsome" daughter, and Darcy forced himself to ignore her mostly one-sided conversation and concentrate instead on his dance partner.

The young woman seemed somewhat amused, and he suspected she knew he had heard her mother's exclamations. He exchanged a few light words with her, and when they had at last completed half of a set, he began to lead her away from the floor.

"You are a fine dancer, Miss Bennet," complimented he. The remark was sincere and even surprised himself.

A smile touched the young woman's face. "For someone who so dislikes the activity, Mr. Darcy, you are certainly not devoid of the skills it requires."

As he took her back to her mother, he reflected that perhaps the whole of the society found in this region was not completely wanting after all. He almost immediately regretted the thought after having to subject himself once more to Mrs. Bennet's presence. As soon as he could free himself from her effusions, he pulled away and engaged in his preferred activity at dances—standing aside, alone with his thoughts.

When the set was over, Bingley and his sister returned to him, the former with a bright smile on his face. "So, Darcy, I see you are not wholly immune to the lure of the dance after all!"

"My dancing was not entirely my design," murmured Darcy. "I am surprised to see you are returning to me rather than to Miss Bennet."

"She is charming, is she not? I actually plan to call on the Bennets tomorrow. Miss Bennet told me her beloved sister is not well and had to stay at home, so I promised I would visit the Bennets' estate to be introduced to her."

"You always had a soft spot for handsome women, Bingley."

"She is radiant, is she not? But her heart, too, is very kind, Darcy. I have never met anyone quite like her. She is certainly an angel!"

"I dare say you shall move on to a new infatuation soon."

"You wound me, Darcy!" cried Bingley. "I can assure you, my friend, this time it will be different."

"Perhaps," said Darcy. He looked to his sister. "Did you enjoy your dance with Bingley?"

"Of course," said Georgiana, giving him a slight smile. "Mr. Bingley is a skilled dancer indeed."

"'Passionate' might be a better word than 'skilled.'"

Bingley laughed. "Come, Darcy! You could certainly use more passion in your life. Come dance with some of these fine Hertfordshire women. You shall not regret it!"

"I prefer to remain as I am, thank you."

Laughing, Bingley soon moved away, presumably eager to place himself once more at the side of Miss Jane Bennet, that he might further converse with his "angel."

Darcy shook his head, watching his friend go. He wished only for the end of the night to arrive and end his misery. He hated dancing.

Chapter IV

Longbourn, the Bennets' estate, was situated only a mile from Meryton, and it was within so easy a walking distance that Mr. Bennet's daughters could often be found walking thither in search of ribbons, books, or even a respite from a mother whose nerves permeated the entire household. Mr. Bennet knew that Elizabeth, as the eldest, tried to assume the role of mentor to her sisters, but her ability to influence them was restricted by their mother's unfortunate tendency to insist upon having the final say in her daughters' educations and affairs—after all, the matron clamored, Elizabeth was merely one of her daughters, while Mrs. Bennet was the mistress of the estate.

Of course, such a circumstance might have been altered if Mr. Bennet had deigned to take his silly wife in hand and correct her flighty behavior. Mr. Bennet, however, knew what trouble awaited such an attempt, and moreover, he had never been a man to immerse himself in the doings of his family, especially since he had been blessed (or cursed, depending on one's point of view) with a succession of five daughters and no sons. Had he perhaps been given a son with whom he could commiserate and whom he could train in the management of the estate, matters might have been different. But they had not been blessed with a son, and since Mr. Bennet had been afflicted with a sickly constitution and ill health, he often felt unequal to the task of doing anything more strenuous than sitting in his personal library with a good book and a glass of port. Indeed, the most basic of estate management tasks were often beyond his ability to handle—or perhaps, to be more accurate, the situation of his health gave him a convenient excuse to avoid tasks he found tedious. He was therefore assisted in the management of his affairs by Elizabeth and Jane, without whom the estate would undoubtedly have fallen into considerable disrepair.

He was reading a book with a glass of port beside him when his eldest daughter found him some time after the departure of the rest of the family to the assembly.

"Ah, Lizzy," said he, "how good of you to join your old father. I must say, your aching head seems to have made a remarkable recovery."

Mr. Bennet knew that Elizabeth was well-acquainted with his moods, his quick and biting humor, and his sarcastic witticisms—in short, he did not doubt that she knew that he was well aware of the reason for her reticence toward participating in the evening's main activity. Her next words proved his supposition.

"Papa, you must know my reluctance to attend the festivities has nothing to do with a headache. Though my sisters enjoy the activity, I take little pleasure in a dance myself. I should much rather stay home and keep you company, thereby avoiding the simpering platitudes and false flattery which seem to be a vital part of any gathering."

"In that case, Lizzy, I quite commend you for refusing to participate in this foolishness."

He coughed lightly, and he saw Elizabeth shift to look at him. With the state of the family—there being five sisters and no brother to break the entail which gave the estate to a most unworthy cousin—Mr. Bennet's slightest cough and every sneeze were scrutinized as causes for great concern, for, as Mrs. Bennet was fond of pointing out, nothing but Mr. Bennet's continued ability to draw breath stood between their comfortable home and their being thrown out to starve. While Elizabeth was concerned for her family's continued well-being, Mr. Bennet's heart was warmed by the knowledge that she cared more about the health of her beloved father than contemplating whatever fate would await her upon his demise.

In light of that fact, it took no great insight for Mr. Bennet to recognize the worried expression on his eldest daughter's face. "Lizzy, do not look at me in such a manner. I do not believe that I shall expire right before your eyes."

Elizabeth shook her head—she had inherited many things from him, but the ability to laugh at such unpleasant thoughts was not one of them. "Papa, you know me better than that. I am not about to bemoan your impending passing or call for my smelling salts."

"I should think you had more sense than that, Lizzy."

"Yes, I believe I do. Papa, now, tell me—are you well? Is the fire warm enough for you, or should I call for the servant to build it up?"

"Believe me, Lizzy, I am well. You will not descend into poverty this night, I should think."

Elizabeth said nothing in response, no doubt knowing from experience there was no talking to him when he was in such a mood. She contented herself with another shake of her head while she sat back in her armchair and opened her book. Mr. Bennet, however, did not remove his eyes from his daughter, nor did his countenance waver from the slightly worried look which he knew had spread over his features. Though his daughter would wish to practice avoidance—indeed, they had oft touched upon the subject which he was about to broach—he could not but press her once more. His affection for her, his favorite daughter, would not allow him to do any less.

"Lizzy, my child, while I commend you for not participating in such foolishness, I do worry about you."

"Papa—"

"No, Lizzy, I will not spare you this conversation. While your mother and most of your sisters spend their days searching for the perfect match, you spend your hours in my study with my books. Though I know we both take pleasure in reading, do you not think your time might be better spent considering your future?"

"My future shall take care of itself—I am in no mood to give myself over to my mother's penchant for fripperies or follow her in her quest to learn the pocketbook size of anyone with trousers. My future will come in good time."

Leaning forward to steeple his fingers in front of his face, Mr. Bennet regarded his eldest daughter with some amusement. "Far be it for me to dispute the accurate picture you paint of your mother, Lizzy. But certainly there are other more proper ways to go about securing the attentions of a worthy young man."

"And I thought it was the duty of a young man to secure the affections of a lady," murmured Elizabeth dryly. "It appears you and my mother have both been remiss in attending to my education."

"Your education has been as sound as I could make it, my dear. You must remember that sometimes young men will not bestow their attention on young ladies without encouragement, and you will certainly never succeed in drawing the attention of any worthy specimen if you continually hide yourself away in my study and refuse to take the time to exhibit as your mother wishes."

When she made no reply, Mr. Bennet continued. "My child, it was almost four years ago. Surely your heart has managed to heal by now. After all, there is nothing a young woman likes better than to be crossed in love. You have even outdone your sister Jane in that regard."

"Please do not worry about the state of my heart, Papa. I shall endeavor to follow your excellent advice, but I am determined to continue to avoid such assemblies—I have no love of dancing, and I cannot imagine that will ever change."

But Mr. Bennet was not about to let Elizabeth put him off. Although he could not by any means be considered one who was intimately concerned with the doings of his family, he was still a caring man at heart, and Elizabeth was his favorite daughter after all. The guilt he felt for not providing for his family properly was one that he experienced from time to time—more often when it was thrust into his consciousness as it was at this particular moment. However, he was not a man to dwell upon anything, especially his failures, to any great extent, and he was rather successful in burying himself in his books and contenting himself with the company of his eldest daughter. Besides, his health prevented him from doing what was required to allow his estate to become prosperous enough to provide him a means of saving for his family. At least, this was what he told himself on occasions such as this when his conscience pricked him for his inaction.

But lately, he had had something else to worry about—namely, the aforementioned eldest daughter. Since her experience those years ago, his Elizabeth had retreated. Whereas she had been willing and eager to meet and dance with young men before, now she rejected the activity altogether, spending time in the library, handling estate matters, and assiduously avoiding assemblies such as the one she had refused to attend that very evening. At first, he had barely noticed the change, and as he had enjoyed the company of his daughter, he had not thought to question her or her reasons.

But the fact was that Mr. Bennet was not becoming any younger—nor was his health improving. Although he had no specific reason to believe he would soon expire, the uncertain nature of his health made him painfully aware that his time could come at any moment. When he finally did perish, his family would face a future fraught with uncertainty, and there was little he could do to prevent it. Therefore, it had become apparent to him that his daughters' future security lay in the path of marriage—if but one of them could make a good match, then that one could provide for the others. Of course, if they could all enter the marriage state, then so much the better, as he was certain that, between them, they would provide for his widow. Jane was, of course, the most likely candidate to marry a rich man, but Mr. Bennet was certain that the right man for Elizabeth existed; if she could only find him, such a man could not fail to comprehend what a treasure he had unearthed.

But Elizabeth seemed determined to avoid all possibility of ever allowing a young man to know her. Indeed, she appeared not only resigned but also determined to maintain her aloof status and never allow another man into her heart. He was puzzled; it was not like his sensible daughter to be so affected so severely.

Which brought him to his current concern. By his count, Elizabeth had begged off the last three assemblies successfully, and although she was becoming adept at running the estate, she would not be able to do that forever. He wanted her secure in a marriage with a man who loved her—and whom she esteemed as her equal. She would not find such a situation sitting in his study while her sisters were out being introduced to rich young men. No, it simply would not do.

"Elizabeth," began he, startling her attention from her book.

"Papa?"

"I treasure your company, but although you tell me not to worry about your future, you must know that I do."

"Papa—"

"No, Elizabeth! You will not put me off again! My dear, you must pull yourself out of this melancholy and enter the world once more. It is one thing for me to sit in my book room while the world passes me by, but you are beautiful and too good to allow yourself to fall into similar straits. Surely there is someone for you, someone who will recognize the exceptional young woman you are. You will not find him in here, my dear. Musty old tomes cannot be a replacement for a communion of hearts with a young man you both respect and esteem."

Elizabeth listened to his argument without comment—without expression, he thought. It was some time before she spoke again.

"Papa, I know of what you speak. Yet I fear you are correct. My heart has been ill-used, and it has been difficult for me to recover."

"But surely, Elizabeth, it is time."

His daughter nodded without enthusiasm. "Again, I must agree. Yet I doubt I shall ever enjoy dancing; it is a reminder—a reminder of what has happened. Perhaps more importantly, it is a reminder of everything that is insincere and false in our world."

"There are other ways to socialize, Elizabeth," chided Mr. Bennet gently.

"Indeed, there are. Papa, I promise you I will try. Whether I will eventually find someone of my own, I cannot say, but if I should be so fortunate as to be granted another opportunity with some young man, I will not let it pass."

"That, my child, is all I can ask."

Elizabeth nodded thoughtfully; then, a playful expression came over her face. "Of course, I could allow Jane to raise our family fortunes. Then I could play old maiden aunt to her gaggle of children."

Laughing at the image, Mr. Bennet reached over and clasped her hand. "I believe Jane would appreciate the assistance, Elizabeth. But then you would deny some worthy young man the privilege of having you for a wife—not to mention denying your unborn children a mother. Do not sell yourself short, my dear, and do not think too meanly of the world. Our society is far from perfect, to be sure, but it is not all darkness and despair. You have much to give. Please do not waste it."

"I promise I shall not."

With that, Mr. Bennet had to be content.

Chapter V

Although Elizabeth did not attend the assembly, her ears were soon filled with so much of it that it almost seemed as if she had.

Lydia was the first to run through the front door of their home. "Lizzy! Lizzy!" shouted the girl as she rushed about.

Elizabeth stood, knowing that the closed door to her father's study would do nothing to deter her enthusiastic youngest sister, and she shortly found herself inundated with the self-centered effusions of Lydia, who proclaimed that there had not been a single dance in which she had not participated. On hearing the girl's hurried descriptions of the assembly, it was all Elizabeth could do to hold back a grimace, knowing that Lydia had likely not behaved in a strictly proper manner.

Before the rest of the family could crowd into his study, Mr. Bennet shooed the two girls from the room, laughingly entreating them to take their discussion of lace and other finery to another part of the house. Indulging him, Elizabeth led her sister from the bookroom into the front parlor, where the other females of her family crowded around her to inform her of the goings-on of the assembly.

"Oh, Lizzy, you should have seen Mr. Bingley!" exclaimed Mrs. Bennet. "He was handsome, polite, kind—and he danced with our Jane *twice*! Such a charming, charming man! I should certainly not mind having *him* as a son-in-law!"

Noting the pink on her sister's cheeks, Elizabeth raised an eyebrow in surprise. Judging by the way Jane was avoiding her twin's gaze, Mr. Bingley had made a favorable impression *indeed*. Elizabeth resolved to ask Jane about it in a more private setting. Part of her was happy at the thought of such a suitor pursuing her sister—assuming, of course, Mrs. Bennet's flattering descriptions could be believed—but there was another part of her that worried. Would a man of four or five thousand a year be able to content himself with marrying someone who would only be able to provide him with one thousand pounds and four per cents—and even that only upon the death of Mrs. Bennet?

After being told about the stern Mr. Darcy and his rejection of the younger Bennet sisters, Elizabeth considered how the man had truly deserved to be taken to task for his temerity. Before she could contemplate it to any great degree, however, she was soon bombarded with her sisters' wishes that she had been there, and she found herself repeating several times that no, she did not regret missing the assembly, and yes, she still found no pleasure in dancing. Her sisters were very excited about the night, and even Mary noted: "As far as such assemblies go, Lizzy, this one was certainly pleasant."

"Pleasant?" said Lydia with a laugh. "It was remarkable fun, Mary. bv it!"

"I even danced with the proud Mr. Darcy, Lizzy!" said Kitty, who was as pleased with the evening as Lydia.

Elizabeth turned sharply toward her mother. "Mama, you let her dance with a *stranger*? And more than that, a man who sounds as if he is determined to be cross with all and sundry? Mama, how could you?"

"I am not a child, Lizzy," said Kitty darkly before Mrs. Bennet could respond.

Mrs. Bennet, oblivious to the thick emotions in the room, waved her hands about dismissively. "Mr. Darcy took a great deal of care with her, I assure you. She could not have been safer had she been in the midst of her family."

"And Mr. Bingley was a good partner for me as well," added Kitty. There was a challenging note to her voice.

"You danced with *two* strangers, Kitty?" asked Elizabeth with obvious disapproval. How could their mother countenance such a thing?

"I did, Lizzy, and nothing untoward happened. You must stop treating me like a child. I am not much younger than you."

"You could have been hurt," persisted Elizabeth. Had Kitty missed a step, it could very well have been disastrous indeed!

"But I was not. You need to have more faith in my abilities, Lizzy. I may be blind, but I am not incompetent. I know the steps of the dances as well as any of you—perhaps even better. You cannot treat me like a child forever."

"Kitty," began Elizabeth, pained.

"Lizzy," returned the other.

"Girls, stop this bickering," said Mrs. Bennet. "I refuse to let you ruin our lovely night! Now—Lydia, did you happen to see Miss Darcy's dress? I dare say it was one of the finest I have rested my eyes on in some time! The lace alone sent my heart aflutter! It must have been made in one of the finest shops in London!" And she then proceeded to discuss the various notable items of clothing which had been featured at the assembly.

Jane looked at Elizabeth and Kitty, obviously wanting to say something to help them make peace, but Elizabeth shook her head with a sad smile. Kitty was correct, of course—she was becoming a woman in her own right, and her sisters would not be able to protect her forever. Should she find a kind and loving man who would treat her well, it would bring relief to the whole family. It would certainly be difficult for Kitty to come across any such suitor if she were only allowed to interact with men who were family friends.

Taking in a deep breath, Elizabeth moved to stand by Kitty, and she squeezed her hand. The gesture was an apologetic one, and Kitty understood, giving her a squeeze in return. The two sisters, no longer cross, were then able to participate in the assembly-related conversation of which Mrs. Bennet was the dominating force. Though made slightly uneasy by Kitty's interest in hearing more about Mr. Darcy—Was he handsome? Did he seem as if he enjoyed dancing with her?—Elizabeth forced herself to become calm and appreciate the fact that perhaps Kitty's future might be a bright one after all.

When Elizabeth and Jane were finally able to escape to bed, Jane seemed so tired that Elizabeth, rather than question her about Mr. Bingley as she wished to do, simply contented herself with teasing: "I will let you rest tonight, Jane, but I expect to be fully apprised of Mr. Bingley's admirable qualities tomorrow."

"I must confess I am not unwilling to have such a discussion," said Jane, blushing.

The bell-like sound of Elizabeth's laughter filled the room.

Chapter VI

The day after the Meryton assembly dawned bright and clear, with nary a wisp of wind, nor with the chill in the air one might have suspected would be present on a mid-October morning. For one such as Elizabeth Bennet, a young lady who enjoyed rambling through the fields and forests surrounding her home, the gift of fine weather this late into the autumn months was almost heaven-sent. Once the winter weather arrived in earnest, she would find her outdoor pursuits severely curtailed, so she attempted to take advantage of the situation as often as she could.

On this particular morning, however, Elizabeth had decided to forego her greatest pleasure in favor of the pleasure of observing Jane. Although Elizabeth had not yet had the opportunity to properly discuss Jane's opinion of Mr. Bingley, Elizabeth knew her sister quite well, and while Jane had looked on other young men with admiring eyes in the past, Elizabeth had never witnessed her sister experiencing quite this depth of reaction to any gentleman before.

Mr. Bingley's promised visit took place soon after breakfast, a meal which was complemented by Mrs. Bennet's fluttering nerves and shrill admonishments to Jane to sit up straight and make the most of her handsome figure. At length, however, once Mrs. Bennet had tolerably composed herself and Mr. Bingley had been shown into the parlor, the visit had commenced.

It was not long before Elizabeth's suppositions from the previous night were confirmed, for Jane, although naturally reticent, greeted Mr. Bingley with the shyest of smiles and the faintest hint of a blush on her fair skin, all of which served as a clear indication to Elizabeth that her sister enjoyed Mr. Bingley's company very much.

For his part, Mr. Bingley looked very much the love-sick swain—or as near as a young man of no more than a twelve-hour acquaintance could possibly approach the condition. He was engaging in his manners and conversation, seeming comfortable with all of the Bennet ladies, yet his eyes wandered back to Jane more often than they would have if he had been unaffected by her presence. Elizabeth noted all of this, and although the acquaintance was a new one, she was content. Elizabeth had always worried some rake would come take advantage of Jane's sweet disposition; it was a relief to see a good and caring young man so enamored with her, especially after such a short acquaintance.

Unfortunately, the presence of Mrs. Bennet made any attempt at sensible talk almost impossible, as she tended to monopolize the conversation with mindless prattle about the previous night's activities, noting who had danced with whom and discussing the lace on Miss Darcy's gown in excruciating detail. Of course, such talk was not interesting to the young man, who quickly suggested walking along the neighboring paths with Mrs. Bennet's daughters (all except for Lydia, who had accompanied her Aunt Phillips to her home for a visit earlier that very morning). This proposal was immediately agreed upon by all—especially Mrs. Bennet, who was not displeased in the slightest at the opportunity to allow her most eligible daughter to spend time with the handsome gentleman—and they busied themselves preparing for the outdoors.

However, they had not gone twenty steps from the house when the door flew open and the Bennet matron's piercing voice arrested their footsteps.

"Girls!" said she, "I simply must have some flowers for the table! Elizabeth, be a dear and fetch me some on your walk."

Elizabeth assured her mother she would do so, and the five quickly made for the gate to the estate and for the freedom which lay beyond.

Very quickly, Elizabeth learned that Mr. Bingley, besides being amiable and charming, was also astute, as he immediately seemed to sense the closeness between the twin sisters and chose to put himself at the side of Elizabeth. Although she initially wondered what this meant,

Mr. Bingley's good-natured conversation and ready attentiveness were accompanied by frequent glances toward Jane. Elizabeth was thus alerted to the fact that Mr. Bingley was attempting to place himself in the best possible light, evidently realizing that gaining the approval of Jane's favorite sister could only assist him in his suit. Far from being displeased at his actions, Elizabeth appreciated him for his sensibility and his consideration, all of which pointed to a sincere, although undoubtedly very new, attachment to her sister.

They walked in this manner for upward of half an hour, Elizabeth conversing in the most animated fashion with the extremely diverting Mr. Bingley while Mary and Jane walked behind, leading Kitty through the woods. Elizabeth, though concentrating on her companion's conversation, had the pleasure of glancing back every so often to see Jane gazing at Mr. Bingley with a shy smile on her face—a smile which transformed to a blush whenever she was caught looking at him by her sister.

At length, the hoofbeats of a horse were heard, and a rider came into view on a large black horse. The rider approached and dismounted before walking forward and leading the horse, his attention fixed upon the entire party. Elizabeth knew immediately this was Mr. Bingley's friend of whom her sisters had spoken the previous evening. He was a tall man—several inches taller than even Mr. Bingley, who was not small by any means. His hair was dark and wavy, and his looks were pleasant; in fact, Elizabeth was able to acknowledge him to be as handsome as her sisters had maintained the night before. His bearing was formal, even approaching aristocratic, and his movements as he led his horse forward were sure and confident. The horse itself was magnificent—as beautiful a horse as Elizabeth had ever laid eyes upon, for although she was not a great rider, she loved the majestic animals and had always wished to ride finer specimens than her father could afford to own.

"Ah, Darcy, so good of you to join us," greeted Mr. Bingley.

Mr. Darcy made no reply, simply sweeping the company with his piercing gaze and finally resting it upon Elizabeth, who, though immediately feeling the urge to blush at his intense scrutiny, nevertheless straightened her back and gazed back in an unwavering fashion. She was determined not to be intimidated by this man!

Mr. Bingley immediately seemed to realize the situation and turned to Elizabeth. "Ah, I beg your pardon. Miss Elizabeth Bennet, please allow me to introduce Mr. Fitzwilliam Darcy

Elizabeth curtsied. "Mr. Darcy."

"Darcy, this is Miss Bennet's sister. She was not at last night's assembly because of an indisposition."

"Miss Elizabeth," said Mr. Darcy with a stiff nod. "I hope you are feeling better."

Elizabeth gazed at the man with a frown for a moment, wondering why he would call her "Miss Elizabeth." She only delayed an instant, however, before she remembered her good manners and replied: "I believe I am, sir. Fortunately, I have a sturdy constitution and recover quite quickly from a mere headache, and there is little indeed which can keep me away from the outside world for long. If I were to receive an ailment which required me to stay in bed for the rest of my life, I should surely succumb to it—the outdoors mean too much to me."

Mr. Darcy peered back at her, as if seeing her for the first time again—Elizabeth suspected he had never been spoken to in such a fashion by any woman of his acquaintance.

"I believe our opinions are very alike in this matter. But there are plenty of entertainments to be found inside. Reading, for example, can be a beneficial exercise for the mind and may help one become truly accomplished."

"Indeed, Mr. Darcy, I think you are quite right, but I prefer to combine my pleasures whenever possible. You are just as likely to see me walking outside with a book of sonnets in my hand as not."

"Well, if you are so fond of books, perhaps you should see Darcy's library at Pemberley," noted Mr. Bingley. "It is very fine and well-stocked."

"It ought to be," allowed Mr. Darcy, his posture to Elizabeth's eyes stiffening visibly. "It has been the work of several generations, and I try to add to it wherever possible."

"Do not be modest, Darcy," cried Mr. Bingley. "Your library has more books than I could possibly read in ten lifetimes."

"Really, Bingley, I do have more than *ten* books in my library." Mr. Darcy's voice was dry and affectionate, an abrupt change from the severe, restrained manners he had shown to that point.

Mr. Bingley only laughed at the insult. "You know me too well, old man. I am afraid I just do not have the patience for books. There is always something else calling my attention away."

"Well, you may have the finest library in all the country, Mr. Darcy," said Elizabeth, "but I have discovered that my father's library suits me quite well, and I frequently reread that which I like best. My father does what he can to update his collection, so I never seem to run out of new material."

"So, you read often, do you?"

"Yes, Mr. Darcy, she does," interjected Kitty. "We have all despaired of her taking interest in any of the more—shall we say—frivolous aspects of a young woman's education. Her penchant to be found with a book in her hands instead of embroidery or some other amusement is a source of some vexation for our mother."

Mr. Darcy turned and favored Kitty with a smile on his face, which she could not of course see, but the genuine pleasure in his voice was evident when he responded. "Good morning to you, Miss Catherine."

Turning her sightless eyes in his direction, Kitty smiled in response. "Mr. Darcy, all my friends call me 'Kitty.' Shall you not do so, too?"

Elizabeth could only gaze at her sister in astonishment. For Kitty, the Bennet sister least likely to part with her trust, to make so open a declaration of friendship to Mr. Darcy after so brief an acquaintance—why, it must have meant that something had happened of which Elizabeth had not been informed.

"It would not be proper to address you in so familiar a manner," replied he. "Perhaps we could compromise at 'Miss Kitty'?"

Kitty inclined her head. "That would be acceptable, Mr. Darcy."

"Then 'Miss Kitty' it is," responded Darcy before turning to Bingley. "I am sorry to disturb you, Bingley, but have you forgotten of our engagement this morning?"

"No, indeed, Darcy," responded Mr. Bingley with a ready smile. "I wished to call briefly on the Bennets this morning to fulfill my promise, but I think you are right—we had best be on our way. But first, we must escort these young ladies home."

At Darcy's acquiescence, Kitty indicated to Mary that she wished to continue down the path, and she started off, with Jane and Bingley following close behind, the former watching her younger sister's footsteps with great care and the latter paying attention to little other than his fair companion. Elizabeth at once realized her sisters had left her to walk with Mr. Darcy, who was leading his horse, and although she was still uncertain what to make of the man, she assented when he motioned for her to precede him down the path.

They walked in silence for several moments until, unaccountably desperate for some conversation, Elizabeth turned to compliment Mr. Darcy on his choice of horseflesh. "Mr. Darcy, I do not think I have ever seen such a fine specimen as your horse. Pray, have you had him long?"

"Since he was foaled. His sire was my father's favorite."

"So your attachment is a long one."

Surprised at her playful tone, Mr. Darcy glanced at her before continuing. "Yes. Am I to conclude that you are an equine lover as well, Miss Elizabeth?"

"Oh, yes, Mr. Darcy. However, I must confess that I have not ridden such a horse as yours. Unfortunately, all my father has on the farm are plow horses and a few carriage horses. I believe riding one such as your beauty would be much different."

"I dare say it would."

"Unless you wish to be regaled with tales of Darcy's stables," said Mr. Bingley, who had heard their conversation, "I would suggest you not encourage him on the subject. Darcy is an excellent horseman and takes almost as much pride in his stables as he does in his library."

But as this was a topic in which Elizabeth held some measure of interest, she took no notice of Mr. Bingley's playful admonishments and addressed Mr. Darcy about his horses, encouraging him to tell her more. The subject of his equine holdings appeared to be a topic for which Mr. Darcy's enthusiasm was boundless, as they spent the rest of the walk to Longbourn in conversation. Indeed, it was with surprise that Elizabeth at length noticed the gates of her home appearing before her, so engrossed had she been in their discourse.

The gentlemen walked them up to the door of the house and bowed, to the sisters' returned curtseys. Then the ladies began to enter their home as Mr. Bingley called for his horse to be brought around from the stables.

However, it was not long before the clamorous voice of her mother reminded Elizabeth of Mrs. Bennet's request for some wildflowers for their dining room table. Elizabeth, unwilling to listen to her mother's excessive lamentations over her thoughtlessness for the rest of the day, determined immediately to repair out of doors to obtain the requested flora. She gathered her bonnet and slipped out the front door, only to find their guests had not yet left the estate. Although she knew listening to the private conversations of others was not ladylike, her interest was caught immediately by their subject matter.

"Are the two eldest Miss Bennets not especially lovely creatures?" asked Mr. Bingley.

"I have seen many a handsomer woman," responded Mr. Darcy, in what Elizabeth took to be his disinterested tone.

"Good God, Darcy, if you have, I should like to know where!" cried Bingley. "I hardly know what to think of this fastidiousness of yours. It seems there is no woman of your acquaintance who can please you. Surely you must agree."

Darcy turned to his friend and affixed him with the sternest of glares. "Bingley, must you continue—"

"I think I must indeed, Darcy. You have been in high dudgeon ever since you arrived. There must be *something* in Hertfordshire which does not cause you distress."

"You are well aware it is not Hertfordshire which distresses me, my friend."

"Well, if you are to be free of such weighty concerns for a time, then you must turn your mind away from your troubles and allow yourself to be diverted. Come now, own it, man—the Bennet sisters have their fair share of beauty, even for a country family, as you are wont to describe them."

Looking as if he would rather not answer the question, Darcy nevertheless afforded his friend a grudging nod. "The elder Miss Bennet is certainly a fine woman."

Seeing Mr. Bingley's face suffused with an affectionately knowing smile, Elizabeth realized that the two men were confused as to who was the eldest sister, which was further testified to by the fact that Mr. Darcy had addressed her as "Miss Elizabeth." All of this passed across her consciousness in an instant, focused as she was on the conversation, and she could almost anticipate the words which next spilled from Mr. Bingley's mouth. Although she knew it would be better to remove herself from the vicinity immediately, she was affixed to the spot, her curiosity afire with the need to know what Mr. Bingley would say next and how Mr. Darcy would respond.

"And what of Miss Elizabeth? You are free with praise for her sister but say not a word of her. Surely you cannot have been so blind to have missed the close similarity between them?"

Mr. Darcy merely grunted in response, his eyes searching around the side of the house for any indication that his friend's horse would soon be brought to him. Elizabeth was certain he longed for nothing more than to be away from Mr. Bingley's persistent questions.

"Oh, I will grant you they have their differences," conceded Mr. Bingley. "After all, Miss Bennet is taller than her sister and has a light and willowy figure. Yet there is something very similar in their faces, and I find Miss Elizabeth's darker coloring and her more petite size very becoming indeed. Can you deny it?"

By this time, Darcy was indeed looking uncomfortable, but he squared his shoulders and looked Bingley in the eye. "I am sorry I cannot agree with you, Bingley, but I must say I find Miss Elizabeth Bennet rather plain."

It was at that moment when Darcy seemed to see past his friend, and his eyes widened as he beheld the subject of his declaration watching him and hearing his every word. Mortified at being caught listening to their conversation—and at the discovery that Mr. Darcy should consider her "rather plain"—Elizabeth disappeared into the house and closed the door firmly behind her.

The door at her back provided some comfort to her in its solidity, and Elizabeth took a few deep breaths to calm herself and consider what she had heard. That Mr. Darcy should not think much of her beauty did not concern her—after all, he had the benefit of moving in the highest circles with the most beautiful of women, so it was of little consequence if she did not excite his good opinion. And it was not as if this were the first time she had been compared to Jane and been found wanting. Elizabeth had never begrudged her sister her admirers or the praise Mrs. Bennet heaped upon her to everyone within earshot. Elizabeth was proud of her sister and took it as a compliment every time her beauty was noticed and commented upon.

However, that Mr. Bingley's friend should have the audacity to mention such a thing in the shadow of the Bennets' own house went completely beyond the pale. Elizabeth chuckled to herself—it was well she was not interested in Mr. Darcy's good opinion, or she might have felt offended at his declaration. As it was, she thought it was magnanimous of her to have fled inside the house to consider his apparent mortification with amusement rather than remaining outside to take him to task for his insensitive words. He certainly would have deserved no less.

Chapter VII

It did not take long for Elizabeth to inform Jane of what had passed between the two gentlemen. As was her wont, she was eloquent in her rendition of the event, her sharp wit more than biting as she flayed Mr. Darcy and his words. Her own culpability of listening at doors, so to speak, she conveniently ignored, enjoying as she was the relating of the tale to her sister.

Jane, however, immediately tried to clear both men of any wrongdoing: "Surely Mr. Darcy would not be so unkind, Lizzy."

Jane was certainly more distressed by such a development than Elizabeth was; the latter was simply amused, and she made no effort to hide her mirth. "I am quite sure that Mr. Darcy meant exactly what he said. The man is utterly proud and disagreeable, and I should be glad never to see his face again."

It was at this point that Kitty burst into the room. "Come now, Lizzy," exclaimed the girl in the doorway, "you are always so quick to see the worst in people. Mr. Darcy may have mortified your pride with his ill-judged words, but perhaps you should try to understand him before condemning him as the worst sort of man!"

"Kitty! Have you been standing by the door this whole time?" admonished Elizabeth.

"It is no more than you have done," retorted the younger girl. She was holding the brown cane she used for navigation against herself, almost as if it were a weapon.

Elizabeth flushed. "I do not understand what you see in that man, Kitty."

"Your conversation with him seemed pleasant enough."

The eldest Miss Bennet just shook her head. "He is too caught up in his pride. But it is of no consequence to me. I am not upset with being so considered by such a disagreeable man, as I have no interest in his ten thousand pounds or anything else he may be fortunate enough to possess. I dare say another woman can submit herself to his foul moods, for I shall have none of them! He may continue to consider me plain—I shall certainly not make any effort to change his mind!"

Jane, upset by the heated nature of the conversation between her sisters, said quietly: "But that is just it, Lizzy—I am not certain that he *does* think you plain. There was an expression on his face when he looked at you—"

"Probably of disgust!" interjected Elizabeth playfully.

"I do not think that was what it was."

"Nor do I," chimed in Kitty.

"In fact," said Jane slowly, "I do not believe he found you unfavorable at all."

Elizabeth shook her head. "You did not hear him speaking to Mr. Bingley. But—for both of your sakes—I shall endeavor to be kind to the man, though I may dislike his conceit so."

But though she was trying to soothe her sisters, her opinion was just as it was before—she found the man's proud bearing worthy only of contempt, and she was certain her feelings on that issue would never change. She only wished that her good friend Charlotte Lucas had not left to become a governess, as Charlotte would surely have been just as amused by Mr. Darcy's comments as Elizabeth was herself. But there were few respectable options available to unmarried women of a certain age, and Elizabeth could not blame her friend (who was seven and twenty) for leaving. Elizabeth thought back to her recent conversation with her father, and she knew that a similar fate might be in store for her, should she not marry within the next seven years.

"Mr. Bingley holds Mr. Darcy in high esteem," pointed out Jane. "I am certain he is a good man—I suspect he has merely experienced some difficulties lately."

"A man with ten thousand pounds having difficulties? Surely you exaggerate matters, Jane."

"Mr. Bingley led me to understand such, though he would not go into any detail on specifics."

"Well, I suppose even wealthy men may have their problems," conceded Elizabeth. "But come, tell me more about Mr. Bingley."

"Oh, Lizzy, I hardly know him."

"But from what I hear, Jane, he hardly left your side last night. Surely that speaks of some kind of attachment. And for Mr. Bingley to come to visit the day after the assembly is no small matter in itself!"

"He is a good man—he is very kind."

"Jane is right," said Kitty quietly. "He made an excellent dance partner—I felt completely at ease with him. My being in his hands was certainly no misfortune."

Elizabeth touched Kitty's arm gently. "Ah, Kitty, it is a shame you cannot see how handsome he is! I am sure you would be well pleased with our sister's new suitor."

"I value his heart more than his looks," noted Jane. She immediately blushed, as though she had exposed more of her feelings than she had intended.

"Oh, I do have high hopes for you, Jane," proclaimed Elizabeth. "I *do*—but I want you to be careful in your dealings with him. Men fall in and out of love all the time. Women are often called inconstant, but I firmly believe that there is no one more inconstant than a man."

"Oh, Lizzy!"

"All I want is for you to watch your footsteps. Mr. Bingley seems charming, and I doubt he would ever willingly deceive you or try to show that which he does not feel. But it is possible that his feelings will change. It has happened before with many other young men."

"You speak as if we were engaged, Lizzy. We have only danced together twice."

"And as I noted, he came to call on you today," said Elizabeth. "He does indeed seem smitten with you, Jane, and his manners are above reproach. Let us hope his feelings remain unchanged!"

"I am sure they will, Lizzy," noted Kitty, "for what man could ever resist our dear Jane!"

Elizabeth laughed. "I am sure you are right, Kitty. The flower of Hertfordshire will always have men falling at her feet!"

"Lizzy!" said Jane with a blush. She was so embarrassed that she was unable to say anything else for several minutes.

Chapter VIII

The front presented to the world by Fitzwilliam Darcy was that of an aloof and arrogant man, one who was pleased with himself and who extended his civility to only a few close acquaintances. To those who did not know him well, he appeared distrustful and disdainful of almost everyone else with whom he came in contact. In town, amongst his social equals, his mien could be said to soften slightly, his countenance becoming less forbidding, yet even with those whom he considered his equals or his betters, he was at best unapproachable and at worst considered arrogant and conceited. But this was not the sole defining attribute of the man.

In truth, Mr. Darcy *was* proud and undeniably arrogant, but it was not this which caused him to remain distant; rather, it was the distinct unease he felt when in the company of strangers and sometimes even when among those with whom he shared an acquaintance. As he had inherited his estate at the tender age of only two and twenty, he had immediately found himself elevated from a young man freshly removed from his final year at Cambridge to the master of a great estate in Derbyshire—and consequently, one of the richest and most eligible young men in all of England. This would not have been considered a hardship to most other young men of lesser means, but to Darcy, who already possessed a serious mind, his sudden ascension to the title of landed gentry had heaped responsibilities upon him for which he had considered himself unready, exacerbating his existing tendency toward seriousness and making him seem dour as a result. It had also made him the target of nearly every single gentlewoman in the entire country of age to marry, and this, of course, did not even take into account the machinations of these ladies' simpering yet calculating mothers. His reputation for arrogance and conceit actually served him rather well, as it helped protect him against socializing with young women seeking rich husbands.

But though Darcy's reputation for aloofness had at times led others to misjudge him, he had never been known to be rude, even to those moving in high society he quite despised, of whom there were not a few. Nor had he ever been known to be a liar. And now, he was acutely aware of the untruth in his statement to Bingley the previous day and of having those untrue words offend a young lady who was in all honesty as handsome as any he had ever laid eyes upon—a woman whose only offense had been her position as the subject of Bingley's less than subtle insistence.

Now, he paced the library, pondering the event and wondering what could be done to resolve the issue without sacrificing his dignity or allowing the woman in question to believe him an unfeeling cad who moved through the world offending every young lady of his acquaintance.

It was while he was thus engaged that Bingley found him, and Darcy could immediately detect a measure of humor in his friend's face which caused his mood to sour even further. After all, if it had not been for Bingley's goading, he would hardly have found himself in such a position.

"Ah, Darcy, there you are."

Darcy merely grunted in response and threw himself in one of the high-backed chairs next to the fire.

"Come, Darcy, what ails you? You have never been overly mirthful in company, but you are beginning to become serious and taciturn—and, I dare say, even disagreeable—in greater measure than before. Your situation cannot be all *that* bad, can it?"

"You are well aware of my situation, Bingley."

"I *thought* I was aware. Perhaps you could illuminate me further—share your burdens, as it were."

The old Mr. Darcy had been rigid and stubborn in his opinions, and one such opinion was the necessity of self-sufficiency for his family, particularly in regard to his son. The younger Darcy had been taught from the earliest days of his childhood to be completely independent and to work out his problems through his own intelligence and industry and to seek the help of others only when a superior or specialized knowledge was required. Personal problems were to be kept to oneself, as to show weakness before anyone, especially someone not of the family, was unacceptable. Because of this, Darcy had always kept his own counsel, never imposing upon his friends for trivial matters which concerned only himself.

Although he was loath to share any of his problems, even with his closest friend, the sight of Bingley standing there—the look of sympathy so evident on his face—caused Darcy to reconsider his father's teachings and to begin to open up with another person for perhaps the first time in his life.

"You have met both of my problems yourself, Bingley," said Darcy as he passed a hand over his face in a weary gesture. "Do you doubt the rest?"

"Yes, I have met them, old man. But I think you highly melodramatic if you refer to two such lovely and amiable ladies as problems."

Darcy snorted with some amusement. "They are both acceptable as prospective brides. However, I shall think you quite the simpleton—or quite blind!—if you persist in calling *one of them* lovely."

"Perhaps you are right," said Bingley with a smile. "But I have often found that talking about a problem to a sympathetic friend can lessen the burden. I would not wish to *increase* your burden by referring to either young lady as less than attractive."

It seemed Darcy had no choice but to capitulate, although he was not distressed by his surrender in this circumstance. Taking a deep breath, he began thusly:

"Having already met the ladies in question, Bingley, you can hardly be at a loss for my present feelings of confusion. I have been taught all my life that duty to oneself, one's family, and one's legacy are paramount and that duty demands that I marry my cousin Anne. Yet you have seen us in company and will no doubt be unsurprised when I tell you that I cannot imagine anyone for whom I could possibly feel less attraction. Anne is everything I do not desire in a wife—she is sickly and frail and is possessed of a cross and serious disposition. I know you would gladly point out that she is too much like myself if I allowed you to, and in this instance, I find that I must agree. We two would suffer for having a serious companion rather than a livelier one who could more easily lighten our own demeanors."

Bingley's soft chuckle was all that greeted Darcy's declaration, and after a moment, Darcy joined in, amused at his own succinct way of describing his troubles.

"As for Miss Baker, she is quite lively and is graced with beauty and gentle breeding, not to mention fortune—in short, everything I find attractive in a partner. Her moments of—how shall I put this delicately?—stupidity are somewhat troubling, yet they are diverting at the same time. I think I should be very happy with her."

By this time, Bingley was openly laughing, and his voice when he spoke could only be understood with great difficulty. "Oh, yes, Darcy—very delicately put indeed."

The room was filled with laughter for several moments before the seriousness of the discussion once more settled into Darcy's heart.

"So, you see, my friend, I struggle between the duty demanded by my heritage and that required by my own inclinations, which lead in a very different direction."

"Well, my friend, it appears you find yourself in a quandary."

"I do, indeed, Bingley. In fact, a chance for some time away from the ladies in question is what prompted me to accept your invitation with such alacrity."

"Then why not enjoy your time away from those two ladies? Anything must be better than wandering assembly halls with a face resembling a thunder cloud and a manner so frigid as to cause the entire party to suffer from frostbite."

Mr. Darcy shook his head at his friend's irreverent manner. "Really, Bingley, having already confessed that my present indisposition is due to a dilemma concerning two young ladies, why would I complicate matters further by adding another to the mix?"

"Did you have any particular young lady in mind?"

Angry with himself for revealing so much, Darcy rose to his feet and planted himself in front of the window, gazing down on the grounds of Netherfield. Bingley was showing entirely too much shrewdness recently, and Darcy could hardly reconcile him with the young man he had originally known. Awed and grateful to be the recipient of friendship from a man such as Darcy, Bingley had been almost vacuous in their early acquaintance, and Darcy had initially despaired of his ever being a companion who could carry his part of an intelligent conversation. But as Bingley had grown more comfortable in his presence and more certain of their friendship, he had begun to show a disconcerting level of astuteness of which Darcy would never have considered his unassuming friend capable.

"Do not fret, Darcy. I doubt any of the Miss Bennets were the wiser, but I have the benefit of a much longer acquaintance with you. Although you seemed to consider Miss Catherine worthy of your attention after your dance with her, I am certain you were more affected by one of her older sisters. Am I not right?"

Darcy merely gave a noncommittal grunt.

Bingley smiled knowingly. "Ah, so I was right! Then, am I to believe you do not find her so plain as you originally stated?"

"You know very well, Bingley, that I said what I did to convince you to hold your tongue about a subject on which I was reluctant to speak. I am distressed not only that she heard me utter so blatant a falsehood, but also that I offended a young lady with my ill-judged words."

"Yes, Darcy," said Bingley, a hint of mischievous humor lacing his voice, "you seem quite able to recommend yourself to any and all Bennets, if your performance of the past few days is any indication."

Darcy shook his head. "Bingley, I am deeply mortified by my actions. Even if I do not consider Miss Bennet to be a pretty young woman, I still could never excuse myself for rudeness."

"So apologize to her," said Bingley in an offhanded fashion while rising to his feet. "After all, you have already had practice in that particular exercise. She is, as you put it, a pleasant young woman and would be willing, I am certain, to accept your offered olive branch should you offer it earnestly. I will warn you, however, that my impression of Miss Elizabeth Bennet is that she is very intelligent and would not appreciate any insincere sentiments. I suggest you mean what you say, not that I would accuse you of dissembling."

With this, Mr. Bingley slapped his friend on the back and then exited the room.

Reflecting upon the last few moments of his conversation with Bingley, Mr. Darcy acknowledged that following his friend's advice was the only proper course he could take.

Chapter IX

The area around the estate of Longbourn was delightful, filled with streams, hills, and small copses of trees. The country air was generally clean, the area being far enough from the ever-present pollution which afflicted London, and the delightfully brisk autumn air lent an even greater sense of pastoral harmony to the area than was normally the case.

Elizabeth Bennet loved her home—she loved every rock and tree and was acquainted with most of them intimately. She was very much a lover of nature and spent an inordinate amount of time wandering through the countryside. Though her sisters also enjoyed nature, they often teased Elizabeth about how essential the outdoors was to her. While it was true that they accompanied her not infrequently, Elizabeth's rambles were generally of a solitary nature. In fact, the walks she took on her own, without anyone accompanying her, were greater in length and covered more ground, taking her further than anyone, even Jane, suspected. If her mother ever learned exactly how far from home she ranged, Elizabeth would undoubtedly never hear the end of her incessant complaining about the wildness of her eldest daughter. In fact, Elizabeth could almost recite her mother's anticipated words verbatim. Mrs. Bennet was nothing if not consistent.

Of course, this did not deter Elizabeth in the slightest. She kept her thoughts to herself and went about the things which gave her pleasure, knowing she had the support of her father.

Why she had walked so far this day, she was not entirely certain—her usual haunts were to the north of Longbourn, closer to Oakham Mount and the delightful views it afforded of the surrounding countryside. However, on this day, she had set out in nearly the opposite direction, skirting the neighboring estate of Lucas Lodge and the town of Meryton and eventually coming to the edge of Netherfield. It mattered little whether she was curious of the inhabitants of that estate or whether boredom with the same scenery in which she had been walking lately had finally caught up to her—regardless of the reason, she soon found herself walking through the woods close to that estate and able to make out the bulk of the manor house in the distance.

Seeing nothing of interest to tempt her further notice, Elizabeth shook her head at her own folly and turned to leave the environs with the intent of returning to Longbourn.

She walked for several moments, reveling in the sunlight shining down through the trees, which were now mostly bare of their canopy of leaves. Feeling the warmth of the light on her cheeks, Elizabeth, on impulse, spread her arms out and began twirling on the path, her eyes closed and her head raised toward the sun.

It was then that she impacted with something quite soft, yet firm and not at all yielding. The air was expelled from her lungs forcefully, and she sat down on the ground, dazed and confused.

Her eyes snapped open, and she saw in front of her a girl in much the same predicament. Neither of them spoke for what seemed like an eternity, and in that time of silence, Elizabeth was able to obtain a clear—if somewhat hasty—impression of the girl. She was no more than sixteen or seventeen and was in possession of a pale complexion and blond hair. She seemed to be a pleasant sort of girl, although sitting upon the ground and contemplating the person with whom you have just forcibly collided was not an effective way to take stock of a stranger.

All at once, they both started to speak:

"Oh, I am quite—"

"I beg your pardon—"

Speaking on top of one another brought them both up short, and they immediately began to laugh as they scrambled to their feet, both brushing off the evidence of their encounter from their dresses.

"I am very sorry," said Elizabeth, trying to catch the other girl's gaze. "I am afraid I was so caught up in the glory of the day that I was not watching where I was going."

The girl glanced up at her and then averted her eyes, her cheeks flushed in embarrassment. "The fault is mine. I was busy searching for flowers and had just turned from picking one when we—"

The sentence remained unfinished as the girl turned her head in mortification. Elizabeth immediately understood that the girl was shy—perhaps more reticent than even Jane, who was well known for keeping her own counsel.

Indeed, as the girl had said, the area around her was littered with small blooms she had evidently picked on her walk.

"Oh, do let me help you retrieve them," said Elizabeth, bending to pick up the flowers from where they had fallen. She and the girl were able to spend the next several moments in companionable silence as they bent to retrieve the flowers.

"Thank you," said the girl shyly once she again held her prize within her hands. "Your assistance is greatly appreciated."

"Do not thank me, for I have done nothing," returned Elizabeth. "After all, it is only fair that I help repair the damage my whimsical actions have caused."

The girl blushed again but then appeared to gather her courage as she gazed back at Elizabeth. "I feel we must agree to disagree in this matter. I am convinced I am as much at fault. I was not attending to my surroundings any more than you were."

Elizabeth laughed and was soon joined by the other girl. "Very well! We shall share the blame."

When their mirth had run its course, Elizabeth glanced at the stranger, only to find herself the object of the other girl's studying gaze. With a slight frown on her countenance she asked, "I am sorry, but are you from the area?"

"Yes," affirmed Elizabeth, "I live at the estate of Longbourn on the other side of Meryton. I often roam these woods."

The girl's eyes widened, and she stared back at Elizabeth. "The other side of Meryton? But that is two miles distant."

"Yes, it is, and Longbourn is another mile beyond."

"Three miles!" cried the girl. "I would never be allowed to walk so far."

Somewhat perplexed and realizing for the first time that the other girl was not native to the region, Elizabeth frowned. "I do not understand. Surely you have walked far from your home this morning."

"Oh, no, I do not live in this area. My brother and I are merely staying in the house of my brother's close friend." She turned and pointed to Netherfield Park in the distance. "We are staying at Netherfield with Mr. Bingley."

All at once, the situation became clear to Elizabeth, and she realized the identity of the young woman, for she had heard stories of Mr. Darcy's beautiful and shy young sister. For an instant, Elizabeth, who still harbored no very cordial feelings toward a certain proud young man, felt a rush of vexation for having accidentally met up with the man's younger sister.

The more rational part of her immediately recognized the young girl was friendly, if a little shy, and could not be held accountable for her brother's excess of pride and ill-judged words. And so Elizabeth put her feelings of ambivalence behind her and smiled.

"In fact, if you have walked so far, perhaps you would like to return to Netherfield for some refreshment?" The words were spoken quickly and breathlessly by the girl, and Elizabeth saw that she was not in the habit of giving invitations, though she was covering her reticence admirably.

"I would be delighted to accompany you," said Elizabeth, "and I thank you for your kind invitation."

Georgiana Darcy, for this was whom Elizabeth believed her to be, inclined her head and gestured in the direction of the manor house. They walked along the path conversing, their conversation ranging from such subjects as Elizabeth's penchant for walking to Miss Darcy's impressions of the area. Although the girl said nothing further of the acquaintances she had made since arriving at Netherfield, Elizabeth was soon given to understand that the girl quite enjoyed the country, for she was effusive in her praise of the estate and the taste of its master in decorating the rooms and making them comfortable and livable after the long period in which Netherfield had remained empty.

During their discussion, Elizabeth kept sneaking glances at her companion, waiting for the realization that they had not yet been introduced. Whatever else he might be—or whatever he might opine within hearing distance of those he was insulting—Elizabeth had taken Mr. Darcy for being rigidly proper and adhering to all rules of polite society. Surely a girl so much younger than he himself—and under his care—would have been instructed in a similar fashion.

But Miss Darcy merely continued to chatter on, heedless of the fact that she had invited a complete stranger to accompany her to a home in which she was merely a guest. The nearer they drew to the house, the more uncomfortable Elizabeth became. Cognizant as she was of

Darcy's opinion of her, she could well imagine him believing she had intentionally withheld her identity from his modest sister for the intent of imposing.

Finally, she could take it no longer. She stopped and turned to regard Georgiana, who halted as well with a look of curiosity on her face.

"I am sorry, but I believe we should make our introductions before we proceed any further. Since there is no one else in the vicinity to perform the task, I fear that we must make do."

Soft, girlish giggling met her ironic words, and the girl inclined her head. "Oh, how thoughtless of me! My name is Georgiana Darcy, and I am sister to Fitzwilliam Darcy, master of Pemberley estate in Derbyshire."

"I believe I have the advantage, then, Miss Darcy. My name is Elizabeth Bennet, and I have previously had the pleasure of meeting both Mr. Darcy and Mr. Bingley."

A shocked silence met her declaration, and she began to wonder whether the girl had heard something of her from her brother. Perhaps Miss Darcy's brother was as effusive in speaking of his disapproval of Elizabeth's appearance to more than just Mr. Bingley, thought Elizabeth, with no little feelings of disdain for the gentleman in question.

"Miss Bennet." Georgiana Darcy curtseyed slightly in greeting, a gesture which Elizabeth returned. "I beg your pardon, Miss Bennet, but you have already met my brother? You were not at the assembly earlier this week, were you?"

"No, indeed," replied Elizabeth. "I was the victim of a small indisposition that night and was unable to attend."

"Then how have you met my brother?"

Elizabeth was surprised by the question, having assumed Miss Darcy had been told of the time the Bennet sisters had spent in the company of the gentlemen the day following the assembly. It appeared the siblings did not share such confidence as she would have imagined. But then again, their age difference was enough that it was not surprising that the elder brother did not confide in his sister as much as Elizabeth and Jane did with each other.

"Mr. Bingley called on my sisters and me the day after the assembly, and I was able to meet your brother at the same time."

Miss Darcy's questioning expression quickly turned to a frown as Elizabeth continued to relate the circumstances of her meeting with the two gentlemen, and by the time she had finished telling the story, Miss

Darcy's lips were pursed, and her face had grown icy and disapproving.

"I see," responded the girl finally, her voice as cold as her face.

Unable to determine the reason for this sudden change in demeanor, Elizabeth searched Miss Darcy's face for any indication of what had displeased her, and she was startled to find a certain resemblance to the expression which had adorned Mr. Darcy's face when he had proclaimed her to be less than handsome—the look was so similar she could well imagine it had been removed from the man's and placed much as a mask over the young girl's face.

Elizabeth attempted to return the conversation to the pleasant discussion it had been before they had introduced themselves, but Miss Darcy merely responded in monosyllabic mumbles. For whatever reason, the girl was now quite displeased and refused to speak with Elizabeth any further.

At length, they came in view of the house, and Miss Darcy proclaimed herself tired and in need of rest, bent in the barest hint of a curtsey, and turned on her heel to march back toward Netherfield without any mention of the invitation which had already been offered. Elizabeth watched her walk off in astonishment—never in her life had she ever been witness to such impertinent rudeness! To invite someone for refreshments and then stalk off without another word was completely beyond the pale.

"Miss Bennet," a voice arrested her thoughts, and she turned to witness Mr. Bingley striding toward her, an anxious expression on his usually jovial features. "My apologies for my presumption—did something just occur between you and Miss Darcy?"

"I hardly know, Mr. Bingley," answered Elizabeth, staring at the retreating figure. "We were conversing quite happily until we made our introductions. When she found out who I was, she almost ran from me."

"Where were you going together? Who introduced you?"

Elizabeth peered up into Mr. Bingley's eyes, mortified that he might consider the altercation to be at her instigation. After the impression she had apparently made on Mr. Darcy, she was not certain she could tolerate the poor opinion of yet another young man.

"We met in the woods, Mr. Bingley, and introduced ourselves since there was no one to perform the task for us."

Mr. Bingley seemed to consider this, but the frown of confusion never left his face. "Miss Bennet, were you going to Netherfield just now?"

"Yes. Miss Darcy had invited me to Netherfield for some refreshments."

"She did what?" Mr. Bingley appeared to be highly agitated, and he began to pace. "Then she left you without a word?"

Elizabeth hesitated, not wanting to agitate him any further, but also not wanting to lie. "I am afraid so, Mr. Bingley."

Mr. Bingley paced for several more moments, running his hands through his hair, before he turned to Elizabeth and bowed deeply. "Miss Bennet, please allow me to apologize for my guest's improper manners. If you will follow me to Netherfield, I assure you we can discover exactly what has prompted this breach of etiquette."

"Believe me—I do not blame you, Mr. Bingley," Elizabeth hastened to assure him. "I would prefer not to make any more of the situation, nor do I wish to mortify Miss Darcy's feelings. I believe I would rather simply return to my home."

Although Mr. Bingley seemed to wish to pursue the subject, he inclined his head in acknowledgment. "If that is your wish, Miss Bennet, then please allow me to set you on your way in my carriage. It is a long way to Longbourn, after all."

"I believe, sir, that I am an excellent walker. I have walked all the way here on my own, just this morning. I assure you, there is no need to concern yourself on my behalf."

"Perhaps not, Miss Bennet, but I insist. Please come with me, and I will order the carriage."

Seeing he was determined, Elizabeth inclined her head and fell into step with him. Their walk to the house was completed in silence, as Mr. Bingley's usual garrulity was absent in response to his concern over Miss Darcy's strange behavior. They reached the house in a few moments, and soon after that, he had handed her up into the carriage. The instructions were passed to the driver and footmen, and then the carriage began to roll away from the park, leaving Elizabeth alone with her thoughts and the puzzle which was the Darcy siblings.

Chapter X

In spite of Mr. Darcy's words regarding Elizabeth, Mary Bennet was the only one of the Bennet sisters who was truly plain, though perhaps it would be a cruel thing to say so openly. The truth of the matter was that she was only considered plain in comparison to her four sisters, who were each very handsome in their individual ways. Mary was actually a pleasant enough girl, with dark hair and a fair complexion, and if she lacked the beauty of the other Miss Bennets, she was certainly far from merely *plain*.

Elizabeth pitied Mary, for she knew that Mary had heard about her sisters' beauty all of her life and—although she was not meant to hear—about her own lack thereof. That it was a less than tactful mother who often lamented this lack simply made it worse. The first time Mary had heard such a thing said, she had taken to her room and cried for hours, only comforted once Elizabeth had come to console her. After Elizabeth had heard the entire story, she had lifted Mary's spirits and shown her the ways in which she could improve her appearance. Elizabeth knew her sister had never forgotten her attention on that day, and while Mary was not a girl to display her emotions openly or express her appreciation in an animated fashion, Elizabeth became Mary's favorite sister—one to admire and to share in such confidences as Mary was able to impart.

Unfortunately, as a consequence of being considered plainer than her sisters, Mary began looking for other ways to distinguish herself. It was then that she discovered moral texts and the pianoforte, and she thereafter bent all of her efforts to become accomplished in the latter while becoming knowledgeable in the former. Her success was mixed at best, a fact of which Elizabeth knew Mary herself was well aware. Mary's passion for sermonizing was often looked upon with annoyance, and while the young woman truly believed the things she read, the general reaction to her tendency toward piety was an exasperated sigh. Although her performance at the pianoforte was competent, it was generally considered to be without passion. Of course, this only spurred her on to greater efforts to achieve that recognition she so desperately craved. Elizabeth suspected that part of the reason for Mary's determination was a deep sense of loneliness. Mary was so different from the rest of her family that she had no one to confide in—despite the fact that she looked up to Elizabeth, the two were truly different people. Unfortunately, her attempts to draw attention were often self-defeating; the more energy she put into her efforts, the less inclined the others of her family became to converse with her.

One morning, she was playing the pianoforte and singing with her weak voice and affected manner when Elizabeth led Kitty into the room, conversing with her as they walked. Elizabeth had decided to confide in Kitty as to the scene which had played out between Miss Georgiana Darcy and herself, for she was quite puzzled as to why the girl had suddenly become so hostile. As Kitty tended to be Elizabeth's confidant in such matters—Elizabeth found she could talk to her about things which Jane would rather not contemplate—Elizabeth approached her to seek her opinion concerning the reason the young lady had become so cold so quickly.

"I am not sure, Lizzy," confessed Kitty in a quiet voice not meant for Mary to hear. "I found Miss Darcy a rather difficult girl to read. She seemed to alternate between coldness and warmth." Louder, she said: "Hello, Mary."

Mary's brow simply furrowed, and she continued to sing without acknowledging the entrance of her sisters.

Kitty, using her cane, moved closer to her sister. "I said 'hello,' Mary."

But Mary just started to play and sing louder.

Kitty finally stepped up beside the pianoforte and reached out in quest for the music her sister was using. Upon finding it, she grasped it to herself. "Come, Mary, will you not greet your sisters?"

The infuriated Mary shot to her feet. "While I am well aware of the proficiency you possess in regard to the pianoforte, Catherine, there are others who wish to benefit from extended study of the play of words and notes upon a page."

"Girls," cried Elizabeth, "please do not fight so! You both have your skills, and there is no need to detract from those of the other by such a disagreement."

Mary grudgingly conceded: "St. Paul *did* tell the Philippians to do all things without murmurings and disputings."

As if on cue, an exaggerated sigh from her younger sister met her declaration, causing Mary to huff irritably in reply.

In a tightly controlled voice, Mary said: "You are right, Elizabeth. There is no need to argue any longer. I am done with the pianoforte, Catherine, should you wish to use it."

After Mary left the room, Elizabeth turned to Kitty with a disapproving frown. "You should not bait your sister so. You know that she struggles to attain her accomplishments and merely wishes to be accepted by those around her."

"I understand that, Lizzy," said Kitty. "But she can be so frustrating sometimes, especially when she pretends she cannot hear us when she is playing. She should know that we accept her as our sister regardless of what others may say—and that those who matter the most do likewise."

Elizabeth could not deny this fact, but she once again stressed the need for sisters to be tolerant toward one another, which Kitty accepted without further comment.

Now that the pianoforte was unoccupied, Kitty did indeed sit down at the instrument, but she did not play immediately. Instead, she asked: "Why are you so curious about Miss Darcy, Lizzy?"

Elizabeth imparted the details of the strange scene she had experienced with Miss Darcy and then said: "I am completely at a loss as to why she became so cold. To offer refreshments and then renege on the offer with nary a word is rudeness beyond anything I have ever witnessed. Even with such a brother, I had thought Miss Darcy of better breeding than *that*."

Kitty ignored Elizabeth's negative comment about Mr. Darcy. "It is indeed peculiar. Do you remember what you said before the change came over her?"

"I do not," said Elizabeth. "But I do remember that it was not worthy of such an expression of rudeness. I did not insult her family or question her bearing. She was quite amiable before being seized by her sudden transformation."

"I suspect there is a good reason behind it. You should take care to examine her in company, for I believe there is something which we are both missing. Now, what shall I play, Lizzy?" Her hands were poised above the instrument in front of her.

Elizabeth touched her sister's shoulder. "Play whatever you would like."

Kitty moved her fingers to the pianoforte and began caressing the keys. Elizabeth, who had the better singing voice, accompanied her.

Even had she retained the use of her eyes, Kitty's skill with the instrument before her would have been viewed as impressive—considering the fact that she was blind, her skill was nothing less than astonishing. The keys easily responded to the gentle pressure of her fingers, revealing the reason why Mary was so jealous of Kitty's skill. Mr. and Mrs. Bennet's second youngest seemed to combine the true emotion of Elizabeth's playing with the technical proficiency of Mary's playing. Though Kitty could not read, she was able to learn music by ear, finding the notes based on what she heard, with only the very rare correction from her sisters. And Elizabeth, possessing the prettiest singing voice of all her sisters, loved singing with Kitty's accompaniment—the effect of the two talents blending together was as fine as the small town of Meryton could boast, and they had often been requested to share their talents at parties and assemblies.

After the song was over, Elizabeth noticed her twin had come into the room and was standing nearby with a smile on her face. "Oh!" exclaimed Elizabeth in surprise.

Jane smiled. "I have not been here for long. Please, continue."

"Play Mozart, Kitty—Sonata in C," suggested Elizabeth, attempting to cover up the embarrassment engendered by having an unnoticed observer.

Kitty turned her head to show her eldest sister a smile. The piece was one of their favorites.

She played the first movement with ease, and her two sisters were pleased to merely stand and listen. Once Kitty began playing the second movement, however, Elizabeth's expression became one of mischief. Kitty passed through a few bars unaccompanied, but finally Elizabeth began to sing again, this time with lyrics which she was creating as she went:

Jane – she was a lovely and nice girl,
Who always thought so kind of everyone.
La da da dee oh da dah dah dee dah doh dee la la la la.

And one day she met a kind man, Bingley,
And it was love at first sight.
Oh, how happy we are that everything is now set aright.

By this point, Kitty and Elizabeth were experiencing such mirth that they were unable to finish the song, while Jane merely stood close by, a rosy blush affixed to her features. It was a common game between the three closest Bennet sisters—the younger and the older trying to provoke a response from the shy and demure Jane, who typically protested and stammered in mortification.

"Girls!" exclaimed poor Jane in embarrassment.

But the two musical conspirators simply continued to laugh.

Chapter XI

Meals at Longbourn had the distinction of being rather confusing affairs if one were not especially acquainted with the Bennets. The dearth of intelligent male conversation was not surprising given the makeup of the family, yet the personalities of the Bennet females was so disparate that their mealtime conversations were often rather muddled affairs, with sometimes two or even three competing discussions occurring at once.

Of course, Mr. Bennet's lack of a son was in many ways made up for by Mr. Bennet's eldest, who in no way displayed the deficiency of conversation shown by her mother and some of her sisters. Instead, Mr. Bennet found conversation with his Elizabeth to be a diverting endeavor. Their shared penchant for laughing at the follies and inconsistencies of their neighbors was more often than not looked upon with complete bewilderment by some of the other occupants of the room. Of course, Elizabeth, although she was Mr. Bennet's dearest daughter, was not the only one with a modicum of sense. Mr. Bennet understood Kitty to be nearest to her in terms of temperament, for Kitty, while she did not have the dry and sometimes caustic wit of her elder sister, was still in possession of a discerning mind which allowed her to laugh at the sometimes humorous manner in which Elizabeth and her father conversed. Jane's understanding was no less than that of her sisters, and Bennet often found conversation with his second eldest, while perhaps somewhat lacking in playfulness, to be satisfying in that she was intelligent and her views were not insipid. Unfortunately, Mr. Bennet had little in common with Mary, and they therefore conversed infrequently with one another. As for Lydia, well, she was so silly and empty-headed that he could not tolerate more than a few moments in conversation with the girl before a headache would manifest itself.

Despite being able to converse intelligently with at least a few of his daughters, Mr. Bennet often longed for a male companion with whom to commiserate. His wife's love of hosting dinner parties was an occasion for relief, but it was unfortunately one which could be a double-edged sword—he did not truly like leaving his bookroom for long periods, and the male companionship of the area was not always sensible. To make matters worse, his ill health prevented him from joining his neighbors in sport as much as he would like, leaving him to starve for the companionship of another man amidst a veritable gaggle of young women.

There was, unfortunately, no recourse to be had, as they were not to be in the company of Mr. Gardiner—Mrs. Bennet's younger brother—and his family until Christmas, and the oncoming visit of another gentleman, although Mr. Bennet hated to use the term considering the ridiculous letter he had received, could hardly satisfy him in his want of intelligent conversation. But such hardships must be endured, and although everything he knew about the man suggested he was pompous and stupid, at least Mr. Bennet would have the pleasure of laughing at the young man without fear of his comments being comprehended.

Shaking off his introspection, Mr. Bennet concentrated on the task at hand. It was necessary for him to inform his wife of the impending visit and then make her aware of the second piece of correspondence which he had recently received. At least it promised to be an amusing development.

The breakfast table was unusually subdued, and the ladies of the house seemed to be concentrating more on their meals than on whatever gossip was now fashionable in the area. Mr. Bennet decided it would be prudent to make his communication at this time—before the conversation erupted in incomprehensible and nonsensical talk about reticules and the like.

"Mrs. Bennet, my dear," said he, "if I might have a moment of your time, I have two letters to discuss with you. One of them contains news of the greatest import."

"Indeed, Mr. Bennet," replied his wife. "And pray, what could that be?"

"Why, that your talents as a superior hostess will soon be put to the test with the arrival of a guest to our family party."

Mrs. Bennet was startled by her husband's assertion and began fidgeting with her napkin. "And might I know the identity of this illustrious personage who will soon require our attention?"

"I have no qualms in telling you, my dear. In less than a se'nnight's time, you will be most fortunate to be able to host the next master of this estate, the illustrious Mr. Collins himself."

"Mr. Bennet!" cried she, "how can you be so teasing? You must know I detest the very sound of the man's name."

"Oh, yes, Mrs. Bennet—I have heard you wax poetic on more than one occasion about your dislike for my heir. In fact, I dare say the entire neighborhood is aware of the lack of esteem in which you hold young Master Collins."

"Personally, I suspect the matter has been canvassed to a *much* larger audience," murmured Elizabeth to Kitty, who snickered.

Mrs. Bennet, however, remained blissfully unaware of her daughter's comment. "And why should I keep my opinion of him to myself? Do you mean to tell me I should feel any differently to know that I will one day be replaced—shunted aside—by that odious man?"

"I am certain Mr. Collins has every intention of personally seeing you thrown out of this house to starve, madam."

"I am certain he has! It is the hardest thing in the world that the estate should be entailed away from your own daughters, Mr. Bennet, and settled on so unworthy a young man. Why should it only pass through the male line? It should go to Lizzy instead, as she seems to have a certain aptitude and liking for estate matters, though heaven knows I do not understand why."

It was an old argument, one which had been debated many times. Unfortunately, the more perceptive members of the family had had no success in convincing the Bennet matron that although there were undoubtedly many estates which were allowed to pass through the female line, Longbourn was not one of them, nor was there anything the present proprietor could do to alter the terms of its inheritance. Privately, Mr. Bennet suspected his wife understood very well the nature of the entail and from whence it had originated. It was, however, an old complaint which she was not capable of releasing, much as a dog protects and worries at a bone. Mr. Bennet was not about to again enter into such a discussion with his wife.

As it turned out, he was saved from having to listen to her rant about the status of the entail by his eldest daughter, who no doubt understood where the conversation was headed.

"Mama," scolded Elizabeth, "I am certain the young man has done nothing to earn your disapproval. He can hardly be faulted for the terms of the entail, which were not of his doing."

"Nor for the accident of birth which made him the heir of this estate," added Kitty.

"Yes, yes, that is all very fine," persisted Mrs. Bennet, though she decided to change her tack. "Yet I fail to understand why we must suffer this loathsome man in our home for an instant more than he is entitled. Why should we allow him to inspect our house with his coveting eyes? I am sure that he will begin to catalog our possessions as though they were already his own the very moment he steps through the door."

Mr. Bennet chuckled, diverted by his wife's indignant and self-righteous lamentations. If nothing else, the time in which Collins would grace their humble abode would not be dull.

Looking at his wife, he smiled at her and said: "I have a letter here from him. Would you not like to hear the method in which he expresses himself?"

"If you must, Mr. Bennet. I must say that I still quite detest the very sound of his name."

Mr. Bennet then began to read:

Hunsford, near Westerham, Kent, 15th October.

Dear Sir,

My purpose for writing to you in this sudden and no doubt unexpected fashion is to attempt a reconciliation between the two branches of our family and restore each other to the convenience and society which must be a blessing and a joy to two most intimately related people such as ourselves. My late father could not often be prevailed upon to discuss the circumstances which brought about this breach in the family, but his abuse of your person on many occasions was such that I was never able to comfortably set my mind to attempt the reconciliation I believed in my heart to be quite necessary for Christian followers of our Lord and Savior.

However, I have recently been referred to the valuable living of Hunsford in Kent and have obtained the patronage and condescension of the most honorable Lady Catherine de Bourgh, who, in her unending Christian generosity, has correctly pointed out that although respect and devotion to one's parents is a commendable and worthy trait, promoting the values of friendship, esteem, and forgiveness is paramount to all clergymen and can only benefit the parish in the manner of showing an example before one's impressionable flock. Her wisdom has greatly humbled me, and I believe that following her advice is the proper recourse for a man in such an influential position as the one I am now privileged to hold.

In doing this, I hope my efforts will not only be viewed as commendable but will also allow myself to rise in your esteem. I hope as well that you shall indulge the second reason for my desire to visit with you and repair the rift between us. I understand that you, Mr. Bennet, are the father of five very pretty and amiable daughters. As my noble patroness has so recently pointed out, my continued status as a bachelor does nothing to promote an example in the parish of the proper respect for our Lord's commandments regarding the sanctity and necessity of the marriage ordinance, and I have determined that I may have a means of making amends to your daughters for being the eventual cause of their removal from the home of their birth by engaging myself to one of them. In doing this, I will allow you the comfort of seeing one of your daughters—who, although I am certain are amiable and all that is good, may never receive an offer of marriage from any young man due to their unfortunately small portions—comfortably settled as the mistress of my parsonage in Kent and later as the mistress of your estate in Hertfordshire after your unfortunate passing. Of course, this arrangement will also satisfy my patroness's demand that I marry soon and will provide me with the joy of having a companion in my life.

If you are agreeable to this design, I propose the pleasure of waiting upon you on Friday, the 25th of October. I shall arrive by four o'clock, and I ask to be allowed to trespass upon your hospitality for a fortnight after this, during which time I will avail myself of the opportunity of making myself agreeable to your daughters and obtaining the promise which I desire and which I know shall be of mutual benefit to us all. We may converse about this matter more upon my arrival. Until then, I wish you all the health and felicity you so richly deserve, and I take this opportunity to state that I hope to eventually claim the honor of calling you my dear father-in-law.

Upon your acceptance of our most necessary reconciliation, I will be, always, your friend and close cousin,

William Collins

The responses from the females of the family were everything Mr. Bennet would have expected, although he was by no means less amused for having predicted their reactions in advance. Lydia's response was, of course, the easiest to predict, as she contented herself with nothing more than an indelicate snort at the thought of marrying a clergyman before returning to her contemplation of redcoats and the recent arrival of a company of militia to the area. Mary, predictably, did some moralizing on the subject and voiced her firm approval for the obvious piety of the young man. Jane could not be moved to respond to the letter, though Mr. Bennet was certain he could detect the slightest tightening around her mouth at the thought of the young man's journeying to Hertfordshire with the intent of marrying her or one of her sisters. Although Jane would never own to thinking ill of someone, Mr. Bennet suspected she could tell from the tone of Mr. Collins's letter that he was not someone who could bring her or her sisters any real measure of happiness. Of course, Elizabeth and Kitty merely snickered and looked to their father in anticipation of his biting comments.

But Elizabeth and Kitty were to be disappointed, for Mr. Bennet's concentration was focused not on making declarations regarding the silliness of his pompous cousin, but on the reaction of his wife to the letter. Mrs. Bennet, although she had just been loudly decrying the imminent visit of the man who was to be the means of rendering her destitute, was silent for several moments as the import of the young man's words made their way through her consciousness. It took slightly more time than her husband would have expected, but once Mrs. Bennet had understood just what the letter meant, her delight was soon almost as violent as her earlier dislike. As a woman who had made it her life's work to marry off her daughters, this opportunity to rid herself of one of them with little effort on her part was enough to send her into raptures.

Of even greater amusement to Mr. Bennet were the calculating looks Mrs. Bennet directed toward her eldest daughter. Elizabeth appeared very aware of her mother's scrutiny and perfectly enlightened as to its meaning. She could not be bothered to dissuade her mother from such a plan, however, as Mr. Bennet knew Elizabeth was confident that he would not consent to anything to which she did not accede.

"What a wonderful thing for our girls!" exclaimed Mrs. Bennet.

"How so, Mrs. Bennet?"

The look she directed at her husband made him want to laugh—she obviously considered the question to be daft. "Why, his expressed purpose in coming to Longbourn is to secure the hand of one our daughters in marriage. Just think of it, Mr. Bennet! With a daughter married to your cousin, our futures would be secured."

"Yes, yes, Mrs. Bennet. I understand his desire and your reasons for enthusiastically embracing his plans. However, before you offer one—or all—of our daughters to Mr. Collins, I suggest you ask their opinions on the matter."

"Their opinions?" cried she. "Of what are you talking? What do their opinions have to do with it?"

"They must give their consent to the match, must they not? Perhaps none of them will develop a regard for the young man."

"They will do their duty!" snapped Mrs. Bennet. Her voice was now gaining in strength and volume, causing more than one member of the family to wince. "In fact, Lizzy, as the eldest, should do her duty and offer herself to Mr. Collins directly when he arrives. Yes, I believe Lizzy will do well as a parson's wife."

"Mrs. Bennet, you will in no way direct your daughter to act so shamefully!" said Mr. Bennet. His voice was as hard as iron, and all the amusement he had felt upon reading the letter was gone. "I will not have any of my daughters married to a man against her will, especially a man whom I suspect to be one of the silliest in all of England."

"But Mr. Bennet—"

"No, Mrs. Bennet! Not another word. If Lizzy should have the misfortune and complete lack of judgment to develop an attachment to my cousin, I will not stand in her way. Otherwise, you will most certainly not browbeat your eldest into accepting a proposal of marriage when she has no inclination for doing so!"

A quiet descended upon the table. Mrs. Bennet knew from previous experience when her husband was not in the mood to be gainsaid; as a result, she held her tongue. Her eyes, however, told a different story, for she continued to regard her eldest daughter, sizing her up for her wedding clothes, if Mr. Bennet was any judge of her character.

Elizabeth, apparently wanting to change the subject, looked at her father and said:

"Papa, you have only spoken of one of your letters. What does the other one say?"

"It is from your Uncle Gardiner. It appears that his business has interfered with their plans to spend Christmas at Longbourn, and he entreats us to join them in London for the holiday."

Predictably, the approbation and general enthusiasm for the idea was unanimous. It was only a few moments before a resigned Mr. Bennet agreed that they should all travel to London for Christmas, although he would not consent to stay as long as the new year. The disappointment rendered by this resolution was momentary, as Jane,

Elizabeth, and Kitty soon conceived of a plan to ask their relations if they might reside with them a little longer, though Lydia loudly proclaimed she would rather return to Longbourn so as to be in company with the officers of the regiment. Mary, who was acting unusually quiet and reflective even for her, stayed completely silent on the matter.

Mr. Bennet knew that he would have nothing to add to the chatter of several female voices talking about the theater, shopping in London, and any number of other anticipated amusements. Therefore, he soon retired to his study, thinking to himself that Gardiner owed him a rather large debt for upsetting his routine and necessitating that he journey to London in the company of his wife and daughters amidst the boisterous cloud of excitement that surrounded them when they went to town.

Chapter XII

On the 22nd of October, a large party was assembled at Sir William Lucas's estate. Sir William was a kind man who had accrued a small fortune in trade. After making an address to the king at St. James's Court during his mayoralty, however, the rank of knighthood had been conferred upon him. This elevation had assured him of his own importance in the world, so he had moved with his family from Meryton to the home about a mile away which was now dubbed Lucas Lodge. At Lucas Lodge, he could live at his leisure without the shackles of business to hold him down, basking in the pleasure of his standing. Yet despite his self-assurance, he was not an unapproachably proud man; rather, he took delight in being very attentive to all those around him.

The Bennets were particularly intimate with the Lucas family, as Lucas Lodge was within a short walk of Longbourn, and at a large gathering such as the one taking place at the Lucas estate, one family could not be found in attendance without the other. That the two families had mothers who loved to gossip, young daughters who were generally of age with one another, and fathers who often took counsel with each other only served to make them even closer friends.

When the Bennets arrived at Sir William's gathering, he warmly expressed his pleasure over the fact that they were able to attend. "And you shall even find," noted he in a jovial and almost mysterious manner, "that the great Mr. Darcy himself has joined us tonight!"

Elizabeth could not help but comment quietly: "I am surprised he should have deigned to come to such a happy gathering. I had begun to wonder if perhaps he delighted in being dour."

"Lizzy!" admonished Jane.

However, Sir William did not appear to have heard Elizabeth, as he was watching the arrival of some new guests, and he excused himself to go greet them without responding. Mr. Bennet had felt well enough to attend an assembly (or perhaps, Elizabeth suspected, he was merely determined to ensure his eldest daughter was not tempted to stay at home), and so he parted from his wife and daughters to seek another kindred soul with whom he could stand aside as an observer. Mrs. Bennet soon left in search of Lady Lucas, though not before she pointed out Mr. Bingley to Jane in a voice brimming with excitement.

Once their mother had hurried off to hold court with the other matrons, the remaining daughters stood as a group for a moment before Lydia exclaimed, "Oh, look!" She pointed to a group of officers standing close by. "I can see Jones and Roberts!" And then, she, too, was gone.

Elizabeth shook her head and turned to Jane. "I am sorry for what I said about Mr. Darcy, Jane," said she, though in reality she did not regret her remark in the slightest. "But I do wonder at him, and it is not just due to the blow he gave to my vanity. If he so detests country manners and cannot take pleasure in speaking with anyone of the company, why attend any of our gatherings at all?"

"Perhaps he does not think so ill of our society as you believe," remarked Kitty.

"You had better be careful, Kitty, or I should start to think that you had an interest in Mr. Darcy of your own," teased Elizabeth.

"Perhaps *you* should pay closer attention to Mr. Darcy, Lizzy," Kitty retorted. "I do not believe that *I* am the one interested in him, and neither is *he* interested in *me*." And with that, Kitty turned away, asking Jane to escort her to visit with some friends.

After watching them leave, Elizabeth looked around in a vain hope that Charlotte Lucas might have chosen to leave her position as governess or, at the very least, that Charlotte might have been able to pull herself away long enough to visit Lucas Lodge. But of course, the young woman was nowhere to be found.

"These gatherings are a good way to lighten the soul," commented Mary, who had remained with her eldest sister.

"Perhaps," said Elizabeth with a sigh, contemplating the fact that a party at Lucas Lodge without Charlotte was an assembly incapable of lightening her soul.

A few seconds later, Mary whispered in warning: "Lizzy."

Elizabeth turned her head to see what had caught her sister's attention, and she nearly gasped as she saw Mr. Darcy's tall and imposing figure walking toward them in determination.

"What can he want?" wondered Elizabeth out loud. Her thoughts darted back to Miss Darcy, to whom Elizabeth was certain Mr. Darcy had related, in full, his low opinion of Elizabeth's person, and she resolved on being cool and firm.

He was soon upon them. After he greeted them, they curtseyed in response, and then he asked a surprising question:

"Miss Bennet, if you would oblige me, might I trouble you for a moment of your time so I may have a word with you?"

Elizabeth, knowing she had little choice, inclined her head in assent. Mr. Darcy bowed his own head in response and gestured for her to precede him. Elizabeth, directing a carefully hidden grimace of distaste for her companion to a clearly unamused Mary, departed from her sister to face the man who had so cavalierly disparaged her.

Elizabeth stole glances at her companion as they left Mary, and though the man let little emotion show in his expression, he was clearly uncomfortable. It seemed unlikely that—given Mr. Darcy's standing and the hauteur he had displayed—he meant to apologize. However, the man kept his face so impassive that Elizabeth could tell nothing further about his feelings or his thoughts. He *did* appear to watch her most intently, but Elizabeth fancied that he was merely attempting to confirm his initial impression of her.

Once they had arrived at a relatively secluded area of the house—presumably so they would not be overheard—Mr. Darcy began to speak. "I wanted to apologize to you, Miss Bennet, for my unkind comments."

Despite her resolution to be cool, Elizabeth found she did not want him to proceed any further with his apology, and she spoke to him with a playful smile. "I assure you, Mr. Darcy, that my ego was not excessively battered by your words. I have far too strong an opinion of myself to allow such a statement to have a lasting effect on me. And surely, sir, you must think that I deserved what I received—after all, I was committing an act of espionage at the time."

"'Espionage' is not the typical word used to refer to such a situation, Miss Bennet. I sense you have a penchant for exaggeration."

"And I sense you have a penchant for speaking out of turn," returned Elizabeth in good humor. "It seems we both have our faults."

And then Mr. Darcy, whose countenance was always so serious, actually gave her a wry smile. "Indeed."

"Why, I am shocked, Mr. Darcy!"

The man's brow furrowed. "What is it, Miss Bennet?"

"I had said you were incapable of smiling. It seems I owe Kitty a new ribbon after all."

"Tell me, Miss Bennet, do you make a habit of forming wagers concerning new acquaintances?"

"Only when they cause as much of a stir among the people of Hertfordshire as you and Mr. Bingley have."

Mr. Darcy lifted an eyebrow. "Am I then to assume that you have made a wager concerning my friend as well?"

Elizabeth gave him an enigmatic smile. "Come now, Mr. Darcy. You cannot expect a woman to share all of her secrets."

"I suppose not." He hesitated before speaking once more. "I want to apologize again, Miss Bennet, and perhaps explain myself further."

But this went against Elizabeth's plans, as she was determined to maintain her dislike of the man. "Mr. Darcy—"

"No, please let me continue. You see, I am not a man who is accustomed to sharing my feelings with anyone, not even people with whom I am well acquainted. That day outside your house, Bingley was pressuring me into owning an attachment which I do not feel. I certainly have not come to Hertfordshire with the desire of participating in such diversions as my friend desires for me. My comment on your appearance was not intended as a slight against you; rather, I was trying to dissuade my companion from making such talk as he was. I am very cognizant of the fact that I should have chosen some other way to induce Bingley to cease his comments. It was very wrong of me to speak so, and I apologize."

"You may consider your apology accepted, Mr. Darcy. Though I am not without my vanity, it is not such that I will stubbornly cling to your former unkind words and refuse your present kind ones."

There was a brief lull in their conversation during which Mr. Darcy looked at her intently before venturing: "Miss Bennet?"

"Yes, Mr. Darcy?"

Mr. Darcy's hesitation was barely perceptible. "Bingley is to have a ball at Netherfield—your whole family will receive an invitation, of course—and I was wondering if I might be given the honor of standing up with you for the first dance?"

Had Mr. Darcy asked Elizabeth for her hand in marriage, she could hardly have been more surprised. "Excuse me, Mr. Darcy?"

"You must promise me the first dance." The man had become stiff, and the seriousness which had seemed to be melting away during the course of their conversation was now back.

"But I quite detest dancing—even had I known before now that Mr. Bingley was to have a dance, I should not have wished to go." She gave him a puzzled look. "I had thought you hated dancing yourself, Mr. Darcy."

The man's mouth was in a hard line. "I am not completely averse to the activity. I merely find that often the company at such dances is lacking."

"You do not have to ask me to dance in an attempt to appease my vanity."

"I am doing nothing of the sort. I am merely asking you to dance with me at Netherfield because I wish it."

Elizabeth hardly knew what else to say, so she agreed to his request. They returned to the more populated area of the house, where he bowed and took his leave of her. She watched his departure with a frown. Mr. Darcy—asking her to dance with him! She did not know what to make of this development.

The man went over to his sister, who looked up at her brother with great pleasure. Elizabeth watched in surprise as Mr. Darcy actually gave Miss Darcy a tender smile. Then he bent over to whisper something in her ear.

Miss Darcy beamed and then made a query which seemed to be: "Who?"

Mr. Darcy spoke softly to her one more time, and a frown spread across her face. Her eyes then lifted to meet those of Elizabeth, who flushed at having been caught staring. Mr. Darcy caught the look his sister gave Elizabeth and bent down to say what must have been an admonishment, for it caused Miss Darcy's face to color.

Throughout the night, Elizabeth found her gaze drawn back to the two Darcys. Mr. Darcy, it seemed, was a happier sort of person when in his sister's presence, as though she lightened the heavy load bestowed on him by his pride. Elizabeth, however, was determined not to like Miss Darcy any better for it. The rudeness displayed by that girl had been completely uncalled for.

Eventually, however, the subject of her thoughts actually came and asked to speak to her alone.

Elizabeth, who had been talking with Lady Lucas about how much

Charlotte was missed, excused herself with some surprise.

Georgiana Darcy turned her head to look at her brother, who gave her a stern nod. "Miss—Miss Bennet," began Miss Darcy. She was trembling and looked as if she were about to cry. "I have come to—to apologize to you." She paused, trying to pull herself together.

Elizabeth could not help but take pity on the girl. Miss Darcy kept looking to her brother, as if desiring that he assist her, but he merely gazed at her firmly. It was obvious she was making the apology at his instigation.

"What I d-did was inexcusable. I—behaved imp-improperly, and I humbly beg you to—to forgive me."

Though Elizabeth had earlier been thinking ill of this girl, she felt the sting of the humiliation Miss Darcy was facing almost as much as Miss Darcy herself. And so, she pressed her hands on Miss Darcy's and told her all was forgiven.

When Georgiana Darcy returned to her brother, Elizabeth saw the latter murmur words of approval. It seemed he was molding his sister into a proper lady. That Elizabeth was the source of that lesson, she did not so much mind, though she still wondered at the drastic change Miss Darcy had made upon learning of her name.

A few minutes later, Elizabeth saw Jane and Mr. Bingley walk over to the Darcy siblings. Bingley's preference for Jane was quite obvious, and Elizabeth noticed, much to her confusion, Miss Darcy looking at the sweet Jane with something close to the coldness she had expressed toward Elizabeth during the encounter for which she had apologized. Elizabeth began to feel overcome by indignation, but a few more seconds of contemplation finally solved a mystery for her. Miss Darcy had feelings of a romantic sort for Mr. Bingley! The realization of that finally made clear why the girl had been so cold to Elizabeth shortly after learning her name. Miss Darcy had been upset that Mr. Bingley was showing interest in someone else—which meant that Elizabeth was implicated simply by her relation to Jane.

Perhaps what was most frustrating about this revelation was that Elizabeth realized she could no longer hold on to her extreme annoyance with Mr. Darcy—he had not laughed about her appearance while conversing with his sister. And as he had apologized for his harsh words and even pressed his sister to apologize for her own rudeness, the only thing of which she could accuse him was a heightened sense of his own superiority. Was that not understandable due to his standing in the world? And was it not ameliorated by the fact that he had not only swallowed his own pride and asked her forgiveness, but he had also insisted that his sister do likewise?

No, she decided. Even though he had apologized for his comment, and she must therefore forgive it, she was determined not to forget it. That she was being unreasonable, she most surely knew. But a wound to vanity is seldom easily forgotten, even should the giver of that blow be ten times as kind as Mr. Darcy had been in requesting forgiveness.

Chapter XIII

Mr. Collins was received at Longbourn at precisely four o'clock on October 25th. His punctuality was very disagreeable to Mrs. Bennet, who, despite his intent to marry one of her daughters, had much rather he had never shown up at all—or at least that he had, through unpunctuality, given her some sort of flaw about which she could moan when not in his presence. Despite Mrs. Bennet's personal feelings, however, Mr. Collins was welcomed with all politeness by the Bennet family. His letter had not done much to endear him to the sensibilities of his cousins, but Lydia appeared to be especially repulsed by him, which was not surprising. Though Mr. Collins was a tall man of five-and-twenty, he was rather heavy and would never have drawn the pleased eye of such a girl as Lydia, particularly as she knew that part of his purpose in visiting Longbourn was to attain a wife.

After greeting Mr. Collins, Mr. Bennet said little, instead contenting himself with watching his cousin and, Elizabeth presumed, taking delight in a study of the man's character. Mr. Bennet murmured to Elizabeth that Mr. Collins was one of those rare types with whom he wished he would come into contact more frequently. Yet Elizabeth knew that her father would desire those times of contact to be of short duration, for, as in the case of Mr. Collins's type of foolishness, a little truly went a long way.

As Mr. Collins passed through Longbourn, he exclaimed over every table, chair, and window; not a view, an item of furniture, or even a cushion on a chair in the Bennet home seemed to go unnoticed. Mrs. Bennet might have been pleased with his attention had she not felt he was surveying everything with the thought that it would all eventually be his. As it was, Elizabeth knew that Mrs. Bennet was using every iota of her will-power to keep from crying out about her nerves and pleading for her smelling salts.

Mr. Collins quickly showed himself to be in possession of very formal manners. When he spoke, he was extremely solemn, as if every word which fell from his mouth were of the utmost wisdom and importance; indeed, he was inclined toward speaking as often as he could without overstepping the more obvious bounds of propriety, though it was to be wondered if he truly understood how sometimes loquaciousness was less desirable than the occasional social misstep.

"I must say, madam, your daughters are simply enchanting," complimented Mr. Collins after he had been seated for but a few minutes. The subject of his cousins seemed to instill a great eagerness in him. "I cannot imagine where I have seen such fine and amiable girls, though I must say that they are nothing to the wonderful daughter of my patroness. Of course, few can match Miss Anne de Bourgh for true nobility, bearing, and beauty. Your daughters, however, are much to be admired, I assure you."

Mrs. Bennet, though not disposed to like the man—and likely a little put out to be told that her daughters could not match up to another's—could not help but respond to his compliment. "I thank you, Mr. Collins. They are praised throughout Hertfordshire, if I may be so bold as to say."

"You may indeed, madam. I have heard great tales of their beauty, but I must say that words simply did not do justice to that which I find before me. You must be very proud of my dear cousins, and I am sure that they will all be happily married in due time."

"We certainly hope they will, Mr. Collins," owned Mrs. Bennet. "Only, I must confess, I am particularly anxious that they do so, for otherwise they will find themselves impoverished, with no place to lay their beautiful little heads. The thought of it breaks my heart."

"I suspect, madam, that you are alluding to the entail of this estate."

"Ah, yes, I suppose I am. It is so difficult for my girls, you know. Though the whole situation brings me much grief, I do not fault you for the matter of this entail. There is no knowing the way estates will be forced to go." Though Mrs. Bennet's words seemed gracious, Elizabeth knew that her mother did, in truth, place the blame on Mr. Collins. Yet even she would never dare to say as much to the man's face.

"I do not wish for you to be concerned that such lovely young ladies will ever find themselves in a situation as bleak as that which you paint. I have come here with the intent to admire them, and I am certain there are many others who wish to do the same."

Lydia snorted, and Elizabeth fixed her with a stern glare. When the younger girl mouthed something mocking concerning their cousin, Elizabeth shook her head in warning.

Jane, likely striving to keep the attention of Mr. Collins away from the quiet interaction taking place between her sisters, spoke up and said:

"We are pleased to find you are such a well-meaning man. Your kindness in attempting to heal the breach between our families is appreciated."

Mr. Collins replied that it was no trouble at all, and he smiled at Jane. The sight immediately alarmed Elizabeth, for there was a sort of unctuous eagerness to his manner when he looked at Jane which was *not* at all pleasing. Of the Bennet girls, Jane was possibly the least able to fend off the attentions of an unwanted suitor. And Mr. Collins, judging by the way he was leering at her, seemed to think already that she was a fitting wife for a clergyman. Elizabeth's conjectures were borne out by the next words to issue from the silly parson's mouth:

"I wonder if my cousin Jane might give me a tour of the grounds?"

He appeared to have missed the look of near-panic which passed across Jane's face. Elizabeth, however, did not.

"I think Jane is a little fatigued today," said Elizabeth, trying to curb the attentions of Mr. Collins. "And as we are all much enjoying your conversation, we would not want you to deprive us of it so soon."

"Indeed," seconded Kitty, "that would be quite a pity."

Mr. Collins completely missed the sarcastic undertone in Kitty's voice. "Ah, well, perhaps I can view the grounds another time. I certainly admire this drawing-room. Have you made many improvements on it since you have been here, madam?"

"This room has always been a fine one," replied Mrs. Bennet, who appeared to feel that Mr. Collins was starting to make himself disagreeable.

"Perhaps we can give you a tour of our home," suggested Elizabeth. She wished to avoid a flare up of her mother's nerves.

"That is a good idea, Lizzy," said Mr. Bennet with an amused smile.

"We should certainly let my cousin see the residence he will one day inherit."

As the group left the drawing room, Lydia somehow managed to slip off. And though Lydia was the only one who was able to effect an escape, the majority of the remaining Bennets also wished that they could be spared the man's civility.

The tour of the house was as disagreeable and ridiculous as Elizabeth could have predicted in advance. Much as in the parlor, nothing was beneath the notice of Mr. Collins—not even the smallest knicknack could escape his hawk-like eyes. And though the assembled Bennets felt they would be exceedingly pleased never to hear his voice again, he kept up an ongoing monologue, praising everything in sight while interspersing his comments on Longbourn with stories of his patroness and her home of Rosings Park. Indeed, his comparisons were often ridiculous, and he never described Longbourn in any positive manner when comparing it with the grand nature of the home of his patroness, though at times that meant his statements were contradictory.

When the party entered one of the sitting rooms and stood before Mrs. Bennet's favorite seat, Mr. Collins told them:

"Ah, this chair reminds me of one currently situated in the servants' quarters at Rosings."

Mrs. Bennet seemed struck speechless, and Mr. Bennet was suddenly filled with mirth, though Elizabeth felt that he hid it admirably.

"A chair such as this is used by servants, you say?" ventured Mr. Bennet.

Since Mrs. Bennet's ability to talk had still not returned, Mr. Collins was able to respond to his cousin's question. "Ah, yes. The fabric of the chair at Rosings is finer, however. This one is rather admirable, though."

Mrs. Bennet finally managed to speak. "We thank you, I am sure."

Even Mr. Collins could sense the discontent in her voice, and he quickly retracted his comment. "Ah, madam, I am mortified to discover I have offended you! You see, the conditions at Rosings are magnificent—almost royal, if I may be so bold as to venture to make such a comment. I did not mean any slight on the furniture at Longbourn, for the situation here is comfortable indeed, but surely you must understand how very grand Rosings is."

And then he began to detail some of the impressive articles of furniture which were to be found in the residence of Lady Catherine de

Bourgh, even going so far as to regale them with tales of the many magnificent windows found at Rosings.

As Mr. Collins continued remarking on the items he came upon, Mr. Bennet occasionally stepped into the conversation to prompt his cousin on some insignificant detail regarding a painting or a sofa at Rosings so he could—with what Elizabeth saw was great satisfaction—witness more of the spectacle that was Mr. Collins.

"If the furniture is so fine," said Elizabeth at last, "I wonder that you are able to sit down at all."

Mr. Collins completely missed the sarcasm of her statement and assured her that the condescension of her ladyship was very great and that her generosity, quite simply, knew no bounds.

"Her ladyship sounds like an ideal patroness," commented Mary, who had heretofore been rather quiet.

"Oh, she is indeed. I am most fortunate to have a patroness who is the very essence of generosity and Christian kindness."

"The Good Lord provideth for his worthy sheep," noted Mary.

Mr. Collins nodded his acquiescence. "He certainly does, does he not, Cousin Jane?"

Jane flushed and indicated her assent. It was all Elizabeth could do to keep from scowling.

"I think Mr. Bingley would agree with that sentiment in particular," said Elizabeth. Her statement was not exactly fitting to the occasion, but she thought that it would be best for Mr. Collins to find out that Jane was already attached to another man.

"Lizzy," hissed Jane under her breath in warning.

But Mr. Collins's attention was caught by a small table, and he was exclaiming over its fine craftsmanship, not having noticed Elizabeth's statement at all.

Mrs. Bennet's countenance darkened, and it was not difficult to guess what was causing her distress: Mr. Collins seemed to be looking at all of the furniture as items which he would one day own. And if Elizabeth had any doubt as to the turn of her mother's mind, if she listened closely enough, she could hear the woman muttering about how the whole world would be much improved if entails did not exist.

Chapter XIV

The day after his arrival, Mr. Collins decided he would speak with Mr. Bennet in private. He was certain it would be proper to talk to the man and once more emphasize his desire for a wife; after all, the matter closely concerned Mr. Bennet and his daughters, and they would surely like some reassurance. Indeed, Mr. Collins was doing such a selfless thing by deciding to marry one of the Miss Bennets that he imagined Mr. Bennet would quickly express how grateful he was at the prospect of having such a generous son-in-law.

An inquiry revealed that the head of the household was in his library, where he was apparently often to be found. The servant had been instructed that he not be disturbed, but Mr. Collins was certain that Mr. Bennet would not stand on such formalities with him—they were soon to become much more intimately connected, after all—and he brushed past the flustered servant and entered the room without any further words.

At the other man's entrance, Mr. Bennet looked up from his book and welcomed him. Mr. Collins basked in the notice he was certain he deserved as a member of the clergy and gave a slight bow to his future father-in-law.

"As a parson," began he, "I am certainly aware of the precious value of one's time, but I assure you—that which I have to say is of the utmost import, and I hope you will oblige me by sparing some few moments in which we may discuss a situation dear to my heart and, I may presume, to yours as well."

Mr. Collins stood even straighter upon seeing Mr. Bennet smile and lean back in his chair. "Please continue, Mr. Collins," said Mr. Bennet.

"I am more than aware of the great hardship which the entail of Longbourn has brought upon your family, and in light of your family's great misfortunes, I have, as I noted previously, come prepared to admire your handsome daughters. I assure you, Mr. Bennet, that you have five very lovely and amiable daughters, each, in her own fashion, possessing attractions which are out of the common way."

Mr. Bennet's smile grew, and he turned back to his book with a nod. "Ah, good. You may join their other admirers then. Young ladies do so enjoy being admired."

Mr. Collins hesitated, wondering at Mr. Bennet's rather lackadaisical and dismissive response. Surely the man understood that he was about to receive the great honor of having one of his daughters taken off his hands! "I confess that I am not wishing to become one entity lost among their admirers; rather, I have a singular object in mind from which my abundant admiration of them flows most readily."

Mr. Bennet raised an eyebrow. "Then your esteem is actually false, Mr. Collins?"

"No, no," assured the other man hastily, not wishing Mr. Bennet to form the wrong conclusions, "my regard is genuine. It is simply precipitated by certain circumstances."

"And what circumstances might these be?"

"My most esteemed patroness, Lady Catherine de Bourgh, has, in her usual Christian generosity and frankness of nature, assured me that it is in my best interests to procure a wife for myself, and I certainly bow down to the infinite wisdom of her kind instruction, as I have already noted to you in my letter."

"You have been directed by the great Lady Catherine herself, have you?" queried Mr. Bennet, and if Mr. Collins had not already been aware of her ladyship's high position in life and her gracious treatment of her social inferiors, he might have thought that his cousin was disparaging her.

"Are you acquainted with her ladyship, Mr. Bennet?"

But Mr. Bennet's reply was mysterious. "Her reputation goes before her, I assure you, Mr. Collins."

Mr. Collins might have chosen to pursue the matter further, but that would not be to his purpose, so he pushed the matter from his mind. "As I was saying," said he, "I flatter myself that my intentions toward your amiable family are highly commendable. Mr. Bennet, I am aware of the poor financial prospects faced by your daughters in the event of your death, and I must own that the matter aggrieves me greatly. The Lord has often admonished us, after all, about the beneficial nature of sacrifice. I am certain you understand it would be a sacrificial gesture on my part, as by tying myself to one of your daughters, I must necessarily be responsible for your entire family once you are gone."

Mr. Collins saw that Mr. Bennet's eyebrows had lifted high indeed, but he continued without letting the older man insert a word, as he wished to ensure that all of his thoughts would be heard.

"No one could deny that all of your daughters are handsome and worthy of admiration, but I am particularly interested in the fine manners exhibited by your second eldest daughter. I am of the stout belief that my cousin Jane would make a fine clergyman's wife—"

Mr. Bennet closed his book with a resounding bang, thoroughly interrupting Mr. Collins's introspection and his pleasant thoughts of Jane Bennet's most excellent future contribution to his humble life. Confused, Mr. Collins gaped at the man, wondering what he was about. Mr. Bennet's next words were most certainly *not* what he had expected to hear.

"Mr. Collins, have you taken leave of your senses?"

"I beg your pardon?"

"I should no sooner have Jane marry you than I should have my Lizzy marry a cockroach. In case you have not heard, Mr. Collins, there is a pleasant young man called Mr. Bingley who has caught Jane's eye. It is generally assumed that they will be engaged before long."

Mr. Collins was most affronted. So what of this other man? Did Mr. Bennet not understand that it was to *all* of his family's benefit to encourage his suit? This Mr. Bingley fellow may not ever offer for Jane Bennet's hand, after all. What reason could Mr. Bennet have for dismissing the suit he had in hand for one which might never come to pass?

Wanting to reason with his cousin, Mr. Collins began: "But Mr. Bennet—"

The other man, however, was in no mood to be reasonable. "Mr. Collins, I must warn you that in the matter of my daughters' happiness, I will not stint. None of them will be forced into an engagement they do not want."

"I am sure that my cousin Jane—" tried Mr. Collins again, but once again Mr. Bennet interrupted him.

"Given what I have seen, Mr. Collins, Jane has already made up her mind. She is *very* receptive to Mr. Bingley, and I have no doubt that she will accept him when he asks. You would do well to turn your attention to another of my daughters, provided you are still earnest in marrying one of them."

Then Mr. Bennet took up his book and began to read, signaling the interview to be at an end. Mr. Collins stared at him for several moments, his outrage at the audacity of this man aroused. When Mr. Bennet paid him no further notice, even to order him from his bookroom, Mr. Collins rose with a huff.

He took his leave of his cousin and went outside to stand beneath a tree, wringing his hands and berating the short-sightedness of Mr. Bennet. What had his cousin been thinking to reject him thus and dismiss him so summarily? Was he not aware of the great peril in which he put his family by turning down such an agreeable offer? Was he insensible to the sacrifice Mr. Collins was making by proposing to the man's most beautiful daughter? He surveyed the house in front of him. It was a good enough residence—modest yet comfortable—and it would be his soon. Why should Jane Bennet not become his wife rather than this Mr. Bingley's? Mr. Bennet's refusal to see reason would almost certainly come back to haunt his family, but that was not Mr. Collins's concern. If Mr. Bennet was this recalcitrant, then it was best that Mr. Collins have nothing further to do with his daughters. Jane Bennet was not *that* handsome, after all.

After sulking beneath the tree for some time, still wondering why Mr. Bennet should conspire against his good-willed offer, he went back into the house, where he was accosted by Mrs. Bennet.

"Ah, Mr. Collins! What have you been doing outside?"

"Admiring the landscape," answered the man curtly.

"Surely you are not already tired of our home, Mr. Collins?"

"I can most humbly assure you that is not the case."

Mrs. Bennet looked at him for a few moments before speaking again. "You know, Mr. Collins, my eldest daughter would make some fine young man an excellent wife. You must acknowledge that Lizzy is very handsome."

He allowed that it was so. Mr. Collins, in truth, was not an admirer of Elizabeth Bennet, not when the beauty of her sister was so immediately available for comparison. He allowed her a pleasant enough aspect, but there was something arch in her manner, something which he was certain would neither suit him in his position as a clergyman nor impress his patroness, whose opinion, after all, was paramount. No, Elizabeth would not do, not when the superior specimen of her sister was readily available.

"And she is very kind-hearted to those whom she cares about," continued Mrs. Bennet, interrupting his thoughts. "The man who marries her will find her to be quite a comfort to him."

"I am certain that my cousin Elizabeth will make an excellent bride," responded Mr. Collins with a dismissive wave of his hand. Why could the woman not focus on Jane? It was almost as though both Bennet parents were plotting against him. "I think her sister Jane, however, is most especially agreeable."

"Ah, yes, I own that Jane is the finest local beauty you shall see gracing the assemblies. But I am afraid I must encourage you to turn your attention toward another of my daughters," here she took on a conspiratorial tone, "for you see, Mr. Collins, I regret to inform you that Jane will soon be engaged to Mr. Bingley. We have simply been waiting for him to make the move."

But Mr. Collins shunted aside his earlier resolution that he would have nothing further to do with *any* of the Bennet daughters, determined now that nothing less than Miss Jane would do. "I thank you for your kind warning, but as I am to understand that she is not engaged yet, there can be nothing to keep me from pursuing her. My situation in life is a most fortunate one, as I am constantly assisted by the guidance of her ladyship, and I know that any wife of mine will find herself in a highly advantageous situation, so I bear no qualms about courting my esteemed cousin."

"Wait, Mr. Collins!" cried Mrs. Bennet. "I really must tell you more about Lizzy!"

But Mrs. Bennet's attempt at dissuasion had provided a boost in the confidence Mr. Collins felt in regard to his ability to woo young ladies, and he waved her protests aside. He proceeded to the drawing-room where his cousins were and immediately placed himself beside Jane, where he remained for some time despite Mrs. Bennet's repeated attempts to extract him from the room. Not even the Bennet matron's constant allusions to Mr. Bingley could convince Mr. Collins to change his plotted course. Mr. Collins was pleased with the progress he made that day—indeed, he felt more than ever that his suit was being well received. It would not be long before what he desired came to fruition. Mr. Bennet would have no choice but to give his consent once Miss Jane had given hers.

Chapter XV

The days after Mr. Collins's arrival at Longbourn seemed to drag on interminably. Mr. Collins's fawning was tiring, and his pompous formal speeches—completely at odds with his obsequious attentions—were delivered without cessation. Furthermore, he appeared to have an opinion about every subject, and he was not overly shy about sharing such opinions. Elizabeth was better read than most of the men of her acquaintance, and this knowledge was matched with a quick wit and a disposition which delighted in learning. Mr. Collins had not been at Longbourn an hour before Elizabeth was convinced of three things. First, that he must be the stupidest and most servile toad in all of England; second, that his understanding of the most basic events of the world was lacking; and third, that it would be merely the trouble of a moment to turn his arguments and expose them for the foolish utterances they were.

She restrained herself, not only due to the fact that he was a guest in her father's house, but also because she felt an apathy toward the man's very existence—in short, while he was here, she would treat him with civility, but the sooner he and his sycophantic flattery were gone, the better she would feel. Of course, her father seemed to harbor no such compunction, baiting the young man and making him look the fool to those of his daughters with sufficient wit to understand. To Mr.

Collins, none of this was remotely comprehensible; it was evident to all that he gloried in his pronouncements, which he thought made him appear to be very civil and attentive. He even seemed to think himself intelligent and learned, though Elizabeth almost laughed out loud at the very idea of applying such terms to him. It *was* true that he was fortunate in his situation in life, but his fortune seemed to have been brought about largely due to no merit of his own. The Bennet girls, it was to be said, were also satisfied with the circumstances surrounding his life—as long as his life was in no way connected to their own.

It fell to poor Jane to suffer the most from the parson's presence. Since he had focused on her as the object of his attention almost as soon as he had entered the house, he became a permanent fixture in her presence. Nothing anyone said could turn him from his pursuit. As a result, Longbourn had become a den of misery for all concerned. Mr. Collins was almost ever-present, and his loud proclamations could be heard in every corner of the house at all times of the day. When Mrs. Bennet's nerves were added to the tense atmosphere of the abode, it was no small wonder that the girls engaged themselves as much as possible in outdoor pursuits—and that the master and mistress of the house kept to their respective chambers as much as they could.

The situation infuriated Elizabeth. She knew that her father had conversed with Mr. Collins soon after he arrived at Longbourn regarding the matter of marriage and that Mr. Collins had been angry for a short time afterward before turning his attentions solely on Jane. Her mother's whining and hand-wringing were having no effect on Mr. Collins, and her father would not exert himself beyond the one admonition against the man's suit. In fact, Mr. Bennet appeared to be amused at the young man's persistence in the face of such a set-down. Although Elizabeth did not for one moment suppose that Mr. Bennet would allow his gentlest daughter to marry the man, she still could not bear her sister's unhappiness. And since Jane was incapable of offending any creature, Elizabeth was obliged to come to her rescue and invent ways for her to avoid the attentions of Mr. Collins.

Several days after the parson's arrival, Elizabeth had almost reached her wit's end. Though all the sisters had assisted Jane in escaping her unwanted suitor (with the exception of Lydia, who remained completely insensible of Jane's plight), Elizabeth was uncertain what more she could do to dissuade the young man aside from insulting him to his face. As Elizabeth was much too well bred to engage in such a breach of propriety—though in truth, she was sorely tempted—she began to look for other means of separating her unwanted cousin from the object of his obsession.

As the day was bright with sunshine, Elizabeth proposed a walk among the paths surrounding Longbourn, with the ultimate intention of climbing the side of Oakham Mount and being calmed by the vistas visible from its peak.

Lydia, caring nothing for such things, declined as was her wont, and Kitty, understanding at least a part of her sister's stratagem, declined as well, stating she would much rather spend her time on the pianoforte than traipsing over the countryside. Jane and Mary, however, agreed with alacrity, and after preparing themselves, they all set out upon their walk.

It came as no surprise when Mr. Collins declared such a walk to be the very thing he had desired—coupling that declaration, of course, with verbose flattery commending his cousins for endeavoring to obtain the proper exercise. What Mr. Collins did not realize was that Elizabeth, knowing the parson possessed a frame not meant for walking, had anticipated his desire to accompany them. Mr. Collins soon found that his cousins set a far brisker pace than any he would have chosen, and not many minutes into their walk, he was puffing like a bellows, which effectively put an end to any coherent murmuring he felt the need to inject into the quiet country morning. Of course, this did not stop him from trying, and more than once Elizabeth had to stifle less than ladylike giggles after hearing his attempts at what he thought were delicate compliments to his cousins, Hertfordshire, and his patroness, all of which came out to be more ridiculous and insipid when interspersed with the deep breaths he made (which sounded not unlike those of a horse). In fact, Elizabeth was highly gratified that she had even seen sweet Jane's lips twitch a time or two at the ridiculous spectacle of Mr. Collins issuing proclamations over the sound of his puffing and wheezing.

Soon, they had reached the lower slopes of their destination, and they began to climb. Oakham Mount was more of a large hill than an actual mountain, but it was the tallest in the area and afforded a splendid view. Mr. Collins, seeing his ordeal was far from over, let out a less than gentlemanly groan but gamely began to climb, although he soon lagged far behind the two eldest sisters. Curiously, it was Mary who stayed behind to escort him, earning herself a questioning look from Elizabeth. At Mary's answering smile and the shrug of her shoulders, Elizabeth and Jane decided to continue, so eager were they to escape the parson's presence for even a moment. If Mary wished to saddle herself with him, it was none of their concern.

The view from the top was marvelous as always, a great sprawling vista of green fields, verdant woods, and broad horizons. Deeply breathing in the autumn air, Elizabeth and Jane shared a look and smiled at their brief but well-earned freedom.

Moments later, they realized that more than just Mary and the struggling Mr. Collins would be soon joining their party. A pair of riders had appeared from another direction and were even now dismounting from their horses and beginning the ascent to the summit. It did not take long for Elizabeth to realize the identity of the newcomers, and glancing beside her for a reaction, she was pleased to see Jane's delighted countenance fixed on their approaching neighbors. They had not seen the two handsome men since the arrival of Mr. Collins at Longbourn, and the opportunity seemed golden to demonstrate the strength of Jane's attachment to Mr. Bingley and dissuade the parson from furthering his hopeless pursuit. At this point, Elizabeth was willing to try anything to spare her favorite sister from the man's attentions.

"Lizzy," said Jane, "I know what you are thinking."

"Do you?" responded Elizabeth in a teasing manner.

"Do not attempt to offend Mr. Collins through the use of whatever interest in me Mr. Bingley may possess. I enjoy his company very much indeed, but Mr. Collins may just frighten him off."

Elizabeth let out a laugh at Jane's impertinence, excessively diverted that her sister—her wonderful and angelic sister, who never had an uncomplimentary thing to say about any human—could obliquely reference their cousin's disagreeable nature in such a manner. "Believe me, Jane, I think it would take more than the likes of William Collins to scare Mr. Bingley away."

Jane's eyes flashed in warning, but there was nothing further she could say on the subject, as the gentlemen had almost reached them. On the other side, Mr. Collins still labored, his pace having slowed considerably, and it was apparent he would not reach them for several more minutes, though he had had considerably less distance to traverse than the two gentlemen.

"Miss Bennet, Miss Elizabeth, good day to you!" began Mr. Bingley in his usual ebullient manner, to which the ladies curtseyed in response. "This is a fortunate meeting."

"Indeed, it is, sir," replied Jane, her brow crinkling at his address. "What brings you so far from Netherfield?"

"Why, having heard so much about the view from this vantage, we determined to see for ourselves the beauties of Hertfordshire. I can assure you, it is just as beautiful as we have been told."

This last was said in reference to the view, Elizabeth was certain, but Mr. Bingley's eyes were affixed on Jane, causing her to blush most becomingly at his hidden meaning. Elizabeth could not be more satisfied in the attention he was showing Jane. He was all that was good and pleasing, and his affections for her favorite sister appeared to be strengthening with every moment spent in her company.

"And you, Mr. Darcy?" said Elizabeth, turning her attention to his friend. Her next words died in her throat as she beheld his eyes fixed upon her, his expression blank but intense. Her heart fluttered alarmingly at his open regard of her person, and she wondered what he was about.

"Yes, Miss Elizabeth?"

Elizabeth gathered herself, determined not to let the man discompose her, regardless of his erstwhile criticisms of her person. A part of her wished to correct him on his method of addressing her and Jane, but she did not wish to seem uncivil. "It was of no consequence, Mr. Darcy. I merely wished to ascertain your reaction to the scenery of Hertfordshire, though I dare say it does not compare with that of your home?"

"Who among us does not believe his home is most beautiful?" said he. "Indeed, I do love the vistas and wilds of the peak district in Derbyshire, which is but a short distance from my home. Hertfordshire is tamer than Derbyshire, but it has many beauties of its own. I do find the view extremely pleasing."

Much as his friend had done with Jane, Mr. Darcy did not remove his gaze from Elizabeth during the recital of his statement, the effect of which was pronounced as a rosy blush spreading across her features. Seeing this, Mr. Darcy seemed to realize what he had said, and he turned his head and gazed out over the countryside. The company was silent, although the contrast between the two couples could hardly be more marked. Jane and Mr. Bingley had eyes only for each other and seemed to be communicating without words, while Mr. Darcy and Elizabeth were studious in their avoidance of one another, both contemplating the nature of their exchange, which their companions appeared to have missed entirely.

The moment, however, was not destined to last, as soon Mr. Collins, still groaning at his exertion, arrived at the top of the hill, the ever-dutiful Mary by his side. His reaction to the view was muted as he became aware of the newcomers to their party, and he could hardly miss the interaction between the object of his attentions and the handsome young man who stood beside her. Privately, Elizabeth was thrilled at the loss of his effusions, so certain was she that she would throttle him if she had to listen to him once more trumpet his approbation for the landscape, Hertfordshire, his patroness, and Elizabeth's eldest sister.

Still, the introduction had to be made, and Elizabeth could only hope that witnessing Jane's partiality for Mr. Bingley would cause Mr. Collins to lose some of his ardor. It was a hope in which she indulged but did not expect to see realized given his willful disregard for every hint which had been made to him by almost every member of the Bennet family.

"Mr. Collins," said she, "you have finally joined us."

"Yes, indeed, I have," was the reply as Mr. Collins studied his rival, though he was still puffing from the exertion. "I see we have also been joined by . . . some acquaintances . . . of yours. Perhaps you would . . . do me the great honor of introducing me to . . . these fine gentlemen."

Unfortunately, though his speech was not, for once, littered with simpering flattery, Mr. Collins appeared to be once again tramping all over the rules of genteel society. As men of higher rank, Mr. Darcy and Mr. Bingley should have been the ones requesting the introduction. To make the situation even more mortifying to Elizabeth, Mr. Collins's less than proper request was interspersed with those heavy breaths which made him seem more like a laboring pack animal than a respectable cleric. Knowing there was little she could do to salvage the situation, Elizabeth did the only thing she could under the circumstances—she introduced the two gentlemen to her cousin.

"But of course. Mr. Collins, allow me to present Mr. Bingley and Mr. Darcy, our new neighbors. Mr. Darcy, Mr. Bingley—Mr. Collins is a distant cousin of my father's and is visiting us for a fortnight."

Mr. Darcy said nothing, merely gracing his new acquaintance with a slight inclination of his head, while Mr. Bingley, in his usual cheerful fashion, responded with assurances of his delight in making the acquaintance of his neighbors' cousin.

Unfortunately, it was a delight which the parson could not share, as his only answer was a curt nod of the head and a short: "A pleasure, I am sure."

Mr. Bingley paused, clearly taken aback by Mr. Collins's abrupt manner, but as the parson was not such a lure to his attentions as was Jane, he soon forgot about Mr. Collins's incivility and turned back to the object of his affections, engaging her in quiet conversation while the rest of the group remained silent, ostensibly admiring the scenery.

Unfortunately, Elizabeth's expectations concerning her cousin's behavior and manners were soon realized. He stood there for some time, regaining his breath and watching the young couple in their easy conversation, and Elizabeth could see the expression on his face move from first displeasure at the young man's attentions to *his* intended and then to jealousy at her responsiveness to Mr. Bingley's suit. His face continued to darken even as Mary attempted in vain to begin a conversation with him. Just as Elizabeth was searching her brain for some way to distract him and prevent his exposing himself and the Bennet sisters to ridicule, he seemed to start, and his gaze was transferred to Mr. Darcy, a look of wonder spreading over his features.

"My cousin Elizabeth," applied he, an urgency evident in his manner, "did I hear you correctly when you introduced this other fine gentleman as Mr. Darcy?"

Astonished at the sudden change in his demeanor and at his imprudent speech, Elizabeth could only nod in response, even while Mr. Darcy turned and gave him the slightest nod.

"Excuse me, good sir, but is it possible I am in the august presence of Mr. Darcy of Pemberley estate in Derbyshire?"

Suddenly, the full weight of Mr. Darcy's implacable gaze rested upon the parson, regarding him as one might look upon a gnat. "Yes, I am he," responded Mr. Darcy, his voice quiet yet stern. "You seem to have the advantage of me, Mr. Collins. In what fashion, might I ask, are you acquainted with me?"

The delight which suffused Mr. Collins's face was only matched by the stupid manner in which he began to bow, which was almost low enough for his knuckles to brush the ground had they been extended. His obeisance was accompanied by the silliest speech Elizabeth had ever heard the man utter.

"Mr. Darcy, I have never—the honor, sir—that is, I must be allowed to state, my dear sir, that in all my wildest imaginings, in even the most stupendous flights of fancy, I would never have imagined that I would meet such an illustrious personage as yourself in so humble a part of England. I cannot begin to inform you, sir, how much of an honor it is to humbly make your acquaintance. To think you would condescend to show my dear cousins the honor of your attentions is beyond anything I would have dreamed, excepting of course, the condescension shown by my most noble patroness, who is all goodness and generosity herself. Truly, her most excellent characteristics must, of a necessity, be those which all of her relations share. Please allow me to say how delighted I am to make the acquaintance of such a preeminent person as yourself."

By this time, even Mr. Bingley and Jane had noticed the long speech and had stopped to stare at the parson, who seemed caught in the midst of a rapturous ecstasy. Elizabeth felt her own cheeks burning at the ridiculously servile fawnings issuing forth from her cousin's mouth, and although she was positive she was the only one who noticed it, the expression of utter contempt upon Mr. Darcy's face was plain for any who cared to look.

"I believe you were about to inform me how you knew me, sir," prompted Mr. Darcy in a low voice.

"My dear sir! Of course, I let my delight at finally making your acquaintance overrule my manners. Allow me to introduce myself more fully—my name is Mr. William Collins, and I have the very great fortune to enjoy the patronage of your noble aunt, the honorable Lady Catherine De Bourgh."

"You are my aunt's new clergyman."

"Indeed, I am, sir. The garden in which my home, Hunsford, is situated lies near the entrance to the great estate of Rosings, allowing me the pleasure of demeaning myself before her ladyship in the greatest of humility. You aunt's generous nature is more than I could have ever hoped for."

"I have visited Rosings, Mr. Collins—I know where Hunsford is."

"Indeed, I believe you must have, sir," said Mr. Collins, his face betraying his happiness. "And I believe I am fortunate in the ability to inform you that her ladyship and her wonderful daughter were in the best of health but four days ago."

Although Mr. Darcy said nothing more, Elizabeth could tell that he considered the churchman absurd and obsequious. For the rest of their time on the mount, while Mr. Bingley and Jane talked quietly together and Mary stayed mostly silent by the parson's side, Mr. Collins carried on a one-sided conversation—though perhaps it was better termed a "monologue"—with the young gentleman in which his silly and long-winded pronouncements were answered with nothing more than monosyllabic replies.

Finally, taking pity on the man who had become the focus of Mr. Collins's parading civilities, Elizabeth advised her sisters they had stayed long enough and proposed they journey back to Longbourn. All at once, Mr. Collins seemed to remember his mission of promoting his suit to Jane and began to move toward her, but Mr. Bingley, delighted to be of use to his lady, had already proposed that he and Mr. Darcy escort the party back to Longbourn and had offered his arm to her, thereby thwarting the parson in his design. Elizabeth noted the glower on Mr. Collins's face and wondered at the audacity of the man who could consider himself a better suitor for a gentleman's daughter than the amiable and wealthy Mr. Bingley. It seemed there was nothing she could do to interrupt his suit, so determined and focused was he on Jane—Elizabeth, after all, was nothing more than a young woman, and a man with Mr. Collins's bloated sense of his own self-worth obviously could not be bothered with the opinions of one he considered his inferior.

Elizabeth snorted at the thought—she, his inferior! At the moment, she considered a garden snake to be *his* superior in all matters.

A movement to her side caught her attention, and she turned to see Mr. Darcy offering his arm, his slightly sly smile in the direction of Mr. Collins a clear indication that the situation and the parson's reaction to Mr. Bingley and Jane had not escaped his attention. Although uncertain of her own regard for the gentleman, she shrugged her shoulders and accepted his proffered arm. Once again, the long-suffering Mary was left to bring up the rear with the insufferable Mr. Collins.

The walk down the mountain was largely accomplished in silence—at least, the last two couples did not have much to talk about. Mary tried to interest their cousin in some conversation, but he was clearly brooding once more about Jane, and he kept his own counsel, completely ignoring Mary as often as not. Though Elizabeth was not as close to Mary as she was to some of her other sisters, she still felt a measure of indignation for the man's poor manners and petulant behavior. As for Mr. Darcy, he had little to say and seemed focused on the couple ahead of them as they carried on a lively and affectionate conversation.

Elizabeth had begun to wonder if this seemingly interminable walk would ever end when all of a sudden, from almost directly overhead, there was a flash, followed soon after by the loud rumbling of thunder. Glancing up at the sky, Elizabeth noticed the angry clouds rolling in and wondered that the entire company had been so distracted that they had neglected to notice the onset of inclement weather.

Seeing Jane's worried glance back at her, Elizabeth smiled hesitantly and looked up at her escort, who was gazing at her with some alarm.

"It appears we have enjoyed ourselves so much that we have not noted the coming weather, Mr. Darcy," declared she, somewhat impudently. "You may wish to escape now—we are quite close to home, and if you are fortunate, you and Mr. Bingley may reach

Netherfield before the storm descends upon us."

"I believe I would not be able to call myself a gentleman if I were to allow you and your sisters to return home without an escort. The weather looks to be somewhat wild."

Not particularly surprised at his declaration, but vastly amused by his inference that Mr. Collins *was not* an acceptable escort, Elizabeth thanked him and suggested they hasten their steps. But it was all in vain, as moments after the exchange, the heavens opened up, and the rain began to pour down upon them.

They were immediately drenched, prompting Elizabeth to thank the fates that the weather was still warm, as they would certainly have been chilled otherwise. Mr. Darcy immediately stopped and, removing his coat, settled it around her shoulders, providing her with a measure of protection from the elements, not to mention protecting her modesty, for with the amount of rain pouring down, she was immediately soaked through, causing her dress to cling to her most improperly.

Elizabeth glanced around, noting Mr. Bingley's treatment of Jane mirrored his friend's. Looking in the other direction, she saw that the situation with Mary and Mr. Collins was so different as to be laughable. Mr. Collins was peering at his cousins with wide eyes, a scandalized expression on his stupid face that vied with the obvious jealousy he felt to witness Mr. Bingley offering assistance to *his* intended. Elizabeth nearly groaned out loud, knowing this would provide fuel for his long-winded and overly pious pronouncements about the proper behavior of virtuous females. It took Mr. Darcy's curt hand motions and calling of his name for Mr. Collins to remember that he, too, accompanied a young lady who needed some protection from the elements.

After Mr. Collins had finally performed his duty with Mary, the three couples once again began walking toward Longbourn, traveling much faster than they had before. It was only a few moments before Elizabeth's words were proven true and the manor house came into view. They were immediately ushered inside for a change of clothes amid Mrs. Bennet's loud wailings regarding how her daughters would catch their deaths due to being caught out in the storm.

Shaking her head at her mother's antics, Elizabeth accepted a blanket to cover her modesty and handed Mr. Darcy's jacket to him, murmuring her thanks for his gallantry. His earnest reply that it was his pleasure startled Elizabeth, but before she could respond or look to him for clarification, he was gone, leaving her to her thoughts.

Mr. Darcy was indeed an enigma.

Chapter XVI

After the two newcomers to Hertfordshire had been forced to submit to the misfortune of a walk with the fawning Mr. Collins, Elizabeth began to wonder if they would ever show their faces at Longbourn again. However, much to Mrs. Bennet's delight and Elizabeth's satisfaction, Mr. Bingley and Mr. Darcy both came to dine with the Bennet family the very day after the torturous promenade. Georgiana Darcy even accompanied the two men, though Elizabeth was uncertain why the girl would have agreed to come with her brother and Mr. Bingley to Longbourn, a place which housed her greatest rival. Of course, perhaps that was the very reason Miss Darcy came—from the young girl's perspective, it would not do to allow Mr. Bingley to interact with Jane without Miss Darcy there to keep a close eye on them. The thought displeased Elizabeth, but she was not one to make a scene, so she simply resolved to watch the girl and ensure no attempts were made to sabotage dear Jane's happiness.

Mrs. Bennet had carefully planned all the courses for the dinner, determined that her visitors would not find anything lacking at her table. She told Elizabeth that she saw this meal as one of the steps to ensuring that three of her daughters would soon become brides. Mr. Bingley was already enamored with Jane, of course, and if Mrs. Bennet had her way, Mr. Collins would soon be falling head over heels for

Elizabeth. As for Mr. Darcy, she had told her exasperated eldest daughter that he and Kitty had looked quite the couple while dancing together. She thought Kitty could do very well in marrying a man with ten thousand a year. Though the Bennet matron believed the sum would have been quite right for her Lydia, she did not wish to subject her favorite daughter to Mr. Darcy's dourness; instead, she thought Kitty would be better suited to counter the man's unpleasant nature. Elizabeth knew better than to argue with her mother; down that road lay futility.

The company had not been sitting at the table very long before the dinner conversation began. It was started, of course, by Mrs. Bennet, who asked:

"How have you found the society in Hertfordshire, Mr. Bingley?"

"I have found it to be quite delightful," proclaimed he, glancing at Jane.

"I am very glad to hear that," said Jane, whose cheeks had reddened. "We have been pleased to have you with us."

Mr. Collins was listening closely to this conversation. He was unusually quiet, but Elizabeth took his demeanor to indicate he was sulking over the presence of Mr. Bingley. Though she preferred this side of the parson to the one which gave lavish details over the furnishings of a building she had never seen, she did not want him to spoil Jane's evening, so she attempted to draw him into conversation on the very subject he seemed to enjoy so much.

"I was wondering if you could tell me again of the many splendors of Rosings, Mr. Collins. And please do not stint when describing the great building's fineness and the number of windows it contains."

But for once, Mr. Collins was not to be distracted by the opportunity to regale her with tales of his patroness and her home. He merely told her the number of windows curtly and then fell back into his brooding silence.

Elizabeth attempted one more time to engage his attentions in something other than Jane and Mr. Bingley, but she met with no success. Holding back a sigh, she let her gaze wander around the table, only to find Mr. Darcy watching her with his dark, intense eyes.

She stared back at him for a few seconds—reminded of how he had given her a similar look on their walk the day before—before coloring and turning her attention to her plate.

Kitty, of course, was unable to see the interaction between her sister and Mr. Darcy, and she asked the gentleman: "Are you well this evening, Mr. Darcy?"

He responded in a pleasant tone that he was, and he inquired as to her own well-being, leading to an easy and pleasant conversation between them. Mrs. Bennet looked on the scene with great satisfaction before turning her attention back to some of the other goings on at the table.

Elizabeth, glad that at least a few members of the dinner party appeared to be enjoying the evening, turned her eyes to Georgiana Darcy. The young lady was staring at Mr. Bingley and Jane, who were all but oblivious to the world as they conversed. Had the girl shouted it out loud, it would have been no more obvious to Elizabeth that Miss Darcy was displeased about Mr. Bingley's choice of conversation partner. Sighing, Elizabeth turned her attention back to Mr. Collins, with whom Mary was speaking in what could only be an effort to spare Jane the indignity of his company. The young woman was talking to him about a religious text of which she had heard him say he was fond, but she appeared to be having no more success in drawing the man into conversation than Elizabeth had.

The dinner continued in this vein until there was a lull in the conversation between Mr. Darcy and Kitty. Mr. Collins leapt upon the opportunity to speak up loudly: "Mr. Darcy, I dare say her ladyship would be proud of what a fine young woman your sister has become."

"It has not been long since we were last in the company of my aunt," said Mr. Darcy stiffly, "but yes, she is always pleased with Georgiana."

Miss Darcy herself gave Mr. Collins a sour look, and the parson must have been cowed for once, as the words he was about to speak actually failed to come out.

Mrs. Bennet, who missed the girl's expression and was unable to be silent for any great length of time, exclaimed: "Ah! It seems cook has outdone herself!"

"Your directions to her were so precise and detailed," said Mr. Bennet in a soft dry voice which nonetheless carried from one end of the table to the next, "that I should be surprised if she had *not* prepared the meal to your tastes. I consider it one of the great mysteries of life that our cook *always* seems to outdo herself on occasions such as this."

Mrs. Bennet continued as if her husband hadn't spoken. "Cook has such a skillful hand in the kitchen—I have never met a cook as talented as ours. I dare say the royal family does not dine so nicely as we! Her meals are simply remarkable!"

Elizabeth's face was flushed in embarrassment, and she could hardly comprehend her mother's words. As if the ridiculousness of Mr.

Collins were not enough, the familial discord between her parents was bound to leave their guests less than impressed. Georgiana Darcy was alternately staring at Mr. Bennet and Mrs. Bennet with a displeased expression, and Mr. Darcy's own face was an unreadable blank, which could not bode well. At least Mr. Bingley did not appear to have been distracted from his attentions to Jane; they were still discussing some of their favorite vistas, heedless of the various happenings around them.

The rest of dinner was a mixed affair, with Mrs. Bennet making a fool out of herself, Mr. Bennet trying to keep her in line with sharp comments—when he was not baiting her—and Mr. Collins switching between sulking about Mr. Bingley, fawning over the Darcys, and attempting to engage Jane in conversation. Of course, this last was another in the man's seemingly endless social blunders, as he kept speaking over several others and cutting off Mr. Bingley in order to address her.

When the dinner was finally over, Elizabeth felt a sense of relief. Unfortunately, she was not given a true respite; the men, rather than remaining while the women withdrew to the drawing room, decided to leave directly with the ladies. Mr. Collins and Mr. Bingley were the obvious leaders of this movement, both desiring more time with Jane. Unsurprisingly, Miss Darcy seemed relieved at this development; Elizabeth suspected the girl was the reason why Mr. Darcy did not seem inclined to pass time drinking with the men in the dining room. Of course, the presence of Mr. Collins likely did not make him any more eager to linger either.

In the drawing room, Mr. Collins and Mr. Bingley both sought to be next to Jane, as did Elizabeth, who wanted to protect her sister from the former and encourage the latter. Though Elizabeth and Mr. Bingley had managed to bracket Jane, Mr. Collins immediately began speaking to the poor young woman from his position on another sofa. Elizabeth tried to draw Mr. Collins away, but she had no success.

A sudden flurry of movement caught Elizabeth's attention, and she turned to see Lydia dancing with a ribbon in her hand around Kitty. "Give it back!" said Kitty, who sounded more amused than upset.

"Only if you sing me a song!" exclaimed Lydia.

Kitty lifted her cane and held it out, obviously trying to make Lydia run into it, but the younger girl saw what she was doing and stopped in place.

Lydia insisted: "All I want is a song!"

Elizabeth turned to her father, giving a pleading look for him to check the actions of his exuberant daughter. He appeared humored by the young girls' display, but he saw Elizabeth gazing at him, and he gave a nod of understanding. "Girls," said he in a voice loud enough to be heard by the entire room, "that is enough."

Elizabeth resisted the urge to close her eyes. Her cheeks were burning. Her gaze moved to rest on Georgiana Darcy, whose distaste for the entire company was so clear that even Mr. Collins could not have mistaken it. Considering Lydia's lack of decorum, Mrs. Bennet's flightiness, and Mr. Collins's ridiculous behavior, not to mention Mr. Bingley's attentions to Jane, it was no wonder she was displeased. Elizabeth was mortified.

The situation certainly did not improve after that. Georgiana Darcy's snobbery only increased, and she slighted any of the Bennets who tried to talk to her. When Elizabeth looked at Mr. Darcy to see what he thought of this impolite behavior, she found him staring at her. Flushing, she realized he did not appear to notice his sister's actions. Unfortunately, Miss Darcy was growing dourer by the minute, and then, when Elizabeth was certain it could not get worse, it did.

"Mr. Darcy," said Mr. Collins so loudly it was almost a bellow, "you must be pleased indeed with the helpful and condescending nature of your aunt, my most esteemed patroness." Here, he stood and, approaching Mr. Darcy, gave an odd sort of bow. "Her every sentence is filled with grandeur, and the kindnesses she bestows on those beneath her are so selfless that I might venture so far as to call her an angel, a gift of God's to an earth which tends to lack the shine given off by such a gem as her ladyship." At this point, the eyes of everyone in the room were on him, and he moved closer to Mr. Darcy and spoke in tones which, while softer, were nonetheless audible to every other member of the dinner party. "It is such a shame that her daughter is sickly and has not inherited her ladyship's many fine qualities. I am certain that must grieve you very much."

The fury on Mr. Darcy's face was so great as to be almost tangible. For Mr. Collins to have insulted his cousin in such a way was a faux pas so great that not even Elizabeth would have believed the parson capable of it. However, one mark of a gentleman was to turn away in silence when another man was impertinent or ridiculous, and that was what Mr. Darcy chose to do. Mr. Collins stared at the back of his social and mental superior for a few moments before returning to walk toward Jane, apparently oblivious to the great insult he had just given.

At last, the Bennets' guests were ready to leave. Elizabeth thought she was going to die of shame, and her heart ached for Jane, who was certain to have lost the most by their relations' display.

But then, the inconceivable happened. Mr. Bingley issued a return invite for the seventh of November. After what had just occurred, he would certainly have been justified in only inviting them to tea, but he actually asked them to dine at Netherfield, stating that his elderly aunt was due to arrive and provide him with a hostess for the event. Elizabeth turned to Jane, whose face was shining with pleasure, and it was all she could do to refrain from hugging her most beloved sister. It appeared that Mr. Bingley had either ignored the many improprieties of her family or had completely missed them in his attention to Jane. Elizabeth could not be more grateful for the blindness of a man in love.

Chapter XVII

If Elizabeth thought that life with Mr. Collins living in the house was insupportable before the dinner party, she soon learned she had not even scratched the surface of the man's ability to frustrate his hosts.

It seemed the gauntlet had been dropped. Witnessing the attachment which subsisted between Mr. Bingley and Jane appeared to spur Mr. Collins on to even greater lengths to earn Jane's favor and, consequently, her hand. However, though his badgering had begun to strain Jane's gentle disposition, not even her pointed disfavor would deter him from his goal. His sights were set upon securing Jane Bennet as a wife, and he would not be diverted from his course.

Of course, Mr. and Mrs. Bennet were of no help whatsoever in dissuading Mr. Collins. When the man had made clear that he was undeterred by Jane's preference for Mr. Bingley, Mrs. Bennet had retired to her room in a fit of nerves and refused to budge, bemoaning fate, entails, and willfully obtuse parsons. And although Elizabeth had brought Mr. Collins's behavior to her father's attention (if indeed he could possibly have missed it), he had refused to do anything about the situation, citing the conversation he had already had with the pompous parson the day after his arrival. However, Mr. Bennet did assure his eldest daughter that regardless of Mr. Collins's attentions to Jane, he would in no way give his consent to the match without Jane's express permission, which was something, he observed wryly, that had less chance of occurring than Mr. Collins had of ascending the throne. Elizabeth, however, was displeased with his response and his determination not to exert himself, and she was not as confident as her father in Jane's ability to refuse the obstinate man instead of giving him her consent for fear of offending him.

Jane's sisters gave her as much respite from his attentions as they were able—or at least, those of Jane's sisters who recognized and were sympathetic to her plight. Elizabeth suspected that Lydia, feeling fortunate that his attentions were not directed at her, was determined to leave well enough alone. But Elizabeth, Mary, and Kitty did as much as they could to discourage his suit, accompanying Jane wherever she went to ensure she was never in a position to be imposed upon by the overly amorous cleric. Elizabeth in particular had taken to acting as Jane's shadow—wherever Jane went, she went. If an outing was planned, Elizabeth was by her sister's side. When the attentions of the parson became too much to be borne, Elizabeth was there to urge Jane to rest in her room.

As for Mr. Collins, though he was as slow-witted as the day was long, Elizabeth knew that her constant presence had even begun to penetrate the fog of his consciousness when—after almost two full days of Elizabeth's following every movement Jane made—he began staring at her with suspicion in his eyes. Elizabeth surreptitiously watched him as he puzzled through her behavior until, suddenly, a candle seemed to be lit in the dimness of his mind, and he directed a smile at her which caused her to shudder in disgust. It was not long after that when he sidled up to her and said:

"My good cousin, I will acknowledge that there is something in your behavior which is very pleasing. Though born a gentlewoman, you are very sensible to the limitations placed upon you by your meager portion. I am not blind to the fact that many in your position would aspire to a much higher match than that of a simple parson, though it would not behoove them to do so."

Elizabeth peered at the man, wondering what he was prattling on about now.

"I do commend you for your interest in wedding a priest. It is truly the mark of a noble woman to content yourself with someone in the reach of your own sphere rather than greedily reaching for the heights. Sadly, however, I must inform you that my affections are already engaged."

Here he stopped and directed a smirk in Jane's direction which he probably intended as a tender glance. Then he returned his attention back to Elizabeth and said: "I am afraid that I cannot return your sentiments, dear cousin."

Trust Mr. Collins to add two and two and come up with five! Elizabeth did not know whether to laugh, cry, or simply bludgeon him with one of her father's books.

"I assure you, Mr. Collins—" Elizabeth tried to deflect him, but the parson was insensible of her words.

"Do not despair, my dear cousin," continued he, speaking quietly so that Jane could not hear. "If you have your heart set upon marrying a member of the clergy, then I would be happy to introduce you to other clerics of my acquaintance. I assure you that when . . . certain matters have been . . . *arranged* to everyone's satisfaction, I shall invite you to my abode forthwith, and I shall see to it that there are others of my rank in attendance, so that you may find a man to your liking."

Elizabeth, though she would have liked to edify Mr. Collins as to her thoughts about his *generous offer,* decided that it was not worth the effort. Besides, his ridiculousness in stating his intentions was such that she had to hold back a most unladylike snort of laughter.

There was one thing of which Elizabeth was certain—the tension was building in the house, and the only way it could be alleviated would be for Mr. Collins to declare himself to his disinterested paramour, thereby allowing Elizabeth to step in and disabuse him of the assumptions he had so zealously cultivated. Although she normally would not have thought a young man would declare himself so soon after making the acquaintance of a lady, Elizabeth also knew that Mr. Collins had been commanded by his patroness to find a wife—and that he had little time away in which to accomplish her instructions. All of this pointed to his needing to either make a proposal within the next few days or risk returning to Kent in failure.

Finally, on the morning of the third day, the tension came to a head, and Mr. Collins made his move. They had just finished breakfast—Mrs. Bennet still refused to leave her bedchambers, and Mr. Bennet was hiding in his bookroom—and the five sisters had retired with their unwelcome house guest to the front parlor to while away the hours of the morning. Elizabeth and Mary had claimed the seats on either side of Jane as protection against her suitor, each taking up needlework while Jane busied herself embroidering a handkerchief. Kitty sat down at the pianoforte and began to play, and Lydia took a seat at the table to trim another in an endless succession of her collection of bonnets.

Mr. Collins, although he appeared as if he had something to say, took up his copy of Fordyce's sermons and settled in, proceeding to fail to turn a single page for the next ten minutes while alternating between staring at Jane and frowning at the sisters sitting on either side of her. Elizabeth had almost begun to think he would not press the matter that morning when the parson closed his book, sat forward on his chair, and addressed them:

"My dear cousins, although the scene before me is pleasing in its domesticity—indeed, you are all to be commended for your piety and adherence to the proper conduct of elegant females everywhere, as expounded upon by our dear Fordyce—I feel I must interrupt your felicity for a matter of utmost delicacy and importance. If it pleases you, I request a moment of my cousin Jane's time—in private." This last was said with a smile at the recipient of his affections. He undoubtedly thought his expression was affectionate and charming, yet it came off as oily and superficial.

Elizabeth quickly came to the conclusion that it was best to oblige him and end the ordeal as quickly as may be. Besides, unchristian though it might have been, Elizabeth was looking forward to putting the parson in his place.

"Mary, Kitty, Lydia," said she, "I believe Mama could use your assistance in the stillroom preparing the last of the summer's blossoms."

The three named girls obediently stood to take their leave. Lydia, for once sensing that significant events were in the offing, led a snickering Kitty from the room, while Mary brought up the rear, clearly reluctant to leave. Mary's behavior became more curious, however, as Elizabeth caught a glimpse of her turning to press her ear against the door before it had even completely closed.

"Ah, my cousin Elizabeth," said Mr. Collins with a condescending smile, "I believe you misunderstood me—I wish to speak with Miss Jane alone. It would please me greatly if you would indulge me this once and spare but five minutes of your sister's time, after which I am certain we will have a most joyous announcement. Of course, in deference to propriety, you may leave the door slightly ajar. As Lady Catherine has often observed, proper comportment in clergy is paramount and should never be neglected under any circumstances!"

Mr. Collins smiled at Jane, who, unless Elizabeth missed her guess, was beginning to wish she had eaten sparingly at breakfast, as the parson's words seemed to be turning her stomach. Elizabeth nearly ground her teeth in frustration, wondering at the man's ability to ignore the signs so clearly visible in front of his face.

"I would prefer that my sister remain," said Jane, her voice almost inaudible.

"Mr. Collins, I am keenly aware of your request and sensible of your desires and your design here today," interrupted Elizabeth before Mr. Collins could gainsay Jane's words. "Jane and I are closer than normal sisters. As twins, we share *everything* with each other, both in our affections and our confidences. I assure you, Mr. Collins, that anything which may be said to Jane may be said in front of me, as I shall surely know of it immediately in any case."

But Mr. Collins was not to be put off. "Really, cousin, although you may share everything with your sister, there are some things which cannot possibly be shared. I have no intentions of acting against the laws of God by paying my addresses to *two* young ladies, and I have already declared to you my attachment to your sister. Therefore, there is no possible reason for you to be obstinate—a few moments of dear Jane's time are all I require, after which she will be at your complete disposal."

By this time, Elizabeth was almost ready to search for something to throw at him. "And *I* assure you, *cousin,* that I have no intention of quitting the room and leaving my sister alone with you. Say what you will. You shall not convince me to go."

Mr. Collins blinked, and his mouth worked in silence as he failed to find the words to respond to such forwardness. He appeared not unlike a beached fish with his mouth waving in the stillness of the parlor air, and although part of Elizabeth wanted to laugh at his ridiculousness, she had no desire to offend him in any overt manner—she merely wished to convince him that his suit was hopeless and thereby bring back a measure of peace to her home. For her, that would be enough.

At length, he seemed to gather his thoughts, and after a few moments of mopping his brow and muttering to himself, he evidently decided it was best to ignore Elizabeth's presence altogether, and he began to address Jane once more:

"Dearest Jane, I am certain you cannot have misconstrued my marked attentions and delicate compliments this past week. As my letter to your amiable parents stated, I have come to Longbourn with the express interest of finding my life's companion. I am perfectly sensible of being the means of ultimately causing hardship to you and your beloved sisters after your father departs from this life. As this situation was caused by none of us, yet you and your sisters were to be the injured parties, I determined the best way to make amends was to choose a bride from amongst your father's progeny, thereby protecting the interests of any unmarried sisters left behind. In this design, I was fully supported by my patroness Lady Catherine de Bourgh, who—in her great condescension—assured me that I had never before voiced anything so inspired."

Jane appeared to be listening intently to the man, but Elizabeth, impatient as she was for him to arrive at the point, nearly interrupted his speech. Still, she managed to keep herself in check, though it was no easy feat.

It was all Elizabeth could do not to release a groan as the parson continued:

"I may say, my dear cousin Jane, that immediately upon entering the house, I was caught by the sight of your loveliness and entranced by your perfect manners and feminine allure. I soon found myself as violently in love with you as a man may be."

By this time, Jane was blushing fiercely, and Elizabeth, although she would have loved to interrupt her cousin, merely narrowed her eyes, realizing that the quickest way to end the ordeal was to allow Mr. Collins to reach the point on his own—even if that did seem unlikely to happen.

"I flatter myself, my dear cousin, in my belief that I am perfectly suited to being your husband, and I dare say that Lady Catherine de Bourgh herself can find no fault in you by way of beauty or temperament and will heartily agree with my choice of bride. You are eminently suitable for the position of a parson's wife and future mistress of this estate, and I hope you will appreciate the comfortable yet modest parsonage which is to be your home while we wait for that sad event which will elevate you to the position of wife of a landed gentleman. You will, of course, benefit in the meantime from the condescension of my most distinguished patroness until that unhappy occasion, which—although we should hope it is far in the future—may in fact be closer than you fear due to your father's poor health.

"Now, I must assure you of my complete devotion and the purity of my affections toward you and ask you in all humility—dearest Jane, will you do me the great honor of accepting my hand and becoming my wife?"

Though Elizabeth was tempted to rail at her cousin for the manner in which he had ignored every suggestion that Jane was *not* interested in him, she knew that her sister, to whom the proposal had been directed, deserved the first right of refusal. And to be perfectly honest, she felt a modicum of curiosity as to how Jane would deal with him—surely the young woman could not be so kind-hearted as to accept the proposal for fear of hurting his feelings. At least, Elizabeth hoped that was the case.

A rather disconcerted Jane paused for several moments, her eyes darting in every direction other than at Mr. Collins before she finally passed a shaking hand over her face and began to respond, still refusing to meet his gaze.

"Mr. Collins—I am . . . thankful for your graciously bestowed favor and . . . generous offer."

The parson bowed in response, his face suffused with the most unctuous smile Elizabeth had ever seen in her life while he preened, his exaggerated sense of self-importance more obvious at that moment than it had ever been before.

"But I believe I must—at risk of offending you, my response must be . . ."

Clearly, Jane was having difficulties coming up with the words which would, in her own mind, hurt the parson. Yet Mr. Collins appeared to have no inkling of this.

"Please, dear Jane," interrupted he, "you need not expound upon how thankful you are or how overwhelmed you feel by my generous offer. I can see it in your eyes, in your manner of speaking—I believe you and I will do very well together."

"I am sorry, Mr. Collins, but I cannot accept your offer!"

The words were dropped onto the parson's head like a bucket of cold water—apparently, Jane, seeing he had taken her hesitance as an acceptance of his suit, was finally spurred into making her refusal. Elizabeth watched Mr. Collins, taking in his sudden, wordless shock; his slightly moving mouth, out of which no sound was forming; and the slight shaking of his head in denial. However, this reaction was only temporary, as after a few moments, his stunned expression transformed into an unpleasant leer.

"My dear cousin, there is no need to retreat into your feminine delicacy—I fully understand that it is common practice to reject at first a man's proposal, but I believe you and I, being family and having become intimately acquainted this past week, are beyond such coquetry. Please give me your assent immediately so we can share the happy news of our betrothal with your excellent parents and all your sisters."

"Mr. Collins, I am not being coquettish!" cried Jane with a squeak of dismay. "I am not in love with you and can in no way see you as my husband—I was perfectly serious in my refusal!"

Mr. Collins shook his head in denial. "My dear Jane, beautiful though you undoubtedly are, given your situation in life and lack of dowry, there can be no surety of ever receiving another proposal of marriage. You must see this. Why do you continue to test my affection for you?"

Jane colored and dropped her gaze to her lap, in which her hands were clasped. Hesitantly, she began: "Mr. Bingley—"

"Mr. Bingley may never make you an offer, while mine is before you," interrupted the parson testily. "I urge you not to try my patience any further, my dearest Jane."

"Mr. Collins!" cried Elizabeth in what was practically a shriek.

If the situation had not been so utterly infuriating, Elizabeth would have found his reaction amusing. His eyes widened, and he stumbled back. His legs met the sofa, and he sat down heavily, looking at Elizabeth with shock and consternation.

"Are you completely without sense, cousin? Jane has already declined your proposal *twice*, yet in your arrogance and your stubborn refusal to see what has been unmistakable since you stepped foot in this house, you cling to your hope like a shipwrecked man to a plank of wood. Jane has become *very* attached to Mr. Bingley, and I believe him to be equally affectionate toward her. Please take your insincere flattery and bestow it upon a recipient more willing. And leave my sister alone!"

"How dare you speak to me in such a manner!" cried Mr. Collins, rising to his feet. "My business with Miss Jane is no concern of yours—I demand you leave this room immediately and cease to insert yourself in affairs which are wholly unconnected to you!"

"I shall do no such thing! Jane is my dearest sister, and as a result, events such as this *are* my concern. You have willfully ignored every indication of her regard for another and have pressed your suit in the most reprehensible manner—and still you continue thus, though she has already told you twice of her disinterest. When shall you be convinced?"

"Cousin," countered he stiffly, "I am afraid you are simply too young to understand such things. I am confident that when your parents confer their blessing upon our union—"

"Those same parents who attempted to dissuade you from charting this disastrous course?" interrupted Elizabeth in a quiet voice. "My mother, who warned you that Jane was partial to Mr. Bingley? Or perhaps my father, who informed you that Jane would not be forced into an unwanted engagement? Are these the people of whom you speak?"

Once again, Mr. Collins was speechless.

"But . . . but . . ." stammered he.

"Mr. Collins, I do not wish to give you offense," said Jane, finding her courage. "But I feel no partiality toward you. I shall not enter into the marriage state with so unequal an affection subsisting between myself and my husband. I am sorry."

"There, Mr. Collins—I believe you have your answer."

Though she was disgusted with his behavior and found him all the more repulsive because of it, Elizabeth could not help feel a stab of pity for the obnoxious man. He was, after all, a relation, however distant, and now that she was certain they had finally penetrated his understanding, there was no further reason to feel upset with him.

"I apologize for my words earlier, Mr. Collins. My sister and I have no wish to see you humiliated, but you must understand the situation and redirect your energies toward wooing a more interested young woman. Please do not take offense."

Confident her point had been made, Elizabeth extended a hand to her sister. "Come, Jane—I believe Mr. Collins requires some time to himself."

Helping Jane to her feet, Elizabeth and her sister quit the room, though not without almost causing Mary to fall over from where she had been pressed up against the door. Mary immediately fled, though Elizabeth thought she saw a hint of a smile upon her face. Before the door shut behind them, Elizabeth chanced a glance back into the room and witnessed a confused and dejected Mr. Collins sinking heavily into the sofa. She was almost able to feel sorry for him. Fortunately, that pity did not extend to allowing him to wed her closest sister.

Chapter XVIII

The rest of that day should have been filled with tension—Elizabeth *expected* it to be so. A man of considerably more than Mr. Collins's mean understanding would have responded to such a rejection with injured dignity, censuring those who had wounded his pride and witnessed his downfall, and she expected no less from the hapless cleric. His reaction to his failure to obtain Jane's hand was almost certain to have been made worse by the manner in which the rejection had been accomplished—Elizabeth knew her role in the matter was hardly a common occurrence and could be considered highly improper.

That was not to say that Elizabeth regretted the role she had played—on the contrary, she would do anything to spare Jane the indignity of being married to such a buffoon as Mr. William Collins. However, she would have preferred that the parson had been successfully persuaded against ever showing a preference for Jane in the first place. After all, the man *was* going to be the next master of Longbourn, and as such, if the worst were to occur, she and her sisters would be entirely dependent on his generosity.

Yet the hostile atmosphere which Elizabeth had expected to descend upon the home did not materialize, for Mr. Collins, rather than rail at the failure of his suit, appeared more confused than upset. During the remainder of the morning and into the afternoon, he wandered about the house and the gardens, alternately talking to himself—presumably going over his actions, perhaps trying to determine where he had gone wrong—and gazing about him with a stunned expression plastered on his face. It was clear that he had never considered the possibility that his proposal might be rejected, although in failing to do so he had shown a blindness far from the common sort. And if Elizabeth had thought his stupidity unattractive, the expression of disbelief and lack of understanding on his face made him appear positively medieval. She could not imagine a man who was less desirable than Mr. Collins was showing himself to be during such moments.

Jane was kept away from him as much as possible. When he was in the parlor cogitating over his failure, Elizabeth escorted her sister out to the grounds for fresh air, and when Mr. Collins made his way to the garden, Jane was ushered into the house and encouraged to remain in her room. Indeed, it had taken little to persuade Jane that this was the best course.

Of course, Mrs. Bennet, when informed of the events of the morning, had been overcome with further protestations of faintness that seemed belied by the volume of her wailing. The explanation that all was well—that the proposal had been refused—had not comforted her, as she was still upset that it had even taken place. She had her heart set on a rich man for Jane, and to have that dream so nearly snatched away from her grasp was enough to send her into paroxysms of grief.

When informed of these developments, Mr. Bennet had merely shaken his head, indulged in a hearty laugh, and waved his eldest daughter from the room, once again engrossed in a book's pages before Elizabeth had even closed the door.

Strangely enough, Mary continued in her efforts to distract the parson, walking with him, listening to his confused mutterings, and trying to bring him out of his obvious unhappiness. It was curious behavior, to be certain, and try as she might, Elizabeth could not account for it. What could Mary mean by it? Was it all tied in to her behavior throughout that entire week? She had accompanied him during their walk, interrupted him during his drawn-out soliloquies to Jane, offered to read the Bible and other religious texts with him, and gone out of the common way to put herself in his company. Was she trying to spare Jane his attention and help him overcome his disappointment, or was there something more to her confusing actions?

It was late that same afternoon when the unthinkable happened—and Mary's intentions became clear.

Jane was in her room, this time with Kitty to keep her company. Lydia had flounced off earlier to walk the grounds, upset that none of her sisters would consent to a walk into Meryton to see the officers. This left Elizabeth and Mary to sit in the parlor with a still-distracted Mr. Collins. Elizabeth had taken up a book, trying to ignore the man in favor of something much more interesting. Yet her mind kept leaving the novel and returning to the flustered parson and the behavior of her sister, which she still could not explain. Though the book was open in front of Elizabeth and she turned a page every so often to give the appearance of her attention upon it, in reality her focus was upon the other two occupants of the room. It was almost as if Mary were leading Mr. Collins through a complex dance to which only she knew the steps, and it was confusing the parson even further.

Mary had successfully turned the clergyman's attention from his failed proposal to some religious subjects to which he had at first paid scant attention. As Mary's efforts continued, however, he warmed to the topic, and he was soon discussing it with her as though nothing momentous had happened that morning. Since Elizabeth found the subject matter dull in the extreme, she concentrated on the interaction between the two, not on the material about which they conferred, though snippets here and there floated up into her consciousness.

"According to Fordyce, a woman should . . ."

"Yes, of course. And in another passage, he states clearly that . . ."

"But what of . . ."

It was not until several minutes later when something her sister said fully brought Elizabeth's attention upon the conversation.

"But Mr. Collins, surely your patroness desires you to secure a wife who is devoted to the behavior and delicacy espoused by our dear Fordyce. Is this not true?"

Mr. Collins paused for a moment, deep in thought. "I do not know whether Lady Catherine has ever read the works of blessed Fordyce. But her ladyship is of such moral character and splendid uprightness that I am certain you are correct. I am of the opinion that the proper social bearing is naturally born in the most righteous and moral of young ladies, though it can, in some cases, be learned by constant study and careful attentiveness."

Mary smiled. "I am certain you are correct, Mr. Collins."

"Then why was I thus refused?" The man's eyes flickered to Elizabeth and seemed to pierce her like daggers, although she feigned obliviousness. "Your sister Jane, with her loveliness and excellent way of conducting herself, must be one of the most elegant and proper females in England. I am certain I have never seen her display anything other than the most seemly manners and good breeding, yet she dismissed me without a by-your-leave. She is all that is good, unlike . . . well . . ."

Rather than being offended by his displeasure, Elizabeth almost laughed out loud. Yet somehow she managed to restrain herself and instead continued to listen, curious as to how Mary would respond.

"Mr. Collins, it is by no means a deficiency in you that made Jane unable to accept your offer."

Elizabeth had to hide another laugh by coughing delicately into her hand. It was *most certainly* a deficiency (or several) in her cousin which had prompted Jane to reject him. His entire person was odious and disagreeable, and Elizabeth could not imagine wishing him upon her worst enemy!

"You simply did not press your suit at the proper time," continued Mary.

With a furrowed brow, Mr. Collins peered at the young woman, trying to decipher her meaning. "Do you mean to tell me I proposed too soon?"

"No, indeed, Mr. Collins. I mean, rather, you arrived in Hertfordshire too late. By the time you arrived, Jane was already attached to Mr. Bingley and he to her—unfortunately, to win her affections when they are already focused on another is an impossible task. You must understand that Jane is very proper, and for her to withdraw her affections from one to whom she has already given them is not a facet of her character. Simply put, once her feelings were engaged by Mr. Bingley, there was no possibility of anyone else turning her head. It would be unseemly."

"Ah, so if I had extended my olive branch even a month or two in advance, I would have arrived here before Mr. Bingley and thus been able to secure her before his arrival."

"I am certain that is the case," said Mary, without even a hint of deception upon her face.

Mr. Collins sighed, the action an exaggerated expression of regret. "In that case, I can only mourn my tardiness in seeking to reconcile with your excellent family. But what of your *other* sister?" This last was said in a much lower tone of voice—almost a whisper—which was accompanied by a glance of distaste in Elizabeth's direction.

It was obvious to whom Mr. Collins referred, and Elizabeth could almost feel the weight of his scorn from across the room. But once again, she affected an insensibility to his words and turned a page.

"They are very close, Mr. Collins," responded Mary in a softer tone, "as close as sisters may be. Elizabeth, being the eldest, looks after us and takes a prodigious amount of care of us all, almost acting as a second mother when required. But the bond between her and Jane as twins is profound. Elizabeth knew of her sister's preference for Mr. Bingley and did as any good sister would have done—she assisted Jane to the best of her ability."

The answering grunt from Mr. Collins was noncommittal.

"Indeed, you must believe me, sir," pleaded Mary. "Elizabeth is the very best of sisters, and although she does not assiduously study texts such as our beloved Fordyce's as I do, I truly believe she is one who has proper manners and morality engraved upon her soul. It was concern for Jane which made Elizabeth act so far from her character this morning. I believe she would have done as much or more for any of the rest of us."

"Of course," conceded Mr. Collins with a slightly injured tone. Then his expression fell, and he slumped forward on the sofa, holding his head in his hands. "But what am I to do? Lady Catherine was most explicit in her instructions—I dare not return to Kent without having completely fulfilled her ladyship's directives. Lady Catherine would be very upset with me if I were to do so."

It was at that moment that the door to the parlor opened and a maid entered the room. "Miss Bennet, the housekeeper wishes to have a word with you."

"Thank you, Sophie," said Elizabeth. "I shall come directly."

The maid curtseyed and turned to leave. Elizabeth closed her book and set it down on the side table before standing and looking at Mary, a slightly questioning expression on her face. Elizabeth was beginning to entertain a suspicion as to where the conversation between her sister and the parson was leading, and she was not certain she liked it.

Mary merely waved her hand. "Do not worry about me, Lizzy. Simply leave the parlor door ajar."

Although she felt she controlled her external reaction admirably, Elizabeth was privately amazed that her sister—Mary, who continually harped upon the proper behavior for young ladies and was not shy about sharing her views concerning how the loss of virtue in a female was irreversible—would dismiss her from the room summarily, allowing herself to be alone with a man. Elizabeth might need to quit their company for the moment, but her suspicions were aroused, and she was determined to discover what her sister was doing.

"Of course," said she. "I will return directly."

Elizabeth was not one to eavesdrop on a private conversation. Yet she found, just as with her previous experience with Mr. Darcy and Mr. Bingley, that she could not turn away from what was about to happen. Besides, while overhearing Mr. Darcy's words had been somewhat of an accident, this situation concerned a sister, and as such, she was not about to leave without knowing what was happening—not when Mary had been making her position known to the parson in a most direct manner.

Therefore, as Elizabeth quit the room, she left the door ajar as promised, but rather than retreating to the kitchen to speak with Mrs. Hill, she instead settled in behind the door slightly down the hallway and listened with growing astonishment to the conversation between her sister and the parson.

"But surely, Mr. Collins, all is not lost. You arrived here with the design of marrying one of my father's daughters, is that not correct?"

"Yes, that is so."

"Then you must realize there are other options available to you. After all, though it is generally allowed that Jane is the most beautiful of my father's children, she is not the *only* available daughter."

The image of molasses slowly flowing down into a bowl filled Elizabeth's head as the silence stretched on—homage to Mr. Collins's particular flavor of slowness.

"Well, your sister Elizabeth *has* been watching me this past week—" began Mr. Collins, only to be interrupted by Mary.

"No, Mr. Collins. She would not make you a good wife."

"But you said—"

"Yes, I did," said Mary gently, "but that does not mean that Elizabeth is fit to be your wife. She is all that is proper and good, but I am afraid she would not fit your requirements. I love my sister dearly, but she is too independent and outspoken to truly immerse herself in your life, not to mention the fact that she would likely clash with your Lady Catherine."

Elizabeth could only agree—based on what she had heard from Mr. Collins, she doubted she would last more than a few moments in Lady Catherine's presence before telling her ladyship exactly what she thought of her. That would certainly not endear her to Mr. Collins if he were her husband. *Husband*—the mere thought of the word connected with the parson was enough to make Elizabeth shudder.

"Perhaps, Mr. Collins, you should look to a different sister for a wife, one a little more like yourself. After all, the secret to a long and happy marriage is a meeting of two minds which are similar in their beliefs, their characters, and their outlook on life. If I may say so, my sisters' characters are far too different from your own for them to be truly happy with you—or you with them. No, you need a wife who espouses your beliefs and ideals."

Mary's impassioned speech all but confirmed Elizabeth's suspicions, and she could almost feel her jaw hitting the floor. Mary actually *wanted* to attach herself to Mr. Collins? As ludicrous as the idea sounded, it appeared to be confirmed in that moment. It took all of Elizabeth's self-control not to barge back into the room and demand her sister discontinue this disastrous conversation. She managed to keep her peace, however, and continued to listen through the open door, imagining the patient expression on her sister's face as Mary waited for Mr. Collins to puzzle through her declaration.

At length, the parson's excited voice floated out into the hallway, and Elizabeth knew her sister was doomed—he had finally figured it out.

"My dear cousin Mary, I believe I have had an epiphany—a veritable inspiration from God Himself!"

"Really, Mr. Collins?" answered Mary's wry voice. "Then you must share it with me—I do so enjoy hearing the word of the Almighty."

"Indeed, I am sure it does you great credit, my dear cousin. But as I was saying, I believe I have gone about my quest to secure myself a companion in the most backwards manner. Upon entering this house, my eyes were immediately caught by the sight of your angelic older sister, and I was enraptured by her, never considering there was another who more properly complemented my situation in life and my need in a wife. I am ashamed to own my weakness, for the appearance of true beauty has overwhelmed my sense and ability to look for the finer attributes in others, and I dare say that since God has now seen fit to illuminate me to my failings, I should change my designs and pursue one who is more suited to me in every way."

Elizabeth could not imagine a more insulting speech. Perhaps Mary was not the most beautiful young lady, but she was not *merely* plain. Furthermore, one did *not* declare oneself partial to a lady while discussing the beauty of her sister—and *certainly not* on the very same day one had made an offer of marriage to said sister. Yet it appeared Mr. Collins was doing just that.

"I believe you have seen the light, Mr. Collins," responded Mary.

"Then I shall pay my addresses posthaste."

It was at this point that Elizabeth, chagrined at hearing her sister actually encourage the parson, decided she had heard enough and moved away from the opening. She was not certain her constitution was up to the task of listening to another flowery proposal from her cousin.

She stepped into the kitchen to speak with Mrs. Hill—who had nothing more than a small question about the evening's menu—before returning to the parlor, hoping Mr. Collins had completed his task so she could speak to her sister.

Just as she was about to enter the room, Elizabeth was nearly trampled by her overly amorous cousin, who was exiting the parlor in a great rush, presumably to go to her father in his bookroom.

"A thousand apologies, cousin," exclaimed the parson as he reached out to steady her. His expression, while not entirely friendly, was not exactly unfriendly either. "I am on a mission of some importance which requires haste, but I most heartily and sincerely apologize for not watching my step and exiting your excellent parlor with due care and attention. I trust I have not inconvenienced you or caused you damage in any way?"

When Elizabeth assured him she was completely well, he bowed and hurried on his way, leaving her standing in the hallway. It appeared Mr. Collins was not about to leave *this* proposal to chance and was determined to secure Mr. Bennet's consent immediately. Shaking her head, Elizabeth turned on her way and stepped into the parlor, her gaze immediately arrested by her sister's slightly stunned expression and rosy complexion, the latter of which was especially abnormal for the normally staid and pale girl.

Walking over to the sofa, Elizabeth sat down and joined her sister, taking one of her hands in her own. "Mary, are you certain you know what you are about?"

"Lizzy, do not start with me, I beg you," responded Mary in a slightly peevish voice.

"I merely wish to ascertain your thoughts. You know what kind of man he is—you have seen daily proof of it since he arrived last week. Are you certain you wish to shackle yourself to such a man for the rest of your life?"

"I can assure you, Lizzy, I know exactly what I am doing. Did it ever occur to you that I am more practical and less romantic than the rest of my sisters? While I am aware of Mr. Collins's many shortcomings, I believe that he can be an acceptable husband if guided by a woman of sense."

Elizabeth considered this, knowing what her sister said was likely true. But it did not account for the constant need to moderate the parson's stupidity and tendency toward social missteps.

"And further, Lizzy, it may have escaped your attention, but he and I share similar interests and views. I presume you listened outside the door as I guided him toward his declaration?"

Elizabeth had the grace to blush at the suggestion.

"It is nothing less than I did this morning when he proposed to Jane, after all."

The two sisters shared a laugh and drew each other into an affectionate hug.

After a moment of commiseration, Mary pulled back and continued. "I was completely serious when I espoused my views to my future husband. I believe a marriage in which the partners possess similar dispositions has a much greater chance to be a marriage of felicity, and since I share many of the same opinions, I believe I shall do very well with him."

Mary turned her eyes on Elizabeth, and her gaze held a slightly pleading quality. "I *want* to marry him, Lizzy. I believe this to be my best chance at happiness. Please support me."

"Of course, Mary," responded Elizabeth, drawing her sister in for another embrace. "I only want the best for you, and if this is what you truly want, I shall not stand in your way."

And so it was done. Shortly after Mr. Collins left to apply for Mr. Bennet's consent, the parson came to tell Mary that her father wished to speak with her, and at her insistence, Elizabeth accompanied her to Mr. Bennet's bookroom. Unsurprisingly, their father was perturbed by the manner and speed in which his cousin's affections were so seamlessly transferred from Jane to Mary, but when Mary spoke of her desire for the marriage and was supported by Elizabeth, Mr. Bennet was forced to give his consent. He expressed, as coherently as can be expected from a man about to lose a daughter to the marriage estate, how happy he was that Mary had found someone with whom she could spend the rest of her life, and he wished her great happiness. Although Mr. Bennet had never been one to show his emotions, the three Bennets shed many a tear at the news, both in happiness and love for one another.

Chapter XIX

Regardless of the impression Georgiana Darcy had made upon the Bennets, she was not a terrible person. She was a devoted sister who loved her brother dearly, and she treated him with the utmost kindness and respect. She had many friends and admirers whom she had gained during her years in a prestigious school in London, and she was very accomplished in her studies. More particularly, she was skilled on the pianoforte, delighting those who were able to hear her play.

Unfortunately, however, the death of her parents had put a heavy burden on her brother's shoulders. Fitzwilliam Darcy had not only become responsible for a large estate and various other holdings, but he had also been thrust into the role of protector of a much younger sister; as a result, he had almost become a father to her rather than an elder brother. Of course, being quite young himself and having no experience rearing a child, he had struggled with raising her as their parents would have wanted. He had done well in teaching her to act properly and with decorum, but he had not been as successful in teaching her to moderate her desires. Considering her economic state in life—and the fact that she had been led to believe that almost anything was hers if she desired it—this was a major failing indeed.

When she had decided she wanted Mr. Bingley, she had assumed that he was hers by right. The kindness of the man had done nothing to dissuade Georgiana from her infatuation, and she had held the brightest hopes for their future until their arrival at Hertfordshire changed everything. Suddenly, Mr. Bingley's attentions had become focused on another young lady. It had made Georgiana heartsick.

But she had quickly rallied. Her brother was a man of action, and he had set a clear example for her. If he wanted a fine horse, he would go out and look for one. If he believed something at Pemberley was not proceeding as it should, he worked to resolve the problem in a satisfactory fashion. Therefore, since Mr. Bingley was not paying the attention that was due to her, Georgiana was determined to follow her brother's example and rectify the situation herself.

Because both of his sisters were married and were not in residence with him, Mr. Bingley had invited Georgiana to act as the estate's mistress in certain matters, with her brother's approval. Unfortunately, however, Georgiana had not yet been presented to court, and Mr. Bingley's gatherings were thus generally intimate ones with only some of their neighbors in attendance.

With the recent arrival of Mr. Bingley's maiden aunt—Mabel Bingley—the residents of Netherfield were able to entertain more extravagantly. The arrival of Mabel had been a true boon to Georgiana. Mabel was a kindly old soul, happy and content with her lot in life, and she had a plethora of amusing stories to tell of Mr. Bingley, as she had largely made her home with her brother and his children during Mr. Bingley's formative years. In addition, she held a special place in her heart for young Georgiana, who had been introduced to her soon after Georgiana's brother and Mr. Bingley had become acquainted, and the girl returned this fond regard with equal measure. The relationship between Georgiana and Mabel was even such that they were on a first-name basis, which was not something undertaken lightly in the Darcy family.

And so when the carriage bearing the elderly lady pulled up the drive to Netherfield manor, Georgiana felt her spirits rise in response. It truly was good to have such a helper and confidante present. The carriage slowed to a stop, and Mr. Bingley, in his ever-irrepressible manner, stepped forward to assist his aunt.

"Aunt Mabel," exclaimed he, "I am absolutely delighted that you have been able to join us here in Hertfordshire. How was your journey?"

"Tiring, as usual, nephew," replied Mabel with a smile. She then stepped forward and pulled Georgiana into a light embrace.

"Georgiana, my dear girl! It appears that you have grown, and your beauty has only increased accordingly. I fear that you must have suitors lined up at your door. Whatever shall your poor brother do?"

Georgiana snuck a quick glance at Mr. Bingley, noting his fond smile. "Oh, Mabel, I am not yet out, as you know."

"Well, we will simply have to prepare you, for it shall not be long." Mabel beamed at her before turning to greet Fitzwilliam. They retired to the sitting room, where they spoke for a few minutes before Mabel excused herself to go to her room to rest before that evening's meal.

Now that Mabel had arrived, it was not surprising that the very first dinner party Mr. Bingley had planned was with his neighbors, the Bennets. Of course, seeing that her young charge had been running the house at Netherfield before her arrival, Mabel was quick to suggest that Georgiana continue to act as hostess, while Mabel would provide guidance as well as the legitimacy of an adult presence to her endeavors.

Now, it could not be denied that Georgiana was less than delighted with the idea of entertaining such a tiresome family as the Bennets, but she intended to ensure they found not a single fault with her table—or, to be more accurate, Mr. Bingley's table.

The servants were given careful instructions, and Georgiana oversaw every detail, with Mabel only providing occasional assistance. Georgiana was determined to impress her brother's friend and show him just what a consummate hostess she could be. Though she wished she could trim a certain person or two off the list, she would at least endeavor to ensure that the evening was a delightful one rather than a horrid one. If she was fortunate, perhaps her aunt's odious parson, Mr. Collins, would propose to Jane Bennet and thereby release Mr. Bingley of his silly temporary infatuation. That would certainly be a proper end to the evening. But even if Miss Bennet remained unattached to the parson, the dinner would not be unpleasant—there would surely be ways to keep her out of conversation with Mr. Bingley. Georgiana even went so far as to hope she could draw the man into conversation with herself despite the fact that she would be at the opposite end of the table from him. It was difficult to talk to him at Netherfield, for he was a very popular man and was frequently invited to have tea or dinner with nearby families. Though her residence at Netherfield resulted in her addition to the party when such invitations were tendered, Mr. Bingley was often too intent upon interacting with their hosts for her to draw him into conversation with her.

Georgiana's thoughts were drawn back to the Bennet family. She simply could not understand what was so alluring to Mr. Bingley about Jane Bennet—the young woman smiled no more at Mr. Bingley than she did at any other man. Georgiana had never witnessed a true sign that Miss Bennet cared for him. Absolutely nothing she had seen had indicated any such extreme emotion as love—and she had watched carefully.

When at last the guests to Netherfield arrived, Georgiana welcomed them with the grace of the perfect hostess, pushing aside her ill feelings toward the Bennets and showing Mr. Bingley how gracious she could be. She was displeased that by and large the Bennet sisters seemed quite taken with Mabel and she with them, but it did not particularly signify, as Mabel was gracious and lively with everyone she met. When they at last moved to the dining room, Georgiana felt positively excited about what awaited them. She moved quickly to her seat, and she smiled as she glanced over to see Mr. Bingley approaching his position at the other end of the table. *This* was how it was meant to be.

As she watched him, however, he did not sit down instantly—instead, he laughed and conversed with Jane Bennet, who did not appear to understand that she was causing Mr. Bingley to remain standing for an impolite period of time. The longer they conversed, the more Georgiana's good humor began to dissipate. When at last the pair separated from their intimate huddle, Georgiana huffed irritably under her breath. She might have been somewhat appeased to see Mr. Bingley finally sink into his chair were it not for the fact that he only did so after he had insisted his dear *Jane* sit to his immediate left.

While gritting her teeth and striving to collect herself, Georgiana happened to glance at Elizabeth Bennet, who had the ghost of a smile on her face. Georgiana pinned Miss Elizabeth with a glare, barely able to believe the audacity of the woman. To be amused at Mr. Bingley's attention to Jane Bennet—and lack thereof to Georgiana—was impertinence of the highest degree!

"Miss Darcy, are you well?" ventured Miss Elizabeth, a hint of a challenge in her voice.

Georgiana did not deign to give her a verbal response, knowing she would say something she regretted. Instead, she nodded stiffly and turned her eyes to her plate.

A few seconds later, the evening became even worse. Mr. Collins appeared delighted to see her, and above the general murmur of everyone's dinner conversation, he began to speak to her. "Miss Darcy, you look especially lovely tonight. Of course, you must know that the eyes of a man in love are colored to enjoy almost everything in his sight."

She stared at him, uncomprehending.

"I am certainly glad that you benefit from contact with your most esteemed aunt and my gracious patroness, Lady Catherine de Bourgh. In encouraging me to come to Hertfordshire, she has enabled me to take advantage of a most fortunate opportunity for domestic happiness. I can only hope that you, too, may one day be so happy as I—or might there already be a man who has stolen your heart away? Of course, you would only marry a man of the utmost strength and character—and naturally, with the guiding influence of her ladyship and your brother, you will never find yourself trapped in the mire that so frequently ensnares young women these days."

As the parson continued to prattle on, fawning over her in the most ludicrous manner imaginable, Georgiana's ill mood grew stronger. Whereas before that day she had severely disliked the Bennets, now she was beginning to loathe them for having subjected her to this obsequious fool. The fact that he was an obsequious fool whom her aunt had seen fit to employ was conveniently forgotten.

Occasionally, Elizabeth Bennet attempted to draw Georgiana into conversation during the times when Mr. Collins paused to take a breath, but Georgiana maintained an icy front, and Miss Elizabeth's efforts soon desisted. Not that the woman seemed to feel the effects of Georgiana's silence—in fact, Georgiana was displeased to see that Mabel had apparently taken a liking to her, and they were conversing as though they were old friends.

Georgiana's mood was not improved by the frequent smiles and laughter coming from Jane Bennet and Mr. Bingley. The two looked utterly content, and it only served to make Georgiana more miserable. The evening, it seemed, could not get worse.

Finally, however, there came some good news. "I dislike to bring an object of sorrow to the attention of such an ebullient party as this one," said Mr. Collins, his voice loud enough to bring everyone's eyes to rest on him, "but I wish to inform everyone, though it pains me to say it due to the unfolding of recent events, that I shall be departing to Kent on the morrow. I know my presence shall be sorely missed—"

Georgiana highly doubted anyone would be missing his presence—not even the Bennets! She began to ignore him completely, reveling in the notion that at least she would no longer be subjected to his company, when something he said broke into her consciousness:

"—and it is, as I have said, my utter delight, nay, my utmost and heartfelt gladness, that leads me to inform you all of the blessed situation in which I find myself: I am the most fortunate of men to have the great honor of announcing that my dearest cousin and soon-to-be life partner, Miss Mary Bennet, has accepted my offer of marriage."

"Thank you, Mr. Collins, for releasing me from the great burden of making such an announcement," said Mr. Bennet dryly, though the parson appeared not to hear him.

Georgiana forced her gaze to rest on the parson's betrothed, and she noted the slight smile tugging at the girl's mouth. However, Georgiana's own almost-smile, which had begun to show at the parson's announcement of his departure, was quickly becoming a frown. She had hoped very much that Mr. Collins would succeed in wooing Jane Bennet, thereby removing her as a threat to Georgiana's rightful claims on Mr. Bingley. But it was apparently not to be. That particular machination had been defeated almost before she had even conceived of it.

It was all Georgiana could do to refrain from flinging her fork onto the floor. The urge to indulge in a tantrum had never been so strong as it was at that moment. She shifted to look at her brother, only to find him staring at Elizabeth Bennet with a strange expression on his face. Was he as disgusted with her country manners as Georgiana herself was? Would that this trip to Hertfordshire had never come to pass! She longed for the precious days spent at Pemberley in the company of her brother and his dear friend Mr. Bingley. If only they could leave Netherfield and return to her home!

When Mr. Collins turned to her and began to comment on how the lace on her dress reminded him of a tablecloth at Rosings, she almost began to cry. How she wished to leave this miserable place!

Chapter XX

Mr. Collins left Hertfordshire the day after the residents of Longbourn dined at Netherfield, returning to Kent as he had originally planned. Elizabeth had no doubt he was eager to report his success to his patroness, and for the most part, the Bennet family was not unhappy to see him go. Mary was the only Bennet who appeared to feel any ambivalence regarding his departure. Although the young woman's stoic countenance betrayed little of her emotions, Elizabeth suspected Mary was eager to extricate herself from a household much more concerned with discussions of reticules and evening gowns than religious enlightenment.

In the days after the parson took his leave, life at Longbourn gradually slipped back into the comfortable routine which had characterized the Bennets' lives before his arrival, but with one significant exception. Since the engagement of her middle daughter meant Mrs. Bennet was finally fulfilling one of her lifelong dreams, her excitement could not be contained, and it manifested itself in a belief that it was incumbent upon her to prepare a celebration the likes of which the small neighborhood had never seen. It did not matter that Mary was perhaps her least favorite daughter (although Elizabeth could also possibly lay claim to that title) or that she was considered the plainest. It was a daughter being married which was important, and Mrs. Bennet would never allow it to be said that she could not plan and execute a wedding breakfast which would have garnered the approval of even a duchess!

It was during these few weeks that Elizabeth felt she was truly coming to know her middle sister for perhaps the first time. Mary had always been quiet and reserved, uncomfortable in genteel society and ambivalent toward some of the social niceties in which other young ladies of her class took great pleasure. She had rarely opened up to anyone—even her sisters—and could not be said to be especially close to any other member of her family.

Elizabeth made a conscious effort to spend much of her time in Mary's company, speaking with her of many things—from their lives at Longbourn and their friends to speculations about what Mary could expect from her new life in Kent. Considering Mary's temperament and interests, the young woman was likely correct in her estimation of her prospects for marriage. Such an opportunity might never have come again for her, and although she had procured this proposal through somewhat unorthodox means, it behooved her to seize the opportunity. Besides, for all Elizabeth knew, a true regard and love could grow between the couple—she had certainly heard of stranger things occurring, though perhaps she could not quite name one offhand.

Other aspects of life at Longbourn also continued to change. Mr. Bingley and Mr. Darcy had become regular visitors, and although Mr. Bingley's growing admiration of Jane made his motivations obvious, Mr. Darcy's own motivations remained unclear. If the grimness that overtook his countenance whenever Mrs. Bennet or Lydia opened their mouths was anything to go by, he still found the company of some of the house's residents tedious, if not downright repulsive. It was a wonder that the man continued to remain in Hertfordshire.

At Longbourn, Mr. Darcy frequently kept his own counsel, often saying nothing of substance for at least the early part of his visit. The windows of the parlor seemed to be his favored location, and he would often stare out of them for some time, observing vistas or contemplating issues to which only he was privy. When he did deign to join the conversation, he surprisingly kept to the company of Elizabeth, although he was not averse to speaking with Kitty and did on occasion appear keenly interested in listening to Jane and Mr. Bingley.

To Elizabeth, his behavior was singular, for although he spoke to her whenever he was able, he always made it clear that his attention was intended as that of a friend, and he took great pains to avoid inciting her expectation that he was motivated by anything other than the enjoyment of conversation with an acquaintance. Yet his actions were not consistent with his continued professions of only friendship. After all, except when it came to Kitty, he spoke no more than perfunctorily with any other inhabitant of Hertfordshire, certainly not to the extent of holding long conversations as he did with Elizabeth.

Their topics of conversation were varied, ranging from literature, to the current state of affairs, to Elizabeth's love of horses. Mr. Darcy's own passion for riding made horses a natural subject which they discussed at length and in great detail. His knowledge was necessarily much greater than hers, and he was eager to share his experiences, conveying a sense of pride in the fine animals which he bred and owned.

One topic they covered was the maintenance of an estate, and Mr. Darcy seemed greatly surprised by the depth of Elizabeth's knowledge on the subject. Since her father was sickly, she had helped with the running of Longbourn for the past several years, learning many things about planting, drainage, and the books her father maintained to record his resources. She knew Mr. Darcy's estate was many times the size of her father's and must also thus be much more complicated to operate, but his admiration for her knowledge could not be feigned—he complimented her on her common sense and skill and gave her advice which she generally found to be good and helpful.

Their conversation would often grow spirited, and he seemed to find her candor and lack of deference for his station refreshing, largely, she felt, due to his interactions with young ladies of society who would no doubt agree with anything he said for the purpose of ingratiating themselves. He often seemed to play devil's advocate, espousing a view which she knew could not be his own for the sake of eliciting a contradictory opinion from her—or, at least, that was how it seemed to Elizabeth. Her sometimes-biting wit and sarcasm did not offend him in the slightest; on the contrary, he appeared to enjoy it when she made some acerbic comment or irreverent observation, and he responded with no few of his own. He was possessed of a keen wit and an impressive understanding, and Elizabeth quickly learned that she could not make sport of him without him instantly understanding the true thrust of whatever she said. Elizabeth's enjoyment of his company and anticipation of their discussions was only tempered by her disappointment—it was often some time before he felt comfortable enough in Longbourn's parlor to engage in conversation, and she believed that this delay in his participation was a great loss.

The slight he had given Elizabeth that day outside her home had been forgiven and forgotten. She saw him now as a confident and intelligent man, someone who was clearly her intellectual equal and who complemented her in his opinions and knowledge of the world. She knew she was not immune to his charms—indeed, he was tall and broad-shouldered, even more handsome a man than his friend Mr. Bingley, and he *had* been very attentive to her. But it was that attentiveness which continued to confuse her; he claimed to be interested in conversing with her due to their shared interests and intellectual debates, but Elizabeth knew that a man did not ignore all others of his acquaintance to spend time with a young woman if he had no admiration for her. After having once been infatuated with a man whose feelings had not fallen in line with hers, Elizabeth was fearful of letting another into her heart, but with this man who had suddenly appeared in her life, she wondered if it were not worth the risk.

Reason quickly asserted itself, however, and she reined in her flights of fancy. Perhaps he *was* paying more attention to her than strict propriety would warrant, but that did not make his claim of friendship any less valid. She had always lamented the lack of spirited conversation in the neighborhood and felt that a man who was accustomed to a much more varied form of society would likely cling to any source of the same, regardless of the person from whom it originated. Mr. Darcy would not lower himself to court a country miss who had little to recommend her, not when he could be assured of so much more.

No, he could not have any serious designs on her, and Elizabeth resolved to think on it no more and to accept his overtures as he had made them, without any expectation of anything further.

Several days after the unlamented departure of Mr. Collins, Longbourn was once again graced by the presence of its estimable neighbors, but this time for another purpose altogether. Though rumors that Mr. Bingley was to throw a ball had been circulating throughout the neighborhood, nothing had been said on that score by the man himself. Elizabeth herself, of course, knew that it was to be held due to Mr. Darcy's request for her hand for the first two dances. But for Elizabeth Bennet to dance at an assembly of any kind would be unusual in the extreme, and as she had no desire to be the recipient of her family's inquisition, she had made no mention of it to anyone.

When Longbourn's visitors had been shown to the parlor and the obligatory small talk had been completed, Mr. Bingley began the invitation thus:

"Mrs. Bennet, our purpose in coming here today is not simply a social one. I wish to invite you—all of you—to a ball to be held at Netherfield on the 26th of November." He punctuated the request by bowing and handing a small and elaborate invitation to Elizabeth's mother.

Now, it was well known that the Bennet matron was not the most observant or clever woman—indeed, her understanding was somewhat weak, and her opinions were insipid. But in the matter of her daughters and eligible young men, her oblivious nature became a keen and observant one; Mrs. Bennet was able to discern a compliment to her daughters and see a potential suitor from several miles away. In the matter of the ball, she quickly determined that Mr. Bingley's motive for delivering his invitation in person—rather than sending the invitation to all the invitees through his servants—was a profession of sorts of his admiration for Jane, and Elizabeth in truth could not fault this opinion. Elizabeth could see her mother become almost giddy with excitement, yet the answer given was somewhat more decorous and calm than might have been expected.

"Mr. Bingley!" exclaimed Mrs. Bennet. "You do us great honor by delivering your invitation in person. We thank you for this very kind gesture and assure you we would be vastly pleased to attend."

"You are very welcome, Mrs. Bennet. I . . . our *families* have become very close, Mrs. Bennet, and I assure you that I am very much looking forward to having the pleasure of your company." Throughout his speech, Mr. Bingley did not take his eyes off Jane once, leading Elizabeth to believe he had wanted to say that he and Jane had become close rather than their "families."

The rest of the Bennet party reacted somewhat predictably—Jane blushed and pronounced her pleasure to accept the invitation; Lydia laughed gleefully and exclaimed over the fun she would have; and Elizabeth, Kitty, and Mary all professed various degrees of acceptance and excitement. Miss Mabel Bingley appeared quite pleased with the idea of a ball, for she was a congenial woman who delighted in the company of others. The reactions of the two Darcys, however, were much more interesting, for they heavily contrasted with each other. Mr. Darcy showed no great emotion, but he did dart a piercing glance at Elizabeth—which caused an unexpected frisson of excitement to move through her—and murmur something about the prospect of an evening in pleasant company. Georgiana Darcy, however, said nothing at all, and her lips were a hard line of displeasure, likely due to the thought of the object of her affections showing preference to another. Elizabeth was uncertain as to whether Miss Darcy would even be allowed to attend, and while she did feel slightly sorry for the young woman, the happiness on Jane's face was enough to put that emotion to rest.

"I do have one other matter to attend to," continued Mr. Bingley when the exclamations of approbation died down. He turned to Jane and favored her with a smile.

"My dear Jane, I would like to take this opportunity to solicit your hand for the first two dances."

Elizabeth was pleased that her conjecture was correct; his asking for her hand for the requested dances in front of her entire family was a bold stroke, and it showed his intentions as clearly as if he had shouted them from the rooftops.

Jane colored and smiled, murmuring her complete willingness to cede the dances to him. Mr. Bingley beamed at her, basking in the success of his mission.

The Darcys, however, appeared to be less pleased. Miss Darcy became as white as a sheet, and a tear escaped from the corner of her eye. Mr. Darcy himself started and peered at Mr. Bingley in shock. It was clear that Mr. Darcy, although he had certainly known of his friend's attachment to the most beautiful Bennet sister, had not expected such a declaration in front of her entire family. Mabel Bingley simply continued to smile at her nephew. She appeared to approve of Mr. Bingley's attachment to Jane wholeheartedly and did not seem to have discovered *Georgiana's* attachment to her nephew, which puzzled Elizabeth exceedingly. She still did not understand how all three of the adults close to the girl could be so blind!

The Darcys would have no choice but to become accustomed to the attachment between Mr. Bingley and her sister, Elizabeth reflected with some amusement. She had known of the young man's regard for some time now, and she doubted there was anything on earth which would prevent him from following his inclination through to its logical conclusion. Elizabeth could not help feeling happy for her sister—it was a wonderful match.

Chapter XXI

The Netherfield ball was held on Tuesday, November 26th. The morning air had been cold and crisp, and a pervasive chill persisted throughout the day. But that did nothing to stifle the excitement of the occasion—if anything, the prospect of being indoors in a warm ballroom rather than outside in the cool air seemed to heighten feelings of anticipation in the Bennet household.

As Elizabeth entered the ballroom at Netherfield, however, she was uncertain as to how she should feel. She had, after all, shunned such assemblies due to an incident in her past better left forgotten. But there was something about being back in the glitter of the ballroom that made her realize it had not completely lost its appeal to her.

When she saw Mr. Darcy and met his gaze with her own, her cheeks colored. She did not believe it had escaped either of their memories as to the identity of her first dance partner. The look in Mr. Darcy's eyes told her that much. The notion of not coming to the ball had occurred to her several times throughout the day, and now the idea of fleeing Netherfield and secluding herself in her father's library was even more appealing. But she had come this far—and she would *not* let herself be intimidated by the prospect of dancing with Mr. Darcy.

She greeted the Netherfield residents in a daze, and from thence, she stepped to the side to gather her composure for the expected ordeal. Before she knew it, it was time for the first dance, and Mr. Darcy was walking determinedly across the floor to claim her hand. Jane was already deep in conversation with Mr. Bingley, so Elizabeth was not even able to garner a sympathetic look from her before she had to turn to her partner.

"Miss Bennet," said he, his voice stiff. His face was unreadable, but Elizabeth suspected he was regretting his application for a set of dances with her. After all, a man of his position could have his pick of any young lady in Hertfordshire—there was absolutely no reason he should have claimed Elizabeth's hand rather than someone else's for the opening dance at his friend's ball. Of course, Elizabeth knew enough about Mr. Darcy to understand that he rarely ever danced, so it was likely he had not even bothered to ask anyone else to accompany him to the floor. Still, the idea of dancing with her certainly did not seem to bring him any joy—he might have been looking over an accounting log rather than addressing a young lady. His face was serious, and his dark eyes, though discerning and intense, did not seem to take any pleasure in observing her figure. He must simply have been acting on impulse when he asked her to be his partner.

"Mr. Darcy," returned Elizabeth politely.

"I believe you promised me the first set," said Mr. Darcy. He appeared uncomfortable making such a supplication, which only further confirmed Elizabeth's suspicion that he had not been thinking clearly when he first made the request.

"That is something I cannot deny, Mr. Darcy," allowed Elizabeth in a teasing tone, "though I confess I wish otherwise. I have long since developed a distaste for dancing. But I have given you my word, and I will not renege on it. The first set belongs to you."

Nothing more was said between them as they moved to the dance floor and stood opposite each other. The music soon began, and Elizabeth studiously avoided looking at Mr. Darcy as he fixedly stared at her. She noticed Jane standing up with Mr. Bingley, both of them as happy as robins in spring, a stark contrast to the heightened emotions that seemed to surround her dance with Mr. Darcy.

They progressed through the opening steps of the first dance in silence, moving down the line in tandem with one another. Mr. Darcy seemed ill inclined to speak—he simply divided his attention between her and the steps, serious and intense as always. They continued in this attitude for some time until, at last, Elizabeth found the silence between her and her companion unbearable, and she endeavored to break it by drawing her tall and quiet partner into conversation.

"Mr. Darcy," said she, "surely you did not invite me to dance with you so we could practice our imitation of church mice."

The corners of his mouth twitched. "Do you always find it necessary to speak while dancing?"

"Why, we should appear strange to the whole party if we danced for the entirety of half an hour without exchanging some small measure of conversation," commented Elizabeth. "For my part, I much prefer speaking to dancing, so I see no reason why I should not exercise my mind as I exercise my feet."

"I suspect both your mind and feet receive plenty of exercise."

"And I intend to keep it that way," noted Elizabeth with a smile. "By speaking with me as we dance, you are helping me with the pursuit of my goal."

"It is a goal you need no help in pursuing. You appear quite able to entertain yourself without my assistance."

They were separated by the dance steps at that moment, and Elizabeth regarded him as they moved closer. When they were near enough to touch hands, she said: "Perhaps you are right. I enjoy splitting my time between roaming the countryside and studying the characters of others. When I am doing one of those things, it is almost impossible for me to be unhappy."

Mr. Darcy paused, turning in the dance, before venturing: "And what do you see in my character?"

"Your character is not an easy one to sketch. I have heard many conflicting reports about you, and I am having difficulty in putting the pieces together."

Mr. Darcy raised an eyebrow. "Then I am a challenge for you?"

"Deciding on your character is a challenge, yes," acknowledged Elizabeth, "but it is one I intend to overcome soon enough."

"I sense you are not one to remain confounded for long," replied Mr. Darcy when they were once more together.

Elizabeth laughed. "That is the impression I prefer to give. I believe you and I are quite similar in that respect."

"How so?"

"Neither of us likes to dwell longer on a subject than is strictly necessary. And you certainly never seem to be a believer in idle chitchat."

A thoughtful expression came over Mr. Darcy's features, and as he moved away from her, he appeared to consider the matter in his mind. When the dance steps brought them together again, he affixed her with his serious stare. "There *are* some subjects that even I dwell on longer than I should," confessed he.

"Ah! Well, those must be close to your heart. I should think you would not wish to share them with me."

"Yes," responded he in a curt voice. Elizabeth had apparently touched on some nerve, and they said little else until the set of two dances ended.

She and her partner curtsied and bowed respectively, and she said with a polite smile: "Mr. Darcy."

He stared at her intently, as if unsure how to respond. Then, suddenly, he spoke: "Miss Bennet, would you care to dance another set?" As soon as the words had been released, he appeared surprised. In fact, the words did not so much come out of his mouth as spill out.

Elizabeth was no less surprised—and she was perhaps even more confused. What had possessed him to ask such a question?

Her mind reeling and her heart pounding, she gently told him: "I should think you were showing me favor, Mr. Darcy. I have been assured that at the last assembly you stood up with only one woman who was not formerly of your acquaintance—and *that* was my sister. And I have it on excellent authority that you only did so to appease my mother. We shall already be the object of a week's worth of gossip as it is now. If we should dance again, the whole month would be filled with discussions of our exploits."

In a tone not devoid of haughtiness, Mr. Darcy responded: "You are quite right. Forgive me for my presumption. I withdraw my application."

As the man stiffly led her away from the dance floor, Elizabeth felt as if her head were throbbing in wonder. Requesting to dance another set was an unmistakable sign of favor toward a young woman. But why would Mr. Darcy—who certainly showed no signs of liking *anything* in Hertfordshire—have been close to making such a misstep? And why had her heart lurched at the idea of actually accepting his request?

Once Elizabeth was escorted to Jane, Mr. Darcy bowed and left with a few muttered words of parting. Elizabeth watched him go, her eyes briefly falling on Mr. Bingley, who was asking another lady to dance. Elizabeth might have been concerned had it not been for the fact that Mr. Bingley's gaze kept returning to Jane.

Mr. Darcy, however, did not seem to have any inclination to ask another woman to stand up with him—instead, he moved to the side of the room, his gaze sweeping over the assembled. His usual unapproachable glare was quite evident for all the room to see.

Elizabeth, after looking at him for a moment, turned to her sister and frowned.

Jane was looking at Elizabeth in puzzlement. "It is very strange that you should dance with Mr. Darcy, Lizzy."

Elizabeth bit her lip. She might have disliked the man at one point in time, but that was certainly no longer the case. Her feelings toward him now were mixed, but she did not want to put them into words. So she merely told her sister: "He asked me for the dance some time ago. I believe it was simply a further apology to smooth over any ill feelings I might still have harbored from our first meeting. He is, after all, a gentleman, if a bit of a standoffish one, and I dare say dancing with him was more pleasant than might have been expected, considering what I have heard of his behavior at assemblies such as this one."

"Lizzy, do you like him?" asked Jane in a hushed voice.

"Jane," said Elizabeth with a smile, "I should sooner marry a mop than Mr. Darcy—I am certain the mop would have more to say!" She let out a light laugh, though she felt even her sister could tell there was something slightly insincere to it. "But come—tell me of your dance with Mr. Bingley! Even now, he can't keep his eyes from you."

Jane flushed, but she willingly began to divulge a few details concerning the inconceivable kindnesses of Mr. Bingley, though they had only a few minutes before the next set began. But as Jane began to sing the amiable young man's praises, Elizabeth could not help but think about Mr. Darcy once again. Though she disliked dancing as a general rule, there was a part of her—a miniscule part that could perhaps be considered as large as a grain of rice—that wished she could have continued dancing with him as he had requested. After all, she told herself, he was an enigma, and she wanted to determine what was behind that somber mask. The fact that she still felt a warmth in her hands where she had been touched by him was simply due to the chill of the winter weather. And the fact that she kept thinking about his curly locks and his dark eyes was only because the former would not stay out of the latter. She had no interest in him beyond that of a character study. None at all.

Now, she simply had to survive the rest of the night. The ball had just begun, and there was absolutely no reason for her thoughts to linger on Mr. Darcy.

Chapter XXII

For Elizabeth Bennet, the rest of the evening took on an almost surreal quality, as if someone were directing her motions like a music conductor at a concert while she sat in a corner and merely observed.

The reason for this, of course, was Elizabeth's level of participation in the evening's festivities. For the previous three years, she had avoided gatherings of this nature, completely eschewing the monthly assemblies at Meryton and generally only attending balls when they were given by one of the local families, as refusal would be a grave insult she was not willing to make—regardless of her distaste for the activity. And even when she *had* been persuaded to attend, she had made it very clear she had no intention of dancing, refusing the first application for her hand and knowing that such a refusal precluded her from participating for the rest of the evening. Soon, word had spread that Miss Elizabeth Bennet could not be prevailed upon to dance, and it had not taken long before the young men of the neighborhood began to focus their attentions on more willing participants.

However, it was not the society which was lacking, but the activity—dancing held far too many less than pleasant memories for her, and she refused to open herself up again in such a manner. She was still lively enough in other ways. Outside the ballroom, she was always eager for conversation, joined in at the card tables on occasion, and could be convinced to display her talents on the pianoforte, such as they were. In the ballroom, however, she would resolutely refuse to dance, though she could often be found sitting alongside the dance floor and speaking with friends who were not engaged for a set. Apart from that, she was primarily a spectator, observing with some interest the ebb and flow of the ballroom, gazing upon the dresses of the women and the coats of the men, or examining the interactions of ladies and gentlemen while occasionally swaying to the music. She would study the characters of people in the room, newcomers and old friends alike, engaging in the pastime of which she and her father had made a game over the years.

Thus, after her dance with Mr. Darcy had concluded, she settled herself in for another night of observing the assembled dancers, confident she had done much more than her duty in standing up for a set—that was to be her sole exertion for the evening. However, the best-laid plans have a tendency to unravel in a most displeasing way. Mere moments after Mr. Darcy had escorted her back to Jane's side, she was approached by one of the local landowners.

"Miss Bennet," said he, "I see you are finally disposed to dance again. May I have the pleasure of the next?"

Aghast at the man's misinterpretation of her intentions, Elizabeth opened her mouth to refuse, only to be interrupted by the sweet voice of her sister.

"Thank you for your kind offer, Mr. Appleton. I am certain Elizabeth would be vastly pleased to stand up with you for a set."

Mr. Appleton appeared somewhat nonplussed for a moment at the strange manner in which his offer had been accepted, but he nonetheless bowed and, thanking Elizabeth, walked away. The next set would begin shortly, but he apparently could tell the two sisters needed a few minutes together alone.

"Jane—"

"No, Lizzy! You spend far too many of these assemblies standing around when you should be dancing with eager young men. You appeared to be content with your partner in the first dance at the very least, so why not continue to dance and enjoy yourself?"

"Jane, you remember what happened—"

"I do, Lizzy," responded Jane, not without compassion. "I also know that it is time you conquered your disappointment and began to live again. It is not right that you should be stuck with this half-existence while that . . . that . . . *scoundrel* who hurt you blithely continues on as though nothing has happened."

Elizabeth was all astonishment as the diatribe continued. She had never known that her determination to avoid the activity had produced such strong feelings in Jane.

A moment later, she was engulfed in her twin's arms. "Lizzy, you must let this go. Do you think you are the only one who has ever been hurt by a man? I want my sister back—that sister who would laugh and dance the night away, amazing every young man in attendance with her wit and intelligence. Can you be that girl again, Lizzy?"

A lump had formed in Elizabeth's throat, but she gamely released her sister from their embrace and smiled, although her smile contained a tremulousness she could not quite suppress. "I shall try, Jane."

"That is all I can ask, Elizabeth," responded Jane, kissing her on the cheek. "Now, here comes Mr. Appleton. Go enjoy yourself, and I shall see you after the set. I am engaged to dance the next with Mr. Goulding."

In a daze, Elizabeth allowed herself to be led to the dance floor, and she was soon immersed in the steps of the dance with her partner. He kept up an ongoing monologue, not seeming to require any answer beyond her occasional murmurs of agreement.

He was, she reflected, not the first choice she would have made in a dance partner, but he was also far from the last. Mr. Appleton was the owner of an estate on the other side of Meryton. It was far enough away that he was not truly considered part of the community, yet it was close enough that he was often included in the invitations to the gatherings of the area. He was a short and portly man, a widower of some years with no children and—if Mrs. Bennet's words held any merit—a need for a wife to correct that unfortunate circumstance. In fact, there had been some speculation that he had admired Elizabeth before *Mr. Darcy* had burst onto the scene, not that she would have ever considered marrying a man more than twice her age. Still, he was kind and proper, and he provided her with the opportunity to consider her situation without having to pay particular attention to his conversation. More importantly, perhaps, he did not appear to be offended by her distraction.

When the set was complete, he escorted her to the side of the room. He opened his mouth to say something further but, for whatever reason, held his tongue and quit her company with a bow.

So began the night for Elizabeth Bennet. Now that she had danced the first two sets, other men found the courage to approach her and ask for their own dances. Elizabeth, remembering her promise to Jane, acceded with as much grace as she could muster, all the while feeling that her previous ambivalence had not entirely departed. Still, it felt good to finally release herself from her self-imposed restrictions and enjoy the moment, which was something that she had not done in many months.

Chapter XXIII

For Charles Bingley, the night was everything he could have imagined. The sights and sounds of the ballroom, so vexing for his friend Darcy, had always been comforting to the outgoing master of Netherfield, and he reveled in the pleasure that fine company and intelligent conversation could bring.

There was also the matter of Jane Bennet—the girl with whom he was rapidly falling in love. Opening the dance with Jane had been pure bliss, and he had immediately taken the opportunity to solicit her hand for the supper dance. Indeed, he would have secured them all had it been proper, but in the end, he was well contented that one of the most important sets of the evening belonged to him.

But that did not end his campaign to win Miss Bennet over. No, there were other members of the family who were almost as important to his suit as winning the affection of his love. So, he made himself available to any and all Bennets, conversing with Mr. Bennet—though his conversation was rife with innuendo and sarcasm, which meant sometimes Bingley had difficulty following him—listening to Mrs. Bennet's excited exclamations, and complimenting Miss Mary on her dress. Though Mr. Bennet was somewhat hard to read—and Mrs. Bennet was a little too *easy* to read—Bingley was glad to know that Miss Mary appeared to be pleased by him, if her rosy-cheeked response was any indication at least. He expected she did not receive much attention, and he was happy to help remedy that, even if only in a small way. Even more important than Miss Mary's direct approval, however, was the fact that he was considered familiar enough with the family to have the pleasure of Miss Kitty's hand for a set. He reveled in the knowledge that he was trusted in such a way, and he was careful to lead her through the steps in such a fashion that no harm would befall her.

But the true object of his campaign was to obtain the favor of Jane Bennet's closest sister, Miss Elizabeth. Seeing her engaged to dance the first set with none other than his friend Darcy had been a shock, but upon considering it for a few moments, he determined this was likely Darcy's way of completing his apology for his unkind statements. And really, he did not know what Darcy had been thinking to have made those statements in the first place, annoyed or not. Miss Elizabeth did not, perhaps, possess the ethereal beauty of her elder sister, but to say she was plain was simply wrong, and tonight, as she was dressed in a fine gown of the palest rose, Bingley had to confess that if he had seen Miss Elizabeth before his dear Jane Bennet, he would have been tempted to fall in love with her instead.

Watching Miss Elizabeth dance with Darcy and then with one of the local gentlemen had been an unexpected but completely welcome boon to Bingley's design to win the young woman's favor. He was puzzled by her consent to dance, as he was aware of the fact that she normally refused to do so. However, thanking divine providence for the opportunity which had presented itself, he immediately put it out of his mind and determined to engage her for a set.

It appeared that other young men of the area had the same thoughts as Bingley, for she was soon besieged by requests, and Bingley felt fortunate to have secured her hand for the set before the supper dance. It was with great appreciation that he finally led her to the floor.

Their conversation began slowly, but Bingley was nothing if not adept at charming members of the opposite sex, and soon she was laughing at his comments and responding with arch looks and amusing anecdotes. Bingley was entranced—surely Darcy was out of his mind to be declaring this enchanting creature merely *plain!* In fact, Bingley had a suspicion that Elizabeth Bennet would not only fill Darcy's need for a wife but also be a far better match for Darcy than—

But no—now was not the time for such thoughts. Darcy needed to come to his own conclusion about his marriage prospects, though Bingley was of course available to offer assistance should his taciturn friend require it. For now, Bingley was determined to focus his efforts on his own future.

"Have you suddenly grown introspective, Mr. Bingley?"

Charles Bingley smiled at his charming partner. "Though I fight against introspection, I must allow that it does affect me from time to time. Normally, I speak too much for my own good, though I am glad to say it is a flaw your dear sister does not seem to hold against me."

"Well, for someone who is without a flaw of her own, Jane does seem quite willing to overlook the foibles of others," teased Miss Elizabeth.

"She is an angel, is she not?" agreed Bingley. He suddenly flushed. He had not meant to verbalize that thought.

"I am glad to hear that your opinion mirrors mine so closely," said Miss Elizabeth amiably, turning his chagrin to pleasure. It seemed to be a fortunate thing that the words had come out despite his intentions. "Your attentions to my sister have certainly been kind." He watched as she gave him a significant look, and he began to suspect it was her way of telling him that she approved of his courtship of her sister. The thought made his heart leap in his chest—if he had the approval of the sister nearest to Jane Bennet's heart, then his chances with her were greater than he had allowed himself to hope.

He glanced across the room and noticed Darcy watching him and Elizabeth Bennet dance. The expression on Darcy's face could almost be termed a glare, and it puzzled Bingley to no end. As the evening progressed, Darcy's mood appeared to have become ever darker. Bingley could not understand the reason for the man's frustration. The only conjecture he could make was that it was perhaps related to Darcy's general dislike of assemblies.

Miss Elizabeth saw his glance and gave Darcy one of her own. She appeared to be echoing his thoughts when she said: "I dare say your friend does not seem happy to be here. He seems to be even less eager than I to dance."

"He nearly always avoids dancing at assemblies," commented Bingley. To himself, he reflected that she only spoke the truth—in that respect, he was similar to Elizabeth Bennet. "I could barely believe my eyes when I saw the two of you dancing the first set together."

Miss Elizabeth's cheeks colored, and she suggested feebly: "Perhaps he is attempting to overcome his dislike of the activity."

"And are you doing the same?"

"I suppose I find it pleasant enough when standing up with a kind partner," said she, smiling at him, "but I do not believe I will ever love dancing as most of my sisters do."

"You never know, Miss Bennet. Perhaps you simply have not yet found the proper partner."

She gave him a small smile. "Perhaps."

Chapter XXIV

Darcy glared across the room at Bingley. He was smiling and laughing with Elizabeth Bennet, and they appeared to be quite happy together. Scowling, Darcy deliberately turned away, intent upon ignoring the scene before him—particularly the young lady who had been on his mind of late. But while he attempted to refocus his thoughts, his eyes continued to seek her out of their own accord.

Though Darcy had initially thought upon meeting the young woman that there was no perfect symmetry to her figure—and he had reflected that her face was hardly in possession of any good features—he now had known for some time that her appearance was made remarkably pleasing by the intelligence found in her dark eyes. Those expressive eyes, he knew, were in possession of no small measure of beauty, and the smile now tugging at her lips was also pleasing to behold. All of the compliments Bingley had bestowed upon Elizabeth Bennet were not without veracity, and her manner, though not the sort Darcy was accustomed to seeing in the more fashionable circles of England, was appealing with its pleasant playfulness. Bingley had been right in singing her praises, and Darcy had been quite wrong when he had insulted her.

But even more important than her beauty and manners, to Darcy's way of thinking, was her intelligence—for the intelligence which shone forth from her eyes was not simply a trick of the light or a show put on for the benefit of others. In Miss Elizabeth Bennet, Darcy felt that he had truly found someone whose intellect could match his own, a woman with whom he could converse while knowing the pleasure he felt in doing so was equally felt. He was confident that she enjoyed their conversations as much as he did, and the knowledge caused him to feel a measure of satisfaction in his ability to please a woman worthy of pleasing. And there was no denying that Miss Elizabeth was worth pleasing.

That knowledge simply made him more frustrated as he watched Bingley and Miss Elizabeth speak together so merrily. Though he knew Bingley was smitten with Jane Bennet, Darcy could not help but be annoyed regardless. Perhaps what was truly annoying him, however, was the fact that Elizabeth—*Miss* Elizabeth—was dancing with so many different partners. It seemed as if every man in the whole blasted room were trying to dance with her! He certainly did not wish to dance with her again, regardless of his nearly drastic social misstep after their set had ended; he simply believed the fact that men were dancing every set with Miss Elizabeth cheapened his initial victory to induce her to dance with him. She was a challenge—that was all. And Darcy was never one to let himself be overcome by a challenge. Even one as enchanting as Miss Elizabeth Bennet.

Darcy danced once more that night; because Georgiana had been allowed to stay for part of the evening, he and Bingley had acted as her only partners before she was sent up to her bed. Afterward, Darcy had decided to linger along the edge of the ballroom as was his wont, watching, observing, and generally hating those who asked Miss Elizabeth to dance, knowing that they were in no way her equals.

He was brooding in this fashion when a nearby conversation accidentally caught his attention.

"Your eldest daughter certainly appears to have put the past behind her," commented Lady Lucas to Mrs. Bennet. "It was an utter shame that the young man left her to marry for money—she is such a wonderful girl."

Darcy had been about to turn his head to gaze at Elizabeth Bennet, but he suddenly froze. He had not realized that Jane Bennet once had a serious suitor.

"We were all heartbroken," said Mrs. Bennet, sniffling a little. "We had hopes that he had some money of his own. And he seemed as if he were such a charming man! But of course, all of that did not signify in the end. I suppose it is just as well she did not marry such a disagreeable man. To think of having such a son-in-law as that!"

"Charming and disagreeable?"

Mrs. Bennet seemed to think Lady Lucas had made a statement rather than asked a question—and she seemed also to miss the amused skepticism hiding behind Lady Lucas's words. "Indeed! I am appalled by how such a charming man could be so disagreeable. Young people in these times can be so very unpredictable. They simply have no sympathy toward their elders—no appreciation for the sacrifices we make for them. It is enough to cause me no small measure of distress. Ah! It nearly tears my heart apart! She has been very greatly affected by it, as I am certain you are aware."

Lady Lucas, who Darcy expected was accustomed to the other woman's temperament, gave a commiserating nod and diverted the conversation: "Well, at least both your eldest daughters appear to be doing well at this assembly. Jane has not sat out a set, and Elizabeth, though I have not seen her dance in a very long time, has matched her dance for dance, unless I am mistaken."

Mrs. Bennet brightened, apparently having forgotten all about her earlier distress. "Mr. Bingley certainly is a charming man, is he not? And he most definitely *does* possess a fine fortune of his own! He would be a wonderful catch for my Jane! She is much more suited to Mr. Bingley than to Mr. Collins. Did you know that he proposed to her?"

"No, I was not aware of that."

"Of course, he does not have nearly as great a fortune as Mr. Bingley! Nor as agreeable a disposition! I dare say my Jane was meant for greater things than to be a mere parson's wife. She will do much better with Mr. Bingley, I am sure. I shall be quite content when she meets him at the altar!"

Darcy's mouth formed a grim line. There had already been no question in his mind that Mrs. Bennet was determined to have Bingley as a son-in-law—even if she had not been so quick to voice her desires, he had long since learned to recognize the covetous gleam that shone in the eyes of mothers with single daughters whenever they beheld him. Of greater concern, however, were the particular feelings of the young lady in question. That, Darcy decided, was something he needed to learn as quickly as possible.

Thus, for the rest of the evening, Darcy watched the young woman as she interacted with other men—particularly, of course, Bingley—to determine whether he could detect some measure of regard for him.

But what he saw was perhaps even more puzzling than ever. He had always known that Jane Bennet was a serene and reserved young woman, but not once did he detect a change in her countenance as she beheld his friend. It was obvious that she received Bingley's attentions with pleasure, but was that pleasure also not bestowed upon other young men with whom she danced and conversed? Where was the special smile meant only for Bingley? Where was the slight tremble when he touched her hand during a dance? Where was the slightly distracted air of a young woman in love? Though Darcy did not have much experience with love himself, he had watched others when out in society, and he had seen that general inattentiveness and incivility toward others were the very essence of someone in love.

None of this was present, and the more Darcy watched Jane Bennet, the more he realized that she was a pleasant and reserved young woman who had been jaded by a less than pleasant experience with a suitor in the past. No, Darcy was certain that she would not give her heart so easily a second time.

A quick glance at the Bennet matron showed her speaking animatedly with another of the local women, and though Darcy could not hear her words, he could guess the content of them. And he suddenly knew that regardless of whether Miss Bennet was inclined to accept a proposal from Bingley, she would not be allowed refuse another proposal—he suspected that the only reason it had been allowed in the instance of Mr. Collins was because Mrs. Bennet had already decided on Bingley as her eldest daughter's future husband.

The situation faced by his friend was worse than he had thought. Not only did the young woman fail to return Bingley's depth of feeling, but she was also a fortune hunter. She had turned down a perfectly reasonable proposal from someone suitable to her station in hopes that she could secure Bingley's wealth. Now, Darcy found himself in a quandary. He had to learn his friend's true feelings for the girl, and then he had to determine what course of action to take. He would not allow Bingley to become trapped in a loveless marriage. Bingley's heart was great, and such an arrangement would surely destroy him.

For the rest of the night, Darcy bent his thoughts toward extracting his friend from the trap the young woman and her mother had set for him. As a benefit of his distraction, he was able to put Elizabeth Bennet out of his head; at least, he did not think about her again more than once or twice.

Chapter XXV

"Blast it!" cursed Bingley as he failed yet again to hit one of the pheasants that were his target. His aim—never good—had been absolutely abysmal that morning.

Darcy's own mood was foul enough that he could not appreciate the fact that he himself had been an excellent shot that day. Despite his present luck in hunting, grouse and pheasants were far from being the object of his concentration; instead, he could not stop thinking about the previous night.

That Bingley was entranced by Jane Bennet . . . well, it was something which Darcy did not doubt. But whether it was serious—or whether it was another one of Bingley's infatuations—was something Darcy could not quite discern. He *believed* Bingley was more partial to this young woman than any before her, but he was uncertain. Regardless of his friend's feelings, however, he was determined to keep the young man from being hurt. And to do that, he had to learn what exactly his friend's feelings *were*.

"Yours was a splendid shot, though, Darcy!" cried Bingley in admiration. He had been in a buoyant mood all morning.

"Some of us do actually try to aim the rifle," returned Darcy lightly.

Bingley chortled. "You are right, my friend. But it is no matter—I feel as though I could defy the world today!"

Seeing his opening, Darcy ventured: "And what precisely is the reason for such an ebullient mood?"

Bingley flushed. "Well—I doubt I have to tell you, Darcy, but I am absolutely captivated by Miss Jane Bennet."

"Indeed?"

"She is a wonderful girl, Darcy, and I have never before felt such feelings for another. She is very handsome, of course, but even more significantly, she has an undeniable innate goodness—why, I said just last night that Jane Bennet was an angel, and I meant it completely!"

As Bingley continued to wax poetic about Miss Bennet and grow even happier because of it, Darcy's mood began to grow even darker. Bingley had at last let the dangerous claws of love entrench themselves in his heart. And he did not have even the inkling of an idea that the object of his utter admiration was someone who cared about the size of his pocketbook and not the contents of his character. It was up to Darcy to tear him away from the fortune hunter, though it pained him to know that his friend's sensitive heart would be bleeding for months afterward. If only he had paid more attention to Bingley and less to Miss Elizabeth, then perhaps he would have seen this coming and managed the separation in a timelier manner!

Bingley had to be removed from Hertfordshire. The Bennets were nothing but trouble, and Darcy knew that he would also benefit from leaving their society. He needed to put some distance between himself and Elizabeth Bennet. He had been facing female problems aplenty before arriving at Netherfield—it was what he had been trying to briefly escape by coming to Hertfordshire in the first place, after all—and he did not need to add that intriguing and fiery woman to the mix. Two women made his life complicated enough without adding a third. He knew what had to be done. It was now merely a matter of convincing his friend that it was in their best interest to go. Unfortunately, given Bingley's apparent fascination with Miss Bennet, it seemed like persuading him would be no easy matter.

"Bingley," said Darcy in a serious and firm voice, "I think it is time we leave Hertfordshire."

"Leave Hertfordshire?" cried Bingley, stabbing the air with his gun. "Why, that is the last thing in the world I should wish to do right now! Did you not just hear me?"

"But it is the first thing in the world you should do," returned Darcy. "You must realize that Jane Bennet is not what you think she is."

Bingley said nothing—he just blinked in confusion.

"Bingley," tried Darcy again, "Jane Bennet is poison to you—"

"Poison! Why, I should say instead that she is an elixir to my soul! Darcy—what the devil has come over you?"

"I do not wish to hurt your feelings, Bingley, but I have been watching Miss Bennet, and I am sorry to say that she has never shown you any special favor."

At this, Bingley lowered his weapon, faltering. "Darcy?" said he in a soft voice. "Is this true?"

Darcy looked away, closing his eyes. "I wish I could give you a more favorable report. But she cares not for you. I—I am truly sorry, Bingley. If you proposed to her, I am certain she would accept—but I also know that she would never be allowed to refuse a proposal, whether or not her regard for you was sufficient to induce her to marry you on her own."

Trembling, Bingley stared at Darcy. Finally, he lifted his chin. "I cannot believe that, Darcy. You are wrong. Jane Bennet, she—she cares for me."

As Darcy gazed back into the defiant face of his friend, he knew he could no longer withhold the details of the conversation he had heard about Jane Bennet. "Last night, I overheard something, Bingley. I learned that Miss Bennet once had another serious suitor—and he left her for a woman of fortune. I believe the experience to have jaded her, and I know Mrs. Bennet will not allow a similar opportunity to escape her daughter's grasp. When Miss Bennet turned down a proposal from Mr. Collins—"

"She turned down a proposal?" cut in Bingley. "Darcy, surely you must realize this means I have hope—"

"No," said Darcy sharply. "You must realize her refusal had nothing to do with her feelings for you—rather, it is your money that she has her eye on."

"That—that is preposterous." But despite his words, Bingley seemed shaky and uncertain. "My Jane—Miss—" he took a breath, "Miss Bennet would not act that way."

In a quiet voice, Darcy told his friend: "I have watched her, Bingley. I wish you were right. But I have watched her. Her smile is not the smile of a woman in love, and it never has been. Her eyes do not sparkle like those of someone facing utter happiness. When she dances with you, she is merely dancing with another well-to-do suitor. My heart breaks for you, Bingley, but I refuse to stand idly by and watch you walk into a loveless marriage. Your heart is too sensitive for that."

"I—I need to go," muttered Bingley, looking as dazed and lost as

Darcy had ever seen him. After dropping his weapon, Bingley began walking at a swift pace toward Netherfield. Darcy gestured to a servant to pick up the rifle and then followed him.

Once they were inside, Georgiana saw them and frowned at the expression on Bingley's face. "Are you well, Mr. Bingley?"

But he simply walked past her with the slightest of gesticulations and disappeared into a sitting room.

Georgiana turned to her brother. "Fitzwilliam, what is wrong with Mr. Bingley?"

Darcy looked after the young man, frustrated. He had to save his friend from the pain of falling any deeper in love with Jane Bennet. Turning, he looked at his sister and studied her for a moment. He hated to bring her into this, but he was desperate. And so—against his better judgment—he began to explain what he had heard and what he suspected about Jane Bennet.

"I am afraid that I have witnessed the very same thing in Miss Bennet," declared Georgiana after Darcy had completed his explanation. "In fact, I consider the Bennets to be nothing more than a grasping, artful sort of family."

Gratified that he found a willing co-conspirator in his sister, Darcy ignored the niggling corner of his heart which told him that *Miss Elizabeth* was nothing of the sort. He hardened his heart against such thoughts, allowing Georgiana's admission to further solidify his resolve.

"Come. Let us speak further so that we can prevent Bingley from making a drastic mistake."

Together, they retired to Georgiana's sitting room, and there they formed a plan to convince Bingley to come to London with them . . . and leave Jane Bennet behind.

At dinner that evening, Darcy asked: "Bingley, have you thought about what I said?"

Bingley's face—which had appeared somewhat disheartened—darkened. "I have, Darcy, and I am certain you are wrong."

"Mr. Bingley," began Georgiana softly, "I think my brother is right."

Mabel Bingley turned to look at the girl and then back at the two men. "I am afraid I do not understand this discussion. Of what are you speaking?"

But rather than answer his aunt, Mr. Bingley turned to Georgiana, and the look on his face pierced Darcy's heart.

Georgiana continued: "I am afraid I have been unable to see any particular regard from Miss Bennet toward you either." She looked down at her hands, her face full of sadness. "I have been so sorrowful for you, Mr. Bingley, as I know you are a man who feels very deeply. But I do not believe Miss Bennet cares for you. I stand with my brother on this issue. I believe her only objective is your fortune."

Though Darcy knew his sister's words would hurt his friend, he was grateful for her speaking them. Every day, she reminded him more and more of their mother, and Darcy was proud of her. Turning to his friend, he pleaded: "Please, Bingley—listen to reason. Come with us to London. We must leave this place."

"Go to London?" echoed Bingley's aunt. "Whatever can you mean by that? Dear Jane Bennet is a lovely girl, and I am afraid I must disagree with both your sister and you, Mr. Darcy. Her objective is not my nephew's fortune."

Bingley bit his lip and stared down at his right hand, which was clenched into a fist on the table. Tapping the bottom of his fist gently against the table and closing his eyes, he said: "Darcy, this is really what you believe?"

Darcy inclined his head, though his friend could not see it. "Yes, it is."

Letting out a heavy breath, Bingley conceded: "I will return to London for a short time."

"Heavens, no, nephew!" exclaimed Mabel Bingley, though her cry was not addressed.

Opening his eyes, Bingley continued: "I will stay through Christmas, and after that—well, I need some time to think."

"Bingley—" began Darcy.

"Please! Say no more. I need time to think about what I want, Darcy—about what I feel for Jane Bennet. I will leave, as you have asked me, and I will consider what you both have said. But other than that, I can make no promises."

Darcy dipped his head. "That is all I ask."

"Far be it from me to argue with the esteemed likes of your friend," said Bingley's aunt, who appeared quite flustered, "but if you do insist upon leaving here, you must be certain not too stay away too long. A girl like that Jane Bennet is a prize indeed, and if you do not take her soon, some other young man will.

"And I will also warn you, Charles," continued she, an uncharacteristically hard expression on her face as she looked at her nephew, "that you must not hurt that poor girl. Tread softly, or I shall not be held accountable for my actions."

"Yes, aunt," whispered Bingley, but his mind was obviously miles away. Perhaps Darcy should have felt somewhat triumphant—or perhaps, to be more accurate, relieved—due to his success in persuading his friend to allow some distance between himself and Jane Bennet for a time, yet Bingley was clearly troubled at the thought of departing Hertfordshire without speaking a word to anyone, and it was difficult for Darcy to feel any happiness over his victory.

The next day, Bingley summoned Darcy to his study, and it was distressing to see just how upset Bingley was. The young man had undoubtedly had difficulty sleeping, as his face was haggard and his mien strangely lifeless.

"I have invested much of myself in hopes and dreams and love during my time in Hertfordshire," Bingley told his friend quietly. "Though you and your sister may believe I hold none of Jane Bennet's heart, she certainly holds mine. To cut our relationship asunder so abruptly without even offering a word would be akin to tearing out my heart, flinging it to the ground, and refusing to give it a backward glance. You have never been in love, Darcy. You may not be able to understand, but despite what you advised, I cannot simply leave like a thief in the middle of the night. I *will not* do it. After having spent so much time with Miss Jane Bennet, it simply shall not do! I *must* go to Longbourn to take my leave of her!"

"I understand your concern, Bingley," said Darcy, "but it is necessary to break away cleanly—you require time to reflect on your circumstances. Would you put yourself once again within the range of Mrs. Bennet's scheming? Seeing Miss Bennet could weaken your resolve to leave Hertfordshire. I do not believe it wise to see her again."

Bingley buried his hands in his hair and then suddenly struck the armrests of his chair with his fists. He stood, his eyes flaring. "What do you suggest I do, Darcy?" cried he. "Wipe away all traces that I have ever been here? Hide my heart away in a cave?" He closed his eyes, taking in a deep breath to calm himself, and then he sunk back into his chair. "I am sorry, friend, but I must bid them farewell at the very least. I owe it to them."

"If you insist on a final communication with them, then write Mr. Bennet a letter," suggested Darcy at last. "Frankly, however, I believe it wiser to say nothing more to them at all."

Bingley shook his head and looked down at his hands, whispering: "I wish you knew how I feel, Darcy. Your heart has only been lightly touched by two young women—you do not know what I am experiencing right now." Bingley looked up sharply and declared with some heat: "It would not be right to leave without saying anything,

Darcy. I have paid enough attention to Jane Bennet that to leave without any word would be improper—and unfair to her. I will not do it." He stared at his friend resolutely. Behind the pungent sorrow of leaving Miss Bennet—and the fear of not truly being loved by her—was a slowly growing strength, one which Darcy could see in his eyes. Bingley had trusted his friend's judgment over his own since nearly the beginning of their acquaintance, lacking a complete confidence in himself due to his extreme modesty, but something was changing. *He* was changing.

Darcy closed his eyes in acceptance, though he certainly wished he could argue with his friend further. "Very well. Write a letter to Mr. Bennet, if you must. I will not try to stop you."

And so, Bingley composed a letter to Mr. Bennet. Though Darcy wished he could see the epistle, Bingley refused to let him have any hand in it. There were perhaps a dozen discarded drafts thrown by Bingley into the fire—each of them splotched with the ink of hesitancy and the occasional fuzzy word caused by a shaky hand—and the final letter might not have been entirely without its blemishes, but at last it was done. The letter was sent. Not long after its departure, Bingley, Darcy, Georgiana, and Mabel left for London.

Chapter XXVI

Whenever an interesting letter came to Mr. Bennet, he usually teased his family with the knowledge of its existence at mealtime before finally reading it out loud to them and providing his opinion—real or feigned—on it. When a letter arrived from Mr. Bingley, however, Mr. Bennet's epistle-sharing was much more subdued. He was aware of the solemnity of the occasion, and as such, he did not attempt to craft an air of excitement and mystery for his own amusement. Instead, he told his family with an uncharacteristic sobriety that he had found it necessary to peruse the correspondence three times before he was certain he had thoroughly processed it, and he gave a sympathetic look to Jane that caused Elizabeth's stomach to clench.

No one said anything as he divulged the contents of the letter. He did not embellish upon any of Mr. Bingley's words or look to see his wife's reaction—in fact, he spoke with as little emotion as possible. When he was at last quiet, so were the females of his family. No one knew how to react. It was as if the floor had been removed from beneath them, and they were now floundering on the ceiling.

Mrs. Bennet was the first to break the silence, wailing suddenly: "How could he leave my poor daughter? My dear Jane! Oh, whatever shall we do?"

As for Elizabeth, the more she considered the letter, the greater her anger became. She could not understand how Mr. Bingley could do such a horrid thing to Jane! He had paid his addresses to her in an unmistakable fashion, making it clear to all of Hertfordshire that Jane meant the world to him. For him to withdraw his affections now was almost like when . . .

She shook her head, trying to clear it. She was not going to make this about herself. It was about Jane. Jane was the one who was hurting now, and it was Elizabeth's job as her twin to take care of her.

Elizabeth turned, and her heart began to break as she saw the tears shining in her dear sister's eyes. Jane was trying to fight them, but she was losing the battle, and it made Elizabeth feel as if her own heart were breaking.

"Jane," said Elizabeth uncertainly. She did not know what she could possibly say to make her sister feel any better—trying to keep Jane from becoming upset would be like attempting to stop a rampaging bull—but she wished desperately that the required words would come.

"Lizzy," returned Jane in a whisper. She tried to lift her chin up—to put on a brave front—but she was unable to fool her twin. She was absolutely miserable. Bingley had shattered her delicate sensibilities more effectively than had he come and shouted at her. If they had spoken harsh words to one another—if indeed Jane could ever be induced to speak in such a manner—then perhaps Jane might have been able to fortify the defenses around her heart and withstand the loss of her beloved. Instead, he had dissolved the bonds between them through a letter and an unexpected trip to London; there was nothing she could grasp onto, nothing save a sudden hole in her heart.

Elizabeth stood and moved to enclose the teary young woman in a hug. "Jane," said she softly, determined to be optimistic for the sake of her dear sister, "he may return. In fact, I think he wanted us to know he will—he leaves the option open quite clearly. Surely a man as much in love as Mr. Bingley will return to the one for whom he cares as soon as may be. I *know* he cares for you, Jane. No one who has seen him with you can think anything else." They were weak words, but they were all she had to give.

Jane shook her head and said what Elizabeth had barely dared think to herself: "But what if he does not?"

Elizabeth looked at her trembling sister's pale face, wishing she knew how to offer some comfort. But nothing she could say would change the fact that Mr. Bingley was going to London. He had not come to talk to them, to ask their opinions—they were helpless. It was done. Jane's dreams had been dashed into the ground, and there was nothing that could be done to recover them.

"Oh, come, Jane! There are plenty of officers who would like to dance with you," scoffed Lydia. "I would not worry about Mr. Bingley. He was not *that* handsome anyway."

Kitty, who had been quiet up to this point, shot to her feet. "Be quiet, Lydia! Mr. Bingley is a man of substance—a true gentleman! He is worth a hundred of your precious *redcoats*!"

"That is not true!" insisted Lydia. "The officers are fine men! And besides, you cannot see what Mr. Bingley looks like anyway. You *are* blind, after all!"

"Lydia!" snapped Elizabeth. "Do not say such say such a thing—that was very unkind, and you should be ashamed of yourself!"

"I was only speaking the truth!" exclaimed Lydia. "I do not know why everyone treats Kitty as though she cannot blow her nose by herself. *I* deserve some of your attention, too! Why, just the other day, I wished for one of you to tell me your opinion on my new dress, and not one of my sisters had anything to say to me about it!"

"Oh, please!" scoffed Kitty. "I am certain that no one in this house cares three figs about what your ridiculous dresses look like!"

"That is not true! Mama, tell her that you care what my dresses look like!"

"Oh, girls, please do not fight," moaned Mrs. Bennet. "Of course I care about your dresses, Lydia, but I do not think my nerves can withstand any more of this! Oh, whatever shall I do now that my dear Jane's Mr. Bingley is gone?"

Lydia sent a vicious glare toward Kitty, who could of course not see it. Then, Lydia flounced out of the room with a disgusted sigh. Kitty simply snorted and shook her head.

Jane slowly rose to her feet. She muttered something about not feeling well and disappeared out the door as well. Elizabeth watched after her for a few seconds before bringing her eyes up to meet her father's. Mrs. Bennet was wailing very loudly at that point, so nothing anyone said could have been heard (had anyone dared to speak), but the sad look she and her father exchanged spoke volumes. They both knew how sensitive Jane was. And they both knew that the likelihood that Mr. Bingley would return was not great. He was probably gone forever. His letter did not seem hopeful—he claimed no urgent business. There was no obvious reason for him to have left unless he simply wanted to put Hertfordshire behind him.

When at last Elizabeth left to attempt to comfort her sister, she found, as she had feared, that Jane was not in the sort of state that permitted comforting. Jane was an intelligent girl, and she was more than aware of the bleak days ahead of her. And nothing Elizabeth could say or do would change Jane's terrible awareness of the severance of what would have been a bright future with Mr. Bingley.

Chapter XXVII

Time passed quickly, but not quickly enough. With Mary's impending wedding, Mrs. Bennet was wasting no time in rushing about making the necessary preparations in spite of her lament over the loss of Mr. Bingley; as a result, there was no peace at Longbourn. If Mrs. Bennet was not exclaiming over ribbons, then she was clucking over food; if she was not clucking over food, then she was obsessing over Mary's trousseau. There would be absolutely nothing missing or out of place at the wedding of her daughter—no one who was at all familiar with the Bennet matriarch could doubt that she would have everything well in hand.

Mr. Bennet found the preparations amusing. He would inquire as to one aspect of the wedding and then watch as his wife fell over herself to explain all the details concerning the proper execution of that element. He would then sit back and observe her as she flitted from one task to another before he brought up another subject and once again observed her as she expounded upon whatever he had mentioned. Though Elizabeth enjoyed examining the foibles of others as her father did, she sometimes wished he would cease pulling her mother's strings like some sort of pitiable marionette.

While Lydia cared more about the buttons on a redcoat's jacket than she did about Mary's marriage—and often could be heard to exclaim that Mr. Collins was boring and stupid—Kitty and Jane, on the other hand, chose to be happy for Mary. Mary herself was pleased with all the attention, and Elizabeth was glad that at least Mary would have this time to look back on. Though Elizabeth was still unconvinced that this marriage was the best choice for her sister, she would not stand in Mary's way.

For Elizabeth, the best part of the impending wedding was the opportunity to see the Gardiners. She relished every chance she had to speak with them and regretted that they did not live closer so that visits could be more frequent and longer in duration. At least she had Christmas to look forward to—her aunt was calm and motherly, and her uncle was intelligent and jovial. A visit with them was always a time to be treasured.

But Christmas had not arrived yet, and so the Bennet daughters had to withstand a flurry of wedding preparations. On one such day when Elizabeth felt she could take no more of her mother's frantic discussions of weddings, she decided she would escape into her room for some peace. However, before she had even made it to her door, she stopped in the hallway at the faint sound of sobbing. The noise was coming from Jane's room, and she knocked and gently twisted the knob, opening the door to find Jane seated by the window.

"Jane," whispered Elizabeth sympathetically, gazing at her sister's back.

"Lizzy," returned Jane in a shaky voice. She did not turn around. It was obvious she did not want her twin to see her.

But Elizabeth came forward nonetheless after shutting the door behind her. She went over to Jane and touched her shoulder, whispering her sister's name.

With no small amount of reluctance, Jane turned, revealing red eyes and a tear-stained face. Elizabeth immediately pulled her into a hug, and Jane started sobbing anew.

"Oh, Jane," whispered Elizabeth, stroking her sister's back. "I am sorry."

"This is—is s-silly of me," managed Jane through her tears. "But I—I miss him, Lizzy. What if Mr. Bingley never comes back from London? What if he is gone for good? What if I shall never see him again? I keep hoping I will, but—" She could speak no more.

Elizabeth pulled back and looked her sister in the eyes. "He is likely involved with some pressing business, Jane. After all, he wrote a letter specifically to us—to the Bennets, Jane!—announcing his intentions, remember? That is a good sign! I dare say he did not give such consideration to anyone else in the neighborhood!" She tried to infuse her voice with confidence, but it was hard to be convincing. Not when her dear sister had been reduced to this wretched state.

"Lizzy," spoke Jane softly, her chest still shaking with her sobs.

"There is still hope. Do not lose hope in him, Jane. Why, if you were to lose hope, then I should think the world was ending!" Elizabeth tried to smile, but her heart was breaking for her twin. She embraced Jane again, and Jane worked on collecting herself.

Finally, Jane was able to say: "I want to hope, Lizzy. Truly, I do. But I do not know if I can. I thought— " Her voice broke, but she began to speak again. "I thought Mr. Bingley had feelings for me, but now I must question my own observations. What if—what if he never did feel any real affection for me, and he realized it and felt he had to take action? What if he does not truly intend to return to Netherfield?"

"He will return," said Elizabeth with a firmness that almost convinced herself. "The esteemed Mr. Bingley would not simply leave you behind without a second glance. You are a treasure, Jane. And if somehow he has failed to see that—well, perhaps he is not the man you thought he was." She gave her sister one last hug and then tugged at her hand. "Come, Jane. Dry your eyes. I think our mother may need your help deciding between two different kinds of lace—you know how she insists that everything must be perfect. I fear a terrible catastrophe if she does not determine the correct lace with the appropriate level of embellishment in Mary's dress!"

Jane gave a half-smile. "Lizzy, I am sure she does not need my assistance. You are exaggerating, as you usually are when attempting to make me smile."

"And I am quite certain she does," returned Elizabeth. "I believe she was saying, 'If only my dear Jane were here to tell me which of these two pieces of lace is of better quality and a lovelier pattern! Why, I believe she is a master lace-chooser, and I do not know what I will do without her help!'"

Jane shook her head at her twin's silliness, but her half-smile had become a real smile. "I promise I will leave this room soon, Lizzy. But I should think Lydia would be the one to turn to for advice. She is the one who is always fixated on lace and ribbons for the purpose of decorating her copious collection of bonnets!"

Elizabeth lifted an eyebrow. "Did my dear Jane just make a joke at the expense of another? Perhaps the world truly *is* ending!"

Jane laughed. "Thank you, Lizzy. I will try to hold on to hope. Perhaps I shall see Mr. Bingley after Christmas!"

"Exactly! And perhaps in a year the two of you shall be married! Though I should hate to see how wretchedly loving your children would be."

"Lizzy!"

Elizabeth smirked. "You two kind souls were meant to be together. Even if Mr. Bingley is apparently a little thick at times."

Jane shook her head, trying to hide a smile. "You can go now, Lizzy."

"My sister is dismissing me? Why, that is a first!"

But Elizabeth, laughing, left the room nonetheless as Jane made shooing motions with her hands. It heartened her to hear her sister's chuckle from the hallway. Still, her thoughts darkened as they turned to Mr. Bingley. If he was not as kind of a soul as he seemed and shunned Jane, then he would receive no quarter from Elizabeth. Jane might have been willing to forgive him in an instant—even if her heart shattered in the process—but Elizabeth was not the same kind of person as her twin. Even though propriety dictated that she be kind to Mr. Bingley regardless of his actions, Elizabeth would exhibit no good will toward him if he split Jane's heart asunder. Elizabeth would be her dear sister's protector—for Jane could not do it herself. While Elizabeth would not call him out for a duel even if she could as a woman—amusing though the thought was—she could be as cold as a sunless winter day.

Chapter XXVIII

The day of Mary's wedding dawned bright and sunny, yet with a distinct chill in the air, as was usual mid-December. The environs of Longbourn were decked with the beauties of the season—hoarfrost coated the trees, and little wisps of snow clung to the ground where they had blown, lending the manor a festive air, as though approving of the first match of the Bennet daughters. And the irony surrounding the wedding was lost on no one—plain Mary, ignored by her mother and the young men of the area in favor of her more beautiful sisters, would be the first of them to marry.

For Elizabeth, it was a day filled with contradictions, both within and without. She was happy she had been able to save Jane from the ignominy of a match with the foolish Mr. Collins, yet she was disappointed with the end result of the man's pursuit of a wife. That Mary actually wanted this union was somewhat comforting, regardless of Elizabeth's doubts about whether her sister could truly be happy with Mr. Collins. Despite any compatibility of interests and character between them, Mary was certainly not stupid—intellectually, she and Mr. Collins were not a good match at all. Though she would never tell her sister as much, Elizabeth suspected Mr. Collins would end up competing with a rock for the greater share of intelligence.

Yet Elizabeth was also sensible of the benefit brought to her family by means of this marriage. Her mother need never again fret about being thrown out of her home, for with a daughter as mistress of Longbourn, she would always have a place to live in her old age should Mr. Bennet succumb to his poor health.

These were the thoughts in Elizabeth's head as she completed her toilette and threw on an old dressing gown, ready to quit her room and see to her sister's preparations. Regardless of the benefits of such a match, Elizabeth would never be able to look back on this day with any positive feelings; however, that did not mean she wanted Mary to feel the same way. Plastering a smile on her face, Elizabeth made her way to her sister's room to help her prepare. Mrs. Bennet was fussing and fidgeting, nervous that everything should proceed as planned. But Elizabeth knew that Mary was already anxious for what the day would bring, and the last thing she needed was their mother's hysterics sounding in her ear. And so Elizabeth carefully deflected Mrs. Bennet's attention to some other task which required her attention and convinced her that Mary's preparations could be completed quite capably by Elizabeth and the maid.

The time they spent taking care of Mary was completed in a companionable fashion. Elizabeth and the maid fussed with Mary's hair, speaking of inconsequential topics and marveling over how radiant Mary looked. Elizabeth had promised herself that she would ensure her sister's appearance was stunning on her wedding day, displaying to the world that the quietest and plainest of all the Bennet daughters was as desirable as any of her sisters.

Elizabeth had finished with the elegant twist of Mary's hair and had begun to curl the ringlets which would frame her face when Mary glanced up at her, a rarely seen look of determination on her features.

"Lizzy, I want to thank you for all you have done for me," began she, a hint of emotion coloring her usually calm voice. "I appreciate the way you have always taken care of your sisters—and I appreciate that you are standing up with me on my important day."

That had been another surprise—Elizabeth had not had any idea her sister looked up to her so much, and the request to be Mary's bridesmaid had astonished her greatly.

"Mary, you are my sister, and I love you. There is nothing more to be said, no more accolades to impart—I have done only what any other would do."

"I believe you underestimate your importance to this family, Lizzy, but I thank you nonetheless. You made me feel like a worthwhile member when our mother had openly disparaged my attractions before the world."

Her face took on a mischievous smile as she continued. "Part of me cannot help but smile and gloat over the fact that *I* shall be married before our mother's favorites."

Elizabeth's raised eyebrow caused a small laugh.

"Oh, I have nothing against my sisters, Lizzy," said Mary, "though I must own that I fear for Lydia. She shall not end well if she is continually indulged as she has been."

"While I hope you are wrong, I have had the same concerns myself," responded Elizabeth. "However, as you well know, Mama will not hear anything against her, and Papa cannot be bothered to check her. Until one of our parents comes to their senses, there is little any of us can do."

They lapsed into a brief silence while the maid completed the final touches on Mary's hair. Elizabeth stepped back and admired their handiwork, reflecting on how very handsome Mary looked. With the effect completed by the modest yet pretty ivory dress which had been procured for the occasion, Elizabeth was certain no one would compare her attractions to any of the other Bennet sisters.

A tender expression settled on her face as she admired her younger sister. "Truly, Mary, you look very well indeed—you shall be the most beautiful of all brides on your special day."

"Thank you, Lizzy," was Mary's reply as tears welled in the corners of her eyes. "You have always been so good to me, even to the point of worrying for me when few others do. I am certain you have thought that I am out of my senses to be marrying Mr. Collins."

Elizabeth began to object, but her sister waved her off. "Do not attempt to deny it, Lizzy. I know you are concerned, and I love you for it. There is no need to worry about me—I am entering this marriage with a full awareness of the problems I am likely to face. I know you and Papa do not have any respect for Mr. Collins's mental capacity, and I am afraid I must concur that he is not the cleverest of men."

Though she would have greatly appreciated the ability to snort in response, Elizabeth held herself in check, earning a wry grin from her sister.

"Well, perhaps that was a slight understatement," continued Mary. "But I firmly believe that I am well suited to be Mr. Collins's wife, not only in temperament but also in our complementary interests. Furthermore, I am convinced that any man may improve with the right woman by his side, and as his wife, I may gently direct him in the manner which may see him grow into a better man. This is all without mentioning the assistance I am providing my family by virtue of this marriage. Surely you have noticed the change in Mama since my engagement."

"I have," responded Elizabeth slowly, thinking of the behavior of their mother. "I do not expect Mama will ever be quiet and introspective, but her exclamations have lost a little of their desperation and shrillness."

"They have," confirmed Mary with a smile. "I knew that *you* of all people could not have missed it. Now, will you accept that I am content with my choice and be happy for me?"

"You know that I will," responded Elizabeth as she leaned over to give her sister a quick hug. "I am already happy for you, Mary—I am simply glad to have your reassurance. And I wish you all the happiness in the world."

"That is well, Lizzy, for I have one more request to make of you."

Elizabeth looked at her sister questioningly. "What is it, Mary?"

"I will be going to Kent today, and I doubt I shall return for some time. I am certain I will find myself missing the company of my family—especially you, Lizzy. I have spoken with Mr. Collins, and he has agreed that I might extend an invitation for you to visit in the spring to help me adjust to life in my new situation. Will you come and stay with me in March? I should feel so much better if I had your support and love to help me, especially as I learn how to handle the infamous Lady Catherine."

The two sisters shared another laugh. "I do not doubt she will be a most attentive neighbor, sister," managed Elizabeth between chuckles.

"Attentive is not exactly what I am expecting," said Mary with a smile. "Meddling sounds closer to the mark."

Elizabeth laughed again. "I most certainly shall come to visit you, Mary. I must own to being very curious to meet the great lady, though I might fear my ability to hold my tongue. But what girl would be satisfied with her life if she was never afforded the opportunity to see the infamous glazing on the windows and the massive fireplace of which your intended speaks? It must truly be a prodigious sight to behold if it can render Mr. Collins to exhibit such descriptions of its elegance."

Mary again laughed, causing Elizabeth to join in, all the while wondering what else she had missed in her interactions with her family.

Later that morning, it was done, and her sister resigned the name of Bennet in favor of her new husband's name. It was a simple yet effective ceremony, completely in keeping with Mary's character and preferences.

The wedding party then went to Longbourn for the wedding breakfast, after which the newly married couple would depart for Hunsford and Mary's new home.

When Mr. Collins learned that it was to be Elizabeth who would visit in the spring (apparently, Mary had not specified exactly *which sister* she wished to invite), his reaction was somewhat amusing. His initial response was one of disapproval, but after he glanced at his new wife and saw her watching him calmly, but with a hint of steel in her eyes, he favored her with an expression that seemed to indicate that he wished to avoid offending her mere hours after their marriage. He then directed a look in Elizabeth's direction and asked Mary: "Dearest wife, are you certain you wish to invite my cousin Elizabeth? Perhaps your sister Jane would be a better choice."

But Mary was adamant, and to Hunsford Elizabeth was to go. As she watched the carriage carrying her sister and new brother-in-law away from Longbourn, Elizabeth prayed that the trip would be as interesting and pleasant as she could hope—and that Mr. Collins would not hold on to his resentment of her interference.

Chapter XXIX

The Bennet household did not change much with Mary's absence. Lydia still chattered constantly about redcoats, Mrs. Bennet still complained continually about her nerves (if less loudly than she once had), and Mr. Bennet still remained hidden in his library from the rest of the family.

Elizabeth felt no small measure of sorrow over the loss of one of her sisters to Mr. Collins, but she had Christmas to look forward to, and that lifted her spirits. They were to go to London to spend the holiday with the Gardiners, and Elizabeth truly desired the change of scenery. Presently, Longbourn reminded her of three men she would rather not think about—Mr. Collins, Mr. Bingley, and Mr. Darcy—and she was always glad to spend time with her kind relatives. With the commotion around Mary's wedding, Elizabeth had not been able to speak with the Gardiners for very long when they had visited for the blessed event, though her aunt had seemed anxious to talk to her in private.

At last, after what had seemed like an interminable wait—though it was in reality a mere three days—the twentieth of December arrived, and the Bennets left for London. Winter travel did not particularly agree with Elizabeth, and as it was a cold Friday, she spent much of the ride bundled under blankets and reading a book, wishing for the journey to be completed so that she could envelop herself in the comfort of the Gardiners' home. But though she was occupied with trying to follow her book, it was impossible not to notice that all Jane seemed to do was stare out the window. Elizabeth felt terrible about her sister's heartache, but what could be done about it? Either Jane would overcome her feelings and her disappointment for Mr. Bingley's departure, or the man would return and lift her spirits. But Jane would not face it alone—Elizabeth was determined to be there for her sister; that was what they always did for each other—and that was the way Elizabeth was determined it would always be.

When they finally arrived in London, they were greeted warmly by their relatives. The Gardiners' home was on an important London thoroughfare, and although it was not the largest house or in the most fashionable part of town, it was quiet and comfortable, tastefully decorated, and welcoming to all who entered.

It did not take long for Mrs. Gardiner to take Elizabeth aside to speak in private.

"Lizzy," said Mrs. Gardiner, looking concerned, "is Jane ill? She is pale and withdrawn—she appears to be even worse than she seemed at the wedding."

Elizabeth clenched her fingers in frustration. She felt so helpless—there was nothing she could do to make Jane feel any better, and it was bothering her exceedingly. "I do not believe she is well at all, though she is not ill. She has had her heart broken by a man we were all certain would make her an offer. I think it has only made it worse that she has been able to hold on to the hope that it will work out."

"What do you mean, Lizzy?"

"Well, the man—Mr. Bingley—left abruptly for London, though I dare say it might have been better for us all if he had gone to Spain instead. Who knows what poor Jane is going through simply by knowing they are in the same city?"

"He left abruptly, you say?"

"Yes. He did not even make a farewell visit. He simply wrote a letter to Papa saying that he was leaving and would return. But we have not heard a single syllable from him since. I do not know if he intends to return at all!"

"Poor Jane! She has too tender of a heart for someone to abandon her like this. Perhaps this Mr. Bingley will return at last!"

"If this is how he handles a trip to London, perhaps it would be better if he did not return," said Elizabeth, her eyes flashing. "I want Jane to be happy, but if this is his normal behavior, then he does not deserve her. I would prefer that she endure heartache and emerge the stronger for it rather than attach herself to someone so unworthy."

"Oh, Lizzy," said Mrs. Gardiner gently, "I think you are allowing your frustration with Mr. Bingley to make you peevish. If Jane has feelings for him, he must be a nice young man."

"That is what I thought initially, but now I am not so certain." Elizabeth sighed. "Still, maybe you are right. There could have been a very good reason for him to have left as he did. I suppose we shall find out sooner or later. But for now, I cannot help but dislike the very thought of him!"

The subject soon passed on to other matters, but the women's hearts remained with Jane.

Unfortunately, as the days passed, the object of their thoughts remained despondent. Elizabeth and Kitty attempted to cheer Jane up, their behavior ranging from silly to kind as they tried to make her smile, but they did not have much success in lifting her spirits.

The behavior of Lydia and Mrs. Bennet in London was predictable. Lydia bemoaned the lack of officers with whom to flirt, whereas Mrs. Bennet lamented Mr. Bingley's departure from Hertfordshire. Mrs. Bennet was particularly satisfied to have a new audience for her complaints now that her excitement over Mary's wedding preparations had run its course.

Though they were frequently busy, Elizabeth found herself with a considerable amount of time in which she had nothing to do but think. One object of her thoughts was Mary's wedding. She still could not believe that Mr. Collins was now her brother-in-law! The thought was enough to make her shudder.

Another item to which her mind kept returning was Mr. Bingley. She simply could not understand how a man who had seemed so kind could be so thoughtless! Was there a good reason for his departure to London? And would he return, as her aunt had hoped?

And finally, she kept thinking about Mr. Darcy.

The harder she tried not to think about him, the more she did. He was an enigma to her.

He had been averse to dancing with anyone at his first ball in Hertfordshire—or so she had heard—and then he had actually been kind enough to dance with Kitty! Later, he had called Elizabeth plain when speaking to Mr. Bingley, only to sincerely apologize and explain himself after he realized she had heard him. And when he had asked for her first dance at the Netherfield ball, it had been enough to shock her beyond belief. He was contradictory and confusing, not the confident and composed young master of a great estate which she had expected him to be. Or at least, he was contradictory with her—sometimes he had acted like a suitor, and at other times he had acted like a cad. She could not make him out.

She had been so certain that he was disgusted by all of Hertfordshire society—and she had included herself in that number. But there had been indications otherwise. Was it simply that he was a shy man who was uncomfortable with the social requirements of his position in society? Was there something hidden behind his pride that resembled a caring human being?

She did not know how to react to him, and as someone who studied character, that was enough to make her very unsettled.

Elizabeth resolved to put Mr. Darcy out of her thoughts for a time. And she soon heard some very pleasant news indeed that helped to banish him from her mind. Since her father disliked London—and since Lydia was more interested in chasing redcoats than experiencing London society—he was going to leave with his wife and Lydia to return to Longbourn on the 28th of December. Jane, Elizabeth, and Kitty, on the other hand, were to stay with the Gardiners. And though Elizabeth worried about being away from Longbourn almost by default, she knew that her father was quite capable, regardless of his sometimes lackadaisical attention to his duties. The estate would be looked after in her absence, and all she had ever done was to assist, after all.

Contrary to what might have been expected, Lydia did not feel slighted by her exclusion from the invitation extended to her sisters. She had no room in her head for such thoughts, as her mind was full of nothing more than men in red coats. Beyond that, Elizabeth suspected that Lydia was eager to have the attention of their parents (or, more specifically, their mother) all to herself, without Jane's beauty, Elizabeth's cleverness, or Kitty's need for protection as competition. Lydia was certainly one who was happy making a spectacle of herself.

Christmas Day passed very happily for Elizabeth when she realized she and her two favorite sisters would be able to relax. They loved their mother and Lydia, but the pair could be rather tiresome. A little time spent away from their excesses was an agreeable prospect.

And since Mr. and Mrs. Gardiner enjoyed having their nieces with them, it was an arrangement that was pleasurable for all. They began making plans for what they would do the next week, and that included watching an opera for which there had been very positive reviews.

Perhaps—or so Elizabeth hoped—the prospect of diversion and society would help Jane overcome her heartache. It could certainly do no harm.

Chapter XXX

In the days following the departure of Mr. and Mrs. Bennet and their youngest daughter, life at the Gardiner home became much more sedate. As a result, the townhouse's occupants were better able to enjoy the time they spent together, which all felt was a blessing indeed

Both the remaining Bennets and the Gardiners settled into a comfortable routine quite quickly. Jane, Elizabeth, and Kitty would assist Mrs. Gardiner with the children—amusing and playing with them when the children were not at their lessons—and with her morning calls, and in exchange, the Gardiners fairly doted on their nieces, ensuring the young ladies' stay was as pleasant as they could possibly make it. Even Jane began to show signs of coming out of her melancholy, for who could continue to be in low spirits when constantly surrounded by the comfort and confidence which subsisted between those sharing the highest affection? Jane still had her moments of quiet and somewhat sad reflection, but on the whole, Elizabeth was pleased with how her sister was emerging from her disappointment.

Their planning for the upcoming opera had also taken up quite a bit of their time, with much of the conversation between the ladies pertaining to what they would wear and what it would be like to see the elegant ladies who frequented the opera and to be seen in turn. Mr.

Gardiner had spared no expense on this occasion, obtaining the use of a box for the night. None of them had ever viewed an opera from the comfort and excellent vantage provided by a box, and all were looking forward to the experience. Even Kitty, despite not being able to see the actors, expressed a belief that the acoustics of the theater must necessarily enhance the quality of the music, and she professed to her family that she was eagerly anticipating the lyrical strains she would hear.

Of course, Mr. Gardiner had to endure constant discussions of fabrics, lace, and jewelry, as he was the only man in the house. He managed himself admirably, allowing the ladies their excitement with many a fond smile, even as he sought the sanctuary of his study when the talk became too much for his taste. More than once, he wondered out loud about his brother Mr. Bennet, who withstood such talk as a matter of course. But Elizabeth knew Mr. Gardiner was quite fond of her and her sisters in spite of all their talk of fashion.

Finally, the day of the opera arrived, and once the preparations for attending had been completed, the party climbed into the Gardiner carriage, eager for the evening's entertainments to begin. It was a tight fit for the five of them in the carriage, but they managed, passing the time during their short journey with a great deal of humor.

The opera house was amazing to the Bennet girls who had never visited it before—their usual opera house was not as fine or as large as the one which they entered on that night. The sights and sounds of the building, the cream of British society all gathered together—it was all enough to take the girls' breaths away.

Their experience on that evening was beyond anything to which they had been subjected previously—beyond anything they could have imagined. Each sister in her own way felt profoundly impressed by what she witnessed. As they had expected, the sound and sight of the players was superior to anything they had seen in their normal opera house, and it was far better than sitting in the rows of seats in front of the stage.

Indeed, so impressed were they that—even without other events to make the evening stand out in their minds—the Bennet girls all exclaimed that it was truly a night to be remembered. However, other events did intrude upon the company which were to have an effect on the two eldest Bennet sisters in particular.

During the first interval, the party descended to the lobby to escape from the box for a few moments. As they stood speaking of the performance, Elizabeth happened to notice a man looking at her with some interest. He was dressed finely, certainly in the type of expensive clothes she would expect to see on a member of the peerage. He was tall and handsome—at least, he would have been handsome if not for the haughty air in which he held himself and the manner in which he stared at her.

Discomforted by his scrutiny, Elizabeth looked away and attempted to put the man from her mind by conversing with her sisters. A few minutes passed before her uncle was approached by an acquaintance who was introduced as Mr. Sykes. The gentleman apparently owned an estate in Surrey and had done some business with Mr. Gardiner to his very great benefit. It was but moments later when the wealthy man Elizabeth had noticed earlier approached the party and spoke thus:

"Sykes, so good to see you this evening. We have not met in several months, unless I miss my guess."

Though Elizabeth thought she detected a certain hesitancy in her new acquaintance's air, Mr. Sykes betrayed none of it in his speech, instead welcoming his friend in like fashion.

The man then looked directly at Elizabeth and requested—and was granted—an introduction.

"Of course, Lord Trenton. May I introduce a friend and business associate of mine, Edward Gardiner. Mr. Gardiner, my neighbor Lord Alastair Trenton, Earl of Winchester."

"I am very pleased to make your acquaintance, Lord Trenton," responded Mr. Gardiner, extending his hand.

"Always delighted to make an acquaintance of my good friend Sykes," replied Trenton, grasping the other man's hand. "Will you do me the honor of introducing your lovely companions?"

The introductions were then made, and Trenton greeted the party affably before entering into conversation with the two other men while the ladies continued to discuss their impressions of the opera.

Soon after, Elizabeth noticed that the earl, rather than attending to the conversation of the other men, was in actuality watching her rather closely. He unobtrusively excused himself from conversing with her uncle and approached, his eyes raking over her form in frank appraisal. Elizabeth was made uncomfortable by his expression, but she forced herself to smile as he approached.

"Miss Elizabeth Bennet, I am very pleased to make your acquaintance."

"I thank you, sir," responded Elizabeth politely.

"I understand from your uncle that your father's estate is quite close to London?"

"Yes, indeed, it is. I am from Hertfordshire, and my father's estate is not more than twenty miles from town."

"And your father? I am familiar with most of the prominent landowners and peers in the kingdom, yet I do not recall ever hearing of the name 'Bennet.'"

"My father's estate is not large, sir," said Elizabeth, annoyed with the man's probing questions. "We are not related to anyone of the peerage, so I am not surprised that you do not know of us."

His face lit up with a supercilious smirk at her response, and Elizabeth felt her opinion of the man, which had not been high to begin with, sink to even lower depths. And her appraisal of him was only to become worse.

"I see," said he with a leer. "In that case, perhaps you would permit me to invite you to my box, so we may become better . . . acquainted."

"You are inviting my party to your box?" asked she, surprised.

"No, I think you mistake my meaning," was his response. "I wish to become better acquainted with you, Miss Bennet—my invitation was for you alone."

Elizabeth was disgusted with this man's familiar and inappropriate invitations. "I am sorry, sir, but as you can see, I am here under the protection of my uncle. It would be inappropriate for me to view the rest of the opera in your box."

"Ah, yes, my apologies," said Trenton. "I was entranced by your beauty, madam, and did not consider the impropriety of the suggestion. Perhaps I could attend you in your box?"

"For that, you would have to ask my uncle, Lord Trenton. Again, I am here with him and under his protection, and I cannot predict how he would respond to such an application."

"Very well then," replied he with a negligent wave of his hand. "I can see you wish to concentrate on the production and not be distracted. I am happy to see that there are others who take true pleasure in the opera."

"I thank you, sir," said Elizabeth, offended by his manner.

"I fear, however, that I cannot allow you to leave tonight without some promise of our meeting again. Will you be so good as to tell me where your uncle's house is so that I may call upon you?" Elizabeth saw a flash of movement, and she turned slightly to watch her uncle's approach. He was coming to gather Elizabeth for the purpose of returning to their box, and she could not be more grateful for the interruption. She curtseyed to the earl and begged his pardon.

"Pray, excuse me, sir—I must return with my party."

She left the man, but not before catching a salacious expression on his face as she walked away. A shudder coursed through her at the thought of that cad's eyes affixed upon her, and she hurried her footsteps, eager to be away from his questing gaze.

Back in the box, she fended off Jane's queries, owning she had not enjoyed her conversation with the earl, but telling her little else. She did not want to worry her sister—or her aunt and uncle, for that matter. She instead focused her attention on the opera.

It was in the aftermath of the performance that the second event of significance took place. The Gardiners and their nieces had exited the theater, their minds and conversation full of what they had seen, and they were waiting for their carriage when an acquaintance stumbled across their party.

The young man had been walking past when he glanced at them and stopped dead in his tracks, a look of shock etched upon his features.

"Miss Bennet!" exclaimed he.

"Mr. Bingley!" replied Jane, just as surprised as he was.

An awkward silence descended upon them, as neither Jane nor Mr. Bingley seemed to know what to say. Mr. and Mrs. Gardiner watched the pair with some interest as their carriage rolled to a stop in front of them.

"I hope—that is to say, I am very surprised to see you here," said Mr. Bingley finally.

"And I you," responded Jane's quiet voice.

"I hope you enjoyed the performance?"

"Yes, sir, it was very moving."

"Good. Excellent."

Silence descended over the group once again, and the Gardiners, seeing Jane's distress, began to shepherd their charges into the carriage. Jane directed one last longing look in Mr. Bingley's direction before entering the carriage and choosing a seat which was hidden from his view. The entire party moved inside the carriage, and in moments, they had departed, leaving a clearly disconcerted Bingley standing in the street, staring after them.

Elizabeth cursed their ill luck—just as Jane had begun to emerge from her melancholy, her erstwhile paramour had appeared to unsettle her, leaving her family to once more attempt to lift her spirits. Jane would have to start again from the beginning.

Chapter XXXI

Darcy stood by the fireplace of his study, listening to his friend rant. Bingley's encounter with Jane Bennet at the opera had apparently made a very strong impression on him, if the manner in which he was now expressing himself was any indication. After weeks of believing Bingley had been rescued from the clutches of that family, all Darcy's work had been destroyed with a single short meeting at an opera. What a thing to have happened at a time like this!

Something Bingley said finally managed to penetrate through Darcy's frustration: "I am telling you, Darcy, she appeared to be as miserable as I have been since I separated myself from her."

"But how can you be certain?" asked Darcy. "She may simply have been suffering from some indisposition which has nothing to do with your departure."

"And this from a man who was not even there to see her! I am telling you, Darcy, she cares for me!"

Massaging his temples in frustration, Darcy took a deep breath and regarded his friend, desperately seeking some way to dissuade him from the disastrous course he was contemplating. The man simply had no concept of what some women would do to secure themselves a comfortable situation—particularly a young woman with as little means as Jane Bennet. Bingley was a prime target for one such as she, and his naturally open and friendly nature was such that he was not suspicious of the motivations of others. Darcy knew he simply had to make Bingley see reason!

"Bingley, I have told you what I heard and what I have seen. She is using you to secure your fortune and obtain a comfortable position, and regardless of her feelings, you know as well as I do that she would not be allowed to refuse an offer of marriage from one in your position whether she wished it or not."

"So say you on the basis of one overheard conversation," spat Bingley, "which you may very well have taken out of context. Not to mention you base the rest of your assertion on a few hours of observing her behavior. I have been in her company for many hours and conversed with her many more times than you have. I believe my observations of her character and her feelings to be superior to yours. She is very demure and barely shows her feelings, I grant you, but I saw her face last night, Darcy. Her mask slipped when she saw me, and her misery was clear to anyone with the wit to see. I am certain of what I am about!"

"Bingley, you *must* hear me. You would be in grave danger from a marriage of unequal affection. Your manner is so open and artless and your nature so affectionate that it would destroy you to marry a woman who did not return your feelings as fervently as you offer them. Jane Bennet is all that is proper and demure, but her feelings are not returned with the same passion—think back and remember her countenance!"

Bingley appeared incensed at the continued attack against the object of his affections, and he stood, beginning to pace the room with no small measure of agitation. "And what of yourself, Darcy?"

Taken aback, Darcy stared at his friend. "To what do you refer?"

"Do you feel deeply? Or is your reserve no more than the lack of feelings?"

"I assure you, Bingley, I feel deeply, though I may rarely display it," responded Darcy, injured at his friend's assertion.

"And I assure you, Darcy," countered Bingley, "that Jane Bennet feels as deeply as you or I, but just as you are reserved, so is she. She is affectionate and caring, but she does not display it for the world to see. And I wish to God that I had thought more clearly about her reactions to me to which only I could be privy—I knew that she cared for me, and I allowed myself to be persuaded otherwise. Too often have I allowed you to dictate my course of action when I should have used my own judgment. It shall not happen again!"

"Bingley, please listen to me—"

"No, Darcy, you must listen to me," snapped Bingley. "I am quite determined and will not be swayed from my purpose. I will seek out my dear Jane Bennet once again and discover for myself whether she cares for me. Continued discussion of this matter is fruitless. You shall not change my mind."

A sigh escaped Darcy's lips. There was, he reflected, nothing more he could do to protect his friend. Bingley was his own man, after all, and regardless of Darcy's continued desire to support him and guide him as to the proper path to take, he needed to make his own mistakes and live his own life. At least Bingley had agreed that he needed to judge for himself what Jane Bennet's feelings were instead of leaping into an engagement without thought of the consequences. It could have easily been otherwise. People in love were seldom logical.

Darcy wanted to argue further with Bingley—he trusted his own observations and knew pursuit of Miss Bennet could only end in heartache—yet if he continued to persist in arguing against him, then he might lose Bingley's friendship entirely. There was a time to stand one's ground and a time to fold. This moment, unfortunately, was one of the latter.

"Do you mean to go soon?" asked Darcy at last. He bit back all his words of protest and attempted to disguise the full extent of his frustration. There was little more to be said.

"I do. I shall go this morning."

"Then go to it," said Darcy. He hesitated, but he was unable to resist offering a few words of advice: "Just make certain you do not raise any expectations which you do not wish to raise. Take the time to observe her before you make any rash moves."

Bingley gave a curt nod, and Darcy suppressed a sigh. It was all he could ask for at this point.

Chapter XXXII

It was the first of January, and Bingley had resolved that with the new year he should be a new man. He had decided—first with trepidation and then with growing resolve—that Darcy had been wrong in his recommendation to spend an extended period of time away from Jane Bennet. When Bingley had seen the young woman after the opera, his heart had leapt within his chest, making him feel alive once more. Her mere presence was enough to fill him with such gladness that he knew without a doubt that their being together *could not* be wrong. She was a gentleman's daughter and an angel!

Still, though his heart sang nothing but Jane Bennet's name, his head knew that he would have to maintain at least a modicum of objectivity. Though he refused to follow his friend's suggestion of distance, he would try to determine for himself whether it was true that Jane Bennet did not care for him—and whether she was a fortune hunter as both Darcys had claimed.

But even as his head reminded him to look for the signs of a woman interested only in material wealth, his heart protested that Jane Bennet was *too good* to be wrapped up in such petty concerns. He was still baffled that the two Darcys could sincerely believe her to be so, for if he were honest with himself, he knew that Darcy's discernment was generally superior to his own. Surely Darcy could see in Miss Bennet that which was so prevalent in his own character—a healthy measure of reserve that by no means indicated a lack of feeling. Darcy's failure to perceive what Bingley did was an inexplicable lapse that seemed almost impossible to explain.

Bingley arrived at the Gardiners' residence in Cheapside with no small amount of anxiety. Miss Bennet deserved more than just a letter to her father noting that he was leaving, and yet that was exactly what Bingley had done, and he still felt guilty over having handled it in such a way. After his boorish behavior of departing Hertfordshire without taking his leave of Jane Bennet in person, would she still have feelings for him? Or had she forgotten the time they had spent together?

Upon entering the house, he learned quickly that the Gardiners and Jane Bennet were out. His disappointment must have showed on his face, for the servant quickly reassured him that they would return soon and asked if he wished to see Elizabeth Bennet. He smiled—perhaps he would look upon Jane's dear face after all!—and agreed that it would be pleasant indeed to see Miss Elizabeth Bennet again.

As he joined the young woman, who was doing some needlework, she stood and curtseyed. But though she greeted him with the utmost propriety, there was a tightness around her eyes and mouth that made him swallow nervously. And then, after the servant had been gone for perhaps a minute, she went and pushed the door until it rested against the frame, though she did not close it, likely to maintain the slightest hint of propriety. The action, however, caused Bingley's unease to grow tenfold.

With a frown, Bingley asked: "Miss—Miss Bennet?"

"I wish to have a private discussion with you, Mr. Bingley," explained she, turning to look at him with a hard gaze. "My apologies if I am too forward, but I simply cannot allow matters to continue as they have been. If you are here to break Jane's heart again, then you had best leave now."

"Miss Bennet," protested he, "I have no intention—"

"She was crushed when you left," said Elizabeth Bennet flatly. "Perhaps I ought not speak to you in such a fashion, but there it is. Mr. Bingley, I must know that your intentions are sincere and that you will not abandon her again. I am not aware of the reasons for your abrupt departure from Hertfordshire, but I ask you to take pity on my dear younger sister and cease calling on her at once if you are not serious in courting her."

"Younger sister?" asked Bingley in confusion, latching on to that simple phrase. His heart had skipped a beat. Elizabeth was the *eldest*

Bennet daughter?

The object of his thoughts gave him a strange look. "Yes. Jane and I are twins, but I am the elder by a few minutes."

Bingley turned away from her. He and Darcy had thought all along that Jane was eldest. If—if Darcy had heard someone speaking about one of the Bennet daughters being a fortune hunter, then it was utterly possible that *Elizabeth* Bennet rather than *Jane*—dear, lovely, sweet Jane!—had lost a suitor to someone more wealthy. Perhaps they had not been discussing Jane Bennet at all!

With that hope, his heart began to sing louder, and he turned to Elizabeth Bennet—*Miss* Bennet, as the eldest!—and told her with the most joyful of expressions on his face: "I have no intention of deserting your sister or breaking her heart, Miss Bennet." Not when Jane Bennet's heart seemed to be his—not when her close sister had nearly told him that much!

"You must understand, Miss Bennet," began he, "that I needed some time to determine the extent of my affection for your sister. But now—now, I feel it is firm! I wish to formally court her—to show her that I am a man who wishes her the greatest of happiness and who desires to share in that happiness for the rest of our lives." He bit his lip, his thoughts turning to Darcy. "So you do not believe me an utter monster, I must confess it was not wholly my decision to leave Hertfordshire. I was—I was influenced by someone who believed your sister did not feel for me as you say she does."

"Pardon me, Mr. Bingley," said Elizabeth Bennet with a hint of ice in her voice, "but I am of the opinion that you should not allow the beliefs of others to direct and determine the course of your life. If you wish to maintain an estate, much less a family, then it will be necessary for you to learn to make your own decisions."

Bingley felt his face flame in guilt and embarrassment, but he knew the censure was deserved. "I assure you, Miss Bennet, I have reached that realization myself, and I refuse to let anyone dissuade me again. I—I care for your sister, and I wish to prove it."

Elizabeth Bennet stared at him, her expression still hard and almost frightening. But then her face softened into a smile, and she walked over to the door to open it, likely in anticipation of the eventual return of her relatives. "I am glad to hear that, Mr. Bingley. You are a good man. I apologize for my unseemly questions and my impertinence in questioning your motives. I merely desired to ensure we both understood what your purpose was in coming here."

"I understand, Miss Bennet. And given the circumstances, I

certainly accept your need to care for your beloved younger sister—and your desire to determine my motives. I am not offended."

They sat and conversed in a more pleasant fashion, and before long, Jane Bennet had arrived, and Bingley was standing and smiling at her so widely that he felt he might burst.

Being the focus of his attention appeared to make her withdraw into shyness, but within only a few minutes, they were completely engrossed in conversation with each other. When he finally had to take his leave, he shot a smile at Elizabeth Bennet, who nodded at him in understanding and approval.

Now that he had seen his angel again, there was one thing about which he was certain.

Jane Bennet cared for him!

Chapter XXXIII

Several hours after the heated conversation in his study with Bingley, Darcy was there once more, staring at a blank piece of paper but unable to remember what missive he had intended to pen. And then Bingley suddenly entered and exclaimed with no delay: "Good day to you, Darcy!"

Darcy could see his friend was in excellent spirits, which, of course, was his usual state of mind despite the events of this past month. His grin extended from ear to ear, and he was whistling—Bingley, who had no talent for music whatsoever, was actually whistling!—as he flung himself on a chair in front of Darcy's desk.

Darcy had been anticipating this visit—dreading it since he and Bingley had parted ways that morning, actually—although he had half expected his friend to be devastated by rejection. But Bingley was not discerning enough to see through another's deception, which was why Darcy made it his business to take care of him. He should have foreseen this outcome.

"Am I to suppose you have visited Miss Jane Bennet as you had planned?"

"Indeed, I have!" confirmed Bingley with the ebullience which Darcy had come to expect from him.

He spoke no further, merely whistling his jaunty tune—which was completely unrecognizable—and slouching in his seat as though he had not a care in the world, all the while grinning across the desk at his friend. *This* was truly a side of Bingley which Darcy despised—he could be unbearably smug when he felt he was right, and he seemed as if he were taking perverse delight in forcing Darcy to extract his news rather than offering it himself.

Passing a hand over his face and praying for patience, Darcy glared at his friend. "And? What was the result of your visit with Miss Bennet?"

"What has happened? Can you not guess, man?"

"I can guess what you *think* has happened, but unless you tell me, I doubt I shall truly know."

"Oh, Darcy, I do declare you can be so annoyingly pompous at times!" exclaimed Bingley.

"And you can be annoyingly disposed to approve of all whom you meet and to accept what they say without reservation. You know what I think of your purpose today, Bingley, and unless you capitulate and tell me exactly what happened, I shall think of you as a simpleton and continue to expect that you are once again being taken in."

Bingley snorted and arose from his chair, crossing to the side table and pouring two glasses of Darcy's port. Handing one to his friend, Bingley sat himself back down in his chair, sipping from his glass in an almost distracted manner. It was all Darcy could do not to rail at his companion—why could he not come to the point?

"If you wish to know of my success this morning, then I shall tell you. It went very well indeed, Darcy, and I am now thoroughly and utterly convinced that not only does Jane Bennet return my affections in equal measure, but that I was a fool to listen to you and your sister when you both recommended I quit Hertfordshire altogether. My Aunt Mabel was correct, and I am very happy to tell you that I was completely justified in my words to you this morning."

Darcy scowled at the reminder of the words they had exchanged. He remembered very well Bingley's resolution to seek Miss Bennet out. He understood that his friend needed to be his own man, but this was an issue for which Darcy was assured he knew the correct recourse. He only wished he could open Bingley's eyes to that.

"Tell me, Darcy," said Bingley suddenly, his voice thoughtful, "when you overheard this conversation which led you to believe Miss Bennet was a fortune hunter, was Jane Bennet mentioned by name?"

Startled out of his reflection, Darcy turned sharply to Bingley, furrowing his brow.

"I am certain Miss Bennet was named, yes."

"No, Darcy," prompted he, "not *Miss Bennet*, but *Jane* in particular. Did they use Jane's name in particular?"

Darcy thought back to the night. From what he could recall, Jane Bennet's name was not used, but they *had* been talking about the eldest daughter, which would certainly refer to her. In his confusion, he stated as much to Bingley, who responded with a triumphant grin, further bewildering him.

"In that case, Darcy, your conjecture was completely wrong. I cannot fathom how we both came to the same mistaken understanding, but *Jane* Bennet is *not* the eldest Bennet daughter—that title belongs to Miss *Elizabeth* Bennet."

Darcy's mouth opened and closed in consternation, but no sound escaped.

"You are in the same condition as I was, my friend," continued Bingley with a hearty laugh. "My information cannot be doubted, as it came directly from Miss Elizabeth Bennet herself. Jane and Elizabeth Bennet are twins, and Elizabeth is the elder."

Darcy finally found his voice. "I cannot tell you how surprised I am. The resemblance is there, but they are so dissimilar—I would never have guessed them to be twins."

"It is true. So, if the *eldest* Miss Bennet was jilted by a young man in favor of a woman of greater means, then it stands to reason that it was Miss *Elizabeth* who lost a suitor, not Miss *Jane*. Therefore, your conjecture about Miss Jane is incorrect."

Though he could not deny that Jane had apparently not been the subject of the discussion he overheard, there was still Mrs. Bennet and her influence and obvious mercenary attitude to consider. Regardless of what Bingley *wished* to believe about the object of his affections, Darcy felt it necessary to make one last attempt at persuading his friend to bow out gracefully.

"Bingley, there is another matter to consider. I may have been mistaken about the daughter of whom they were speaking, yet I am certain that the *substance* of my information is correct. Your Miss Jane may not have lost a suitor, but her sister did, and it has obviously affected the whole family, if indeed they were not already disposed to be mercenary due to their financial situation. I urge you most strongly to reconsider this reckless path. It will only lead you to heartache!"

But Bingley, it appeared, had had enough of the conversation. He drained the remainder of his port in one swallow and set the glass on Darcy's desk while rising to his feet.

"My mind is made up on the subject, Darcy. As I told you before, I shall not be dissuaded."

He turned and walked to the door, opening it and making to leave. Before he departed, however, he turned and peered at Darcy with a determined gleam in his eye, the likes of which Darcy had never before seen on his friend's face.

"Darcy, I thank you for your assistance in introducing me to society and for your friendship. However, I must warn you that I feel strongly about this—so strongly that I will not brook any interference from you in the matter of my life and future happiness. For the sake of our friendship, I urge you to cease your efforts to induce me to abandon my path. If I am making a mistake, it is mine to make.

"If you are truly concerned about my welfare, I invite you to accompany me when I next visit Miss Jane tomorrow morning. You may then observe my beloved and see for yourself. I mean to leave at ten in the morning—if you wish to accompany me, please send me a note, and I shall fetch you on the way."

The door closed behind Bingley, leaving Darcy to his thoughts and feelings. Though he was afraid Bingley was making a mistake, he was also proud of his friend for standing up for his convictions. Determined that the only thing he could do was to see for himself, Darcy decided he would send Bingley a note that evening indicating his intention to accompany him to visit Miss Jane. He would discover the truth himself.

Chapter XXXIV

Time seemed to pass by very slowly as Elizabeth waited for the opportunity to speak to Jane alone. Though Mr. Bingley had come by during the fashionable time for visits and the rest of the day lay before her, Elizabeth could not find the opportunity which would allow her to approach her sister. It was not as if Jane were avoiding her; rather, Jane kept to company for the rest of the day, and Elizabeth did not feel comfortable with raising the subject of Mr. Bingley in the presence of any other members of their family.

She did, however, have the occasion to watch her sister, and what Elizabeth saw gave her the confidence that she had acted in Jane's best interests by speaking with Mr. Bingley in what was truly an inappropriate manner. Jane literally glowed with vitality due to the knowledge that her beloved was not indifferent to her after all. It made Elizabeth long to disclose the words that had passed between her and Mr. Bingley even more strongly.

Finally, the hour grew late enough that Elizabeth could excuse herself for bed, and she gave her sister a pointed look that encouraged her to do the same.

They climbed the stairs together in silence, and when they had closed the door behind them and were at last alone, Elizabeth gave Jane a sudden embrace. "Your Mr. Bingley has returned for you, Jane!"

Jane flushed. "Oh, Lizzy. He is not *my* Mr. Bingley—"

"Jane, he came here for you," said Elizabeth firmly, "and I made certain that he knew what the expectations were for his presence."

Jane's forehead furrowed. "What do you mean, Lizzy?"

Elizabeth felt a flash of embarrassment for having been so brazen, but she pushed through it and spoke confidently: "I had a discussion with Mr. Bingley in which I let him know in no uncertain terms that he was to leave immediately if he were not serious in his pursuit of you."

"Lizzy!" exclaimed Jane in horror. "How could you talk to Mr. Bingley so?"

"I did not want him to break your heart once more," whispered Elizabeth. She did not want to see her sister so desolate ever again.

Jane turned away from her, obviously upset. "That—it is not done, Lizzy. You should not have spoken to him in such terms. You have—you have revealed my feelings to him. What if he thinks me just a silly girl?"

Elizabeth moved toward her sister and hugged her from behind. "Jane, Mr. Bingley obviously cares for you. If anything, I wonder whether perhaps he needed more of an indication of your feelings for him than you had provided in Hertfordshire. Men can be infuriatingly oblivious sometimes, and you *are* very reserved, after all."

Jane had stiffened when Elizabeth first put her arms around her, but she slowly melted, unable to maintain even a hint of antipathy toward her sister for long. "I suppose you had only my best interests at heart, Lizzy."

"Oh, Jane, you know I did!" exclaimed Elizabeth. "But come, dearest Jane. Are you not excited that he means to pay court to you?"

Jane turned and gave her a small smile. "You know I am. My love for him is so great that his absence . . . it has hurt me." She turned away from her sister and spoke quietly. "It was so wonderful to see him again—to not have my last memory of him be that glimpse after the opera. But I am . . . fearful of the unknown." She moved back to look at her sister. "Lizzy, what if he breaks my heart again?"

Elizabeth gazed at her sister fondly. "Why, if he should do that, then I suppose he would have to do any further courting in a most uncomfortable manner. It will be truly unfortunate for him, I suppose, but such events are all too common, I understand!"

Jane peered at Elizabeth suspiciously. "To what do you refer, Lizzy?"

Assuming a studied look of nonchalance which she knew Jane would see through, Elizabeth said: "It is truly unfortunate, as I said, but it would be amusing to watch Mr. Bingley attempt to court a young woman while itching most ferociously!"

"Oh, Lizzy," said Jane with a smile, obviously understanding what Elizabeth meant, "we cannot put cow itch in Mr. Bingley's clothes. That would be too cruel a punishment."

"I do not believe it would be!" proclaimed Elizabeth. "If he breaks my sister's heart, then making him appear the fool for all to see would be an apt punishment! Of course, *he* is not the only fool who will need to be disciplined."

"What do you mean, Lizzy?"

"Mr. Bingley let slip that someone else influenced his decision to leave Hertfordshire. He did not come to that decision on his own. In fact, I strongly suspect he would not have left Hertfordshire at all were it not for this person of whom he speaks, and that vexes me greatly. But I told him he should not tolerate the direction of others when it comes to the course of his life, and he acknowledged himself to be a changed man in that regard."

Jane stared at her sister, surprised. "You were certainly direct with Mr. Bingley, Lizzy." She looked away. "I suppose I should be thankful he did not conceive the notion on his own, but I find my pain little assuaged. I am worried—"

"Well, you *should not* be," said Elizabeth with a steady voice. "Mr. Bingley cares for you. I believe he is becoming his own man, Jane, and I think you should give him every opportunity to prove himself to you." And she truly did believe that. Mr. Bingley had realized that he had made a mistake, and he seemed to have every intention of correcting it. He no longer deserved Elizabeth's censure, so she had determined not to question him any longer. No, the other person of whom he spoke was the one on whom her resentment should be focused.

The two sisters discussed Mr. Bingley—and Elizabeth teasingly spoke of their future children—for a few minutes more before preparing themselves for sleep.

But as Elizabeth lay in bed, her thoughts refused to remain still.

It was possible—and, indeed, likely—that Mr. Darcy was the reason Mr. Bingley had left Hertfordshire. Mr. Bingley seemed to think highly of his friend, and there were few others whom he held in close confidence in Hertfordshire that would have wielded such sway over him. She supposed Mr. Bingley's aunt could have influenced him to leave, but as Mabel Bingley had seemed to support his suit and had generally behaved in an agreeable manner to Elizabeth's family, it did not seem likely.

As for Georgiana Darcy, perhaps she had played some part in Mr. Bingley's decision. The girl appeared to harbor strong feelings for Mr. Bingley and would have likely jumped at the opportunity to remove her rival from the equation. Nevertheless, Miss Darcy's opinion alone would not have been enough to alter Mr. Bingley's course. Mr. Darcy was surely the force behind Mr. Bingley's departure. He must have believed the Bennets beneath his friend's notice, and that made Elizabeth fume. Mr. Bennet was a gentleman who descended from a line which, although not rich or titled, had held Longbourn estate for generations! They were certainly good enough for Mr. Bingley, whose fortune had come from trade.

But though Elizabeth had suspicions about Mr. Darcy's role in Mr. Bingley's departure from Hertfordshire, she had no proof. It was possible there was someone else important whom she did not know or had not considered. Still, she felt in her heart that Mr. Darcy was at fault, and it made her bitter.

But though she was furious with the man, she could not help but remember how it had felt to dance with him. He had made an excellent partner, his hand soft on hers, his feet missing no steps, his gaze intense and never wandering. But just because he was a good dancer did not mean he was a good man. His pride colored everything he did.

And it had likely influenced his decision—assuming it *was* him—to encourage Mr. Bingley to leave Hertfordshire. If any man deserved Elizabeth's censure, Mr. Darcy did. She was certain of that.

Chapter XXXV

The day after Mr. Bingley's first visit to Gracechurch Street saw the gentleman once again coming to present his card to be announced at the Gardiners' residence. However, this time he was accompanied by an obviously reluctant Mr. Darcy. Mr. and Mrs. Gardiner were not present, having left earlier to visit an acquaintance, which meant the three sisters were required to entertain their gentlemen callers themselves. If their visitors had been almost any other gentlemen in town, it would not have prudent to receive them without Mrs. Gardiner at home, yet Elizabeth believed they were all well acquainted enough that she could be comfortable in allowing them entrance.

The visit was certainly not a trial for one of them—Jane, upon spying Mr. Bingley through the window, had sat brimming with excitement over the attentiveness of her soon-to-be-official suitor. Of course, her placid demeanor hid her anticipation from the casual viewer, though Elizabeth could quite easily detect her sister's excitement by examining the smile which adorned her features and the way she fidgeted slightly in her seat.

As for Elizabeth herself, she was cheered by this display of constancy from Mr. Bingley. What did not please her was the appearance of his friend by his side, as she wondered what could be meant by it.

The uncharitable thought, however, caused Elizabeth to reprimand herself—she did not, after all, have any real proof that Mr. Darcy had effected Mr. Bingley's flight from Hertfordshire, regardless of her suspicions and Mr. Bingley's words, and Elizabeth's inherent good manners would not allow herself to slight him on mere suspicion. She therefore joined her two sisters in welcoming the gentlemen to the Gardiners' home and called for refreshments while they all sat down to visit.

Jane, unsurprisingly, was commandeered immediately by Mr. Bingley, who had seated himself by her side to engage her in earnest conversation. Elizabeth, knowing how delighted Jane was to be receiving his attentions, smiled fondly at her sister, glad that her dreams appeared to be on the verge of coming true. Confident that matters between Mr. Bingley and her sister would proceed in the manner in which they should, she turned her attention to the man's friend.

Mr. Darcy was as withdrawn as he had initially been in Hertfordshire, which was quite the departure from his later behavior when he had sought her company often. Seeing the return of his taciturnity left her with no congenial thoughts toward the gentleman, but she endeavored to be cheerful, and with Kitty's aid, she did succeed in drawing him into a brief discussion of his stay in London.

Even that conversation, though, was stilted and difficult, as for the first few minutes, Mr. Darcy seemed more focused on Mr. Bingley and Jane while they spoke to one another. The two objects of his scrutiny, however, remained oblivious to the rest of the room. Elizabeth had difficulty in accounting for his behavior. Did he wish to protect his friend from Jane, or had he developed some tender feelings of his own? The latter possibility hardly seemed likely, as he had never distinguished her with any particular favor during his time in the neighborhood. No, perhaps he still considered Jane to be Mr. Bingley's inferior and sought to point out her faults by paying close attention to her. Or perhaps he thought to protect his sister's interest in the man. Elizabeth's suppressed anger suddenly flared to life again, as she felt insulted on Jane's behalf.

The arrival of the tea and cakes forestalled any possibility of Elizabeth's simmering resentment being unleashed on the young gentleman, and she busied herself with the serving of the refreshments, and in the process of occupying herself, she was once more able to bring her anger under control.

When her task was complete, she focused on Mr. Darcy, only to find that he had turned his attention away from the couple and was now caught up in conversation with Kitty. Surprised, Elizabeth snuck a glance at Jane, finding her still deep in a discussion with Mr. Bingley, before turning back to the enigma of a man who sat before her. She was given to know through Kitty's discussion with Mr. Darcy that his sister was away at Ramsgate. It seemed that Mr. Bingley's aunt, Mabel Bingley, had gone to Ramsgate for a brief holiday, and she had insisted that Miss Darcy accompany her. The young girl had acquiesced and had soon departed London for Ramsgate in the company of Mr. Bingley's elderly aunt. In addition, Miss Darcy had been joined by her companion, who, Elizabeth was given to understand, had not been present at Netherfield with Miss Darcy the previous autumn due to the birth of her granddaughter. Elizabeth was relieved—it was good to know that one meddling influence was now separated from Mr. Bingley.

Mr. Darcy *did* exert himself to take greater part in their discourse, but he was still somewhat taciturn—and, to be blunt, even a little surly—although he hid his poor mood behind a mask of indifference. Yet Elizabeth could tell that he had no wish to be there and was fighting to retain his good temper.

The morning took a turn for the worse shortly after the two gentlemen had arrived. They were sitting in the aforementioned manner, engaged in their conversations, when the doorbell rang once more. It was a matter of moments before the butler answered the door and then entered the room to speak with Elizabeth.

"There is a Lord Trenton to see you, Miss Bennet," said he, handing her the earl's card.

Elizabeth was shocked that the man had come to visit them—especially since it was not strictly proper for such a new male acquaintance to be calling on Elizabeth specifically rather than her aunt—but then the memory of his repulsive attentions at the opera intruded upon her recollection, and she realized that it was no surprise that he should seek her out.

Though she would have liked nothing more than to refuse him entry, she was well aware that it was not advisable to do so—as an earl, he undoubtedly wielded significant influence in society, and he would not hesitate to use it. So Elizabeth reluctantly gave her consent to allow him entrance, and the butler left to guide their newest visitor to the parlor.

Elizabeth stood to greet the man, and the moment he entered the room, her anger rose at the insolent grin he directed at her. He was, she reflected, perhaps the only man in England she wished to see less than Mr. Darcy.

Lord Trenton appeared taken aback at finding other gentlemen callers already visiting the home, but he masked his reaction quite quickly with a smile.

"Darcy!" cried he, stepping forward to greet the gentleman. "Fancy meeting you in a place such as this."

Mr. Darcy appeared to be as pleased to see Lord Trenton as the reverse—which was to say, not at all. Elizabeth could not help but think that was a mark in Mr. Darcy's favor, especially since Trenton had, by greeting Darcy first, snubbed Elizabeth as the senior of the Bennet daughters in attendance—his first greeting should have gone to her.

"Lord Trenton," replied Mr. Darcy, standing and offering a bow. His eyes briefly met Elizabeth's, and she knew he had certainly not missed the slight against her. The grimness of his countenance, however, surprised her.

"I did not know you were acquainted with the Bennet sisters," exclaimed Lord Trenton.

"Nor I you," murmured Mr. Darcy in response.

"Come, man, since we appear to be in similar straits, you should tell me—how did you come to be acquainted with them?"

"I stayed at the estate of a friend near their father's for some months in the fall."

Mr. Darcy stepped back and motioned to Mr. Bingley, who stood in response. "Charles Bingley, let me introduce Lord Alastair Trenton, the Earl of Winchester. Bingley is an old friend from Cambridge, Lord Trenton, and it was at his invitation that I stayed in Hertfordshire."

The two men bowed to each other, and Lord Trenton raised an eyebrow at the other man. "Bingley, is it? And your estate is in Hertfordshire?"

The man's tone was all impertinence, much to Elizabeth's frustration, but Mr. Bingley managed to respond with perfect composure: "It is a rented estate only. Darcy here was assisting me in learning the management of an estate, for which I am in his debt."

The unpleasant sneer on the lord's face grew substantially, and his features took on an arrogant cast. "So, this is the infamous Mr. Bingley, is it, Darcy?" said he with a sly glance. "So good of you to involve yourself in the affairs of such . . . people, Darcy. I commend you."

He then turned away and paid no more attention to the men, both of whom did not even attempt to hide their distaste. Lord Trenton, however, seemed decidedly oblivious to the decrease in the room's temperature, focusing his attention on Elizabeth instead.

Elizabeth was left with a dilemma. Bingley and Jane occupied the loveseat on the far side of the room, while Mr. Darcy and Kitty had been seated upon the sofa. Elizabeth had been sitting in one of the chairs, leaving the other chair close by as the only seat for Lord Trenton. Though she had no desire to be anywhere near the man, she did not see any way to avoid sitting in close proximity to him.

Taking the only action available, Elizabeth motioned him to one of the chairs while seating herself in the other. As she did so, however, she gave Mr. Bingley and Mr. Darcy a pleading look. Since another caller had arrived, the two men were expected to leave shortly without making it seem obvious that the new arrival was their reason for doing so. Yet Elizabeth did *not* want to entertain Lord Trenton with only her sisters to protect her.

Mr. Darcy's intense stare and slight nod of understanding made Elizabeth sigh in relief. He recognized her concerns and would not abandon her. Her gaze went to Lord Trenton, and she heard him give a gentle snort that made her realize he knew very well what the silent communication between her and Mr. Darcy meant, but he made no protests, instead simply smiling knowingly.

This began a most unpleasant half hour in which Elizabeth was forced to withstand the attentions of the insistent Lord Trenton. He acted exactly as Elizabeth would expect of a man who was certain of his own worth and considered himself well above his company, curling his lip and looking down upon everyone. But when Mr. Darcy spoke, Lord Trenton at least gave him the courtesy of his attention. Mr. Darcy was the scion of an earl—though untitled himself—and Elizabeth suspected that Mr. Darcy was made worthy of the lord's notice by virtue of that fact alone. But even so, it seemed Trenton scarcely wanted to give him that.

Elizabeth found herself the recipient of most of Lord Trenton's attention, and though she would have preferred almost anything rather than to be forced to endure his company, at least they had the arms of the chairs in between them. Lord Trenton was overly familiar with her even as things stood—had they been seated on the same piece of furniture, she might have been afraid for her virtue.

The conversation was generally carried by the earl, as Elizabeth attempted to give him as little encouragement as possible. She was curious, however, as to how he had located her, and she said as much.

"I have my contacts," was his smug response. "It was no great feat to determine the residence of your uncle, given that I knew his name and the fact that he was a man of *business*."

The last was said as a sneer, and Elizabeth, annoyed as she already was by his manners and arrogance, felt her patience beginning to fray.

"I am sorry, sir," said she, "but I find myself quite at a loss as to why you would seek us out. After all, we are not of your sphere. What can you mean by it?"

"Nothing weighty, Miss Bennet," responded Lord Trenton with a studied look of nonchalance. "I rarely meet persons who intrigue me as much as you do. And as your sisters do, of course."

His last sentence was spoken in an offhand manner, and privately, Elizabeth doubted Lord Trenton had any interest whatsoever in her sisters; he had as yet not spoken more than two words to either of them.

"Actually, I do have a purpose for being here, Miss Bennet," continued he. "I would like to invite you," he swept the room with his gaze, "all the Miss Bennets, of course, along with your uncle and aunt, to my Twelfth Night Ball, which is to be held at my house here in town."

He produced the invitation with a flourish, handing it to Elizabeth.

"I am afraid I did not fathom that I would meet you here, Darcy," said he, looking at the other man. "Yours I have already sent by post."

He sneered in Bingley's direction. "Of course, I would not mind in the slightest if your friend Mr. Gimbley were to accompany you."

"Bingley," stated Mr. Darcy with a scowl.

"Yes, yes," replied Lord Trenton, waving his hand in the air. "Of course, as it is a Twelfth Night celebration, it shall be a masquerade ball. Therefore, you shall have to come wearing a mask, and your partner for the evening will be chosen by lottery."

Elizabeth considered the invitation, wondering if there were any way to refuse it politely. The fact that he was delivering such an invite in person put her in an especially awkward position. To be singled out by such a man was the last thing she wanted! She looked to her sisters, but Jane, though she had heard the invitation, appeared to have no opinion regarding it, and Kitty's attendance was, of course, doubtful.

Deciding that tact was required, Elizabeth regarded the lord once again and said: "I thank you for the honor of your invitation—"

"Good!" exclaimed Lord Trenton. "Then it is settled."

"I believe Miss Bennet was not finished," said Mr. Darcy.

Elizabeth regarded him again with a grateful nod. At the same time, she saw his glare at the earl and wondered what he could mean by it. He was providing her assistance, of course, but she did not understand his ill-concealed hostility for the other man. Was there some longstanding disagreement with the earl?

"Indeed, Mr. Darcy is correct," continued Elizabeth finally. "As my uncle is responsible for our care while we are in town, it will be his decision as to whether or not we will be able to attend. I am certain you understand."

"Of course," replied Lord Trenton. "Please tell your uncle that I would be happy to call upon him if he is uncertain of the sincerity of my invitation. I shall hope to see all of you in attendance—though, of course, I shall not necessarily know you due to your masks."

He chuckled delightedly at his jest, while Elizabeth was only able to summon the barest of smiles in response. She hoped her uncle would refuse the invitation; she was not certain she could bear to see the man's face again, even if it *were* obscured by a mask.

The gentlemen stayed for only a few moments longer before all departing at once. Elizabeth, needing to retreat into solitude, mustered up a farewell before sighing and escaping to her room. At least Jane's relationship with Mr. Bingley appeared to be deepening as she had thought it would.

As for herself, she had begun to wonder if being in London was worth the drawback of subjecting herself to the company of arrogant young men.

Chapter XXXVI

When the Gardiners returned, Elizabeth was summoned to meet with them. Sighing—she still felt unsettled due to the visit from the gentleman callers from that afternoon—Elizabeth put aside the book she was reading and exited the room.

She made her way down the stairs to the drawing room, where she could hear the voices of her family. As she went inside, she learned her sisters were acquainting their aunt and uncle with the details of what had passed in their home earlier that day.

"*Lord Trenton* has invited us all to his Twelfth Night Ball?" said Mrs. Gardiner in disbelief. "Why, I am surprised that we should receive such an invitation from an earl—and in person no less."

"I think it may have something to do with Lizzy," ventured Kitty.

Elizabeth looked at her sister in surprise. Kitty would not have been able to see Lord Trenton's leers, but she appeared to have gleaned something regardless. Sometimes, Elizabeth forgot how discerning Kitty could be.

With a frown, Elizabeth said: "The partners are to be chosen by lottery. As such, Kitty should not go. I do not believe it would be fair for us to attend and leave her behind." In truth, she did not want to have any part in the ball.

Kitty shrugged in indifference. "It *is* a masquerade, and I would be missing a crucial part of the experience were I to go. I do not mind remaining at home while you all attend. I should like to spend some time with my young cousins anyway."

"It is rather short notice," persisted Elizabeth. "We do not have time to prepare regardless."

"Nonsense, Lizzy," said Mrs. Gardiner. "In the time we have, we can ensure that you girls make a spectacular appearance. Why, I might almost think you do not want to go, Lizzy." Here, her aunt pinned her with a stare.

Elizabeth looked away. "My dear aunt, I think . . . I think perhaps we should refuse this invitation."

Mr. Gardiner spoke up: "I am not sure that would be wise, Lizzy. This is a prominent social event. To attend could prove to be of some assistance to your family in the long run."

Elizabeth gazed at her uncle. He might as well have said, "If you go, you will become better known in society, and it may make you more marriageable." He would never have been so callous as to state so much in such a blunt way, but she took his meaning nonetheless.

"But it is to be a masquerade ball," protested Elizabeth. "Even should I go, no one will know who I am!"

"I dare say that by the end of the ball, those paired together become acquainted with the identity of their partners, Lizzy," said her aunt. "You may even have the good fortune to be paired with someone who strikes your fancy."

"And besides," added her uncle, "your aunt and I are too old to engage in such frivolity. Therefore, though we shall also be wearing masks, it will be necessary to make ourselves known, and if we become better known in society, that can only help your chances."

Sighing, Elizabeth conceded: "Very well. Perhaps we should go. However, I am not certain how I feel about this lottery."

"Maybe you will receive a partner such as Mr. Darcy," said Kitty brightly.

Elizabeth shook her head, thinking that surely Fate would not be so cruel as to pair her with that man at the dance. "My partner shall probably be someone I have never met," said she. "But I will not mind so long as Jane is paired with Mr. Bingley."

Jane flushed. "We do not even know whether he is attending, Lizzy."

Elizabeth smiled at her. "If he thinks you will be, then I am sure he shall attend."

Soon afterward, the conversation turned into a discussion of proper clothing, and Mr. Gardiner excused himself. It did not take much longer before Kitty also bored of the conversation and left to go play with the Gardiner children.

Jane was inattentive to the discussion taking place between her aunt and elder sister, sitting quietly with a soft smile on her countenance, and Elizabeth finally told her: "You should retire to your room, dear sister. You shall need your beauty rest in case you should see Mr. Bingley again tomorrow."

"Oh, Lizzy!" exclaimed Jane in exasperation, but she left the room regardless. Perhaps she sensed that Elizabeth and Mrs. Gardiner needed to converse in private.

Mrs. Gardiner watched the young woman disappear before turning to her eldest niece. "I am glad to hear Mr. Bingley came to visit Jane. Do you believe his intentions to be genuine this time, Lizzy?"

Elizabeth smiled to herself, recalling her words of warning to the kind young man. "Indeed, I do."

"And you say his friend Mr. Darcy was with him?"

"Yes. He was. But I rather wished he had not been!"

Her aunt frowned. "What do you mean, Lizzy?"

"The man is infuriating! I believe that he was the one who convinced Mr. Bingley to leave Hertfordshire. Mr. Bingley said someone pressured him into doing so, and I think Mr. Darcy is the only one who could have held such great influence over him as to convince him to leave the woman he cares for so deeply!" She threw her hands in the air. "He is cold and proud and taciturn, and he cares for no one but himself. If he was indeed the one who convinced Mr. Bingley to leave, then I doubt he did it for any reason but to distance himself from our family and the other families in Hertfordshire. Company such as ours is beneath him!"

"Lizzy!" said Mrs. Gardiner sharply. "You are being very uncharitable, and I think perhaps you do not know Mr. Darcy so well as you think."

"Believe me, my dear aunt, I know his kind very well indeed. As for Mr. Darcy in particular, I believe I know him as well as I should ever wish."

Mrs. Gardiner affixed Elizabeth with a stern expression—the kind of expression with which she rarely favored any of her nieces, save for Lydia. Elizabeth had only seen it a few times, and it meant that her aunt was seriously displeased with the way she was acting.

"You know Mr. Darcy well, do you?" demanded she, her tone suggesting that Elizabeth was acting like a petulant child. "Did you know that Mr. Darcy and Mr. Gardiner have been business partners for several years? In fact, Mr. Darcy has dined with us many times."

Elizabeth stared at her aunt in astonishment. Was it true that Mr. Darcy had actually lowered himself to deal with *tradespeople*? If so, then perhaps country company was not as abhorrent to him as she had believed. Yet it still made the most sense for him to have been the one to extract Mr. Bingley from Hertfordshire. Elizabeth was confused, but since her aunt was expecting a response, she managed to murmur: "I had not realized that."

"He has more progressive views than you think, Lizzy," admonished her aunt, though her tone was much softer now. "He knows he will eventually need to supplement his income, as times are changing, and he has thus been investing in new technologies and companies such as your uncle's. He is truly a good and caring person. I have no doubt of that."

Chastened, Elizabeth looked down to her hands, which were wringing a handkerchief. Stilling them, she lifted her head. "I must own that I wonder a little whether we are speaking of the same person. Mr. Darcy rarely smiles, much less laughs, and he speaks only when it appears that he must. How could he be this good and caring person of whom you speak?"

"Lizzy," said her aunt gently, "obviously I cannot say anything of Mr. Darcy's behavior in Hertfordshire, but I would counsel you to withhold your judgment. I am not, of course, privy to Mr. Darcy's concerns, but I suspect he may have some important matter weighing on him. He is of an age where several critical decisions are ahead of him. Perhaps he believes he must soon seek a wife."

Elizabeth colored and lowered her eyes back to the handkerchief. "Have you met his sister before?"

"A few times," replied her aunt. "She seemed to be a very affable sort of person, though she was rather shy."

"Hmm," said Elizabeth noncommittally. "Well, I suppose I could take the time to look at Mr. Darcy a little closer. Perhaps I have indeed misjudged him."

"Please do, Lizzy," replied her aunt. "He truly is an admirable man."

Elizabeth stood, ready to go to bed. "Maybe one day I shall see him as you do, my dear, dear aunt," said she with a smile.

"I hope so."

As Elizabeth walked away from her aunt, her mind was drawn to the thought of Mr. Darcy. Could the man be as multi-faceted as his sister? It was possible. But she refused to take the thought any further beyond that.

Chapter XXXVII

Sometimes the passage of time could be ever so frustrating, Elizabeth reflected. When one was awaiting a much anticipated event, time seemed to move at an interminable pace. Dreaded engagements, however, always seemed to come upon one swiftly.

Normally, a ball would be an occasion which *could* be looked upon with some anticipation, for although Elizabeth preferred to avoid dancing, she would still be able to indulge in her pastime of observing others at the ball, laughing at their antics and speaking with her friends. Elizabeth was—and had always been—a social creature.

Lord Trenton's masquerade ball offered none of these pleasurable activities, and Elizabeth regretted the necessity of attending. There was something about the earl which put her on edge, something in his eyes when he looked at her. At times, she wondered if the feelings his gaze engendered in her approximated those of a field mouse being eyed by an owl. She would not put it past him to try something distasteful at this ball of his, and she was not certain she would be able to withstand his attentions.

All of this did not even take into account that a Twelfth Night masquerade ball was traditionally a time for the cream of society to shed their normally proper behavior and engage in revelries with much less restraint than was their wont. Despite the low chance of having to deal with Lord Trenton himself as a partner, the appeal of spending the evening in the company of some other dandy interested in nothing more than pointless flirtation and other less respectable activities was sadly lacking.

However, the arguments the Gardiners had used to persuade her of the need to attend were impeccable, the result of which had her sitting in the carriage on the way to Lord Trenton's opulent London home, wishing she had stayed in the Gardiners' townhouse.

Less of a surprise was the attendance of Mr. Darcy and Mr. Bingley—the next day's visit by both gentlemen had revealed the Bennet sisters' intention to attend, which of course necessitated Mr. Bingley's presence at the evening's entertainment. Although he would undoubtedly be paired with someone other than Jane, his motives were clear. Mr. Darcy's motives, however, were not, and Elizabeth would likely have puzzled more over his behavior if the circumstances had not been so unsettling for her.

The carriage pulled up to the house, and the Bennet sisters were immediately impressed by the elegance of the earl's home and the casual opulence which was displayed. It was by far the most impressive home Elizabeth had ever seen, and though she was not in a position to judge these things, having grown up in a much more modest setting, she felt that his taste was actually quite good. She had assumed that such a rich man would have tried to bludgeon his visitors over the head with displays of wealth, but the earl did not necessarily seem to be that sort of man. It improved her opinion of him—very slightly.

It appeared that many from the highest circles of London society had turned out for the event. The entrance to the house was crowded as the invitees to the soirée made their way to the ballroom, and Elizabeth was awed by the fabrics and cuts of the gowns. She was suddenly glad that her aunt had insisted upon using Mr. Gardiner's contacts to ensure they had new dresses created for the occasion; even the finest of the dresses she had brought from Hertfordshire would have paled in comparison to what she was witnessing that evening, though the dress would have been considered dreadfully ostentatious for all but the most formal engagements back at home. Here, her new gown made her fit in with this crowd—barely. There were dresses here which would have cost a sizable chunk of her father's yearly income.

Elizabeth's own dress was a deep burgundy in color, and while perhaps it was not as expensive as most of the other dresses there, she made a good showing. The eye-slits of her mask were lined with red, and the golden color covering the nose of the mask spread upward above the eyes like eyebrows. There were pointed strips of orange, red, and gold along the sides of the mask which bore a slight resemblance to tongues of fire, and it was exotic without being overly ostentatious. As for Jane, she wore a royal blue gown and a simple blue mask. The modest simplicity of the ensemble was very much representative of Jane herself, and Elizabeth thought she looked lovely indeed.

Mr. Bingley had insisted on conveying the Gardiners and the two Bennet daughters in one of Mr. Darcy's large carriages, and they were therefore able to study each other's costumes in some detail, even if it might have been a little crowded in the coach with all the ladies' finery.

The appearances of Mr. Bingley and Mr. Darcy certainly could not be any more different. Mr. Bingley was dressed in a green suit which was a little lighter than a deep forest color, but it was one that—though it was easily recognizable—did not induce a headache. It rather spoke to a sense of flamboyance and playfulness—he had apparently decided to put great effort into his costume. His mask was a contrasting mint green, with plumes of feathers streaming out from its top, waving about his head like a peacock's plumage. The effect was slightly silly, but somehow the effervescent Mr. Bingley managed to pull it off. Mr. Darcy's own outfit was not as flashy. He wore a cobalt-colored coat with cream-colored trousers, and his mask was the same muted color of deep blue. Elizabeth might have found herself swooning at his debonair appearance had she not already acknowledged to herself that he was a handsome gentleman. The effect of his outfit was one of mystery, unlike the silliness of Mr. Bingley's ensemble—their appearances were certainly reflections of their contrasting personalities.

Both the two young men and the two young ladies were ready for the masquerade in terms of their appearance, though Elizabeth did not feel prepared for it mentally and emotionally. Nonetheless, she was resolved to face the evening with a pleasant countenance—though she would likely be gritting her teeth the entire time.

At the entrance to the ballroom, a group of the earl's servants were greeting the partygoers and offering small slips of paper, each with a number printed upon them. This, obviously, would be the means by which her companion for the evening would be determined.

A comment from Jane distracted her, and she leaned to hear her sister's voice, all the while marveling at the splendor on display. A sudden sense of being watched turned her attention away from Jane, and she peered toward the servants' table, only to see the swirl of a dark cloak as a man departed from amongst the servants. Deciding her nerves were getting the better of her, Elizabeth took a deep breath and calmed herself, ensuring her mask was firmly in place.

When they had made their way to the table through the press of the crowd, they were urged by the servants to draw a number from the bowls provided for the occasion. The Gardiners declined, preferring to remain together, and although Elizabeth would have liked nothing more than to do so herself, she was urged to choose her number and enjoy the evening. Her aunt and uncle disappeared after admonishing them once more to enjoy themselves, and Elizabeth saw that there were several couples emulating the Gardiners' example. There were, however, many others—some of them older by far than her father—who joined the festivities by choosing their own numbers. It appeared that the revelries were not only for the young and unattached.

Elizabeth gathered her courage and stepped forward, directed toward a bowl by the servant, and after she had plucked a card from the bowl, she opened it to reveal the number "64."

The servant who had provided the number gestured to the card she held and said: "You are to display the card so the gentleman with the same number—who will become your partner for the evening—can find you in the crowd. If you cannot find your partner within the first thirty minutes of the ball, then you should return to the table to draw a new number."

Elizabeth expressed her gratitude for the instructions, and then, with Jane beside her and Mr. Darcy and Mr. Bingley following behind, she made her way into the ballroom.

If Elizabeth had been impressed with the house before, the magnificence of the ballroom raised her appreciation even higher. It was decorated with ribbons and garlands and with holly and ivy, all in keeping with the season, while sparkling icicles and snowflakes hung on wires from the ceiling. The orchestra was clearly of the highest quality, and it played prelude music which echoed over the din of the speaking masses. On the far side of the room, the scents of wine and punches drifted lazily—yet enticingly—through the air, and delicacies of every sort to tempt the palate stood on tables which were already surrounded with guests partaking of the bounty with relish. It was the most incredible scene which Elizabeth had ever beheld, and for a moment, she was actually glad she had come.

The party stood as one group for several moments, scanning the crowds for their companions for the evening—at least, Elizabeth did so. Jane and Mr. Bingley appeared to be focused more on each other and their disappointment at not being paired, while Mr. Darcy seemed as if he were concentrating on displaying his most imperious and intimidating stare to the room.

It was not long before a young man approached and bowed to Jane, displaying the matching card to Jane's own. Although Elizabeth was only in his presence for a moment, he appeared to be cheerful and friendly, and soon Jane was swept away with him after she gave a low murmur that Elizabeth needed to enjoy herself for the evening. Mr. Darcy and Mr. Bingley left not long after to search for their own partners, though Elizabeth did notice that Mr. Darcy seemed to be staying nearby. Elizabeth could only wonder at his behavior—the man obviously wished he were somewhere else, so why had he deigned to attend the ball at all? She was once again forced to suppress her less than charitable feelings for him due to her dear aunt's portrayal of his character.

Several moments later, she was approached by a tall man dressed all in black who bowed and presented her with a card which contained the identical "64" emblazoned upon its surface. His feathered black mask covered his eyes and nose but left his mouth easily visible. Silver surrounded the eye-holes and curved upward, while tufts of delicate black feathers were scattered along the top of the mask. The effect was somewhat sinister.

"Good evening, madam," stated he. "It appears that I am to be your companion for the evening."

Elizabeth started and stared at the man, hoping against hope that the suspicion which was beginning to form in the back of her mind was not about to be confirmed.

"Sir," responded she with a curtsy, her good manners overcoming her misgivings.

The man grinned devilishly at her and, taking her arm, directed her toward an out-of-the-way corner of the room. "I am very pleased to make your acquaintance, Miss . . ."

Fury took hold of Elizabeth. It was clear—from the voice, the assured movements, the supercilious manner—that she had the complete misfortune to be paired with none other than the detested Lord Trenton!

Shocked and unable to account for this stroke of ill luck, Elizabeth was silent, glancing down at the floor and praying for the strength to make it through the evening. Or rather, to withstand the machinations of the man, she thought savagely. It was nigh impossible that this could be a coincidence—somehow, he had managed to influence the lottery so that she would be forced into a night in his company! There was no other explanation!

"Madam? Are you well?"

The words were not spoken in the solicitous tone Elizabeth would have expected given the circumstances; instead, they were spoken with all the arrogance of a lordling who had an overblown assurance of his own importance and lacked any measure of real concern for her wellbeing. Her eyes darted to his face, and although it was obscured somewhat by his mask, Elizabeth could see the haughty look which adorned his features. He was obviously aware that she had figured out his interference, and he was not bothered by the fact. The nerve and pride of the man!

"I am very well, thank you," bit out Elizabeth in response. "I thank you for inquiring."

"I am glad to hear it. I should not like to be deprived of the opportunity to spend the evening with such an enchanting young woman due to some small ailment."

Elizabeth colored. "I thank you, sir. But perhaps you should reserve judgment upon my person until you have known me longer than a mere five minutes."

A most unpleasant grin spread over his face, and he leered down at her, nearly causing her to shudder in revulsion.

"I do not doubt that you will be an agreeable partner, miss. But come now—shall you keep me guessing about your identity for the entire evening? I should very much like to know the name of my companion."

Though she knew that the earl was in no doubt of her identity, Elizabeth would not give him the satisfaction of calling her by name. "Perhaps not," responded she coyly. "I believe I should like to keep you guessing, sir—it may very well be the only power over you which I possess."

His answering grin was almost feral. "Very well then, miss. I shall enjoy attempting to divine your identity. All I ask is that you be more forthcoming if I have not had any success by the supper hour."

Elizabeth would have given almost anything to be able to deny him even that, but she was forced to agree with his condition.

The music changed, and couples began moving to the dance floor for the opening set. Lord Trenton bowed to her and grasped her hand, pulling her with him while giving her a lusty look. "I believe this is the first dance, and I must have the pleasure of experiencing it with you."

It was, quite simply, the most horrible dance to which Elizabeth had ever been subjected, and it was almost enough to induce her to completely swear off the activity anew. Though she was well aware of the follies of certain men and the means by which they would attempt to flatter a young woman and try to gain her favor—not to mention the methods a man would use to encourage the woman to indulge in more than idle flirting—she had never been witness to, much less the center of, such base behavior herself. Lord Trenton proved to be the most rakish and improper partner Elizabeth could have imagined. Even Mr. Darcy, stiff-necked and proud as he was, would have been a more agreeable man with whom to spend an evening!

Lord Trenton used every trick in his considerable arsenal. He flattered her vanity with outrageous compliments, lingered closer to her than necessary, and held her hand longer than was proper, all the while staring at her with unbridled desire. Elizabeth felt he was veritably undressing her with his eyes!

The dance seemed interminable, but when it was finally over, he led her to the side of the room for some more "private conversation," and Elizabeth begged off, indicating she needed to visit the retiring room. His smug assurance that she would be back was evident in his voice as he declared himself to be anticipating her return.

Chapter XXXVIII

Elizabeth only spent a few moments in the retiring room, conscious as she was of the other women present—it would appear odd for her to stand there doing nothing while other ladies entered and exited.

She tried to sneak unobtrusively from the room and immediately made her way to another part of the house where various entertainments had been set up. There were card tables, comfortable lounges where couples gathered to speak, and rooms with tables fairly groaning due to the wide variety of refreshments topping them. There were also other—more esoteric—amusements to be found, most of which she would not linger over.

Not wishing to be discovered by the house's master, Elizabeth kept moving through the crowd, hoping to find Mr. and Mrs. Gardiner and induce them to leave the celebration early.

She had exited the house into a small courtyard when she espied the earl enter from the opposite side, his eyes affixed upon her from the moment he made his appearance. Stifling an unladylike curse, Elizabeth darted back into the house and quickly made her way through several rooms before ducking out onto one of the balconies. Sighing, she leaned against the balustrade, wishing for a polite way out of her predicament.

Not a moment later, she heard the soft fall of a footstep and whirled around to see the smirking visage of the earl as he stepped out onto the balcony.

"Ah, there you are," intoned he, his voice smug. "You must have had difficulty in locating me after your brief respite from the ballroom."

The conceit of the man was beyond belief—he was completely cognizant of the fact that Elizabeth had been avoiding him, yet he ignored her antipathy as though it were of no moment. And how had he managed to locate her so quickly? Had he ordered the servants to report her movements?

"But perhaps this happenstance is fortuitous," continued he, approaching her as a predator approaches its prey. "I would relish the opportunity to know you better away from prying eyes."

Moving quickly, certain her virtue was at risk, Elizabeth darted to another entrance to the house, drawing him in her wake. "I should much prefer to dance," exclaimed she by way of explanation, regretting that she needed to say anything to him at all.

His manner in response to her ploy was all insolence—she could see his determination and his confidence that he would eventually have his own way. Not willing to put herself in any sort of private situation with him from that point forward, Elizabeth led him to the ballroom, but not before he caught up with her and firmly placed her hand upon his arm, escorting her as though they were close confidantes and almost seeming to indicate to the gathering that she was his possession. Elizabeth nearly withdrew her hand and left him right there, but she kept her composure with some difficulty and swallowed the biting words she wished to say to him.

As they entered the ballroom, Elizabeth happened to notice Mr. Darcy standing to the side, watching her as she entered on Lord Trenton's arm. His displeasure at seeing them was more than evident. But Elizabeth scarcely had time to consider the matter before Lord Trenton was once more sweeping onto the dance floor.

The second dance with the arrogant lordling was similar to the first, but the discomfort it caused her was magnified by Lord Trenton's increased aggressiveness. His eyes were now blatantly on the bare skin above the low neckline of her dress, and his hand lingered upon hers with a series of almost sensual caresses. It was when his fingers "accidentally" brushed against her waist during one exchange that Elizabeth's anger flared. She stopped abruptly, much to the confusion and stumbles of the nearby dancers, and after imperiously glaring at her escort through her mask, she turned and stalked off the dance floor. She had no doubt she was making a spectacle of herself, but her mask and relative anonymity made her bold—she would not endure another moment with this man, not even if she were to face the censure of the entire room!

Furious, Elizabeth strode forward, determined to find her aunt and uncle and demand she be allowed to return home and escape this farce of an event.

She made it to the refreshment tables before her arm was grabbed roughly from behind and she was spun around to face her attacker.

"What precisely is wrong with you?" demanded Lord Trenton.

"*You* are what is wrong!" cried Elizabeth while wrenching her hand from his grasp. "I do not know to what behavior you are accustomed, sir, but I can assure you that I will not be treated in such a cavalier manner!"

"And what manner is that, madam?" challenged the earl. "I was under the impression that we were to be partners for the evening. Is not a certain amount of familiarity expected in such cases?"

"A certain amount, perhaps, but decorum must also be maintained. I do not appreciate your overly amorous attempts to seduce me or your efforts to force me into a situation which would compromise me. I do not welcome your attentions, sir!"

The sneer which came over his face was quite unpleasant. "You are a commoner, and as such, you are worthy only of being a plaything to your betters. Why can you not simply accept your role and appreciate coming to the attention of one such as I?"

In that moment, Elizabeth's already frayed temper snapped, and before she could even recognize any conscious thought, her arm was swinging forward to connect with the egotistical man's cheek with a resounding smack. Elizabeth had just slapped a man for the second time in her life!

Unfortunately for the earl, he was clearly not expecting her reaction, whether it was due to his pride and sense of superiority or his overwhelming confidence that he would ultimately prevail in obtaining what he wanted. Whatever the reason, her hand connecting with his cheek caught him completely by surprise, and he stumbled backward, colliding bodily with a nearby table of refreshments and knocking it over, depositing a tray of delicacies and a bowl of punch all over his expensive suit.

Pain shot through Elizabeth's hand, and she cradled it while watching the reactions of the surrounding revelers, who were clearly shocked at her impulsive act. Not all those around her appeared to be displeased, she learned, for the earl's mask had been knocked askew, revealing his identity for all to see, and she saw more than one person smile in satisfaction at the sight of the man drenched in his own punch. If Elizabeth had been in any state to enjoy the scene, she would have been forced to acknowledge that his predicament was highly diverting.

As tears began to stream down Elizabeth's face, Jane rushed up to her and hugged her, providing all the comfort of a beloved sister. Behind her, Mr. Darcy also approached, the look on his face mirroring the general astonishment of the room, although his countenance held a certain satisfaction mixed in with the surprise. Elizabeth, however, had no time to think about the enigmatic man.

"I want to go home, Jane," sobbed she as the tears began to fall in earnest.

"Of course, Lizzy," whispered Jane in response.

A look passed between Mr. Darcy and Jane. Mr. Darcy excused himself and rushed off into the crowd while Elizabeth was led away by Jane, who whispered words of comfort into her ear as they walked.

"How dare you?" broke out the enraged voice of the earl over the crowd.

Elizabeth and Jane turned to see Lord Trenton struggling up from the floor, his efforts hampered by the slickness of the punch-coated floor and the delicacies which squished most unpleasantly under his shoes. His mask had been discarded and now lay in a puddle of punch, and when he at last gained his feet, his face was suffused with an expression of such murderous fury that Elizabeth momentarily felt afraid he would do something unthinkable to seek vengeance.

He made no move toward the sisters, however, merely bellowing for his servants, several of whom came rushing forward.

"Throw these harlots from the house directly!" ordered he.

As the servants turned toward the two frightened sisters uncertainly, Mr. Darcy and Mr. Bingley emerged from the crowd and rushed to their sides. Mr. Darcy took one look at the shaking young women and turned on his heel, affixing Lord Trenton with a cold stare while motioning the servants to stand clear.

"You will do no such thing!" said Mr. Darcy, his voice calm, controlled, and icy cold.

"Who are you to order me in my own house?" cried Lord Trenton. "This trollop has drawn me in and humiliated me in front of all my guests. I will not have her remain here, ruining this event!"

"It is your own doing, Trenton," said Mr. Darcy in response. "I have watched you throughout the evening. You have behaved in a most ungentlemanly manner, forcing your attentions on a young lady who did not want or welcome them. Then you besmirched her good name by declaring her to be nothing more than your plaything. *If* I considered you enough of a gentleman, I would call you out for such dishonorable behavior."

The earl paled at Mr. Darcy's words before his expression once again hardened. "Get out! You will all leave this house immediately!"

"Nothing would please me more!" cried Elizabeth, who had regained her voice, before turning and marching from the room, closely followed by her sister and the two gentlemen.

They moved through the foyer and gathered their coats and wraps. Mr. Darcy spoke softly to one of the servants, instructing him to find Mr. and Mrs. Gardiner and inform them of their immediate departure. Then he and Mr. Bingley escorted the two young women from the house and into the carriage, which the former had ordered moments before.

"I am so sorry to ruin your evening, Jane," said Elizabeth through suppressed sobs. "I simply could not abide another moment in his company."

"It is nothing, Lizzy," replied Jane, stroking Elizabeth's hair. "The young man with whom I was paired was pleasant, but he was not the one I wished to have as a companion."

Her reference was not lost on any of the carriage's occupants; Mr. Bingley's face was suffused with a beaming smile, and even the corners of Mr. Darcy's mouth twitched upwards in response to her declaration.

"Whatever shall I do?" wailed Elizabeth as the reality of her situation entered her awareness. For a brief moment, she forgot that there were men near and could think only of her future. "After that altercation, I will be ruined. The earl will almost certainly brand me as a scarlet woman and temptress to all."

"Miss Bennet," interjected Mr. Darcy gently, "I believe you need not concern yourself on that account. I doubt you were recognized, and Lord Trenton will certainly not wish to publicize his disgrace at the hands of one he considers to be so much lower in consequence to himself. I am sorry to pain you with that description, but I can assure you that his own feelings will mirror my words in every particular."

Elizabeth smiled gratefully at him, and as coherently as she was able, she gave him to understand that she was sensible of his words and appreciated his concern.

"I should think that nothing will come of this," continued he once she had thanked him. "As long as you do not declare your identity, the scandal sheets will gleefully report Trenton's humiliation at the hands of an 'unknown lady,' but they will soon lose interest as other scandals come to light. There is little to worry about."

The Gardiners appeared a few moments later, and after assuring themselves that their niece was unharmed, they gave the order to leave, and the coach departed. The Gardiners invited the gentlemen to their house for a light repast, which was gratefully accepted, and the passengers settled in for the trip home.

It had been, Elizabeth reflected, the most horrid night of her life. But the pain of her sprained wrist was somewhat offset by the memory of seeing the insufferable man covered in the remains of his own refreshments.

Chapter XXXIX

London kept Bingley very busy. If he was not visiting Jane at the Gardiners' home, then he was attending to the other social engagements required to keep up an appearance of respectability and propriety. He begrudged the social visits that took him away from Jane Bennet, but he had come to London with Darcy and would not shun or shame his friend, who had many acquaintances in the city, even though those people did not capture Bingley's attention as had once been the case.

The reason for that lapse was obvious, and Bingley did not think on it to any great degree. No, what had recently commanded his attention were his closest friend and the puzzle of his behavior. Bingley had known Darcy for several years, but he had never seen him behave in the way he had as of late. While a few hours of observing Miss Jane should have been enough for Darcy to convince himself of the sincerity of the young woman's affection for Bingley, still Darcy continued to accompany Bingley on nearly all of his visits to Gracechurch Street. The only reason for Darcy's doing so which Bingley could conceive was the notion that Darcy was attracted to Elizabeth Bennet. Darcy had certainly proved himself quite the rescuer to Miss Bennet from her unenviable situation at the Twelfth Night Ball, though Bingley realized the woman had mostly been able to extricate herself from her own predicament. He still found it difficult to get the image of a refreshment-covered Lord Trenton out of his mind. Even Darcy had managed half a smile afterward and commented: "I believe punch looks good on Trenton."

Pushing his thoughts of the upper classes and Trenton aside, Bingley concentrated once again on his friend, reflecting that while he had seen Darcy interact with many different women in their time together, his friend had never seemed *this* distracted. In fact, Bingley knew the reason Darcy had been so eager to leave Rosings and come to Hertfordshire was to distance himself from two women and think carefully about his future. But if Bingley's suspicions were correct in regard to Miss Elizabeth Bennet, then Darcy was merely becoming more distracted than he had been before he went to Hertfordshire.

Bingley looked across at his friend, who was standing by the window and looking outside. Darcy had always kept his feelings close, and it was generally impossible to know what he was thinking.

"Is London proving a suitable distraction from the troubles that await you in Kent?" Bingley asked, failing to hide his amused smile.

"Somehow, I cannot escape from my thoughts," said Darcy in a detached voice. He did not even notice the knowing expression on his friend's face.

Bingley smiled to himself and shook his head. He did not envy Darcy his position and did not doubt that the man was reluctant to return to Kent to face the two women who had been the impetus for Darcy's trip to Hertfordshire. While Bingley knew there were a variety of factors to be considered by a young man seeking a wife, he was of the opinion that romantic affection was of the utmost importance. Unfortunately, Bingley feared that Darcy did not think such a consideration merited more than a few moments of thought.

The first woman Darcy saw as a suitable marriage candidate was his cousin Anne de Bourgh. Bingley knew Darcy cared for her in his fashion, but he did not believe his friend felt more than cousinly affection for her. Nevertheless, the man of duty in Darcy appeared to be seriously considering proposing marriage to Miss de Bourgh. Of course, Bingley did not know why exactly it *would* be a duty, for although Lady Catherine was vociferous in her insistence that Darcy marry her daughter, Darcy had privately confided to him that he knew of no such agreement from his mother's side. Still, there could be an amount of sympathy or even pity wrapped up in Darcy's consideration of the matter, for the young woman was oppressed by her overbearing mother and was generally a sickly, colorless sort of creature who required a white knight to ride in and save her from the drudgery of her life. Privately, Bingley did not consider pity to be an adequate inducement to enter into the marriage state.

The other woman Darcy had been considering seriously in Kent was Miss de Bourgh's friend, Elia Baker. Miss Baker was certainly a handsome, lively, and kind-seeming woman, but even Bingley thought she was too obtuse for the intelligent Darcy. For reasons Bingley did not understand, however, Darcy appeared to be amused by the woman's slightly stupid moments. It was something that did not sit well with Bingley, who was reminded in no small way of how Mr. Bennet laughed over his wife's lack of sense.

Bingley had feared when they left Rosings that a part of Darcy fancied himself in love with Miss Baker. But Bingley did not believe Darcy could truly find happiness and fulfillment from such a marriage. Miss Baker's status in life was certainly above that of Mr. Bennet's daughters, so on those grounds, she would make a suitable wife for Darcy. However, Bingley felt the amusement she provided his friend was not of a healthy sort. Unlike Elizabeth Bennet, Elia Baker did not challenge Darcy.

If Darcy *was* attracted to Miss Bennet, then he must have felt troubled as to what he should do. A man of his wealth and position was expected to choose a proper bride. Considerations such as the woman's dowry and familial connections had to be taken into account, and the expectations of a man's family could also not be completely ignored. Darcy's aunt had certainly been more than clear about her wishes for Darcy to marry her daughter. Fortunately for Darcy, the rest of his family would not be upset if he did not wed Miss de Bourgh, but he had to be feeling pressured nonetheless. That particular young woman would bring no small dowry.

"Here, Darcy, what do you say to some Scotch?" asked Bingley of his friend, trying to catch his attention. He lifted the bottle in the air.

"Yes, please," murmured Darcy, not moving away from the window.

Bingley withheld a sigh and poured two drinks. Darcy's character had always held a slightly brooding quality, but he had never been this uncommunicative. Bingley was just glad *he* did not have to choose from three women as his friend did. Bingley's happiness was wrapped up in Miss Jane alone. He never needed to look with hope and trepidation at another woman again.

Bingley carried the drink to Darcy, who accepted it and returned his gaze to the outside world with a mumbled thanks.

Bingley just shook his head and then poured a drink of his own. After the disaster that had happened when Darcy interfered in Bingley's love life, Bingley was determined to keep his opinions to himself. Unless Darcy specifically asked him what he thought about any of the three women occupying his thoughts, Bingley would not say a word.

Still, Bingley knew he would not be unhappy to have Darcy for a brother-in-law—and not just because he would enjoy calling Darcy "brother." Elizabeth Bennet conjured up extreme emotions in the normally serious Darcy, and Bingley believed that was good for his friend. Furthermore, Bingley felt that Miss Bennet was an excellent match for Darcy. She was not simply someone his friend could respect—she was someone with whom Darcy could find the deep connection Bingley had found with his dear Jane. But Bingley himself would not say anything. Darcy was the only one who could decide what his future would look like. Bingley could not do it for him.

As Bingley took a sip of his Scotch, his thoughts turned to Jane. Now, *there* was something much more pleasant about which to think.

Chapter XL

For Elizabeth, Jane, Kitty, and their aunt and uncle, there were many visits to be made and assemblies to attend in the days and weeks which passed after the unpleasantness with Lord Trenton. On the twenty-ninth of January, they even went to an ice-skating party. Ever since the Twelfth Night ball, the Gardiners were more cautious in what invitations they urged their nieces to accept, but they quickly deemed this event a harmless one, and their nieces were eager to attend. Many was the winter day that the girls had glided across a pond on their father's estate. The gentle scraping of skates across the ice—combined with the pleasure of cheeks warmed by their exertions and the sheen of the thin frosty layer left behind in their wake—created an effect that was altogether pleasurable.

There was some debate as to whether Kitty should accompany them—she was as accomplished a skater as her sisters, but she would be unable to see the other ladies and gentlemen on the ice—but Jane and Elizabeth insisted they would assist her, so the Gardiners relented.

They dressed warmly in scarves, gloves, caps, shawls, and the other accoutrements of winter, and then they took a carriage to their destination.

The party was to be held at a frozen tributary near the home of Mr. Davidson. He was a wealthy man with an estate in Wiltshire, and Mr.

Darcy knew him from Cambridge. Mr. Darcy had, in fact, introduced Mr. Davidson and his wife to the three Bennet girls at an assembly. Though the Davidsons had spoken to the Bennets only briefly, they had declared that they must meet the young ladies again; the Davidsons' invitation for them to attend the ice-skating event therefore did not come as a surprise.

When they arrived, Mr. Davidson greeted them jovially. "Ah, such pictures of loveliness! I do hope you have dressed warmly enough—if not, my home is open to any who wish for a chance to warm themselves." He made a gesture to the street, drawing their attention to a side entrance to his home. "You will find cakes, pastries, tea, and all manner of refreshments inside."

"We thank you for your hospitality," said Mrs. Gardiner with a smile.

"It is our pleasure," offered Mrs. Davidson.

After glancing at the frozen tributary, Mr. Davidson asked them: "Are you all skilled on the ice?"

"We have skated many times at our home in Hertfordshire," answered Elizabeth.

"Ah!" said Mr. Davidson, sounding disappointed, though there was a twinkle in his eye. "I must own that I had hoped otherwise—I would relish the chance to teach young ladies such as yourselves the proper method."

"My husband is a skilled skater," said Mrs. Davidson kindly. "He was teaching our children some of the finer points of skating earlier today."

"We shall be certain to ask if we need assistance," said Elizabeth.

"Good, good!" exclaimed Mr. Davidson. And then he moved on with his wife to greet more of their guests.

Elizabeth smiled to herself. Mr. Davidson seemed to be an amiable man, but it was a little strange to her how Mr. Darcy appeared to surround himself with open and jovial people like Mr. Bingley and Mr. Davidson. She might have thought he would be interested in people of a disposition more similar to his own.

Shrugging, she helped Kitty affix her skates to her shoes and then did the same for herself. Then, she and her two sisters went to the ice. There were already several skaters gliding around, and Jane and Elizabeth each took one of Kitty's arms and joined them.

"Skating is so freeing!" cried Kitty.

Elizabeth smiled. "It makes me feel like a bird!"

"A silly bird without feathers," said Jane warmly.

Elizabeth raised her eyebrows in shock. "Why, my dear sister Jane is teasing me!" She laughed. "If I were a bird without feathers, I should imagine all the other birds would not wish to accept me! If I were able to fly—despite not having any feathers—then I would go far away from London to seek out other featherless birds."

"And if you never found anyone like you?" ventured Kitty.

"Then I should simply have to find someone who accepted me as I am. Surely there is someone interested in silly featherless birds like myself!"

"Oh! There are Mr. Darcy and Mr. Bingley!" exclaimed Jane.

Elizabeth looked to where Jane was pointing with a free hand. Mr. Darcy had on skates of his own, and he was struggling to move onto the ice without falling. Mr. Bingley was standing beside him and grinning widely, as though it brought him great pleasure to see his friend was actually unskilled at something.

Mr. Bingley saw them looking at him, and he came skating over to them as they slowed almost to a stop.

"Miss Bennet, Miss Jane, Miss Kitty," greeted he happily. "You appear to be fine skaters."

"Mr. Darcy seems to be having some difficulties," noted Elizabeth with a mischievous smile. "I might wonder why a man who lives in the frozen north of Derbyshire would not know his way around on a pair of skates."

Mr. Bingley laughed. "I do not know, but I *can* tell you that Darcy barely knows a skate from a stirrup, and he only knows *that* because he is a fine rider! I dare say he is in desperate need of an instructor, though he is probably too proud to accept one."

Elizabeth looked over at Mr. Darcy, whose face was dark as he tried to move forward, his arms hovering in the air in a fashion that was almost birdlike as he tried not to slip and fall.

Elizabeth smiled to herself. Then, remembering how her aunt had wanted her to look more closely at Mr. Darcy, she said to the man's friend: "Mr. Bingley, if you will assist Jane with Kitty, then I shall go take Mr. Darcy under my wing."

"Certainly!" agreed Mr. Bingley.

"Your featherless wing!" exclaimed Jane.

"What shall Mr. Darcy do with a bird which cannot fly?" said Kitty playfully.

Elizabeth, however, affected not to notice her sisters' teasing, though their giggles followed her as she skated over to Mr. Darcy.

"Miss Bennet," greeted he, his face red.

"Mr. Darcy," returned Elizabeth, trying to refrain from laughing at his obvious embarrassment. "I am told you have not much experience in the art of ice skating."

The man glowered at his friend, who was cheerfully helping Jane escort Kitty. "It appears Mr. Bingley has exposed my secret to the world."

This time, Elizabeth allowed herself to laugh. "Oh, it was no secret, Mr. Darcy. Your lack of practice was obvious even to the untrained eye."

"I suppose I should have agreed to let my sister teach me a few years ago when she offered," mumbled he.

"Well, fear not, Mr. Darcy. You have a new instructor at your service." Elizabeth punctuated her words with a little curtsey, which she executed regardless of the fact that she was on skates.

He actually favored her with a tiny smile at that. "I suppose you are taking this task upon yourself?"

"Indeed, I am. I refuse to allow you to sully your reputation by plunging to the ice. Now, come." She offered him her arm.

He stared at her with those intense dark eyes for a few seconds, and she felt her breath catch in her throat. But then he took the arm she was offering, and she forced her gaze away and her mind to the business at hand.

At first, they merely talked in low voices about skating, her coaxing him along and giving him tips about how to hold himself and what to do with his feet.

Before long, however, he had grown comfortable enough with the activity that they were able to speak of other things.

"Are you enjoying your time in London?" inquired Mr. Darcy.

"I am," affirmed Elizabeth. "But I do miss my walks at Longbourn."

"Surely in the winter you cannot walk as you do in the summer," commented he.

"That is true, yet I do nonetheless engage in such exercise when the day is not too cold. The hills may not be covered in green, but there is a beauty to the paleness of winter nonetheless."

"Yes, there is," murmured Mr. Darcy. Though she was not looking at him, she could feel him staring at her, and she flushed. He made a slight noise to clear his throat and then said:

"Hertfordshire is pretty, I grant you, but I prefer the beauty of Pemberley in the spring. I am certain there is no greener place in all of England."

"You love your home, then?"

"Yes. I do."

They both became quiet then, listening to the gentle scraping of skates and the conversation and cries of laughter of the other guests.

Elizabeth felt terribly confused. There was a part of her that enjoyed their time together—he was an intelligent man, and though he was often taciturn, she occasionally saw flashes of intense emotion from him. Those flashes made her feel unbalanced and made her want to reconsider her opinion of him.

But how was she to reconcile this man—the one who accepted assistance in learning how to skate, the one who had attempted to extricate her from the disaster at the Twelfth Night Ball, the one who threatened to take her breath away—with the man who she was almost certain had nearly destroyed her sister's happiness by taking Mr. Bingley from Hertfordshire?

She did not know how to feel or what to think. She only knew that she enjoyed being in his presence, even if he was—on occasion—utterly infuriating.

Chapter XLI

When Elizabeth Bennet finally returned to her sisters, Darcy left the ice, his head and his heart both muddled. Why did this woman stir him to such passions? The last thing he needed was to have this intoxicating woman always on his mind. But the more he saw her, the more he needed to see her. Even when he tried to sleep, he would visualize those playful eyes looking back at him. Somehow, Miss Bennet had become ingrained in his life without his conscious permission, and regardless of his current uncertainty about his choice of a marriage partner, he could not bring himself to repine having come to know her.

Despite the overheard conversation about the eldest Miss Bennet—which he now knew to be Elizabeth—he was certain that Elizabeth Bennet was no fortune hunter. After what had happened at the Twelfth Night Ball, there was no question about what sort of person she was. A well-bred woman who wanted to improve her chances for marrying well would never go so far as to drench a rake with his own refreshments due to his lack of boundaries. In fact, very few daughters of gentlemen would be able to conjure up the audacity to make such a bold move regardless of wealth and social standing; many would, in fact, have tried to engineer the situation to result in such a compromise of virtue that it would have required a swift marriage. Trenton was, for all his bluster and his dissolute ways, a very rich and tempting catch for any woman, let alone one from so humble a background. The sort of reaction that had been provoked in Miss Bennet painted her as a truly unique woman. Even though it had surprised him, he should have expected nothing less.

It was extremely troubling to Darcy that he should care whether or not Miss Bennet was seeking to marry to improve her fortunes. He should not have been interested in the slightest, as he intended to wed either his cousin Anne or Miss Elia Baker, and he meant to consider no other women when it came to his marriage prospects. Yet despite all reason, the knowledge that Miss Bennet was not seeking a suitor for his wealth made him feel an inexplicable sense of relief. It was as if some invisible burden had been lifted from his shoulders.

He was staring at the object of his thoughts—watching her laugh at something one of her sisters said, her eyes bright and her cheeks pink from the cold of the day—when Mr. Davidson approached and startled him from his reverie.

"She is a lovely woman."

Darcy turned to his friend. Trying to keep his voice level, he asked: "Who is?"

Mr. Davidson gave a slight shake of his head, the corners of his mouth lifting slightly. "Come now, Darcy. You know who I mean. Miss Elizabeth Bennet."

"She is certainly handsome," acknowledged Darcy.

"More than that," said his friend with a snort. "If I were not already married, I would be seriously tempted to try my hand at courting her—though I imagine she is a prize that would take some effort to win."

"I am certain whoever she marries will be fortunate indeed."

"Yes, he will. The question, however, is *who* will see her for the jewel she is and remove her from the marriage market permanently. Do you know anyone of our acquaintance who will step up and do the honors? He would need to be one with a fine fortune, of course, and the ability to treat the dear young woman like royalty."

Startled, Darcy looked over at his friend, wondering what Davidson was suggesting. Surely he was not insinuating that Darcy himself should make a simple country miss the toast of London by offering for her. Unsure, he decided to change the tone of the conversation slightly.

"I imagine that this time she is spending in London society is not helping in that regard as she might wish," said he in a dismissive tone. "She is, after all, nothing more than the daughter of a country gentleman, and she cannot have high expectations for a marriage partner. She is essentially dowerless, you know."

His obfuscation was clearly not effective, as Davidson turned back toward him with incredulity written across his face. "I cannot believe you would speak such nonsense, Darcy. Surely the worth of a woman is to be measured on a scale where the size of her dowry is only a small consideration."

Darcy raised an eyebrow. "And did you not marry a woman who came with a handsome fortune?"

"Indeed, I did," said Davidson, narrowing his eyes, "but you should know me better than to suppose that was my primary consideration. I would have married my Julia had she lacked a shilling to her name.

"Listen to me, my friend," continued Davidson as he directed a serious gaze at Darcy, "do not fall for our circle's typical inducements into matrimony. The love of a good woman is not to be underestimated—nor is the ability of a shrewish woman to make your life miserable. Choose a woman with your needs for emotion and companionship in mind, not how much wealth she brings to the union. The latter may perhaps provide extra security, but it is not the dowry which will be sitting at the dinner table with you every night. Nor will her money keep you company, assist in rearing your children in a proper fashion, or help you resolve life's day-to-day problems with alacrity."

Darcy paused for a moment, carefully mulling over his friend's words to determine whether they had a hidden meaning. Finally, he said: "So you would compel me to marry Miss Bennet?"

"Of course not," said Davidson, though his tone made it sound as if the notion were not as preposterous as Darcy seemed to think. "I speak in general terms, though I must I own I *have* noticed your interest.

"Do not attempt to deny it," said Davidson, waving him off when he would have protested. "I believe I have known you long enough to divine your looks and manners. I am in no way suggesting you propose to the girl straightaway, only that you take great care when choosing your future companion, whether it be Miss Bennet or another deserving young woman. Life is a fleeting instant, but even that instant can seem very long indeed if one's companion in life is not chosen correctly."

After giving Darcy a final slap on the back, Davidson departed to speak with his other guests, leaving Darcy alone with his thoughts. But though he was certain his friend spoke from experience and gave good advice, Darcy was a creature of duty, and he knew that marrying Miss Bennet would not in any way satisfy his duty. No, he would not court

Elizabeth Bennet. He would forget her and marry another lady who was infinitely more suitable—one whom there would be no censure for marrying.

Even if he could not get Miss Bennet's fine eyes out of his mind.

Chapter XLII

The more time Elizabeth spent in London, the more confused she became—and it was all courtesy of Fitzwilliam Darcy. She found the situation similar to the one which had existed when Darcy had departed Hertfordshire. In fact, it was almost more blatant—in Hertfordshire, she had suspected him of gravitating toward her because he found her company more agreeable than any other available in the area. In London, however, his attentions did not wane, and although he did not allow himself to excite her expectation by showing any level of affection, he still appeared to prefer her company, even though his preference at times seemed to be at the expense of others of his acquaintance, particularly the many young ladies who were intent on becoming the next mistress of Pemberley.

It was not long before Elizabeth felt she was becoming somewhat of an unpopular figure at many of the events she and her sisters attended through his influence, and more than once, she found herself the recipient of an exasperated or unfriendly expression or even a veiled cutting remark, though that was always delivered when Mr. Darcy was least likely to overhear. Mr. Darcy appeared not to notice how the hopeful young ladies were acting; he paid no special attention to any of the women with whom he came into contact and never danced a second time with any young lady. In fact, at many events, he did not dance at all.

Still, Elizabeth was painfully aware of their disparity in stations. Indeed, if not for Mr. Darcy and his influence, she and her sisters—and Mr. Bingley, for that matter—would never have been able to attend the breadth of higher society engagements they were given the good fortune to experience that winter. Of course, Mr. Bingley was also helpful in finding them engagements, but it was apparent that he simply did not possess the influence of Mr. Darcy.

Elizabeth was truly enjoying her time in London, if she were to be honest with herself. Operas and the theater had always been favorites of hers, but her connection with Mr. Darcy meant she was able to view them from the incredible vantage of a private box which Darcy made available for use by Elizabeth and her sisters. And the high society balls and parties which they attended were events which overwhelmed her, so fine were the musicians, the refreshments, and the fabrics of the dresses which swirled and waved around them. Elizabeth had enjoyed assemblies in Meryton in her youth, and she felt she could do so again, but she had to acknowledge that they could in no way compare with those found in London.

The other effect of all these events was the attention that the Bennet sisters received from other members of high society. While Elizabeth could understand why she herself was not exactly popular with the young ladies with whom they came in contact, more surprising was the fact that Jane was not much more so. Elizabeth attributed this to Jane's beauty and poise and to the disinclination those ladies felt for one whom they considered a rival.

When it came to the young men, however, the newly introduced ladies found themselves to be the center of attention. Jane, of course, had already been claimed by Mr. Bingley, and though a formal courtship had not been announced, his protectiveness toward her was evident and could hardly be missed. Indeed, Elizabeth was amused on more than one occasion by the sight of Jane's beau staring down a member of a much higher social sphere while protectively holding her hand on his arm.

With Jane out of the picture—and the family's protectiveness toward Kitty—Elizabeth found more and more of the male attention directed toward her. She rarely sat out a set at a ball, though many times she would have preferred to have been given that opportunity, and she was subjected to the company of a great many young men who were eager to secure her hand for dinner dances and the subsequent repasts which followed.

Unfortunately, this appeared to have a negative effect on Mr. Darcy's mood—Elizabeth noticed he would frequently brood after learning her hand had once again been secured for dinner—and he eventually started to request her hand for dinner dances, often securing such a set before an assembly had even begun. He showed no outward signs of jealousy or protectiveness, only that same maddening intensity which she felt she could interpret in several different ways. And though they began to garner attention due to his actions, he did not—or affected he did not—notice. Elizabeth finally dismissed it as his feelings of manly pride driving him to protect one of the female persuasion. The incidents with Lord Trenton must still be as fresh in his mind as they were in hers, and he, far more than Mr. Bingley due to his position in society, was in a position to protect her.

Then there were the dinners that they attended. Though they were at times invited to dine with other acquaintances, they primarily rotated dinner invitations between the Gardiner, Darcy, and Bingley townhouses, and they generally kept those dinners as small affairs. Elizabeth learned that there was much more to the connection between the Gardiners and Mr. Darcy than she had ever considered before. Her dear aunt had informed her of their business dealings, but beyond that, there appeared to be a true friendship and confidence subsisting between them. In addition, she learned that the town in which her aunt had been raised was no more than five miles from Mr. Darcy's estate and that therefore they knew many of the same families and locations. The fact that they both considered Derbyshire to be the most beautiful of all counties was merely the best part of their mutual friendship.

It was during this season of invitations and engagements that another event of some note took place. Late in February, only a week before Elizabeth was to depart for Kent, they were attending another ball when Elizabeth had the misfortune to run into someone she had hoped to never see again.

Soon after they entered the ballroom to the familiar scene of splendor and society, Mr. and Mrs. Gardiner had become separated from their nieces in the crowd. Elizabeth and Jane led Kitty to an out of the way corner, where they waited for the gentlemen to bring them some punch. It was not two minutes later when Elizabeth heard a sharp intake of breath and turned to see the blazing eyes of Lord Trenton boring into hers.

He approached, bringing to Elizabeth's mind a predator stalking its prey, and situated himself directly in front of her, an accusatory expression on his face.

"What are *you* doing here, trollop?" demanded he.

"I am attending a ball to which I have been invited, Lord Trenton," responded Elizabeth quietly. "Now, if you will excuse me—"

"I shall not! You, a mere commoner, have the audacity to strike a member of the peerage, and then you show your face before proper society as though nothing has happened?"

Elizabeth would have preferred to avoid him altogether, but her sense of outrage was aroused. The presence of her two sisters gave her the courage to respond to her tormentor. "And you, who lay claim to the respectability of a gentleman, have the nerve to attempt to assault a gentlewoman and then place the blame on her?"

The expression on Lord Trenton's face was almost murderous. "I should strike you where you stand."

"Perhaps you should," said Elizabeth, affecting a confidence she did not feel. "Prove to all in attendance just what manner of man you are. You are no gentleman, Lord Trenton. Your attentions were most improper and unwanted, and I would appreciate it if you would cease your attempts to harass me."

"There will be no harassment or striking of any woman here, Trenton."

Elizabeth had never been so happy to hear Mr. Darcy's voice. Lord Trenton, however, experienced the opposite reaction, and he immediately turned toward this new threat, an expression of intense distaste etched upon his face.

"And what do you have to say on the matter, sir?" hissed the earl.

"As Miss Bennet is a member of my party, I believe I have plenty to say. Your continuing presence is uncalled for and unwanted."

Lord Trenton sneered. "I suppose I should not be surprised to know that *you* are the champion to this—this—"

"Be careful what you say, Trenton," interrupted Mr. Darcy. His significant glance about the room left no doubt of his meaning—they had begun to attract an audience.

"And *I* should not be surprised that you would continue to behave in such a base and ungentlemanly manner!" continued Mr. Darcy. "Miss Bennet has every right to resent your actions, sir. I suggest that you leave her be."

Lord Trenton appeared to wish to push the matter further, but he glanced around and drew himself to his fullest arrogant manner.

"Very well. I shall overlook the slight. But I, for one, would very much prefer to never see you again."

"Believe me, sir, the feeling is very much reciprocated," replied

Elizabeth coolly.

Lord Trenton cast one last imperious glance in Elizabeth's direction before stalking off in high dudgeon.

Once he was gone, Elizabeth allowed herself to sag in relief. Her arm was immediately taken by Mr. Darcy, who escorted her to a nearby chair.

"Are you well, Miss Bennet?" inquired he, pressing a flute of wine into her trembling hands, though she was not certain when he had procured it.

Elizabeth nodded shakily and sipped on the wine. "I am, thank you. I merely need a moment to regain my equilibrium."

The Gardiners had rushed to her at the end of the altercation, and they were standing nearby with her sisters, appearing rather worried.

Elizabeth nodded at Jane, who was regarding her with particularly strong anxiety. "Jane, the music is about to start. I know you are set to open the ball with Mr. Bingley—please do not concern yourself on my account."

Though reluctant to leave, Jane appeared to realize that there would be no arguing with her sister, as she agreed and allowed herself to be led to the dance floor. The Gardiners, however, were loath to leave their niece.

"I feel I must apologize for failing to protect you again, Lizzy," intoned Mr. Gardiner. "I should have been by your side so that I could protect you from that cad."

"I pray you say nothing further," disagreed Elizabeth. "You should not be expected to hold my hand at every assembly as one would a child's. There was nothing to be done."

The Gardiners continued to try to take the blame for the incident, but Elizabeth would have nothing of it. It was the middle of the opening dance before she was able to make the party relax slightly by convincing them of the return of her composure.

"Miss Bennet," said Mr. Darcy after some moments had passed, "I commend you for your bravery and ability to stand up to that man. Your fortitude is never to be underestimated, or whoever does so shall pay the consequences."

"Oh, Lizzy has always been thus," spoke up Kitty from Elizabeth's other side. "All the gentlemen of Hertfordshire have a healthy respect for her strength of character."

Elizabeth could feel her cheeks become pink at the praise. "Please, Kitty, do not embarrass me."

Kitty's soft chuckles were her only reply.

For the rest of the evening, the members of Elizabeth's party kept a close watch upon her, never allowing her to wander far and risk facing Lord Trenton alone yet again. Elizabeth was grateful for their care and attention—she wanted nothing further to do with the man.

Chapter XLIII

Finally, the time for Elizabeth to depart for Kent drew near.

On the one hand, she would be happy to see Mary again. Mary's letters to her had been written with the attempt to be optimistic, yet there was something that made them melancholy in nature. Elizabeth attributed this tone to Mary being away from her family for the first time in her life—the young woman was undoubtedly feeling their absence keenly. Elizabeth was looking forward to being able to impart some measure of cheer to her sister and provide her with companionship, which was undoubtedly somewhat lacking both inside the parsonage with Mr. Collins and outside the parsonage with the infamous Lady Catherine de Bourgh.

On the other hand, Elizabeth wished that she could have remained in London and that the magical winter could have continued for the rest of her life. Despite a few less than welcome events—meeting Lord Trenton came to mind!—it had been an incredible assemblage of activities which sometimes almost blended together to create one majestic picture. While there had not been enough invitations to keep her and her family busy *every* night of the week (although it had often seemed to be so!), there *had* been enough that they were kept busy several nights of every week, a stark contrast from their past stays in London.

Elizabeth had never witnessed such a spectacle and had certainly never expected to take part in a season in London. Whatever her feelings for the gentleman from Derbyshire were, she could not help but feel thankful for the notice he had shown her and her sisters.

Elizabeth's final dinner in the company of Mr. Darcy was soon to take place at Mr. Bingley's townhouse, and Elizabeth was dreading it and anticipating it at the same time. After her departure from London, she was certain that nothing would ever again be as it was. In her mind, this would be the last time she would dine with Mr. Darcy in London, and her feelings on the finality of that dinner could not be deciphered. Yet she was also looking forward to conversing with him, for there was truly no other man of her acquaintance whose intelligence, interests, and wit matched hers so well.

She had learned from her aunt that there were to be a few additions to their normal party that night, for Mr. Bingley's two elder married sisters were also to be in attendance that evening.

"But what can you tell us about them?" asked Elizabeth. Mrs. Gardiner and her three nieces were gathered together in the parlor, discussing the dinner invitation.

"Little enough," was the reply. "I have not actually *met* them, after all."

"But surely you can tell us something of them," persisted Kitty. "Are they amiable like Mr. Bingley?"

"I *could* tell you something. But perhaps I should hold my tongue and let you all form your own opinions."

A chorus of protests and supplications met her declaration, especially from Jane, who was intensely interested in—and a little worried about—the family of the man she hoped to marry.

"I suppose you must have it, then," continued Mrs. Gardiner with an exaggerated sigh.

Elizabeth was not fooled for a moment—her aunt was undoubtedly enjoying provoking her young relations. For her to tease the three young ladies, Mrs. Gardiner must have had some interesting gossip indeed.

Elizabeth affixed a stern glare upon her aunt, who returned the look with a laugh of delight before speaking thus:

"Mr. Bingley has two sisters, and neither is in any way like their brother. The elder sister—Louisa—has been married to a Mr. Hurst for these last four years. Mrs. Hurst is a quiet soul who rarely expresses an opinion of her own which has not already been conveyed by her younger sister. Mr. Hurst is a landowner, and he is apparently fond of little other than food and drink, cards, and his hunting rifle.

"But it is the other sister who is the more interesting of the pair. Caroline is her name, and though I have never met her, I almost feel that I know her due to the fact that Mr. Darcy has spoken of her—or, dare I say it, *complained* about her—for several years now."

Jane appeared perplexed. "About what would Mr. Darcy have to complain? She is Mr. Bingley's sister after all."

"Mr. Darcy has never told me as much outright, you understand—he is too much the gentleman to ever say such a thing—but from what he *has* said (and perhaps more importantly, what he has left unsaid), I suspect that Miss Bingley is a most devious social climber." Mrs. Gardiner paused and laughed. "After Mr. Bingley graduated from Cambridge and she met Mr. Darcy, she had the idea fixed in her head that she was to be the next Mrs. Darcy, and she pursued him shamelessly."

Elizabeth snorted, earning a reproving glare from her aunt, who said: "I had thought you were reevaluating your feelings for Mr. Darcy, Lizzy."

"Oh, it is not that, my dear aunt," protested Elizabeth. "It is just that I have seen many a young lady set her cap at Mr. Darcy these past few months, and if his reaction to Mr. Bingley's sister was anything like his reaction to *them*, I can safely say that she could not have been pleased."

Somewhat mollified, Mrs. Gardiner agreed. "I believe you are correct, Elizabeth. Because Mr. Bingley is a very close personal friend, Mr. Darcy tolerated the young lady's attentions, though he was always careful to never give her any encouragement. Unfortunately, she required no such support.

"It all came to a head nearly two years ago. It appears Mr. Darcy had invited Mr. Bingley to Pemberley for a visit, and as a courtesy, he invited Mr. Bingley's family to accompany him. The visit was a nightmare."

The three girls were on the edge of their seats, Elizabeth and Kitty interested in the story and—in no small amount—the follies of Mr. Bingley's sister, whereas Jane listened with a certain morbid fascination about the in-laws she was hoping to obtain. It was good that Mr. Bingley was so amiable, as it did not sound as if his sisters would in any way be a pleasant part of a life spent with him.

"From what Mr. Darcy told us, Caroline Bingley was arrogant and condescending, acted as if she were the mistress of Mr. Darcy's estate, and in every way made the visit difficult for not only Mr. Darcy and his other guests, but also for the servants. Before they left, Mr. Darcy took her aside, along with Mr. Bingley, and told her in no uncertain terms that he was not interested in her and would never make her an offer of marriage."

The stunned Bennet sisters gaped at Mrs. Gardiner, each privately wondering how a woman could be so oblivious and blind. Her behavior sounded almost as though it had been lifted from the pages of a novel.

"Surely not," spoke Jane into the ensuing silence.

"I am afraid so, Jane," said Mrs. Gardiner. "In fact, it becomes worse. The young woman would not believe him and continued to act much the same way in company as she ever had—she clung to him, fawned over him, and reacted badly to him paying attention to any other lady.

"Finally, after repeated attempts at restating his intentions, he resorted to cutting her at a London event to force her to cease her possessive behavior."

The three sisters gasped almost in unison—being cut by a man of Mr. Darcy's standing was a serious blow to any young lady.

"I had no notion that you were as intimate with Mr. Darcy as your account seems to suggest," said Elizabeth.

"And you would be correct," responded Mrs. Gardiner. "Normally, Mr. Darcy would not share such confidence with us, but as the event was much discussed in society, Mr. Darcy felt compelled to explain the matter to us so our opinion of his actions would not be adversely affected."

"But if that is the case, how does she now receive an invitation to dine at his house?" asked Elizabeth.

"She has lately been married," began Mrs. Gardiner, "and—"

"—is thus no longer a threat," finished Elizabeth.

"Exactly, Lizzy, my dear. I do not know much of the man she married. His name is Smith, and he has a small estate in Norfolk. The Smiths and the Hursts have just returned from an extended tour of the continent, which is why we shall see them tonight. However, I also suspect there is a desire on the part of Mr. Bingley to introduce a certain young lady to his family."

Jane blushed very becomingly, a fact which caused her sisters to tease her mercilessly until it was time for them to dress for dinner.

Chapter XLIV

They reached Mr. Bingley's townhouse at the appropriate time and found they had arrived before Mr. Darcy, which was an oddity of sorts—usually, when one of the gentlemen hosted the evening, the other would arrive before the Gardiners and their nieces. The Gardiner party was shown into the drawing room, where Mr. Bingley proceeded to introduce his two sisters and their husbands. They were much as Mrs. Gardiner stated: the elder sister, Louisa Hurst, greeted them quietly, while the younger sister, Caroline Smith, spoke to them with a little more confidence. Elizabeth was somewhat wary of the latter, however, for the expression on Mrs. Smith's face appeared to be one of something not unlike contempt. Yet Mrs. Smith's features quickly changed, and she spoke to the newcomers with composure, though not overt warmth. Their husbands were more innocuous—Mr. Hurst was portly, and his greetings were perfunctory, while Mr. Smith was a short man with pleasant, though not handsome, features.

It was shortly after—once Mr. Darcy had been announced—that the true spectacle began. Elizabeth had hardly been given the chance to form any sort of opinion of her new acquaintances when a shrill voice rang out across the room: "Mr. Darcy! How wonderful it is to see you—it has been far too long!"

Elizabeth saw a streak of lime cross the room and attach itself to Mr.

Darcy's arm, earning a raised eyebrow from the man.

The woman chattered on for several minutes, her comments full of how she had missed her "dearest friend" and had simply been longing to see him. These statements were supplemented by her inexhaustible supply of praise for his person, his state of dress, and countless other insignificant factors vaguely concerning him. In fact, it reminded Elizabeth somewhat of Mr. Collins's descriptions of Rosings Park.

Elizabeth exchanged glances with Mrs. Gardiner, who was barely suppressing a laugh, and Jane, whose eyes were wide and disbelieving, before looking at Mr. Darcy, who was in the act of trying to disengage his arm from the young woman clutching it.

The sound of a throat clearing loudly drew everyone's attention, and Elizabeth turned her head to see Mr. Smith glaring across the room at his wife, who held Mr. Darcy's arm as though she would never let it go.

"Caroline, my dear," called he, his voice tight and unhappy, "will you please join me here?"

Mrs. Smith immediately seemed to recollect herself, and with a slight blush on her face, she curtseyed to Mr. Darcy and returned to stand with her husband. They moved into Mr. Bingley's parlor, where the group fell into quiet and stilted conversation. Mrs. Smith's unseemly display had put a damper on the company, and it was difficult to recover from it.

A few moments later, however, they were saved by the announcement of dinner. The company stood to go to the dining room, and Mr. Smith quickly caught his wife's hand and said:

"Let us not stand on ceremony, Bingley. I believe I desire Caroline's company this evening."

Though he appeared surprised at this irregular request, Mr. Bingley was clearly willing to fulfill it. After all, not only had they been sitting as they wished during the dinner arrangements that had taken place between the small group of friends, but the change in plans also allowed him to claim Jane's arm to escort her into the dining room. Mr. Gardiner at that moment moved to his wife and Kitty and gallantly offered to escort them. Elizabeth, who had been standing near Mr. Darcy, soon found herself on the gentleman's arm, and when they entered the room, they discovered that Mrs. Hurst was already sitting in the hostess's chair at the foot of the table, her husband by her side. With the Smiths sitting across from Mr. Hurst, that left the only seats for Elizabeth and Darcy on the opposite side of the table next to Mr. Bingley. After they sat down and the first course of the meal was served, conversation began once more.

Elizabeth was somewhat surprised to see that both the Hursts and the Smiths were disinclined to speak during the meal. While Mr. Hurst seemed fixated upon the food as Mrs. Gardiner had indicated—and Mrs. Hurst seemed rather quiet in general—the Smiths appeared to be going somewhat against their own natures by brooding, presumably on the exchange that had just occurred in the drawing room. Before long, however, Mrs. Smith withdrew from her contemplation to regard Elizabeth with what could only be termed a glower. Unsettled and wondering what she could have done to earn the woman's enmity, Elizabeth endeavored to ignore her.

"Is Mrs. Smith bothering you, Miss Bennet?" asked a voice quietly.

Elizabeth glanced gratefully at Mr. Darcy before shaking her head. "She appears angry about something, Mr. Darcy, but as I know of nothing I have done to cause her disapprobation, I shall not give it another moment's thought."

"It is probably for the best," replied he. "I suspect she is unhappy that she is not occupying a seat closer to me, but she should not be quite so upset about it. She *is* married now after all."

Elizabeth laughed. "She is at that."

"I assume your aunt acquainted you with the details of her situation?"

"She did, indeed, Mr. Darcy," confirmed Elizabeth in a low voice. "I just never thought I would see such a display now that she is married. Was it much like that before?"

He responded with a grimace. "Worse, if you can imagine it. I believe her behavior has been so firmly ingrained that she forgot herself for a moment—either that or she wanted to repair her 'relationship' with me so she would continue to be welcome in my company."

"And what of Mr. Smith? What kind of man is he?"

Mr. Darcy frowned. "He is a good enough fellow, I suppose, but to be honest, he is a little dull."

Elizabeth stifled an unladylike snort of laughter at Mr. Darcy's blunt opinion, and Mr. Darcy chuckled. "He is a good landowner," clarified he. "He takes care of his tenants, makes a good profit on his land, and is open to new ideas. But if you try to talk to him about anything else, he proves himself to be outmatched immediately. It is almost as though he *did not* spend four years at Cambridge. *You* would tire of him very quickly."

"And how would you know this?" was Elizabeth's arch reply.

His gentle smile caused the breath to catch in her throat. "Have I not conversed with you many times these past months? Have I not come to know your opinions and your intellectual capacities? I assure you, Miss Bennet, that you would be bored within minutes of beginning a conversation with him."

After dinner, Elizabeth learned that Mr. Darcy was entirely correct. Once the gentlemen rejoined the ladies, she found herself in close proximity to Mr. Smith, and after being given a blank look in response to her proffered opinion about a piece of Shakespearean poetry, Elizabeth decided right then and there never to subject him to so taxing a discussion again.

Still later, Elizabeth found herself near Mrs. Smith. After a short and somewhat frosty exchange of pleasantries, Mrs. Smith said something utterly unexpected.

"You must think the worst of me, Miss Bennet," said Mrs. Smith bluntly.

Though surprised at the other woman's manner of expressing herself, Elizabeth gathered herself to respond. "I assure you I do not, Mrs. Smith. I have only met you this evening and cannot claim to be able to form an opinion of another so quickly."

The woman's answer was bitter. "Oh, I do not doubt that you have been made aware of the way I behaved in the past."

"I have heard something of what passed between you and Mr. Darcy, but I assure you that I am more than willing to base my opinion of you on your own merits rather than hearsay."

Mrs. Smith's expression was unreadable. Elizabeth felt herself scrutinized—weighed and measured, much as a rack of lamb at the butcher's—before the woman finally relented and dropped her gaze to her folded hands with a sigh.

"I was certain that I was destined to be Mr. Darcy's wife, but now that I look back on it, I realize that I never truly knew him. It is humbling, I assure you, to know that the man who I determined would be mine never had a jot of interest for me." She shook her head. "It is strange, but even after all this time, I still have trouble accepting the fact that Mr. Darcy may have an interest in another woman."

Mrs. Smith's pointed glance at Elizabeth was not missed, causing Elizabeth's own cheeks to blush in response. But before the unmarried young woman could stammer out a reply, Mrs. Smith continued:

"Miss Bennet, I must tell you that I have never seen Mr. Darcy gaze at any other woman with such interest as he does you. Though he has been speaking with my brother these past ten minutes at least, I do not think his eyes have left your face the entire time."

Elizabeth's blush deepened, and she glanced up at the man, confirming that his eyes were affixed upon her, just as Mrs. Smith had asserted. She gathered her courage and responded:

"I assure you that you are mistaken, Mrs. Smith. Mr. Darcy and I enjoy our conversations, but that is the extent of our friendship. Mr. Darcy feels nothing more for me than I do for him."

An indelicate snort was her response. "And *I* assure *you*, Miss Bennet, that if Mr. Darcy had even once glanced in my direction with the intensity that he has directed at you all evening, I would not have hesitated to purchase my wedding clothes immediately.

"Still," continued Mrs. Smith, "I have no cause to repine, and I shall not allow my previous fancy for Mr. Darcy to affect me again. I am married to a good man who cares for me, and he has given me every reason to be happy."

Mrs. Smith rubbed her hand over her flat stomach, which caused Elizabeth to smile delightedly and extend her congratulations for the happy news. They fell into conversation, and by the end of the evening, Elizabeth felt she had gained some understanding of the other woman. Although she did not feel they would ever truly be close confidantes, she found Mrs. Smith to be intelligent, agreeable, and truly willing to put her past actions and opinions to rest.

Elizabeth could not help but ponder Mrs. Smith's assertions of the gentleman's affections. It was true that Mrs. Smith had misconstrued Mr. Darcy's interest in *herself*. Why, then, should Elizabeth place any weight in what Mrs. Smith had said?

Yet there was a part of her which hoped—a part which wondered whether Mr. Darcy's near-constant gaze and friendly conversation were significant in ways that went beyond the purely social. She had begun to push past her suspicions of his interference with Mr. Bingley and see the unexpected warmth that Mr. Darcy brought to her life. The man she had once considered to be so cold had somehow integrated himself in her daily routine. She looked forward to seeing him, remembered fondly their time on the ice (when she had discovered the formidable Mr. Darcy was *not* perfect at everything!), and thought sadly of that fact that her visit in London was almost at an end.

But even as she tentatively acknowledged to herself that he had become important to her—that his intent gaze could make her heart skip a beat—she feared that *she* could never be anything more than a friend to *him*.

Though she was a gentleman's daughter, she had nothing to offer him. As the scion of an earl, how could Mr. Darcy *ever* be interested in her? There was too much of a chasm between them for that to ever happen—even if perhaps he desired it as much as she feared she was beginning to—and it was foolish to allow her fledgling hopes to rise. The moment those hopes lifted into the air, they were certain to be dashed onto the ground.

But she could not help but turn and look at him once more. His eyes met hers, and she gave him a slight smile before turning back to Mrs. Smith. But it was difficult to concentrate on the rest of their conversation . . . especially since she felt Mr. Darcy's gaze on her the entire time.

Chapter XLV

"I shall miss you, Lizzy," proclaimed Kitty as she hugged her sister fiercely.

"I shall miss you, too, Kitty," said Elizabeth, her eyes more than a little moist.

"Must you really leave?"

"I am sorry, Kitty, but I really must. Mary needs me." Elizabeth lowered her voice so only Kitty could hear her. "I cannot imagine how she must feel right now being married to that odious man!"

Kitty managed a light chuckle, but her sightless eyes were just as misty as her eldest sister's. Elizabeth squeezed her once more before turning to Jane.

"Oh, Lizzy!" was all Jane managed before tearfully embracing her. As twins, Jane and Elizabeth hated being parted from each other—yet there was an even greater parting looming on the horizon for them that Elizabeth could not bear to consider until she was ensconced in the privacy of the carriage.

"I shall miss you, Jane," said Elizabeth to her sister, "but we shall see each other again before long."

"Of course," acknowledged Jane warmly. But despite her attempt to demonstrate her fortitude, there was an unmistakable shakiness to her voice which Elizabeth, who knew her better than anyone else did, could easily detect.

"Watch over Kitty, Jane," whispered Elizabeth.

"I shall."

Trembling a little herself, Elizabeth turned and said farewell to her aunt and uncle, thanking them for allowing her to stay in London.

Mrs. Gardiner told her: "You are always welcome in our home, Lizzy. You know that."

And then Elizabeth was stepping up into the carriage the Gardiners had provided for her journey to Kent, settling in and waving goodbye to her relations as the horses began to move. When they were out of sight, she gave a slight nod to the maid provided by the Gardiners for her journey, and the girl smiled back at her.

Elizabeth did not trust herself to speak, so she wrapped herself in her thoughts.

Jane and Mr. Bingley seemed to be well on their way to an understanding—she only wished she could be present when it happened. She could easily picture the glow on her sister's face and the smile on Mr. Bingley's—truly, they made each other so very happy, and she was glad that what had been torn was now mended.

But there was a part of her which selfishly shunned the notion of her sister's marriage. A married woman's first duty was to her husband, and the confidences Jane and Elizabeth shared would dwindle in number when Jane was finally wed. A married woman could not invite her family to her estate every day—and certainly, Jane must not wish to do so, for even her patience was tried by Mrs. Bennet's effusions. Furthermore, it would not be right of Elizabeth to constantly visit the couple herself—they needed time with each other. And when they had children, they would find themselves even busier.

Still, despite knowing that she and her dear twin would lose precious time together, Elizabeth truly was happy for her sister. Jane deserved the kind Mr. Bingley, and theirs would be a life of bliss. Elizabeth could not have asked for a better man for her sister. Elizabeth felt new tears spring to her eyes, but if the maid saw them, she did not comment.

Thinking about Mr. Bingley made her thoughts turn toward his friend. She was not certain exactly what her feelings toward him were. He remained a mystery—if he was not staring at her, then he was either engaging her in lively conversation or studiously avoiding saying anything to her at all. And then, after the last dinner at Mr. Bingley's London home, he had told her that he would be going to Rosings—and that he went there for an Easter visit every year.

That information had surprised her. She had not realized she would likely be seeing him in Kent, and she found it strange that he had waited so long to tell her. Should the information not have been casually imparted days before? He had not mentioned he would be visiting Rosings any of the times she had spoken of her upcoming trip to see her newly married sister. Why would he withhold his own visit from her?

For someone who took such pleasure in sketching the characters of others, Elizabeth found she could barely make even an outline of Mr. Darcy. His behavior was puzzling, to put it lightly, and she was not certain how she should feel toward him. Should she be flattered by his scattered attentions? Should she be wary of his long silences and peculiar behavior?

She let out a light sigh, staring out the carriage window. What she needed to do was clear Mr. Darcy from her mind entirely. Whatever he was feeling, he could never seriously pursue her. There was no sense in even thinking about him as anything more than an acquaintance—and perhaps a friend.

Rosings would surely be an end to the familiarity between them. Once he was with his aunt, he would likely feel that with the superior company of his closest relations at hand, his attentions to her would no longer be necessary. And of course, one so exalted as Lady Catherine—not to mention meddling, if Mr. Collins's account was anything near the truth—would likely not wish to encourage her nephew to be in conversation with a woman of Elizabeth's stature as much as had been his wont this last month. Perhaps that was why he had waited so long to mention his visit to Kent. He did not want her to anticipate seeing him again so soon when everything would be so different.

Yet even as she had those thoughts and began to think that this journey would be a way to put that chapter of her life behind her, she could not help but wonder in the back of her mind if she was being too uncharitable to Mr. Darcy.

She shook her head. Everything would change, and she needed to accept that.

END VOLUME I

Read an excerpt from the upcoming sequel to *Words in the Darkness*,

Echoes at Dawn

Meryton. It was the same old town he remembered from five years before, and those intervening years had not changed it in the slightest. Of course, Meryton was typical of any other small market town which could be found in every corner of the kingdom, containing dusty streets which turned into a veritable quagmire after a rainfall, small shops with little or no quality or charm to them, and dreadfully ordinary locals whose lives were just as drab and boring as the town in which they lived.

Still, Meryton—and any other town like it—was nothing more than a means to an end for an enterprising young man such as himself. And at this point in his history, enterprising was exactly what he needed to be.

Though he had never been rich—no thanks to *someone* he could name—he had been holding his own until recently, with the freedom to do as he pleased. Then, after a streak of bad luck with cards and a few poor choices at the horseracing track, his hard-won resources had been all but depleted. With no other choice before him and a mountain of debts behind him, he had left his establishment and set out into the world to make his fortune . . . again.

But he did not let the repetition darken his mood. He could always find people to swindle, credit to run up, and a few widows or maidens with whom he was duty-bound to share his charms. And if the females with whom he cavorted had money, then so much the better.

In some respects, however, the chase and all that came with it was a bother. Feminine delights could be readily found at the many establishments he frequented, and as for the other things involved in the chase, he would just as soon spend his time at the gaming tables. No, the chase was a means to an end, not the end itself, and though he would have preferred not to be bothered by it again, his circumstances and appetites—not to mention his tendency to go through money as if it were water—necessitated his imminent performance.

Because the chase had been difficult and fruitless thus far, he was ready to break from his search to conduct a conquest which promised more than a little pleasure. That was the reason he had come to Meryton.

Over the past five years, he had often found his mind wandering back to this insignificant little speck which barely appeared on any map. And somewhat surprisingly, it was not the thought of past triumphs, conquests, or extraordinary luck in gaming that kept the town on his mind. It was the girl who had managed to escape him. Few had ever evaded him after he had set his sights on them, which was, he supposed, why his thoughts had returned to her so often despite the passage of time.

She had been a pretty little thing less than five years before, and the period he had spent "courting" her had been most enjoyable, for she was not like most other young women of her age. For one, she was not a bashful young lady who blushed prettily while agreeing with every word which proceeded out of his mouth—his wife, to his mingled amusement and disgust, had been *very much* that sort of woman. No, this girl he remembered had been intelligent and unafraid to show her intelligence by challenging his opinions and stating her own with decided confidence. *That* in and of itself set her apart from just about any other young lady of her station . . . and made the idea of her surrender all the more satisfying.

Now, after five more years of maturity, he could hardly imagine how she would appear, but he was wagering that her youthful prettiness had grown into an uncommon beauty, and he very much wished to sample the delights she had to offer. It truly was a shame that she had lacked the monetary inducements necessary to satisfy his needs.

He strode into town with the confident strut he had carefully cultivated over the years, and he frequented a few of the shops, just enough to observe and gather information. It was at a taphouse that he finally heard all he needed to know; he then quietly left town, mounted the horse he had left tied to a tree just on the city's outskirts, and took the road heading north.

The journey was barely a mile from Meryton and took him only a few minutes on horseback. When the manor came into his view, he smiled to himself before schooling his features into his customary charming demeanor. He dismounted in front of the door and knocked, handing his card—one of the few he still possessed—to the maid who answered.

In only a few moments, the maid had returned, and he was led into the well-remembered parlor to greet the inhabitants.

"Mr. Wickham!" exclaimed the matron of the house.

Also from
One Good Sonnet Publishing:

Due to the machinations of Lady Catherine de Bourgh, Fitzwilliam Darcy faces a longer road trying to secure the hand of Elizabeth Bennet. Though he is quite willing to demonstrate his fortitude for the one he loves, is it possible for him to succeed amid the onslaught of rumors and the interference of others?

About the Authors

Jann Rowland

Jann Rowland was born in Regina, Saskatchewan, Canada. He enjoys reading and sports, and he even dabbles a little in music, taking pleasure in singing and playing the piano.

Though Jann did not start writing until his mid-twenties, writing has grown from a hobby to an all-consuming passion. His interest in Jane Austen stems from his university days when he took a class in which *Pride and Prejudice* was required reading.

He now lives in Calgary, Alberta with his three children and his wife of almost twenty years.

Lelia Eye

Lelia Eye was born in Harrison, Arkansas. She loves reading and misses the days when she was able to be a part of the community theater group in Harrison.

Lelia has enjoyed writing since she won a short story contest in the sixth grade, and she graduated from the University of Central Arkansas with a Master's degree in English. It was while she was obtaining her undergraduate degree at Hendrix College that she took a Jane Austen class which sparked her interest in *Pride and Prejudice*.

She now lives in Conway, Arkansas, with an adorable toddler, her husband, three dogs, and two cats.

Their blog may be found at
rowlandandeye.com

Printed in Great Britain
by Amazon